Praise for Our Authors

USA TODAY Bestselling Author
Lynne Graham

"Lynne Graham delivers an engaging, sensual tale."
—*RT Book Reviews*

"Once again Lynne Graham delivers another keeper...
a mesmerizing blend of wonderful characters,
powerful emotion and sensational scenes."
—*RT Book Reviews* on *The Winter Bride*

USA TODAY Bestselling Author
Carole Mortimer

"Carole Mortimer dishes up outstanding reading
as she blends dynamic characters, volatile scenes,
superb chemistry and a wonderful premise."
—*RT Book Reviews* on *Married by Christmas*

"[This] novella...is an excellent example of this
international bestselling author's storytelling prowess!"
—*Cataromance* on *Snowbound with the Billionaire*

Favorite Author
Marion Lennox

"Marion Lennox pens a truly magnificent tale.
The romance is pure magic and the characters
are vibrant and alive."
—*RT Book Reviews* on *A Royal Proposition*

"Marion Lennox's second Castle at Dolphin Bay story
resonates with deep emotions,
relieved by flashes of wit."
—*RT Book Reviews*

Christmas PROMISES

LYNNE GRAHAM

CAROLE MORTIMER

MARION LENNOX

H HARLEQUIN®

entertain, enrich, inspire™

ISBN-13: 978-0-373-83767-0

CHRISTMAS PROMISES

Copyright © 2012 by Harlequin Books S.A.

The publisher acknowledges the copyright holders of the individual works as follows:

THE CHRISTMAS EVE BRIDE
Copyright © 2001 by Lynne Graham

A MARRIAGE PROPOSAL FOR CHRISTMAS
Copyright © 2004 by Carole Mortimer

A BRIDE FOR CHRISTMAS
Copyright © 2006 by Marion Lennox

Recycling programs for this product may not exist in your area.

www.Harlequin.com

Printed in U.S.A.

CONTENTS

THE CHRISTMAS EVE BRIDE

Lynne Graham

CHAPTER ONE

ROCCO VOLPE was bored and, as it was not a sensation he was accustomed to feeling, he was much inclined to blame his hosts for that reality.

When the banker, Harris Winton, had invited him to his country home for the weekend, Rocco had expected stimulating company. People invariably went to a great deal of trouble to entertain Rocco. But then he could hardly have foreseen that Winton would miss his flight home from Brussels, leaving his unfortunate guests at the mercy of his wife, Kaye.

Kaye, the youthful trophy wife, who looked at Rocco with a hunger she couldn't hide. His startlingly handsome features were expressionless as his hostess irritated him with simpering flattery and far too much attention. He had never liked small women with big eyes, he reflected. Memory stirred, reminding him *why* that was so. Swiftly, he crushed that unwelcome recollection out.

'So tell me…what's it like being one of the most eligible single men in the world?' Kaye asked fatuously.

'Pretty boring.' Watching her redden without remorse, Rocco strolled over to the window like a tiger sheathing his claws with extreme reluctance.

'I suppose it must be,' the beautiful brunette then agreed in a cloying tone. 'How many men have your power, looks *and* fabulous wealth?'

Striving not to wince while telling himself that if he ever married *his* wife would have a brain, Rocco surveyed the well-kept gardens. Fading winter sunlight gleamed over the downbent head of a gardener raking up leaves on the extensive front lawn. There was something familiar about that unusual honey shade of blonde that was the colour of toffee in certain lights. He stiffened as the figure turned and he realised it was a woman *and...*?

'Your gardener is a woman?' Not a shade of the outraged incredulity and anger consuming Rocco was audible in his deep, dark drawl. But someone ought to warn Winton that he had a potential tabloid spy working for him, he thought grimly. Harris would never recover from the humiliation of the media exposing one of his wife's affairs.

His keen hostess drew level with him and wrinkled her nose. 'We have trouble getting outside staff. Harris says people don't want that kind of work these days.'

'I imagine he's right. Has she been with you long?'

'Only a few weeks.' The brunette studied him with a perplexed frown.

'Will you excuse me? I have an urgent call to make.'

Amber's back was sore.

It was icy cold but the amount of energy she had expended had heated her up to the extent that she was working in a light T-shirt. She could hardly believe that within ten days it would be Christmas. Her honey-blonde hair caught back in a clip from which strands continually drifted loose, she straightened and stretched to ease her complaining spine. About five feet three in height, she was slim, but at breast and hip she was lush and feminine in shape.

It would be another hour before she finished work and she couldn't *wait*. Only a few months back, she would have said she loved the great outdoors, but working for the Wintons had disenchanted her fast. Nothing but endless backbreaking labour and abysmally low pay. Her rich employers did not believe in spending money on labour-saving devices like leaf blowers. On the other hand, Harris Winton was a perfectionist, who demanded the highest standards against impossible odds.

'Brush up the leaves as they fall,' he had told her with a straight face, seeming not to grasp that, with several acres of wooded and lawned grounds, that was like asking her to daily stem an unstoppable tide.

You're turning into a right self-pitying moan, her conscience warned her as she emptied the wheelbarrow. So once she had had nice clothes, pretty, polished fingernails and a career with a future. She might no longer have any of those things but she *did* have Freddy, she reminded herself in consolation.

Freddy, the pure joy in her life, who could squeeze her heart with one smile. Freddy, who had filled her with so much instant love that she could still barely accept the intensity of her own feelings. Freddy, who might not be the best conversationalist yet and who loved to wake her up to play in the middle of the night, but who still made *any* sacrifice worthwhile.

'*Buon giorno*, Amber…what an unexpected pleasure!'

At the sound of that dark, well-modulated voice coming out of nowhere at her, Amber jerked rigid with fright. Blinking rapidly, disbelief engulfing her, she spun round, refusing to accept her instinctive recognition of that rich-accented drawl.

'Strange but somehow extraordinarily *apt* that you should be grubbing round a compost heap,' Rocco remarked with sardonic amusement.

A wave of stark dizziness assailed Amber. As she focused in paralysed incredulity on the formidably tall, well-built male standing beneath the towering beech trees a few yards away, her heart was beating at such an accelerated rate that she could hardly get breath into her lungs. She turned white as milk, every ounce of natural colour evaporating from her fine features, her clear green eyes huge.

Rocco Volpe, the powerful Italian financier, once christened the Silver Wolf by the gossip columns for his breathtaking good looks and fast reputation with her sex. And there was no denying that he *was* spectacular, with his bronzed skin and dark, dark deepset eyes contrasted with hair so naturally, unexpectedly fair it shone like polished silver. Rocco Volpe, the very worst mistake she had made in her twenty-three years of life. Her tummy felt hollow, her every tiny muscle bracing in self-defence. But her brain just refused to snap back into action. She could only wonder in amazement what on earth Rocco Volpe could possibly be doing wandering round the grounds of the Wintons' country house.

'Where did you come from?' she whispered jaggedly.

'The house. I'm staying there this weekend.'

'Oh…' Amber was silenced and appalled by that admission. Yet it was not a remarkable coincidence that Rocco should be acquainted with her employer, for both men wielded power in the same cut-throat world of international finance.

Tilting his arrogant head back, Rocco treated her to a leisurely, all-male appraisal that was as bold as he was. 'Not good news for you, I'm afraid.'

Amber was as stung by that insolent visual assessment as if he had slapped her in the face. *Grubbing round the compost heap?* The instant he bent the full effect of those brilliant dark eyes on her, she recalled that sarcastic comment. But a split second later thought was overpowered by the slowburn effect of Rocco skimming his intense gaze over the swell of her full breasts. Within her bra, the tender peaks of her sensitive flesh pinched tight with stark awareness. As his stirring scrutiny slid lazily down to the all-female curve of her hips, an almost forgotten ache clenched her belly.

'And what's that supposed to mean?' Amber folded her

arms with a jerk, holding her treacherous body rigid as if by so doing she might drive out those mortifying responses. Only now she was horribly conscious of her wind-tossed hair, her lack of make-up and her workworn T-shirt and jeans. Once, she recalled, she had taken time to groom herself for Rocco's benefit. Suddenly she wanted to dive into the wretched compost heap and *hide*! Rocco, so smooth, sophisticated and exclusive in his superb charcoal-grey business suit and black cashmere coat. He had to be wondering now what he had *ever* seen in her and her already battered pride writhed under that humiliating suspicion.

'Why are you working for Harris Winton as a gardener?' Rocco asked drily.

'That's none of your business.' Pale and fighting a craven desire to cringe, Amber flung her head high, determined not to be intimidated.

'But I am making it my business,' Rocco countered levelly.

Amber could not credit his nerve. Her temper was rising. 'Being one of the Wintons' guests *doesn't* give you the right to give me the third degree. Now, why don't you go away and leave me alone?'

'You really have changed your tune, *cara*,' Rocco murmured in a tone as smooth as black velvet. 'As I recall, I found persuading *you* to leave *me* alone quite a challenge eighteen months ago.'

That cruel reminder stabbed Amber like a knife in the heart. Indeed, she felt quite sick inside. She had not expected that level of retaliation and dully questioned why. Rocco was a ruthless wheeler-dealer in the money markets and as feared as he was famed for his brilliance. In automatic self-protection from that cutting tongue, she began walking away. Eighteen months ago, Rocco had *dumped* her. Indeed, Rocco had dumped her without hesitation. Rocco had then refused her phone calls and when she had persisted in daring to try and speak to him, he had finally called her back and asked her with icy contempt if she was now 'stalking' him!

'Where are you going?' Rocco demanded.

Amber ignored him. She had been working near the house. Obviously he had seen and recognised her and curiosity had got to him. But it struck her as strange that he should have acted on that curiosity and come outside to speak to her. A guy who had suggested that she might have stalking tendencies ought to have looked the other way. But then that had only been Rocco's brutally effective method of finally shaking her off.

'Amber…'

Bitterness surged up inside her, the destructive bitterness she had believed she had put behind her. But, faced with Rocco again, those feelings erupted back out of her subconscious mind like a volcano. She spun back with knotted fists, her small, shapely figure taut, angry colour warming her complexion. 'I hate you…I can't *bear* to be anywhere near you!'

Rocco elevated a cool, slanting dark brow. He looked hugely unimpressed by that outburst.

'And that is not the reaction of the proverbial woman scorned,' Amber asserted between gritted teeth, determined to disabuse him of any such ego-boosting notion. 'That is the reaction of a woman looking at you now and asking herself how the heck she could ever have been so *stupid* as to get involved with a rat like you!'

Alive with sizzling undertones and tension, the splintering silence almost seemed to shimmer around them. Glittering dark golden eyes flamed into hers in a crash-and-burn collision and she both sensed and saw the fury there that barely showed in that lean, strong face. No, he hadn't liked being called a rat.

'But you'd come back to me like a bullet if I asked you,' Rocco murmured softly.

Amber stared back at him in shock. 'Are you kidding?'

'Only making a statement of fact. But don't get excited,' Rocco advised with silken scorn. 'I'm *not* asking.'

Unfamiliar rage whooshed up inside Amber and she trembled. 'Tell me, are you trying to goad me into physically attacking you?'

'Possibly trying to settle a score or two.' With that unapologetic admission, Rocco studied her with cloaked eyes, his hard bone-structure grim. 'But let's cut to the baseline. You can only be working here to spy on the Wintons for some sleazy tabloid story—'

'I beg…your pardon?' Amber cut in unevenly, her eyes very wide.

Ignoring that interruption, Rocco continued, 'Harris is a friend. I intend to warn him about you—'

'What sleazy tabloid story? Warn him about *me*?' Amber parroted with helpless emphasis. 'Are you out of your mind? I'm not spying on anyone… I'm only the gardener, for goodness' sake!'

'*P-lease,*' Rocco breathed with licking contempt. 'Do I look that stupid?'

Amber was gaping at him while struggling to master her disbelief at his suspicions.

'How much money did you make out of that trashy kiss-and-tell spread on me?' Rocco enquired lazily.

'Nothing…' Amber told him after a sick pause, momentarily drowning in unpleasant recollections of the events which had torn her life apart eighteen months earlier. A couple of hours confiding in an old schoolfriend and the damage had been done. What had seemed like harmless girly gossip had cost her the man she loved, the respect of work colleagues and ultimately her career.

Rocco dealt her a derisive look. 'Do you really think I'm likely to swallow that tale?'

'I don't much care.' And it was true, Amber registered in some surprise. Here she was, finally getting the opportunity to defend herself but no longer that eager to take it. But then the chance had come more than a year too late. A time during which she had been forced to eat more humble pie than was good for her. She had stopped loving him, stopped hoping he would contact her and stopped caring about his opinion of her as well. After he had ditched her, Rocco had delighted the gossip columnists with a series of wild affairs with other women. He had provided her with the most effective cure available for a broken heart. Her pride had kicked in to save her and she had pulled herself together again.

'You already have all the material you need on the Wintons?' Rocco prompted with strong distaste.

The rage sunk beneath the onslaught of sobering memories gripped Amber again. 'Where do you get off, throwing wild accusations like this at me? What gives you the right to ignore what I say and assume that I'm lying? Your *superior* intellect?' Her green eyes flashed bright as emerald jewels in her heart-shaped face, her scorn palpable. 'Well, it's letting you down a bucketful right now, Rocco—'

'My ESP is on overload right now. I don't think so,' Rocco mused, studying her with penetrating cool.

A hollow laugh was wrenched from Amber's dry throat. 'No, you naturally wouldn't think that you could be wrong. After all, you're the guy who's always one hundred per cent right about everything—'

'I wasn't right about you, was I? I got *burned*,' Rocco cut in with harsh clarity, hard facial bones prominent beneath his bronzed skin.

I got burned. Was that how he now viewed their former relationship? Amber was surprised to hear that, but relieved to think that the hurt, the embarrassment and the self-recriminations had not only been hers. But then he was talking about his pride, the no-doubt wounding effect of his conviction that she had somehow contrived to put one over him. He wasn't talking about true emotions, only superficial ones.

'But not enough,' Amber responded tightly, thinking wretchedly of the months of misery she had endured before she'd wised up and got on with her life without looking back to what might have been. 'I don't think you were burned half enough.'

'How the hell could you have expected to hang onto me after what you did?' Rocco demanded with a savage abruptness that disconcerted her. His spectacular eyes rested with keen effect on her surprised face.

'Only two possible explanations, aren't there?' The breeze clawing stray strands of her honey-blonde hair back from her flushed cheekbones, Amber tilted her chin, green eyes sparkling over him where he now stood only feet from her. 'Either I was a dumb little bunny who was indiscreet with an undercover journalist *or*...I was bored out of my tiny mind with you and decided to go out of your life with a big, unforgettable bang!'

'*Dio*...you were *not* bored in my bed,' Rocco growled with raw self-assurance.

Rocco only had to say 'bed' in that dark, accented drawl and heat pulsated through Amber in an alarming wave of reaction and remembrance. Punishing him for her own weakness, she let a stinging smile curve her generous mouth. 'And how would you know, Rocco? Haven't you ever read the statistics on women faking it to keep tender male egos intact?'

The instant those provocative words escaped her, she was shaken by her own unusual venom. But she was even more taken aback by the level to which she had sunk in her instinctive need to deny even the physical hold he had once had on her. Ashamed of herself and furious with him for goading her to that point, she added, 'Look, why don't you just forget you ever saw me out here and we'll call it quits?'

'*Faking* it…' His brilliant dark eyes flared to stormy gold, his Italian accent thick as honey on the vowel sounds of those two words. He had paled noticeably below his bronzed skin and it was that much more noticeable because dark colour now scored his hard masculine cheekbones. 'Were you really?'

Connecting with his glittering look of challenge, Amber felt the primal charge in the atmosphere but she stood her ground, none too proud of her own words but ready to do anything sooner than retract them. He was sexual dynamite and he had to know it. But he need not look to any confirmation of that reality from her. 'All I want to do right now is get on with my work—'

Without the smallest warning, Rocco reached for her arm to prevent her from turning away and flipped her back. 'Was it *work* in my bed too?' he demanded in a savage undertone. 'Did you know right from the start what you were planning to do?'

Backed into the constraining circle of his arms, Amber stared up at him in sensual shock, astonished at the depth of his dark, brooding anger but involuntarily excited by it and by him. Mouth running dry, breath trapped in her throat, she could feel every taut, muscular angle of his big, powerful body against hers. She shivered, conscious of the freezing air on her bare arms but the wanton fire flaming in her pelvis, stroked to the heights by the potent proof of his arousal, recognisable even through the layers of their clothing. The wanting, the helpless, craving hunger that leapt through her in wild response took her by storm.

'I wouldn't touch you again if I was dying…' As swiftly as he had reached for her, Rocco thrust her back from him in contemptuous rejection, strong-boned features hard as iron.

Her fair complexion hotly flushed, Amber turned away

in an uncoordinated half-circle, heartbeat racing, legs thoroughly unsteady support. 'Good, so *go*—'

'I'm not finished with you yet.' Leaving those cold words of threat hanging, Rocco strode off.

In a daze, she watched him walk away from her. He had magnificent carriage and extraordinary grace for a male of his size. He soon disappeared from view, screened by the bulky evergreen shrubs flourishing below the winter-bare trees that edged the lawn surrounding the house. Amber only then realised that she was trembling and frozen to the marrow, finally conscious of the chill wind piercing her thin T-shirt. She grabbed her sweater out of the tumbledown greenhouse where she had left it and fumbled into its comforting warmth with hands that were all fingers and thumbs.

What had Rocco meant by saying he wasn't finished with her yet? She tried to concentrate but it was a challenge because she was so appalled by the way he had made her feel. Suppressing that uneasy awareness, she tensed in even greater dismay. Only minutes ago, he had told her that he intended to warn Harris Winton about the risk that she could be spying on him and his wife in the hope of selling some scandalous story to a newspaper.

Dear heaven, she could not afford to lose her job, for it might not pay well but it *did* include accommodation. Small and basic the cottage might be, but it was the sole reason that Amber had applied to work for the Wintons in the first place. Indeed, the mere thought of being catapulted back into her sister Opal's far more spacious and comfortable home to listen to a chorus of deeply humiliating 'I told you so's filled Amber with even more horror than the prospect of grovelling to Rocco!

CHAPTER TWO

Rocco was certain to be lodged in the main suite of the opulent guest wing, Amber reckoned. Just to think that she had probably fixed that huge flower arrangement in there purely for Rocco's benefit made her wince as she headed for the rear entrance to the sprawling country house.

Helping out the Wintons' kindly middle-aged housekeeper, who had been run off her feet preparing for guests the previous month, had resulted in Amber finding herself landed with another duty. The minute that Kaye Winton had realised that their gardener had done the magnificent floral arrangement in the front reception hall, she had demanded that Amber should continue doing creative things with flowers whenever she and her husband entertained.

A time-consuming responsibility that Amber had resented, however, was now welcome as an excuse to enter the house. How on earth could she have let Rocco take off on that chilling threat? His suspicions about her were ridiculous, but she knew *why* he believed the Wintons might be the target for media interest of the most unpleasant kind. Harris Winton was an influential man, who was often in the news. But, for goodness' sake, the whole neighbourhood, never mind the staff, knew about Kaye Winton's extra-marital forays! Sometimes, men were so naïve, Amber reflected ruefully. A newspaper reporter would only need to stop off in the village post office to hear chapter and verse on the voracious brunette's far-from-discreet affairs!

Catering staff were bustling about the big kitchen. Leaving her muddy work boots in the passage and removing the clip from her hair to finger-comb it into a hopeful state of greater tidiness, Amber hurried up the stone service staircase in her sock soles. With a bit of luck, Rocco would be in his suite. If he was downstairs, what was she going to do? Leave him some stupid note begging him to be reasonable? Grimacing at that idea, Amber wondered angrily why Rocco was allowing his usual cool common sense and intelligence to be overpowered by melodramatic assumptions.

I got burned. Well, if Rocco imagined the slight mortification of that newspaper spread on their affair eighteen months back had been the equivalent of getting burned, she would have liked him to have had a taste of what she had suffered in comparison. Her life, her self-respect and her dreams had gone down the drain faster than floodwater.

In the guest wing, she knocked quietly on the door of the main suite. There was no answer but, as she was aware that several rooms lay beyond and Rocco might be in any one of them, she went in and eased the door closed behind her again. She heard his voice then. It sounded as if he was on the phone and she approached the threshold of the bedroom with hesitant steps.

Rocco's brilliant dark eyes struck her anxious gaze and she froze. Clearly, he had heard both her initial knock and her subsequent entrance uninvited. Her skin heated with discomfiture when, with a fluid gesture of mocking invitation, he indicated the sofa several feet from him. He continued with his call, his rich dark drawl wrapping round mellow Italian syllables with a sexy musicality that sent tiny little shivers of recall down her taut spinal cord. She recognised a couple of words, recalled how she had once planned to learn his language. With a covert rub of her damp palms on her worn jeans, she sat down, stiff with strain. He lounged by the window, talking into his mobile phone, bold, bronzed features in profile, his attention removed from her.

He stood about six feet four and he had the lean muscular build of an athlete. Broad shoulders, narrow hips, long, long powerful legs. His clothes were always beautifully tailored and cut to fit him like a glove. Yet he could look elegant clad only in a towel, she recalled uneasily from the past. Her colour rising afresh at the tone of her thoughts, she looked away, conscious of the tremor in her hands, the tension licking through her smaller, slighter frame.

They had been together for three months when Rocco had ditched her. For her, anyway, it had been love at first sight. He had called her 'tabbycat' because of the way she had used to curl up on the sofa beside him. When he had been out of the country over weekends and holidays, he had flown her out to join him in a variety of exotic places. Her feet hadn't touched the ground once during their magical affair. All her innate caution and sense had fallen by the wayside. Finding herself on a roller coaster of excitement and passion, she had become enslaved. When the roller coaster had come to a sudden halt and thrown her off, she had not been able to credit that he'd been able to just abandon what *she* had believed they had shared.

That was why she had kept on phoning him at first, accepting that he was furious with her about that ghastly newspaper story, accepting that that story had been entirely her fault and that *she* had had to be the one to make amends. Loving Rocco had taught her how to be humble and face her mistakes.

And how had he rewarded her humility? He had kicked her in the teeth! Her delicate bone-structure tightened. She pushed her honey-blonde hair off her brow, raking it back, so that it tumbled in glossy disarray round her slim shoulders. Her hair needed cutting: she was letting it grow because it was cheaper. At the rate that her finances were improving, she thought ruefully, she would have hair down to her feet by the time she could afford a salon appointment again. Loving Rocco had also taught her what it was like to be poor…or, at least, how utterly humiliating it was, after a long period of independence, to be forced to rely once more on family generosity to survive.

Her tummy churning with nerves, she focused on Rocco again, noting the outline of his long, luxuriant black lashes, comparing them to Freddy's… Freddy's hair was as dark as Rocco's was fair, black as a raven's wing. She squeezed her eyes tight shut and prayed for concentration and courage. •

'To what do I owe the honour of this second meeting?' Rocco enquired drily. 'I thought we were just about talked out.'

Worrying at her lower lip, Amber tilted her head back. But she could still only see as high as his gold silk tie because he had moved closer. In a harried movement, she stood up again. 'If you tell Harris Winton that there is the slightest possibility that I might be spying on him for some newspaper, I'll get the sack!'

Rocco studied her with inscrutable dark eyes. In the charged silence that he allowed to linger, his lean, powerful face remained impassive.

'I can't understand why you should even *think* such a thing of me…it's nonsensical!'

'Is it? I remember you telling me that you once very much wanted to *be* a journalist…'

Amber stilled in consternation and surprise. *Had* she told Rocco that? During one of those trusting chats when he had seemed to want to know every tiny thing about her? Evidently, she had told him but she hadn't given him the whole picture. During her teens, Amber's parents had put her under constant pressure to produce better exam results and, when they'd finally realised that she was not going to become a doctor, a lawyer or a teacher, she had been instructed to focus on journalism instead. They had signed her up for an extra-curricular media studies course on which she had got very poor grades.

'*And* how desperately disappointed you were when you couldn't get a job on a newspaper,' Rocco finished smoothly.

For the first time it occurred to Amber that, eighteen months back, Rocco had had more reason than she had appreciated to believe that the prospect of media limelight might have tempted her into talking about their relationship. She was furious that one insignificant little piece of information casually given out of context could have helped to support his belief that she was guilty as charged.

'Do you know the only reason I went for that job? My parents had just died... It was *their* idea that I should try for a career in journalism, not my own. And what I might or might not have wanted at the age of sixteen has very little bearing on the person I am now,' Amber declared in driven dismissal.

Rocco continued to regard her in level challenge. 'I can concede that. But when we met, you were employed in a merchant bank and studying for accountancy exams. Give me one good reason why you should now be pretending to be a gardener?'

'Because, obviously, it's *not* a pretence! It's the only job I could get...at least the only work that it's convenient for me to take right now.' In a nervous gesture as she tacked on that qualification, Amber half opened her hands and then closed them tight again, her green eyes veiling, for the last thing she wanted to touch on was the difficulties of being a single parent on a low wage.

'Convenient?' Rocco queried.

'I live in a cottage in the coachyard here. Accommodation goes with the job. My sister lives nearby and I like being close to her—'

'You never mentioned that you *had* a sister while I was with you.'

Amber flushed a dull guilty red for she had allowed him to assume that she was as alone in the world as he was. Rocco was an only child, born to older parents, who had both passed away by the time he'd emerged from his teens.

'So explain why you kept quiet about having a sister,' Rocco continued levelly.

But there was no way Amber felt she could tell him the honest truth on that score. She had been terrified that Rocco would meet her gorgeous, intellectual big sister and start thinking of Amber herself as very much a poor second best. It had happened before, after all. It didn't matter that Opal was twelve years older and happily married. People were always amazed when they learnt that the highly successful barrister, Opal Carlton, was Amber's sibling. From an early age, Amber had been aware that she was a sad disappointment to her parents, who, being so clever themselves, had expected equally great things from their younger daughter as well. Her best had never, ever been good enough.

'Well, I have a sister and I'm very fond of her,' she mumbled, not meeting his eyes because she was ashamed that she had kept Opal hidden like a nasty secret when indeed she could not have got through the past year without her sister's support.

'Why are you feeding me this bull?' Rocco demanded with sardonic bite. 'Nothing you've said so far comes anywhere near explaining why you should suddenly be clutching a wheelbarrow instead of fingering a keyboard!'

Amber swallowed hard. 'Within a month of that kiss-and-tell story appearing in print, I was at the top of the hit list at Woodlawn Wyatt. They said they were overstaffed and, along with some others, I lost my job.'

'That doesn't surprise me,' Rocco conceded without sympathy. 'Merchant banks are conservative institutions—'

'And the regular banks are still shedding staff practically by the day so I couldn't find another opening,' Amber admitted, tight-mouthed, hating the necessity of letting him know that she had struggled but failed to find similar employment. 'I also suspect that, whenever a reference *was* taken up with my former employers, the knives came out—'

'Possibly,' Rocco mused in the same noncommittal tone. 'But had you stayed in London—'

'Being out of work in a big city is expensive. I hadn't been with Woodlawn Wyatt long enough to qualify for a redundancy payment. I moved in with my sister for a while—'

'This is a rural area but it's also part of the commuter belt. Surely you could have found employment *more*—'

Her patience gave out. 'Look, I'm happy as I am and I only came up here in the first place to ask you to back off and just forget you ever saw me!'

Rocco lounged back against the polished footboard on the elegant sleigh bed, bringing their eyes into sudden direct contact and somehow making her awesomely aware that they were in a bedroom together. 'Do you really mean that?'

Amber blinked but it didn't break the mesmerising hold of his arresting dark golden eyes for long enough to stifle the terrifying tide of sheer physical longing that washed over her. Memory was like a cruel hook dragging her down into a dangerous undertow of intimate images she was already fighting not to recall. Rocco tumbling her down on his bed and kissing her with the explosive force that charged her up with the passion she had never been able to resist; Rocco's expert hands roving over her to waken her in the morning; the sheer joy of being wanted more than she had ever been wanted by anyone in her entire life.

'What are you t-talking about?' Amber stammered,

dredging herself out of those destabilising and enervating memories.

'Do you really want me to forget I ever saw you?' Rocco viewed her steadily from beneath inky black lashes longer than her own.

'What else?' Already conscious of her heightened colour and quickened breathing, Amber was very still for every fibre of her being was awake to the smouldering atmosphere that had come up out of nowhere to entrap her.

'Liar...' The effect of the husky reproof Rocco delivered was infinitely less than the sudden sensual smile of amusement that curled his wide, eloquent mouth.

Images from a distant, happier past assailed Amber: the sound of a smile in his deep voice on the phone, the feeling of euphoria, of being appreciated when he looked at her in just that way. What way? As if there were only the two of them in the whole wide world, as if she was someone *special*. Before Rocco came along, nobody had ever made Amber feel special or important or needed.

Her breath catching in her throat, she stared back at him, wholly enchanted by the charisma of that breathtaking smile. 'I'm not lying...' she muttered without even being aware of what she was saying.

Rocco reached out and closed his hands over hers. At first contact, a helpless shiver ran through her. Slowly, he smoothed out her tightly clenched fingers, one by one. Like a rabbit caught in car headlights, she gazed up at him, heart banging against her ribcage, aware only of him and the seductive weakness induced by the heat blossoming inside her. He eased her inches closer. His warmth, the feel of his skin on hers again, the powerful intoxicant of his familiar scent overpowered her senses.

'I said I wouldn't touch you again if I was dying *but...*'

The rasp of his voice travelled down her responsive spine like hot, delicious honey.

'But?'

'Dio...' Rocco husked, drawing her the last couple of inches. 'I believe I could be persuaded otherwise, tabbycat...'

The sound of that endearment made her melt.

'However, you would have to promise to keep it quiet—'

'Quiet?' All concentration shot, she didn't grasp what he was talking about.

'I don't want to open a newspaper on Monday morning to find out how I scored between the sheets again—'

'Sorry...?'

Without warning, Rocco released her hands and, since he was just about all that was holding her upright on her wobbling lower limbs, she almost fell on top of him. He righted her again with deft cool. 'Think about it,' he advised, stepping away from her.

For an instant, Amber hovered, breathing in deep, striving to get her brain into gear again. She did not have to think very hard. 'Apart from the obvious, what are you trying to imply?'

'I'm bored this weekend and you challenged me.'

In considerable emotional disarray as she appreciated that she had been standing there transfixed and hypnotised, entirely entrapped by the sexual power he had exercised over her, Amber spun round. 'I beg your pardon?'

Rocco sent her a sizzling glance of mockery. 'Maybe I want to see you *faking* it for my benefit.'

Amber reddened to the roots of her hair. 'No chance,' she said curtly and stepped past him to hurry back out to the sitting room.

Without the slightest warning whatsoever, the door she was heading for opened and Kaye Winton walked in. At the sight of Amber, she frowned in astonishment, pale blue eyes rounding. 'What are you doing up here?'

Mind a complete blank, Amber found herself glancing in desperation at Rocco.

Brilliant dark eyes gleaming, Rocco said, 'I asked for someone to remove the flowers.'

'The flowers?' the beautiful brunette questioned.

'I'm allergic to them.' Rocco told the lie with a straight face.

'Oh, no!' Kaye surged over to the centre table as if jet-propelled. Gathering up the giant glass vase, she planted it bodily into Amber's hastily extended arms. 'Take them away immediately. I'm so sorry, Rocco!'

Her sweater soaked by the water that had slopped out of the vase with the other woman's careless handling, Amber headed for the corridor at speed, her shaken expression hidden by the mass of trendy corkscrew twigs and lilies she had arranged earlier that day. It was ironic that she should be grateful for Rocco's quick thinking, even more relieved that her employer's wife had not come in a minute sooner and found her in his bedroom. How on earth would she ever have explained that?

Indeed, how could she even explain to *herself* why she had allowed Rocco to behave as he had? She had acted like a doll without mind or voice and offered no objection to his touching her. Sick with shame at her own weakness, Amber disposed of the floral arrangement and pulled on her work boots again with unsteady hands. Rocco was bored. Rocco was playing manipulative games with her to amuse himself. Dear heaven, that *hurt* her so much. And she knew it shouldn't hurt, knew she should have been fully on her guard and capable of resisting Rocco's smouldering sexuality.

Wasn't she supposed to hate him? Well, hatred had kept her far from cool when he'd turned up the heat. And there she was blaming him when she ought to be blaming herself! Rocco had made her want him again...instantly, easily, reawakening the hunger she had truly believed she had buried for ever. But with every skin-cell alight with anticipation, she had just been desperate for him to kiss her. And he hadn't kissed her either, which told her just how complete his own control had been in comparison to her own.

Well, she was going to spend the rest of the weekend at her sister's house and stay well out of Rocco's way, she told herself impulsively. Then she recalled that she *couldn't* do that. True, she was babysitting at her sister's that evening, but she had to work Saturdays and would have to turn in as usual. Harris Winton was usually home only at weekends and the reason Amber got a day off mid-week instead was that her employer insisted that she be available for his weekly inspection tour of the grounds.

She trudged round to the old coachyard and climbed into the ten-year-old hatchback her brother-in-law, Neville, had given her on loan, saying it had been a trade-in for one of the luxury cars he imported, but not really convincing her with that less-than-likely story. Furthermore, the car was on permanent loan, Amber reflected heavily, once again reminded of just how dependent she *was* on Neville and Opal's generosity.

The independence she had sought was as far out of her reach as it had ever been, she conceded heavily. Her sole source of pride was that she was no longer living under her sister's roof. But she was only able to work because she shared the services of the expensive but very well-trained nanny her sister employed to look after her own child. Amber's low salary would not stretch to full-time childcare or indeed towards much of a contribution towards the nanny's salary. So she kept on saying thank you to her family and accepting for Freddy's sake, striving to repay their generosity by making herself useful in other ways. It occurred to her then that she could have wiped the sardonic smile from Rocco's darkly handsome features with just a few words.

As she drove over to the exclusive housing development where her sister lived, she asked herself why she hadn't spoken those words to Rocco when she had finally got the opportunity.

'Rocco Volpe is pond scum,' her sister, Opal, had pronounced on the day of Freddy's birth. 'But I'd sooner cut my throat than watch you humiliate yourself trailing him through the courts to establish paternity and win a financial settlement. Rich men fight paternity suits every step of the way. The whole process can drag on for years, particularly when the father is not a British citizen. He could leave the country and stonewall you at every turn. Keep your pride… that's my advice.'

Her pride? The very thought of telling Rocco that she had given birth to his child flicked Amber's pride on the raw. Rocco had pulled no punches when he'd ended their relationship. Amber's troubled thoughts took her back in time an entire eighteen months. Had she had proper pride and sense, she would never have got as far as a first date with Rocco Volpe…

CHAPTER THREE

WHEN she was seventeen, Amber had started work as clerk in an accountant's office. She had gratefully accepted the offer of day release and evening classes to study for accounting qualifications; it had been four years before she'd moved on. At twenty-one she had applied for and got a job at the merchant bank, Woodlawn Wyatt, where she had become second in command in the accounts department; her salary had doubled overnight.

'You're the token woman,' her section senior had told her patronisingly.

But Amber hadn't cared that she'd had to work with a male dinosaur, angry that his own choice of candidate had been passed over. Finally having got her foot onto a promising career ladder with that timely move and promotion, she had been happy to work long hours. Busy, busy, busy, that was what she had been, little time for friends or a man in her life, falling into bed exhausted night after night, driven by a desperate need to prove herself and terrified of failing.

She had met Rocco when Woodlawn Wyatt had thrown a big party for the outgoing managing director. Sitting with a fixed smile during the speeches, she had surreptitiously been drawing up a study schedule on a napkin in preparation for her next exam. She had not even noticed Rocco at the top table and when the lights had lowered and the dancing had begun, she had been on the brink of going home, having made her duty appearance.

'Would you like to dance?'

Rocco came out of nowhere at her. She looked up with a frown, only to be stunned by the effect of those spectacular tawny eyes of his. 'Sorry…who are you speaking to?' she mumbled, not crediting for one moment that it might be her.

'You…' Rocco told her gently.

'I don't dance…I was about to leave, actually—'

'Just one dance—'

'I've got two left feet,' she muttered, getting all flustered. 'Did one of my colleagues put you up to this for a joke?'

'Why would anyone do that?'

As it was her responsibility to keep a choke hold on business expense claims, Amber knew herself to be disliked by executive personnel, who loathed the way she pursued them for receipts and explanations of extraordinary bills. It was an unpopular job but she told herself that she wouldn't be doing it for ever.

Embarrassed then by the low self-esteem she had betrayed with her foolish question, she found herself grasping Rocco's extended hand and rising. And from that moment, her safe world started tilting and shifting and becoming an unrecognisable place of sudden colour and emotion. Nothing that followed was within her conscious control. After midnight, she left the party with him, aware of the shaken eyes following in their wake, but it had truly been as if Rocco had cast a spell over her. She had *still* been with Rocco at lunchtime the following day.

'What attracted you to me?' she had asked him once, still mystified.

'My ego couldn't take not being noticed by the one woman in the room worth looking at?'

'Seriously…'

'You had your shoes off under the table and you have these dinky little feet and I went weak with lust—'

'Rocco.'

'I took one look and I wanted you chained to my bed, day and night.'

Had she initially been a refreshing novelty to a sophisticated male accustomed to much more experienced women? Sinking back to the present, Amber parked at the rear of her sister's big detached house and went inside. As they often did, her sister and brother-in-law were staying on in London to go out for the evening with friends before returning home. Amber was booked to babysit as it was their nanny Gemma's night off.

The red-headed nanny was sitting in the airy conservatory with the children. Amber's two-year-old niece, Chloe, was bashing the life out of an electronic teaching toy while Freddy sat entranced by both the racket and the flashing lights.

Freddy…with the single exception of hair colour, Freddy was Rocco in miniature, Amber conceded. He had black hair, big dark golden brown eyes and olive skin. She studied her smiling baby son with eyes that were suddenly stinging. She loved Freddy so much and already he was holding his arms up for her to lift him. As Gemma greeted her while attempting to distract Chloe from the ear-splitting noise she was creating, Amber crouched down and scooped Freddy up. In just over a week, when Christmas arrived, Freddy would be a year old. She drank in the warm, familiar scent of his hair, holding his solid little body close to her own, grateful that she didn't need to worry about taking him back to her cottage at the Wintons' for at least another twenty-four hours.

'You're very quiet. Don't tell me you're still worrying about your car not starting,' her brother-in-law, Neville, scolded as he dropped her off in the cobbled coachyard at the Wintons' early the following morning. 'Look, I'll have that old banger of yours back on the road by this lunchtime. One of my delivery drivers will run it over here for you.'

Sheathed in the fancy black designer dress that she had borrowed from her sister's dry-cleaning bag because she had forgotten to pack for her overnight stay the evening before, Amber climbed out of Neville's Mercedes sports car, and gave him a pained smile. 'Yes, as if it's not bad enough that I have to drag you out of bed on a Saturday morning to take me to work, I now wreck the *rest* of your day by sentencing you to play car mechanic—'

The older man gave her a wry grin. 'Give over, Amber. I'm never happier than when I'm under the bonnet of a car!'

Yeah, sure, Amber thought, guiltily unconvinced as he drove off again. Maybe that was true if the car was a luxury model, but she could not credit that a male who owned as successful a business as Neville did could possibly enjoy working on an old banger. Barefoot and bare-legged because she hadn't wanted to risk waking her sleeping sister by going in search of shoes and underwear to borrow, a bulk, heavy carrier bag containing the previous day's clothes weighing down her arm, Amber rummaged for her keys for the cottage.

She got the fright of her life when a slight sound alerted her to the fact that she had company. Head flying up, she focused in astonishment on Rocco as he stepped into view out of the shadowy recesses behind one of the open archways fronting the coachyard. Casually, if exclusively clad in a husky brown cashmere jacket and tailored beige chinos, luxuriant silver fair hair tousled in the breeze above his devastingly attractive dark features, Rocco literally sent her composure into a downward tailspin.

'So it's *true*,' Rocco pronounced with grim emphasis. 'You've got a middle-aged man in a Merc in tow.'

The hand Amber had extended towards the keyhole on the cottage door fell back limp to her side. 'What are you d-doing out here at this hour?' she stammered, wide-eyed, still to come to grips with his first staggering statement.

Rocco vented a humourless laugh. 'You should know I never lie in bed unless I've got company—'

'But it's barely eight in the morning.' Amber didn't really know why she was going on about the actual time. She only knew that she was so taken aback by Rocco's sudden appearance and her own inability to drag her eyes from that lean, darkly handsome face that she couldn't think straight.

'I've been waiting for you. I want to know if what Kaye Winton said about you after dinner last night was a wind-up,' Rocco bit out flatly, raking brooding dark eyes over the short fitted dress she wore, lingering in visible disbelief on her incongruously bare legs and feet. '*Dio mio*...he chucks you out of the car half naked in the middle of winter. Where have you been? In a layby somewhere?'

Shivering now in the brisk breeze, Amber was nonetheless welded to the spot, frowning at him in complete incredulity. 'What Kaye Winton *said* about me? What did *she* say about me?'

'She warned me to watch out for you coming onto me as you were the local sex goddess...only she got rather carried away and didn't manage to put it quite that politely.'

Amber's generous lips parted and stayed parted. 'Say that again...' she finally whispered shakily when she was capable of emerging from the severe shock he had dealt her with that bombshell.

'I believe you enjoy a constant procession of different men in flashy expensive cars and regular overnight absences...' Rocco grated in seething disgust, striding forward to snatch her keys from her loosened grasp and open the door. 'Go inside...you're blue with cold!'

'That's an absolute lie!' Amber exclaimed.

Rocco planted a hand to her rigid shoulder and thrust her

indoors, following her in to slam the door closed again in his wake. 'I think it's past time you told me what's going *on* with you—'

Amber flung down her carrier bag and rounded on him. 'Now, let me get this straight…Kaye Winton *told* you—'

'After what I've seen with my own eyes I wouldn't swallow a denial,' Rocco cut in angrily. 'So don't waste your breath. Are you hooking to support some kind of life-threatening habit?'

Amber closed her eyes, outraged and appalled that he should even suggest such a thing. 'Are you insane that you can ask me that?'

Rocco closed his hands over hers and pulled her closer. 'Amber, I want the truth. I was tempted to close my hands round that vicious shrew's throat last night and squeeze hard to silence her! I honestly thought it was sheer bitching I was listening to—'

'I want to hear this again. In front of witnesses, that woman—'

'*No* witnesses…the other guests were at the far end of the room when she chose to get confidential—'

Only a little of Amber's growing rage ebbed at that clarification. 'Right, I'll have it out with her face to face—'

'It would be wiser to keep quiet than encourage her to spread such tales further afield—'

Amber lifted angry hands and tried to break his hold. 'Let me go, Rocco. I'm going to tip that dirty-minded besom out of her bed *and*—'

Rocco held fast to her. 'Looking like you're just home from a rough night at a truck stop, that will be *so* impressive!'

'How dare you talk to me like that? How dare you suggest that I might be…that I might be a whore?' Tears that were as much the result of distress as fury lashing her eyes,

Amber slung those words back at him with the outrage of raw sincerity.

'I'm sorry if I've offended and hurt you, but I need to know.' Releasing her with relief unconcealed in his brilliant dark incisive eyes, Rocco expelled his breath in a stark hiss. 'So when *did* you get into men in the plural just for fun?'

Amber swept up the jampot of dying wild flowers on the small pine table and flung it at him. The glass jar hit the stainless steel sink several feet behind him and smashed, spattering shards all over the work surface.

'That was buck stupid when you have no shoes on,' Rocco pointed out with immense and galling cool.

'I wish it had hit you!' Amber launched wildly, but the truth was that she was already calming down out of shock at what she had done. She breathed in slow and deep. 'I don't have any life-threatening habits to support either…have you got that straight?'

'I'm very pleased to hear it. But I do wish you had retained the same exclusive attitude to sex.'

Ignoring that acid response, Amber fought to get a grip on her floundering emotions and understand why Kaye Winton, who had never demonstrated the slightest interest in her private life but whose husband bought their cars through Neville's business, should have muddied her reputation in such an inexcusable way. Had the other woman somehow sensed in Rocco's suite the day before that more was going on between Amber and Rocco than she had seen? Amber had never subscribed to the general local belief that Kaye Winton was an air-head. That might well be the impression the brunette preferred to give around men, but Amber was unconvinced and, recalling the manner in which she herself had automatically looked at Rocco for an inspiring excuse or being found upstairs with him, she suppressed a groan.

'I bet Kaye Winton noticed the way I glanced at you for

support yesterday. Strangers don't do that.' Amber sighed. 'But as for the rest of her nonsense…'

It only then occurred to Amber that it was true that she spent regular nights away from the cottage and that it was equally true that she might often have been seen climbing in and out of different cars. Between them, Neville and Opal owned five luxury vehicles. Neville often picked her up on his way home if she was coming over to stay and just as often dropped her back in the morning. Someone watching from an upstairs window would not be able to tell that the driver was always the same man. Even so, she was shattered by the apparent interpretation the brunette had put on what she had seen, yet surprised that the other woman did *not* appear to have mentioned that Amber was also an unmarried mother.

Amber breathed in so deep, her full breasts strained against the fabric of her sister's dress which was too snug a fit under that pressure. She glanced across the room. Rocco had his attention riveted to her chest. She reddened, feeling the sudden heaviness of her own swelling flesh, the tautening of her sensitive nipples. 'Stop it…' she muttered fiercely before she could think better of it.

'Tell me *how*…' Rocco invited in a raw undertone, fabulous cheekbones taut and scoured with colour, eyes like burning golden arrows of challenge on her lovely face.

'I need to get dressed for work—'

'Or you could get *undressed* for me. In fact, you don't need to move a muscle,' Rocco murmured roughly as he closed the distance between them. 'I'll do it for you—'

'But—'

He caught her into the circle of his strong arms and she gazed up at him, heart beating fast and furious in the slight hiatus that followed. She told herself to break away but somehow she did precisely nothing. He lifted her up against him with easy strength. She wrapped her arms round him. He meshed one fierce, controlling hand into the fall of her honey-blonde hair and brought their mouths into hungry devouring collision.

It was like being shot to sudden vibrant life after a long time in suspended animation. With a strangled gasp of shock at the intensity of sensation surging through her quivering frame, she kissed him back with a kind of wild, clumsy, hanging-on-tight desperation. If she stopped to breathe, she might die of deprivation, she might stop *feeling* everything she had thought she would never feel again. A soaring excitement thrummed low in her pelvis, awakening the dulled ache of a physical craving way beyond anything she could control.

But, breathing raggedly, Rocco dragged his expert sensual mouth from hers and stared down into her shaken green eyes with febrile force. 'You're wearing next to *nothing* under that dress—'

Aghast that he had realised that reality, for she had scarcely clothed herself for entertaining, Amber mumbled in severe discomfiture, 'Well...er—'

Rocco dumped her down on a hard chair by the table. 'How many ways did he have you in the Merc? And when the hell did you turn into such a tramp?' he ground out wrathfully.

'For your information, that was my brother-in-law driving that car!' Amber shot at him furiously.

'Tips you out barefoot at dawn on a regular basis, does he?'

'When my car breaks down and I've spent the night at my sister's home...*yes*!' Amber hissed back. 'And I wasn't going to put a pair of dirty workman's boots on with this dress *and* without clean socks, was I?'

'I suppose all these guys in the expensive cars you've been seen in are married to *sisters* of yours?' Shooting her a look of splintering derision, pallor spread round his ferociously compressed mouth, Rocco strode to the door.

'Two minutes ago, you didn't much care!' Amber heard herself throw at his powerful back in retaliation.

Rocco swung back and surveyed her with shimmering golden eyes. '*Per meraviglia*...who was it who called a halt? I didn't come here to get laid—'

Enraged by that assurance, Amber threw herself upright again. 'I'm still waiting to hear why you did come here because I sure as heck didn't want you anywhere near me!'

'Then isn't it strange that you should find it so difficult to say that one little word, "no"?'

Amber paled and turned away, biting her lip to prevent herself from making some empty response which would only prolong her own agony of mortification.

'After what I heard last night, I was concerned about you—'

Amber whirled back. '*You* concerned about *me*? Give me a break!'

Rocco stared at her with cold, dark eyes of censure. 'I would do as much for any ex if I thought they needed a helping hand. And don't curl your lip like that. I'm serious,' he spelt out with chilling cool. 'If you need financial help to get yourself out of what appears to be a crisis period in your life, I'll give it to you...no questions asked and *nothing* expected in return.'

The silence hung there like a giant sheet of glass waiting to crash and smash when the seething tension broke. She stared back fixedly at him. A shaken and hollow laugh was wrenched from her convulsed throat. 'So where were you, Rocco...when I *really* needed you?'

A tiny muscle pulled tight at the corner of his expressive mouth and he did not pretend not to follow her meaning. 'I was very angry with you eighteen months ago—'

'*So* angry you couldn't even take a phone call?' Amber squeezed out the reminder with burning bitterness.

His lean, powerful face clenched. 'You knew how much I valued my privacy. I won't apologise for that. You destroyed us when you decided to share salacious details of our relationship with a muck-raking journalist. I could never have trusted you again after that.'

'I gave no salacious details whatsoever, but those sort of details are fairly easily guessed when it comes to a guy with your reputation…and I did not *know* I was talking to a journalist—'

'Amber,' Rocco incised flatly, 'I don't know what you're trying to prove but it's way too late to make the attempt.'

But whose fault was it that it was now too late for her to speak in her own defence? Hatred as savage as the hunger he had roused only minutes earlier flamed into being inside her. 'I'll never forget what you did to me back then,' she said without any expression at all, her heart-shaped face pale but composed. 'You're right. It's way too late to discuss any of that now. Go on…take your precious charity and your nauseatingly pious offer of help out of here and don't you dare come back!'

Stubborn as a rock and contrary in the face of an invitation he should have been all too keen to take in the circumstances, Rocco stood his ground. 'I wasn't being pious and I wasn't offering you charity.'

'You're talking down to me, though, and I won't stand anyone doing that to me.'

'Better that than dragging you back into bed,' Rocco murmured in a savage undertone that shook her as he yanked open the door again.

'I wouldn't *go* to bed with you again!'

His arrogant silvery fair head turned back to her, a searing sexual hunger blatant in the all-encompassing appraisal he gave her. 'If it's any consolation, no woman ever gave me as much pleasure as you—'

'*Consolation?*' Amber almost choked on that mortifying word and what followed very nearly sent her into orbit with frustrated rage.

'But I need a woman to be exclusively mine—'

'Only you're not so scrupulous yourself,' Amber heard herself remark. 'After you dumped me, according to the gossip columns you were like a sex addict on the loose!'

Taken aback, Rocco froze, and then he sent her a smouldering look of what could only be described as sheer loathing.

Reeling in shock from that revealing appraisal, Amber went white and she could not drag her stricken gaze from his lean, strong face. 'Rocco…?' she whispered unsteadily.

'*You* did that to me,' he imparted with savage condemnation.

The door thudded shut on his departure, leaving her trembling and in more confusion and turmoil than she had ever thought to experience again.

CHAPTER FOUR

AN HOUR later, just as Amber was ready to go outside and start work, a brisk knock sounded on the cottage door.

She was stunned to find Kaye Winton waiting outside. The brunette, clad in a skin-tight green leather skirt suit, her beautiful face stiff, took advantage of Amber's surprise and strolled in uninvited.

'I'm going to lay this on the line,' Kaye told her curtly. 'If I catch you coming on to one of our guests again, I'll inform my husband.'

Amber gave her an incredulous look. 'Coming *on* to one—?'

'Rocco Volpe. Oh, I don't blame you. In your position I might have done the same. Rocco's a real babe and some catch,' Kaye cut in with a tight little smile, green as grass with envy and resentment. 'But you needn't think I didn't work out that when I interrupted you both yesterday, you were walking out of his bedroom—'

Amber found herself in the very awkward position of being guilty as charged on that count of inappropriate behaviour. And while she had initially intended to confront the other woman about the hatchet job done on her own reputation, nothing was quite that simple. Admitting that Rocco had repeated the brunette's allegations to her would reveal that Amber was much more intimate with Rocco Volpe than she was prepared to admit. Indeed, so fraught was the entire situation with the risk that she could end up losing her job or, at the very least, be forced into making personal confidences in her own defence, Amber had not yet decided what to do for best.

'Mrs Winton, I—'

'I did my best to limit the damage last night and turn his attention away from you,' Kaye revealed, surprising Amber with that blunt admission. 'When all's said and done, Rocco's just another testosterone-charged bloke on the lookout for sexual variety, but he's *not* going to find it with our gardener. Is that quite clear?'

'I believe you've made yourself very clear,' Amber said grittily, fingernails biting into her palms to restrain her from saying anything she might later come to regret.

The other woman nudged the tiny toy train lying on the tiled floor by the table with the toe of her stiletto-heeled shoe. 'I forgot about your kid…where do you keep him, anyway? Does he only visit you? Now that I think about it, I've never laid eyes on him.'

'I'm sure you're not interested.' Having wondered why Kaye had neglected to inform Rocco that Amber had a baby, Amber concealed her relief at the casual admission that the other woman had simply forgotten Freddy's existence. It was hardly surprising, though, when at the outset of her employment Harris Winton had warned her that he didn't expect to see her using the grounds of the house outside working hours.

Kaye shrugged her agreement. 'You're taking this well—'

'Maybe…maybe not.'

Opening the door again, the brunette dealt her a wry glance. 'I've done you a favour. My husband would have sacked you yesterday. Harris has Victorian values on staff behaviour.'

Since it was a well-known fact that Kaye Winton had once been a lowly groom working at the riding stables owned by her husband's first wife, Amber could barely swallow that closing comment.

'Men…' Kaye laughed in frank acknowledgement of that hypocrisy. 'Can't live *with* them, can't live without them!'

It was noon when Kaye's husband, Harris, finally came in search of Amber. A small, spare man with a very precise manner, he was much quieter than usual and he cut short his usual lengthy inspection tour by pointing out that he had guests staying. As the rain was coming on heavily by then, Amber was unsurprised at his eagerness to head back indoors again. Resigning herself to a day spent skidding on muddy lawns and getting soaked to the skin, for the rain always found its way through her jacket eventually, Amber got on with her work. Around lunchtime she went back to the cottage and made herself a sandwich before returning outside.

Never had she been more conscious of the vast gulf that had opened up between herself and Rocco. There he was snug indoors on his fancy country-house weekend, being waited on hand and foot, entertained, fed like a king by special caterers and lusted over by his shapely hostess. And here *she* was, in the most subservient of positions with a list of instructions from her employer that she would be lucky to complete in the space of a month, never mind over the next week!

In addition, Rocco *hated* her. So why was that making her feel as if the roof of the world had fallen in around her? She relived that look of his at the outset of the day…violent loathing. She shivered. He went out pulling women as if he had only days left to live and went out hell-raising for an entire six months before sinking into curious obscurity and then he had the neck to say to her, '*You* did that to me!'

Louse! Not the guy she recalled, but then there was no denying that she had had a very rosy and false image of Rocco until reality had smacked her in the teeth. That first night they'd met they had stayed up talking until way past dawn in a variety of public places. Her brain had been in a tailspin. She had let him take her home for breakfast and he had seduced her into bed with him. Well, possibly, she had been fairly willing to be seduced for the first time in her cautious existence. After all, she had only been in love once before Rocco and that had been nothing but a great big let-down.

She grimaced, recalling Russ, whom she had fallen for the year before she'd met Rocco. Meeting Opal over dinner one evening, Russ had taken one stunned look at her beautiful sister and had barely noticed Amber's existence from that point on. Sitting there like a third wheel while the man she'd thought she'd loved had ignored her and flirted like mad with her sister, Amber had stopped thinking he was special. That very night, Amber had been planning to surrender to Russ's persuasions and acquire her first experience of making love. But by the time Russ had finished raving about how gorgeous and how totally fabulous and fascinating Opal was, Amber had known she never, ever wanted to see him again. Opal turned heads in the street with her flawless ice-blonde perfection. As Amber had learned to her cost, a lot of men couldn't handle that.

Rocco had never got the chance to make the same mistake.

Their first day together, Rocco had woken Amber up about lunchtime and told her that he had been looking for someone like her *all* his life. Well, all his life from the night before, she could only assume in retrospect. Rocco, who had stood outside his own locked bathroom door swearing that it was *so* romantic that she had fallen into his bed within hours of meeting him, declaring that he did not have one-night stands, that he would never, ever *think* of her in that light and finally, in desperation, apologising for not having kept his far-too-persuasive hands off her. On the other side of the door, she had been biting back sobs of chagrined self-loathing and struggling into her clothes with frantic hands.

'I'm not letting you go,' Rocco told her when she emerged. 'I'm hanging onto you.'

Three months of excitement and joy, interspersed with occasional violent rows that tore her apart at the seams, followed. No longer did she want to work endless overtime: she wanted to be with Rocco but she valued her career. Rocco offered her a position on his own staff at much more than she was earning. She didn't speak to him for two solid days. Such a casual proposition insulted all that she had achieved on her own merits. Rocco had made the very great error of allowing her to see how unimportant and small that job of hers was on his terms.

Crazy about him, she stopped having lunch and taking breaks at work and socialised equally crazy hours, burning the candle at both ends. She fell asleep on him once over dinner in a busy restaurant.

'Such a compliment,' Rocco quipped.

When she appeared in photos by Rocco's side in the gossip columns, she began receiving pointed cracks and knowing looks from her male co-workers. One of the directors provoked a chorus of sniggers the day he thanked her for giving Woodlawn Wyatt so much free publicity. Her working environment was one where men lived in eager hope of seeing a manipulative woman using her body to get ahead. Having an affair with a wealthy and powerful international financier was not the ticket to earning respect.

'Why won't you give me the chance to meet Rocco?' Opal demanded of Amber repeatedly. 'A quick drink early some evening…an hour, no big deal, Amber.'

Amber viewed her sibling's pure, perfect face and her heart sunk for she knew she could not compete. Not in looks, not in wit, not in *any* field. 'It's not cool to confront guys with your family. It might give him the wrong message—'

'You're very insecure about him. I suppose you can't believe your good luck in attracting a male of his calibre and are still wondering what he sees in you,' Opal remarked with deadly accuracy. 'But if he's a commitment-phobe, better to find out now than later. Don't do what I once did. Don't waste five years of your life making excuses for him and chasing rainbows.'

And that was the surprising moment when Amber learned that her sister, whom she had naively assumed to be ultra-successful in *every* way, disabused her of that notion. Prior to meeting Neville, Opal had apparently been strung along by an older man she'd adored and then been ditched when she'd least expected it. That confession of vulnerability allowed Amber to feel close to her older sister for the first time. But the one person she could have trusted with her confidences, she refused to trust.

By the time she had been with Rocco an entire three months, Amber was literally bursting with the simple human need to verbally share her happiness with someone. It was sheer deprivation to have no friend in whom to confide the news that Rocco was the most romantic, the most wonderful guy in the world. Years of attending evening classes several nights a week and working long hours had left Amber without close friends. Dinah Fletcher had gone to school with Amber, made the effort to get Amber's phone number from Opal and rang up out of the blue to suggest a girly get-together, a catching-up on old times…

Deep in her disturbing memories of that disastrous evening with Dinah, Amber hoisted herself up onto the low, sturdy branch of a giant conifer and braced her spine against the trunk. At least everything was still dry below the thick tree canopy, she reflected ruefully, staring up at the loose dead branch pointed out to her by her employer and wondering how best to dislodge it. Reaching down for the leaf rake, she clambered awkwardly higher.

Hearing the rustling, noisy passage of something moving at speed through the undergrowth, she stiffened in dismay, recalling her experience of being cornered by a very aggressive dog a few weeks back. The owner, a guest of the Wintons', had called the animal off, boasting about what a great guard dog he was, not seeming to care that Amber had been scared witless. But now when she peered down anxiously from her perch, she saw that it was Rocco powering like an Olympic sprinter into the clearing below. Her tension ironically increased.

'What the hell are you trying to do to yourself?' Rocco roared at her from twenty feet away. 'Get down from there!'

Amber assumed that now that the rain had quit he was the advance guard of a larger party getting the official tour of the woods, and her teeth gritted in receipt of that interfering demand. 'Why are you trying to make me look like a clown when I'm only trying to do my job?' she snapped in a meaningful whisper. 'Do you think I'm up here for fun?'

Lean, bronzed features stamped with furious exasperation, Rocco strode up to the tree, removed the leaf rake dangling from her loosened grasp and pitched it aside. 'If you knock that hanging branch down, it's going to smash your head in!'

'I'm as safe as houses standing here!'

'Don't be bloody stupid!' Rocco reached up and simply snatched her bodily off her perch. As he did so, the branch on which she'd stood bounced and sent a shiver up through the tree. With a creaking noise, the loose branch above them lurched free of its resting place and began to crash down.

Rocco moved fast, but not fast enough to retain his balance when he was carrying her. Sliding on the soft carpet of leaves below the trees, he went down with her on top of him. Weak with relief that neither of them had been hurt, Amber kept her face buried in his shirt-front, drinking in the achingly familiar scent of him that clung to the fibres, listening to the solid thump of his heartbeat.

'So how are you planning to say thank you?' Rocco enquired lazily.

Amber pushed herself up on forceful hands and scrambled backwards and off him as if she had been burnt. 'Thank you? When you almost killed both of us?'

'I saved your life, woman.' Raw self-assurance charging every syllable of that confident declaration, Rocco strode over to survey the smashed pieces of wood strewing the ground. 'Winton should have hired a forester or a tree surgeon for this kind of work—'

'He's too mean to pay their rates.' Her uncertain gaze followed him and stayed with him. In a dark green weatherproof jacket, his well-worn denim jeans accentuating his lean hips and long, powerful thighs, the breeze ruffling his luxuriant silver fair hair above his lean, dark, devastating features, Rocco looked so sensational, he just took her breath away. 'How come you seem to be out here on your own?'

'I'm escaping some *serious* Monopoly players.' Rocco leant back with fluid grace against the tree trunk and surveyed her with heavily lidded eyes, his gaze a golden gleam below dense, dark lashes.

'Monopoly? You're kidding me?' Amber said unevenly, wandering skittishly closer, then beginning to edge away again as she registered what she was doing.

'I'm not into board games.' He stretched out his long arms and captured her by the shoulders before she could move out of reach. 'You're pale…all shaken up.'

'Maybe…' Amber connected with his stunning dark golden eyes and she wanted to say something smart, but all inventiveness failed her.

Rocco tugged her to him with easy strength. 'I'll be gone in a couple of hours.'

'Gone?' In the act of forcing herself to pull back from him, Amber stilled in shock. She wasn't prepared for that shock,

either. Indeed the shock came out of nowhere at her like a
body blow. He was a weekend guest, *of course* he was leaving.
'But it's only Saturday,' she heard herself muttering weakly.

'Twenty-four hours of the Wintons goes a long way, tabbycat.' Framing her taut cheekbones with long, sure fingers,
Rocco extracted a hungry, drugging kiss as if it were the most
natural thing in the world.

Amber was defenceless, all concentration already shot
by the knowledge of his imminent departure. Leaning into
him, she slid her hands beneath his jacket to rest against his
crisp cotton shirt. Shivering, desperate hunger had her in a
stranglehold. Going, going, gone... I can't *bear* it, screamed
a voice inside her head. Her heartbeat racing at an insane rate
beneath the onslaught of that skilful kiss, she blocked out that
voice she didn't want to hear.

'While one minute of you doesn't last half long enough,'
Rocco husked, and let his tongue pry between her readily
parted lips, once, twice, the third time making her shiver as
though she were in a force-ten gale.

He stopped teasing and devoured her mouth with plundering force. She pulled his shirt out of his waistband, allowed her seeking fingers to splay against the warm smooth
skin of his waist, felt him jerk in response. He dragged her
hand down to the hard, thrusting evidence of his very male
arousal. Her fingertips met the rough, frustrating barrier of
denim. He pushed against her with a muffled groan of frustration, angled his head back from her, feverish golden eyes
glittering, to say with ragged mockery, 'No sheet to hide
under out here, *cara.*'

'Rocco...' Cheeks flaming, she was assailed by bittersweet
memories that hurt even as they made her shiver and melt
down deep inside where she ached for him. And the combi-
nation released a flood of recklessness. She stretched up and
claimed his sensual mouth again for herself and jerked at his

belt with trembling fingers. He tensed in surprise against her and then suddenly he was coming to her assistance faster than the speed of light, releasing the buttons on his tight jeans.

The feel of Rocco trembling like a stallion at the starting gate was the most powerful aphrodisiac Amber had ever experienced. Her own legs barely capable of holding her up, she slid dizzily down his hard, muscular physique onto her knees.

She pressed her lips into his hard, flat stomach and then sent the tip of her tongue skimming along the line of his loosened waistband. His muscles jerked satisfyingly taut under that provocative approach and he exhaled audibly. 'Don't tease...' he begged her, Italian accent thickening every urgent syllable. 'I couldn't stand it...'

'Stop trying to take control...' Taking her time, she ran her hands up his taut, splayed thighs, loving every gorgeous inch of him, loving the way just touching him made her feel. As she eased away the denim, dispensed with the last barrier, Rocco was shaking, breathing heavily. Finding the virile proof of his excitement was not a problem. The extraordinary effect she was having on him was turning her so hot and quivery inside, she was sinking deeper and deeper into a sensual daze.

As she took him in her mouth, he groaned her name out loud, arching his hips off the trunk in surging eagerness. She felt like every woman born since Eve; she felt a power she had never dreamt she could feel. He was *hers* and he was out of control as she had never known him to be. It gave her extreme pleasure to torture him. He meshed his hand into her hair, urging her on, and then he cried out in Italian and he shuddered into an explosive release when she chose, not when he chose.

In the aftermath, the birdsong came back to charge a silence that still echoed in her sensitive ears. She was so shaken up, her body so weak, she felt limp.

Rocco hauled her up to him to study her with dazed and wondering dark golden eyes and then he wrapped his arms round her, pulled her close, burying his face in her hair. He held her so tightly she could not fill her lungs with oxygen, but she revelled in that natural warmth and affection of his, which she had missed infinitely more than she had missed him in her bed. He muttered with a roughened laugh, 'So...I sack the gardener at my own country estate. I hire you...I get into rustic daily walks...no problem, *cara*!'

Amber went rigid and, planting her hands against his broad chest, she pulled free of him like a bristling cat.

'Joke...' Rocco breathed when he saw her furiously flushed face. 'Obviously the wrong one.'

Amber wasn't so sure: Rocco had a very high sex drive. Rocco was still surveying her with stunned appreciation. Rocco always just reached out and took what he wanted. But she wasn't available; she wasn't on offer and never would be again.

'No encore. Goodbye, Rocco.'

'So you weren't in a joking mood—'

Amber crammed her shaking, restive hands into the pockets of her jacket as she backed away from him. 'Your days of being stalked by me are over...OK?'

'I openly admit that I was stalking *you* today, *cara*.'

'Do you think I didn't work that out for myself?' She forced a jarring laugh for she was actually only making that possible connection as he admitted it. 'But I turned the tables—'

'Yes. You also turned *me* inside out...' Rocco rested his intense golden eyes on her, a male well aware of the strength of his own powerful sexual appeal.

Amber dealt him a frozen look of scorn that took every ounce of her acting ability. 'So now you know how that feels.'

CHAPTER FIVE

THE instant Amber believed she was out of sight and hearing, she broke into a run, her breath rasping in her throat in a mad flight through the trees.

It was only four but it was getting dark fast. As Neville had promised, he had had her car brought back. She blundered past it into the cottage, shedding her jacket in a heap, pausing only to wrench off her boots. Not even bothering to put on the lights, she was heading up the stairs when she noticed the red light flashing on the answering machine. With a sigh, she hit the button in case it was something urgent.

Opal's beautifully modulated speaking voice filled the room. Opal and Neville had gone to visit friends, were staying on there for dinner with the children and were planning on a late return. 'Freddy's getting loads of attention,' her sister asserted. 'He won't get the chance to miss you. I'll put him to bed for you when we get back home.'

The prospect of hugging Freddy like a comforting security blanket that evening receded fast. Eyes watering, Amber hurried on upstairs. In the tiny shower room, she switched on the shower and pulled off her clothes as if she were in a race to the finish line. Stepping into the cubicle, she sent the door flying shut and stood there trembling, letting the warm water flood down over her.

What had got into her with Rocco? Sudden insanity? She didn't know what was happening inside her head any more and she was too afraid to take a closer look. All she remembered was feeling as if she were dying inside when Rocco had said he was leaving. So had she somehow had a brainstorm and imagined he was going to move in with the Wintons for ever? Rocco playing board games? Rocco, who was so full of restive, seething energy you could get tired watching him?

She sank down in the corner of the shower, letting the water continue to cascade down over her still-shivering body. What had come over her out in the woods? She didn't want to know. He was gone, he was history…he was *gone*. A horrendous mix of conflicting feelings attacked her. Rage…fear… pain. She hugged her knees and bowed her head down on them.

Rocco had come in search of her. He had admitted that. To say goodbye? Impossible to imagine the Rocco she remembered planning to take advantage of her smallest show of weakness and drag her down into the undergrowth to make love to her again. She would have said no anyway, she *definitely* would have said no, she told herself. He hadn't laid a finger on her, she reminded herself with equal urgency. But then, bombarded by erotic imagery which reminded her precisely why Rocco had been so unusually restrained, she uttered a strangled moan of shame. Rocco not having touched *her* was no longer a source of reassurance or comfort.

She hated him, she really did. She was over him, over him. She hadn't even been kissed in eighteen months, had conceived a violent antipathy for every male her brother-in-law had brought home to dinner in the hope she would take the bait and start dating again. Maybe that had something to do with how she had behaved with Rocco. Or maybe she just loved his body. *Yes*. Wanton, shameless…starved of him? *No*, she swore vehemently to herself. Just a case of over-charged emotions, confusion and an overdose of hormones out of sync. She stayed in the shower until the water ran cold.

Wrapping herself in a towel, she padded out of the shower

room. She frowned at the sight of the dim light spilling from her bedroom out onto the landing. She hadn't even been in her bedroom yet. Had she left the bedside lamp switched on all day? If so, why hadn't she noticed it when she'd come upstairs earlier? Acknowledging that she had been in no state to notice anything very much and that she still felt hollow and sick inside, Amber pushed the door wider and walked into her room.

On the threshold, she froze. Rocco was poised by the window.

'How on earth—?'

'You didn't hear me knock and your front door was unlocked—'

'Was that an invitation for you to just walk on in?' Amber snapped, thinking how very lucky she was that he had not gone into Freddy's little room next door to hers first. Had he done so, he would hardly have failed to notice the cot and the toys in there.

He had changed out of his designer casuals. Sheathed in a formal dark business suit, his arrogant head within inches of the ceiling, Rocco looked formidable.

Agitated by the severe disadvantage of having a scrubbed bare face, dripping hair in a tangle and only an old beach towel between herself and total nudity, Amber added, 'And walk right up into my bedroom?'

Rocco gave her a cloaked look. 'Since I've already said my goodbyes to my host, I didn't think you'd want me to advertise my presence by waiting downstairs in a room that doesn't even have curtains on the windows.'

Amber flushed at that accurate assumption. 'I haven't got around to putting any up yet,' she said defensively.

'I think a woman living alone and secluded by a big empty courtyard should be more careful of her own privacy and safety—'

Amber lifted her chin. 'You're the only prowling predator I've ever known. So what are you doing here?'

'When you turn me inside out, you take the consequences,' Rocco murmured with indolent cool.

'What's that supposed to mean?'

'That what you start, you have to finish.'

'We *are* finished,' she said breathlessly.

'I'm not hearing you...' Rocco sidestepped her and pushed the bedroom door closed like a guy making a pronounced statement.

'Rocco—'

'You want me...I want you. Right now, when I'm flying out to Italy for three days, everything else is superfluous.'

A tide of colour washed up over her heart-shaped face.

The expectant silence rushed and surged around her.

'Unless you say otherwise, of course,' Rocco spelt out with soft sibilance. 'I can't say goodbye to you again.'

Rocco wanted her back. She couldn't believe it. He had wrongfooted her, sprung a sneak attack, thrown her in a loop. She had had no expectations of him at all. She had said goodbye and she had meant it. But her saying goodbye had been kind of pointless when no other option had been on offer, an empty phrase that nonetheless could rip the heart out of her if she thought about it.

'You have incredible nerve...' she mumbled shakily, wondering what had happened to all that stuff about him never being able to trust her again, fighting to focus her brain on that mystery, utterly failing.

'No, I'm a ruthless opportunist.'

She saw that, could hardly miss that. Show weakness and Rocco took advantage. He had taught her that within twelve hours of their very first meeting. A brilliant, ruthless risk-taker whom she had once adored and could probably adore again, but the prospect terrified her. Freddy...what about her son, *their* son, Freddy? He didn't know about Freddy and she didn't think that it was quite the right moment to make that shock announcement. Rocco seemed to believe that the clock could be turned back and, dear heaven, she wanted to believe that too, *but…* A baby made a difference; Freddy *would* make a difference.

'So…' Rocco was studying her as she imagined he would study an opponent in the boardroom. With a cool, incisive intensity that sought to read the thoughts on her face. 'Do I go…or do I stay?'

No, it really wasn't the moment to ask him how he felt about being a father and, since it was his fault she had fallen pregnant in the first place, he was really just going to have to come to terms with Freddy. Oh, yes, Rocco, she thought with helpless tender amusement, unlike you once assured me, it *is* that easy to get pregnant. He might reign supreme in every other corner of his organised, fast-moving existence, but fate had had the last laugh in the field of conception.

'You've got a big smile in your beautiful eyes,' Rocco drawled with a wolfish grin that twisted her vulnerable heart.

He jerked loose his silk tie.

'You could be taking a lot for granted,' she said, trying to play it cool.

'I took you for granted until I had to get by without you. When I saw you last night, I became a very fast learner,' Rocco asserted, shimmying his wide shoulders back with easy grace and casting off his superb tailored suit jacket.

'No servants here, Rocco… I'm not picking up after you,' Amber whispered, heart hurling itself against her ribcage, making her feel dizzy.

Rocco vented a rueful laugh. 'So I'm not tidy.'

It had been so long since she'd heard him laugh like that, she wanted to tape him; she wanted to capture the moment, stop time dead, just look, listen, rejoice. She picked up his jacket; she couldn't help it. She couldn't bear to see expensive clothes treated like rags of no account. She hugged his jacket to her, happiness beginning to soar like a bird taking flight inside her. Thank you, God, she chanted with silent fervour, thank you.

As far as she was concerned, Rocco's slate of sins was wiped clean. Within the space of twenty-four hours, Rocco had transformed himself from being a stubborn, angry, unforgiving louse full of wild allegations back into the charismatic lover she had lost. Hadn't he just said that he had taken her for granted until he had had to get by without her? Had he been too proud to seek her out after his anger had ebbed?

He flung his shirt on the chair where she was draping his jacket. She gave him a sunny smile of approval. 'Did you drive yourself down here? Where's your car?' she asked.

'Parked in the back lane...this is like having an illicit assignation.'

She tensed. 'And how much do you know about that?'

'I don't mess around with married women.'

At that grounding admission, a little of her buoyancy ebbed. 'But you haven't exactly spent the past eighteen months *pining*...let's be frank.'

Stilling, Rocco sent her a slanting glance of scorching hunger.

She was vaguely surprised that her towel didn't go up in flames, but the pain she was suppressing wouldn't let go of her. 'Stop evading the issue...'

A faint rise of dark blood accentuated his fabulous high cheekbones. His equally fabulous mouth tautened. 'I was on the rebound...I was trying to replace you. I don't want to talk about that,' he completed with brooding abruptness, lush black lashes lifting, stormy golden eyes challenging her.

Was that guilt or regret she was hearing? Or back off, mind your own business? Amber turned away. A split second later, he was behind her, tugging her back against him with possessive hands. 'So how many other men have there been?' he said in the same tone he might have utilised to read a weather report, but his big powerful frame was so tense it betrayed him.

'Back off…mind your own business,' Amber heard herself say.

'But—'

'I don't want to talk about it.' She flung back the same words he had given her.

'Sooner or later you'll tell me,' Rocco forecast, and swept her right off her feet in a startling demonstration of his superior strength to carry her over to her own bed. 'You tell me *everything.*'

'Not quite everything…no one tells everything.'

He settled her down on the bed and then lifted her again to yank the duvet from beneath her. He came down beside her, like a vibrant bronze image of raw masculinity, and detached the tuck on her towel with long brown fingers. Smouldering tawny eyes scanned her hectically flushed face. 'I'll get it out of you, tabbycat.'

She lifted an unsteady hand to trace the course of one hard, angular cheekbone. 'Don't call me that unless you mean it,' she whispered helplessly. 'I don't want you hurting me again.'

He caught her fingers and kissed them, ridiculously long inky lashes screening his gaze from her. 'I would never set out to hurt you and I never say anything I don't mean.'

In receipt of those assurances, her attack of insecurity ebbed, but she was already very conscious of her own intense vulnerability. She had got by without Rocco by persuading herself that she hated him. Now the scary truth was blinding her. She was still crazy about him. Her barriers were down. Putting them back up would be impossible for her a second time.

CHAPTER SIX

'YOU'RE so serious, *cara*,' Rocco censured huskily.

And tonight, 'serious' was obviously not what was required, Amber interpreted without much difficulty. That *wasn't* like him, she thought uneasily, but she suppressed that suspicion and concentrated instead on being seriously happy.

'Smile…' Rocco urged, tumbling her back into the pillows and arranging himself over her, so that not one inch of her was bare of his potent presence.

Amber smiled brighter than the sun because she was with him again. He kissed her in reward. She even tried to smile under his marauding mouth and her heart sang, her senses flowering to the taste and the touch and the scent of him again. Every fibre of her being was on a knife edge of delicious anticipation.

He found her breasts with a husky sound in the back of his throat that was incredibly sexy. Her sensitised flesh swelled into his shaping palms and she trembled in response. He rested appreciative eyes on the full, pouting mounds. 'I swear that though the rest of you has got thinner, your gorgeous breasts…*per amor di Dio*—just looking at you makes me ache,' he ground out with thickened fervour. 'You're every erotic dream I have ever had, *cara*.'

Amber was aware that pregnancy *had* changed her shape. She tensed, but Rocco chose that exact same moment to give way to temptation and send his dark head swooping down to capture a throbbing pink nipple in his mouth. Her ability to think was wrenched from her at speed. Her eyes squeezed tight shut and her spine arched. As he teased at the stiff, tender buds begging for his attention, nothing existed for her for long, timeless moments but the all-encompassing surge of her own writhing response. She had always been intensely sensitive there. Pulsing waves of intense pleasure cascaded through her quivering body as she yielded to his erotic mastery.

'I *missed* you so much…' she gasped, mouth dry, throat tight, breathing a challenge.

He reclaimed her reddened lips with fierce, plundering passion, his hands knotting into her damp honey-blonde hair, lifting her to him as if he could never get enough of her. His tongue delved deep into her mouth and her thighs clenched together on a need that already felt shockingly intolerable. He kissed her until she was moaning and clinging to him and he only paused to catch his own breath.

He studied her passion-glazed eyes with intense male satisfaction. 'When I saw you getting out of that car this morning, I felt violent,' he declared with raw force as he shifted with innate eroticism against her, acquainting her with the bold, hot proof of his hard arousal. 'I wanted to rip that guy out of his Merc and beat him to a pulp. Then I wanted to drag you off like a caveman and imprint myself so deeply on you that you would never look at another man again!'

'Neville's my brother-in-law,' Amber reminded him, aghast.

'They can't *all* have been relatives—'

As Rocco loomed over her, all domineering male, Amber ran worshipping hands up over his magnificent hair-roughened torso, adoring the hard strength and beauty of him, and he shivered, rippling muscles pulling taut. But shimmering stubborn golden eyes still gazed down into hers. 'I only want a number…I've no wish to talk about them—'

'No…someone as possessive as you are doesn't want a

number either,' Amber whispered, a rueful giggle tugging at her vocal cords, even as his hand tightened on her hip and dragged her closer and her wanton body turned liquid as heated honey.

'Ballpark figure?' he pressed with roughened determination.

Amber exerted pressure on his big brown shoulders to tug him back to her again. It would be so easy to admit that there had never been anyone else, but the mean streak in her wouldn't let her tell him that yet. If, and when, he deserved that honesty.

'*Dio mio*…it's driving me crazy thinking about you with other—'

'Shush…' Amber came up on one elbow and pressed her tingling mouth to his again.

Rocco went rigid and then he vented a hungry groan and he responded with devastating, driving sensuality. She laced her fingers into his thick, tousled hair, weak and quivering with a hunger as unstoppable as a floodtide. Every time her sensitised skin came into glancing contact with any part of his lean, hard frame, the heat building inside her and the tormenting ache for fulfilment increased.

'Rocco…' she moaned as he thumbed the aching buds of her breasts and lingered there, giving her ruthless pleasure with indolent ease.

Skimming sure fingers through the silky fleece of curls at the junction of her thighs, he pressed his carnal mouth to the tiny pulse flickering at her collarbone, making every skin-cell leap. Her blood started roaring through her veins, her heart thundering in her own ears. As he explored the hot, damp welcome awaiting him, she could not stay still and all control was taken from her. There was only Rocco and what he was doing to her with such exquisite expertise, the burning need that sent her hips rising from the bed, the choked sounds wrenched from her with ever greater frequency.

'Please...' she sobbed.

He pulled her under him, spread her thighs with an urgency that betrayed his own urgent need. She collided with feverish golden eyes and a great wave of love infused her.

'I never thought I would *be* with you again...' Rocco groaned with raw, feeling intensity as he tipped her up and drove deep into her moist satin sheath.

She arched up to receive him, a stunned cry of response torn from her for she had forgotten just how incredible he could make her feel, forgotten that bold sensation of being stretched to accommodate him. He set a pagan rhythm and with every fluid thrust he excited her beyond bearing. Every hot, abandoned inch of her revelled in his strength and masculine dominance. His passionate force drove her wild with excitement until at last he allowed her to surge over the final threshold. That shattering climax felt endless to her, splintering through her writhing body in long, ecstatic waves of release. Utterly lost in him, mindless with delight, she whimpered and clung as he shuddered over her and slammed into her one last time with a harsh groan of very male pleasure.

'Nobody can make me feel like you do, tabbycat...' Rocco vented an indolent sigh of satisfaction. Smoothing her hair from her brow, he stole a tender, lingering kiss from her swollen lips and hugged her close.

She kissed his shoulder, drowning in the hot, damp smell of his skin, loving him. It felt like coming home. She could not credit that he had only come back into her life the night before, for it now felt to her as though they had never been apart...as though the whole dreadful nightmare of that cheap and sleazy spread in a down-market newspaper had never happened. 'When did you start appreciating that I must have been set up by Dinah Fletcher?' she murmured curiously.

His big, powerful frame tensed. Lifting his tousled fair head, he rested dark as midnight eyes on her, superb bronzed bone-structure taut. He was still in her arms but she recognised his instantaneous withdrawal by the impassivity of his gaze. It was as if he had slammed a door in her face. 'We haven't got time to talk. I have to be out of here in fifteen minutes.'

As Rocco rolled free of her and sprang out of bed, Amber was stunned. 'You have to be out of here in fifteen *minutes*?'

'What began as an excuse to extract me from this weekend early turned into the real McCoy,' Rocco quipped on his way out of the room. 'I have to work out a rescue package for a hotel chain which belongs to friends of mine by Tuesday.'

Obviously he had known that before he'd come to see her. She just wished he had mentioned how little time he had to spend with her. On the one hand, she felt hurt and disappointed, but she was also aware that Rocco's talents were always very much in demand. It was also exactly like him to drop everything to go to the assistance of a friend. She listened to the shower running, knew he would find very little, if any, hot water.

'I'm not a fan of primitive plumbing, *cara*,' Rocco commented with a feeling shudder on his return to the bedroom. 'I'll organise a car to move you out of here tomorrow.'

'Move me *out...*of here?' Amber prompted unevenly, immediately wondering if he was asking her to live with him and wondering how she would answer him if that was what he meant. Everything felt as if it was happening way too fast for common sense, but it had always been like that with Rocco.

Rocco dropped the towel wrapped round his lean brown hips. Attention straying, she swallowed hard. He was magnificent: the lean, muscular power of a very fit male laced with the overwhelming appeal of a very sexual animal. Her cheeks burned. He was drop-dead gorgeous but gaping at him made her feel embarrassed for herself in spite of the renewed intimacy between them.

'I *have* to come clean with you,' Rocco murmured with rueful emphasis. 'I'm afraid I overreacted when I first realised you were working for the Wintons yesterday...'

Amber nodded agreement, glad he was admitting that reality.

His expressive mouth tightened and then he breathed in deep. 'But by the time you came indoors to reason with me, I had *already* called Harris and warned him that you might only be marking time here in search of a story worth selling.'

Amber turned pale with horror at that most belated confession.

'I'm sorry.' Rocco spoiled his seemingly sincere apology, however, by adding, 'But it's not really a problem now, is it?'

'What did Mr Winton say?' Amber demanded tensely, only now recalling how cool the older man had been with her earlier in the day, but she hadn't even suspected that there might have been anything personal in his apparent preoccupation.

'He'll be looking for grounds to sack you and get you off his property as fast as possible.' Rocco followed that devastating assurance with a shrug of incredible cool. 'But since this is not a convenient neck of the woods for you to live when I'm based in London when I am in the UK, it hardly matters—'

'It hardly matters...' Amber parroted in a shattered tone of disbelief. 'You tell me that you've virtually got me the sack and that I'm likely to be kicked out of this cottage...and you *think* that's no big deal?'

Rocco elevated a dark, imperious brow. 'Like you really love that wheelbarrow and living in this dump!' he derided.

'I won't even dignify that with an answer!' she said in reproach, appalled by his seeming indifference to the plight he had put her in.

His white shirt hanging open on his bronzed, hair-roughened chest, Rocco strolled over to the bed and crouched down to her level. Tawny eyes rested on her shaken and furious face. He closed his big hands over hers, strenuously ignoring her attempt to pull free of his grasp. 'It goes without saying that, from this moment on, I will take care of *all* your expenses so you really do have nothing at all to worry about.'

She stared back at him in astonishment.

Rocco released his hold on her and lifted lean brown fingers to brush her hair back from one taut cheekbone in a soothing, but nonetheless very confident, gesture of intimacy. 'It's the only thing that makes sense and you know it—'

Pale as death, Amber compressed bloodless lips, but she couldn't stop herself trembling. 'You never brought money into our relationship before—'

His lean, powerful face clenched. 'It was a different relationship.'

'Different?' Amber echoed and she could hear her own voice fading away on her, for this terrible fear was building inside her that she had entirely misunderstood what he had meant by coming back to her.

In an abrupt movement, Rocco vaulted back upright again.

The silence stretched into infinity.

'Explain that word "different" to me,' Amber whispered tightly.

'It would be hard to quantify it.'

'Oh, I think I can quantify it *for* you,' Amber muttered in an agony of humiliation, but she didn't speak her thoughts aloud. She had given him sex and he had come back for more sex and the foreseeable future would include only very much more of the same. Being a wanton in the woods had rebounded on her. He thought he could have her back on any terms now.

'We can't pretend the past never happened. Naturally

things have changed. But there's nothing wrong with my wish to look after you.'

'Look after me...with a view to what in the future?' Amber asked shakily.

Rocco chose that exact moment to turn his back to her searching eyes and duck down low enough to use the dressing mirror and straighten his tie. 'Whatever happens, I'll be there for you. I don't turn my back on my responsibilities. You're making a fuss about nothing.'

Amber was so crushed she couldn't think straight. She was thinking of Freddy: Freddy who was very much Rocco's responsibility. Somehow Amber did not think that Rocco would be quite so keen to reacquire a lover who had already given birth to his child.

'I won't be your mistress, your kept woman, whatever you want to call it,' she stated curtly. 'I thought you cared about me—'

'*Santo Cielo*...of course, I care about you! Stop dramatising the situation,' Rocco whipped back round to rest his stunning dark gaze on her in cool challenge. 'Be practical. Right now you're as poor as a church mouse!'

Amber lost even more colour and studied her tightly linked hands.

'No doubt if I was as poor as a church mouse and on the brink of being unemployed and homeless as well, *you* would offer to keep *me*!' Rocco continued in a very specious argument, attempting to present the unacceptable in an acceptable guise.

'You would starve sooner than take me up on the offer. Furthermore,' she countered tightly, 'you dug yourself into a hole when you phoned Harris Winton and screwed up my job security, so you can hardly walk away *without* having me on your conscience—'

'Couldn't I?' Rocco shot her an exasperated appraisal. 'I

could have just handed you a cheque in compensation. Are you coming to London or not?'

She swallowed the thickness in her throat. *'No...'*

Rocco withdrew a gold pen from his jacket. 'I'll leave my phone number with you—'

'No...'

'I'm not about to grovel,' Rocco grated.

'You're refusing even to discuss that newspaper story last year!' Amber condemned.

'If we talk about it, I might just wring your neck!' Rocco sent her startled face a flashing look of censure. 'I did not appreciate being publicly labelled a five-times-a-night stud—'

'But I never *said* that...I didn't make one tiny mention of even sleeping with you!' Amber gasped strickenly.

'So how come it was true?' Rocco growled, unimpressed by that plea of innocence.

'Lucky guess?' she muttered chokily.

'The day after that trash was printed, I walked into a Mayfair restaurant with a client and a bunch of city traders at the next table stood up and gave me a slow handclap.' The banked-down rage in his stormy gaze at that unfortunate recollection flailed her.

Amber just cringed.

'But I could have got over that...it was the sense of betrayal I couldn't take,' Rocco spelt out fiercely. 'I trusted you. When you really care about someone, you're loyal and you don't discuss that person with anyone else!'

'If you still believe that I would've discussed our intimacy with anybody, then get out of here because I don't want you near me!' Amber told him feverishly, but she was horribly impressed by his definition of caring.

'If you can't take the heat, you should have stayed out of the kitchen, tabbycat,' Rocco responded with silken derision.

'Don't start thinking that giving me a great time in bed automatically wipes out what you did last year!'

Amber stood up on hollow legs. At that crack, an uneven laugh escaped her. 'I am *so* much more forgiving than you are—'

'What have *you* got to forgive?'

Just at that moment, Amber felt dead inside, as if he had killed all her feelings. 'You didn't love me enough. I can see that now…odd, how I refused to face that at the time. A man who *really* loved me would have given me the chance to explain myself.'

His darkly handsome features clenched. 'Amber—'

Amber turned away. 'Please leave—'

'I haven't got time for this right now,' Rocco delivered, his tone sufficient to tell her that he wasn't taking her seriously.

'So *go!*'

'You don't mean that.'

Amber breathed in so deep, she marvelled that she didn't explode and fizzle round the ceiling above him.

Rocco reached the door and spread fluid and confident hands. 'You'll be on the phone within twenty hours—'

Amber's teeth gritted together.

'You need me.'

'No, I needed you eighteen months ago,' Amber countered fiercely. 'But I *don't* need you now. I got by without you once and I will again. If I get in touch with you in the next few days, Rocco…I warn you, it won't be about *us*.'

Rocco sent her a sudden vibrant grin of amusement. 'I'll see you in London, tabbycat.'

Only if she went, she wouldn't be arriving alone, Amber thought heavily. She listened to the slam of the front door downstairs and hugged herself. He didn't listen; he *never* listened to what he didn't want to hear. It wasn't that he had a huge ego. No, Rocco had something much harder to deflate:

immense and boundless confidence. In addition, he had once been tremendous at second-guessing her every move. Only this time, he was miscalculating because there was a factor he didn't know about. *I would never set out to hurt you.* Stinging tears burned her eyes. She felt even more alone than she had felt when she had finally appreciated that she was pregnant by a man who wouldn't even take a phone call from her. Why, oh, why had she been such a fool as to imagine that the clock could be turned back when Rocco had never loved her in the first place?

CHAPTER SEVEN

IT WAS ironic that Harris Winton could not conceal his dismay when Amber went up to the house and tendered her resignation without notice early the following morning.

'I'm not a media spy, Mr Winton, and I'm not leaving because I have some poison-pen article written either,' Amber declared with wry humour and, now that she was leaving, not caring what opinion she left in her wake, continued, 'Rocco gets a little carried away sometimes. I'm going because it no longer suits me to work here.'

After the turmoil of the night, a strange accepting calm settled over her as she drove over to her sister's house. It had been a pretty awful job and she hated being so dependent on Opal and Neville's charity and seeing so little of her son. Freddy was growing fast and he wouldn't be a baby for much longer. It was time to make fresh choices and leave pride and personal feelings out of the question. The guy who had sworn he didn't turn his back on his responsibilities was about to find out that he *had.* How he felt about that, she didn't much care at that moment.

Opal was rarely taken by surprise. Reclining on a sofa in her elegant drawing room, looking very much like a fairy-tale princess with her flowing pale blonde hair and her exquisite face, she smiled with satisfaction when Amber announced that she had given up on gardening. 'You can move back in here immediately. It was very convenient having you here as second in command with the children. It suited you too. You saw much more of Freddy.'

'Thanks, but I've decided to move back to London.' Amber drew in a deep breath as Opal's fine brows elevated. 'I'm going to tell Rocco about Freddy—'

Her sister sat up with a start. 'Are you crazy?'

Amber would have much preferred not to admit that Rocco had been staying with the Wintons earlier that weekend but in the circumstances it wasn't possible. As she completed her halting explanation about having 'got talking' with Rocco and certain fences having been partially mended, while refusing to indicate *which* fences, her sister wore her most cynical expression of freezing incredulity.

Opal then looked at her in outright disgust. 'So Rocco Volpe just snaps his fingers and you throw up everything and go running—'

'It's not like that—'

'Isn't it? You didn't *tell* him about Freddy and we both know why, don't we? But what was the point of keeping quiet? The guy will laugh in your face if you try and pin a kid on him!' Opal forecast.

Amber paled.

'You'll humiliate yourself for nothing. He'll walk out on you and if you hear one more word from him, I guarantee it will be through his lawyer!' Opal continued.

'Maybe…but I'm doing what I should have done a year ago,' Amber declared tightly. 'Not for my sake, but for Freddy's. I want the right to tell my son who his father is and not have anybody laugh in my face *or* his.'

'Tell me, are you imagining that Rocco will open his arms to your child and turn into Daddy of the Year?' Opal demanded with total derision.

Amber studied her sister with hurt, bewildered eyes. 'I

don't have *any* expectations at all. I don't know how he's likely to react. But I thought you'd think I was doing the right thing.'

'You're making yet *another* big mistake.'

'I don't think so.' It took courage for Amber to stand up to her sister.

'Why don't you tell Amber the truth about why you feel the way you do, Opal?' Neville had appeared in the door-way, his frank blue eyes pinned to the wife he adored with rare disapproval.

'Stay out of this, Neville—'

'I'm sorry, I can't.' The older man sighed. 'You're too prejudiced. The man who let *you* down was a married man—'

Amber stilled at that revelation and looked at her sister in astonishment. 'The man you told me about, the commitment-phobe you were with for five years, was *married* to another woman?'

Twin highspots of furious colour now burned over Opal's cheekbones.

'And like most married men having an affair, he couldn't run far enough when your sister told him she was expecting his child,' Neville completed heavily.

'Is this true?' Amber questioned her rigid and silent sister. 'You were pregnant?'

'I miscarried…fortunately,' Opal admitted curtly. 'But those facts have no bearing on the advice I've given you.'

Amber could not have agreed with that appraisal. She had just seen in Opal's rigid face the depth of her sister's bitterness, her sister's own memory of humiliation and rejection at the hands of the married man she had loved. Naturally that experience had coloured the forceful opinions which Opal had given Amber. 'I'm sorry you got into a situation like that,' she said awkwardly. 'But I wish you had told me the whole story.'

Ten minutes later, Freddy crawling round her feet in pursuit of a wooden car, Amber called the number Rocco had left with her. She got an answering machine and all she could do was leave a message.

However, within an hour Rocco called her back. Having answered the phone, her still-frozen-faced sister extended the receiver to Amber as if it were an offensive weapon.

'When do you want to travel?' Rocco asked, disconcerting her with that prosaic opening question, for she had expected a variety of greetings and that had not been one of them.

'The day you're coming back,' she said stiltedly. 'But I'll drive myself up—'

'You sound terrified. You won't regret this,' Rocco swore huskily.

'I think you *will*,' Amber muttered tautly. 'I'm just warning you...OK?'

'When did I contrive to forget that you're a pessimist, who nourishes negative expectations of anything new and different?' Rocco loosed an extravagant sigh.

'You haven't even told me where we...' She stumbled in dismay. 'I mean, *I'm* going to stay—'

'No, that's why you have to be collected and you can't drive yourself. I very much want to surprise you—'

'I don't like surprises.'

'Within a week of Christmas, that is *not* good news, tab-bycat.'

'Don't call me that,' Amber told him woodenly.

'Whatever you say,' Rocco drawled with scrupulous po-liteness. 'We'll cancel Christmas too, shall we? Obviously you're not in the mood for it either.'

'Look, I've got to go,' Amber muttered, blinking back hot tears and swallowing hard. 'I'll see you when you get back to London.'

CHAPTER EIGHT

Two days later, a long, opulent limousine drew up to collect Amber from her sister's home.

The uniformed chauffeur was somewhat disconcerted to be confronted with a disassembled cot, a baby seat, a buggy, two bulging suitcases and a laundry basket full of toys and other unavoidable essentials.

'Will you get it all in?' Amber asked anxiously.

'Of course, madam.'

Before leaving for work, Neville had pressed a mobile phone on her. 'I think you should've given Rocco fair warning of what's coming. I'll be working late at the car showroom tonight. If there's a problem, wherever you are just call me and I'll come and collect you and Freddy.'

Opal had been even blunter. 'Don't be surprised if Rocco takes one look at Freddy and slams the door in your face! I cannot credit that you are doing this. It's *insane*…it's like something a foolish teenager would do.'

Amber only began to question what she was doing and how she was doing it on the drive to London. That was when she recognised her own bitterness and her own seething desire and need to confront Rocco. It would have been more sensible to tell Rocco about Freddy without Freddy around. But then, in such circumstances, there really wasn't a right or an easy way, was there?

When the limo headed for Holland Park and turned beneath an imposing arched gateway and came to a halt in front of a picturesque Georgian mansion set within lush lawned grounds, Amber at first assumed it was a hotel. Realising that it was a private residence, she was taken aback. Was this where Rocco now lived? Eighteen months ago, he had been living in a penthouse apartment, opulent and impressive if not remotely cosy, the perfect backdrop for a single male.

An older woman greeted her, introducing herself as the housekeeper. Freddy was much admired. Rocco had been held up in Rome, Amber was informed, and was not expected back before nine that evening. As it sank in on Amber that Rocco had had her brought to his own home, her nervous tension began increasing. Of course, it didn't mean that he had plans for her to stay under the same roof for more than one night.

By eight, Freddy was tucked into his cot in a charming guest room and fast asleep after a more than usually active day. Almost an hour later, Amber heard a car pulling up outside. She was wearing a fitted burgundy skirt suit and high heels, her hair conditioned within an inch of its life to fall round her shoulders in shining waves. She wanted to knock him hard with what he had done to her life, but she definitely didn't want him looking at her and thinking that dumping her again would be no great sacrifice.

Rocco strode through the door of the drawing room as Amber reached it. She had only a single enervating glimpse of his startlingly handsome dark features before he hauled her into his arms, clamped her to his big, powerful frame and crushed her startled mouth beneath his with a groan of uninhibited hunger.

That passionate onslaught knocked her sideways. The taste of him after a three-day-long fast was too much altogether for her self-discipline. Every prepared speech just went out of her head and she clung to him to stay upright on knees that had turned weak. As he sent his tongue delving between her readily parted lips to search out the moist, tender interior in explicit imitation of a much more intimate invasion, Amber's temperature rocketed into outer space. Her whole body went into sensory overload in reaction, her breasts pushing against her bra, straining peaks pinching into taut, erect buds, a stirring desperate ache making her clench her trembling thighs together.

'It's a torment to stop and breathe, *cara*,' Rocco growled against her reddened mouth, gazing down at her with smouldering golden eyes. 'I just want to jump you like an animal. Three days can feel like half a lifetime, especially when I wasn't *sure* until the very last minute that you would come here.'

'Weren't you?' Blinking rapidly, Amber studied her clinging hands, which were pinned to his shoulders, and dragged them from him in an abrupt guilty motion, face burning.

'I would've driven down to fetch you if you had backed out on me. In any case, I ought to meet your sister and her husband,' Rocco stated without hesitation.

Amber stiffened and dropped her head at that unwelcome announcement. Why on earth did she have this terrible fear of Rocco meeting Opal? And then the answer she had long avoided out of her own reluctance to face it came to her. Opal would set out to charm and enchant and hog centre stage because Opal always did that with men. Neville's adoration alone wasn't enough to satisfy her sibling's ego.

'And right now,' Rocco continued as she focused on him again, 'there is nothing I want to do more than carry you upstairs and make mad, passionate love to you *but*—'

'Rocco…' Amber was back on track again and striving to muster the words for her big announcement, and then she just blundered on into it before she lost any more momentum. 'When you ditched me, eighteen months back, I was *pregnant*!'

His black luxuriant lashes semi-screened his intent dark

gaze, but his bone-structure had clenched hard. He stared at her with riveted attention. 'You can't have been—'

'I was actually two months pregnant by then, but I'm afraid I had no idea. I was losing weight, I wasn't eating properly or even sleeping enough, and my cycle had never been that regular. When we were still together, it didn't even occur to me that I might be pregnant because I never had the time to stop and think and worry,' Amber said in a driven rush. 'My life then was just one mad whirl.'

Rocco had been listening to her with an intensity as great as the stunned light growing in his dark as midnight gaze. 'Pregnant…'

It seemed to her that he could hardly bring himself to speak that word out loud and she could see for herself how appalled he was.

'But you were taking the contraceptive pill,' he continued hoarsely.

'I had only been taking it for a couple of weeks,' Amber reminded him uncomfortably. 'And if you cast your mind back—'

'I don't *need* to have my mind cast back,' Rocco interposed tautly, pacing over to the window to stare out at the street lights glowing behind the belt of trees surrounding the house, his wide back and powerful shoulders taut with strain beneath his tailored dove-grey suit jacket. 'You warned me that the doctor had said you needed to take extra precautions. It was the middle of the night and I had nothing left to use and *I* said that it wasn't that easy to get pregnant.'

Amber had certainly not expected such perfect recall of events.

'Famous last words,' Rocco conceded in a dark, roughened undertone. 'Famous *stupid* last words. Even as I spoke them I was wincing for myself, but I couldn't resist temptation long enough to do what I should have done. It was always like that with you, *bella mia*.'

'I could have said no,' Amber found herself pointing out in all fairness. 'But I didn't. I was irresponsible too.'

'I was your first lover and I'm seven years older and a life-time more experienced,' Rocco countered harshly, swinging back to face her. He had turned a sort of ashen shade beneath his bronzed complexion and his strong facial bones were rigid. 'But after a few weeks had passed and you showed not the slightest sign of concern, I assumed we'd got away with our recklessness and I didn't think of the matter again.'

Amber flushed. 'I thought about the risk even less than you did.'

'It's not a risk I've ever taken with any other woman,' Rocco muttered heavily, his lean, strong hands clenching into fists and then slowly unclenching again as if he was willing himself into greater calm. 'So this is what changed in you, this is why you told me I might regret you coming here…everything is falling into place. *Porca miseria*…I have been in-credibly slow on the uptake. Your bitterness and your anger were there for me to see. But there I was, believing like a plaster saint that only I was entitled to such feelings.'

'Rocco…'

Rocco lifted his hands and spread them in an almost aggressive silencing motion. 'I need a drink.'

He had already worked it all out, Amber registered. And although she had not expected him to react as if he had received the good news of a lifetime, she had equally well not been prepared for him to turn pale as death and head for the drinks cabinet.

'Do you want one?'

'No…'

'Neither do I.' With a hand that was noticeably unsteady, Rocco set the glass he had withdrawn back into the gleam-

ing cabinet and thrust the door shut again as if he was ward-
ing off temptation. He settled sombre dark eyes on her. 'I'm
afraid I don't know what to say to you—'

'You're speaking pretty loudly without saying very much.'
Amber thought that his shock, horror and pallor gave her a
fair enough indication of his feelings on finding out that he
was a father. Certainly, a woman with a young child was
no candidate for a free-wheeling affair and frequent foreign
travel. But then she wasn't about to have an affair with him,
she reminded herself urgently.

'Shock... I think I could have better stood this happening
with anyone but you—'

As that statement sank in on Amber, the seemingly ulti-
mate rejection, her tummy gave a sick somersault. 'How can
you openly say that to me? *How?*'

'How *not*? Do you think I can simply shrug off what you've
told me as if it never happened? Don't you think that just like
you I'm going to be remembering this for the rest of my life?'
Rocco demanded, more emotional than she had ever seen him.

Her brain fogging up in her efforts to understand what he
was telling her, Amber gazed blankly back at him.

'Well, maybe *not* just like you,' Rocco adjusted, meeting
her questioning eyes with frowning force. 'But surely taking
such a decision was deeply upsetting?'

Amber had had just about enough of trying to follow a be-
wildering dialogue in which Rocco appeared to have lost his
ability to put across clear meaning. 'Would you please pause
for a moment and just tell me in plain English what you're
talking about?'

'*What?* I was trying to be tactful. I didn't want to distress
you,' Rocco ground out between clenched white teeth. 'But
you don't seem to be that sensitive on the subject, do you?
No, scratch that. I *didn't* say it...you *didn't* hear it. I swear I

am not judging you. I wasn't there to offer support. I know that. I accept that—'

Amber tilted her honey-blonde head to one side and stared at him with very wide but no longer uncomprehending eyes. 'Tell me, is the word you're dancing all around but avoiding…abortion?'

Rocco went sort of sickly grey in front of her, a sheen of perspiration on his skin. He nodded jerkily and breathed in very deep.

'Did I accidentally speak that word without realising it?' Amber prompted on a rising note of incredulity.

Rocco shook his head in negative.

'So you just *assumed* that if I fell pregnant I would *naturally* rush off for a termination, did you?'

The silence sizzled like a live electric current.

His full attention welded to her, Rocco's brows pleated. 'Didn't you?'

'Didn't I?' Amber sucked in a vast amount of oxygen like a woman ready to enter a pitched battle with extreme aggression. 'No, I darned well didn't go off and have an abortion! You have got some *nerve* just arrogantly assuming that that's what I chose to do!'

'Right…right,' Rocco said again, evidently getting his brain back into gear but not, it had to be said, at supersonic speed. 'You didn't have an abortion…you gave birth to our baby?'

He was recovering a more natural colour and straightening his shoulders again, Amber noted. Huge relief was emanating from him in perceptible waves. Amber was utterly transfixed and fascinated. She had never been able to read Rocco as easily as she did that moment.

'For that, I am very grateful,' Rocco asserted thickly at nowhere near his usual pace and making a visible effort to shake free of his shock. 'The other conclusion…it would have haunted my conscience for ever and we might never have come to terms with it. So, obviously, you gave our child up for adoption—'

'Excuse me?' Amber's temper was on a knife edge because she was so wound up.

'The thought of that breaks my heart too...' Rocco's dark, deep drawl shook slightly as he made that emotive admission.

'Really?' Amber was back to being fascinated and paralysed to the spot again.

'But it was very brave of you to go through the pregnancy and face that alone and a situation I will simply have to learn to live with,' Rocco framed like a guy picking every word while walking on ice likely to crack under him and drown him at any minute. 'I can...I will, but it is such a terrible loss for both of us, *bella mia.*'

'Yes, I suppose it would have been...at least, it would have been for me, certainly,' Amber heard herself mumbling. 'And I'm beginning to get the message that it would have been a terrible loss for you too. *So*—'

Rocco raised and spread fluidly expressive hands in an appeal for a pause in revelation. 'No more until I have had a drink. I am all shaken up.'

Amber watched him pour a brandy with a great deal less than his usual dexterity. 'So you like children.'

'I think so...I haven't met many,' Rocco said hoarsely, carefully, and passed her a drink without being asked. 'But that time I thought I might have got you pregnant, I liked the idea.'

'Oh...did you?' Amber studied his clenched profile, recognised that he was still firing on really only one cylinder, and her heart overflowed. 'That's good, Rocco. Because, for what it's worth, your idea of what I would do when I found myself unexpectedly pregnant and without support is very badly off target.'

He focused on her with grave dark eyes, his strain palpable. 'How...off target?'

'Well, I didn't go for abortion and I didn't go for adoption. Oh, and before you make yet another wild deduction, I did not abandon my baby either or have him placed in foster care,' Amber informed him gently. 'In fact, my baby—*our* baby—is upstairs right now...OK?'

The balloon glass dropped right out of Rocco's hand and fell soundlessly to the carpet. But it smashed noisily when he stood on it in his sudden surging step forward.

'If that is a joke, it's a lousy one,' he breathed raggedly.

Amber folded her arms. 'Unlike you, I don't crack jokes at the most inopportune moments. Freddy's upstairs sleeping in one of your guest rooms.'

Rocco gazed at her as if she had taken flight without wings before his eyes. He was totally stunned. 'Say that again... *Freddy*?'

'Your son, Freddy...I called him after my grandfather, who was about the only role model I wanted him to follow in my own family,' she said shakily.

'Upstairs...*here*?' Rocco shot at her incredulously, suddenly recovering his usual energy without warning. 'In my own home? I don't believe you!'

'You want to see him?'

Rocco wasn't waiting. He was already striding out into the hall. Amber followed his forceful surge up the stairs. 'Room at the foot of the corridor... Rocco, if you wake him up before midnight, he'll scream blue murder. After midnight...even around two or three in the morning, he's bouncing about his cot and positively dying to socialise.'

'I'm not going to wake him up...OK?'

Amber insinuated herself between him and the door which had been left ajar. She pushed it wider. Light spilled in from the landing and, in concert with the nightlight Amber had

brought with her, it shed a fair amount of clarity on the oc-
cupant of the cot. There Freddy lay in his all-in-one sleeper
which was adorned with little racing car images.

Rocco mumbled something indecipherable in his own language and peered down into the cot, lean hands flexing and
then bracing again on the side bars. Freddy shifted in his
sleep, looking incredibly angelic with his dark curls and fan-
shaped lashes. Rocco's expression of sheer, unconcealed wonderment filled Amber with enormous pride, but there was no
denying that she was in a stupor of shock at the way matters
appeared to be panning out.

Like a man in a dream, Rocco was slowly sinking down
to crouch by the side of the cot so that he could get an even
closer look at his sleeping son. 'The throwback gene didn't
get him,' he muttered absently.

'Sorry?'

'His hair is dark. He's not going to get the life teased out
of him at school as I did,' Rocco extended with pronounced
satisfaction. 'He has my nose and your mouth.'

Amber nodded in silence at news that was not news to
her, but which she had not expected him to pick up on quite
so quickly.

'Also my brows—'

'He got your eyes too.' Amber was in a total daze. Where
were the doors slamming in her face, the denials of paternity, the demands for birth certificates, DNA testing and all
the other supporting evidence she had somehow expected?
Well, maybe not all of that, but at least one or two elements,
she conceded dizzily.

'Where was Freddy when I was stalking you in the woods?'
Rocco murmured.

She explained about her sister's nanny.

'Freddy is *really* something else,' Rocco declared of his son.
'He won the beautiful baby competition at the village

fête last summer,' Amber heard herself saying with pride. 'Opal was furious and couldn't hide it. She was expecting her daughter...my niece, Chloe, to win.'

Rocco sprang fluidly upright again and cast her a veiled appraisal. 'We need to talk.'

CHAPTER NINE

Rocco only walked to the big landing above the stairs and cast open a door there.

'You've accepted Freddy's yours, haven't you?' Amber enquired nervously. 'He's a year old next week but he was born prematurely... I had an awful pregnancy.'

'How awful?'

Scanning the spacious bedroom as he switched on the lights, Amber wondered why they weren't going downstairs again and asked.

'I want to hear Freddy if he wakes up.' Rocco studied her with stunning dark golden eyes. 'Awful...you were saying?'

'Well, I wasn't exactly fighting fit to begin with,' she pointed out, edgily pacing away from him. 'I was sick morning, noon and night as well, so I lost more weight. I couldn't find another job and I couldn't afford the rent on my flat either, so I had to move into a bedsit. I didn't have blood running in my veins by that stage, I only had stress.'

She spun back. Rocco was really pale, his bone-structure rigid.

'Had enough yet?' Amber prompted.

'No...' he framed doggedly.

'Well, my blood pressure was too high and I ended up in hospital because I was threatening to miscarry. So there I was flat on my back and not allowed to do anything for weeks on end. It was like a living nightmare. No privacy, no visitors, no nothing, just me and my thoughts—'

'What about your sister?'

'If you knew Opal like I know Opal, you wouldn't have been in any desperate hurry to contact her and confront her with your messy mistakes either.' Amber sighed. 'But I finally had to call her because I needed my bedsit cleared out and she was really wonderful.'

'And I was nowhere—'

'I started hating you in that hospital bed,' Amber admitted.

'Am I allowed to ask why you didn't contact me?'

Amber surveyed him in outrage. 'After you accused me of stalking you?'

'Did you know you were pregnant at that stage?'

'No.'

Rocco just closed his eyes and swung away. 'I was a bastard. On Saturday, you said I wouldn't discuss that newspaper story and that that wasn't fair. You were right, so let's get it out of the way now and then never talk about it again.'

Unprepared for that subject to be raised, Amber groaned. 'I went to school with the journalist who wrote that story.'

In astonishment, Rocco froze. 'You went to *school*—'

'With Dinah Fletcher, yes.' Amber explained how the other woman had contacted her. 'She said she had only recently moved to London to start a PR job—'

'A *PR* job—?'

Amber kept on talking. 'She was always great fun at school and I was delighted to hear from her. She came over with a bottle of wine. I told her about you but I never gave her a single intimate detail. It was girly gossip, nothing more—'

Rocco sank down heavily on the foot of the bed. 'She got in touch with you because she already knew that I was seeing you. She set you up,' he breathed in a raw undertone.

'Yeah and I fell for it.' Amber could feel the tears threatening because she still felt sick at the awareness that she had actually enjoyed that evening. She had had no suspicion that

Dinah was a junior reporter, ambitious to make her mark, regardless of who got hurt in the process. 'A couple of days after the story appeared, she phoned and said she hoped that there were no hard feelings and that she was only doing her job. I asked her if it was also her job to tell lies about what I'd said but she just put the phone down on me.'

Rocco viewed her with haunted dark eyes and vented a distinctly hollow laugh. 'I was planning to tell you tonight that I was now big enough to take a joke—and that at least you hadn't informed the world that I was lousy in bed and you had to fake it all the time...' His deep, dark drawl faltered. 'Now I don't know what I can say.'

'Not a lot in your own defence,' Amber agreed in a flat little tone, but the most appalling desire to surge across the room and put her arms round him was tugging at her. He was badly shaken and suddenly she was no longer feeling vengeful satisfaction. Only as she saw that within herself did she appreciate that she had so badly wanted revenge. The nasty part of her had enjoyed hammering him with all the bad news.

'I was naive...I was indiscreet and probably I deserved to get dumped because I caused you so much embarrassment,' Amber conceded in a sudden rush. 'But it was the way you *did* it—'

Brilliant dark eyes shimmering, Rocco sprang upright again. 'I was on the brink of asking you to marry me. Then that sleazy article hit me in the face and I really thought you'd been taking me for a ride!'

Amber's feet had frozen to the carpet. It was her turn to go into shock.

'Nothing had ever hurt me so much and I couldn't face seeing you again. I saw no point,' Rocco admitted heavily. 'I could see no circumstances in which that story could've been conceived without your willing agreement and participation.'

Amber stared at him with shaken eyes. 'You were going to ask me to marry you?'

Rocco pushed a not quite steady hand through his bright silvery fair hair and shrugged, but it was a jerky movement that lacked his usual grace. 'I felt you'd made such a fool of me. There I was ready to ask you to be my wife... I was in the process of buying a house, I even had the engagement ring... and then *bang*! It all fell apart in my hands.'

'But couldn't you have once stopped and thought that I wouldn't have done such a thing to you?' Amber pressed helplessly, if anything even more aghast at the discovery that she had lost so much more than she had ever dreamt. Rocco had loved her, planned to marry her. Rocco would have been pleased about Freddy. Rocco would have been there for her every wretched step of the way had not that newspaper story destroyed his faith in her.

'When I'm hurt I lash out and nothing I can do or say can alter the past. You will say I didn't love you enough...I would say I loved you *so* much, I was afraid of being weak and ending up back with you again,' Rocco bit out in a roughened undertone.

'Would you?' A glimmer of silver lining appeared in the grey clouds that had been encircling Amber until he spoke those final words. 'And all those other women?' she asked on the strike-while-the-iron's-hot principle.

'Anything to take my mind off you and it didn't work. I didn't sleep with anyone else for a very long time...and that was lousy too. In fact...' Rocco hesitated and then forced himself on, dark blood rising to accentuate his carved cheekbones. 'Everything was lousy until I looked out Harris Winton's front window and saw you and felt alive again for the first time since I dumped you.'

'I just love you saying that when you couldn't *wait* to phone the man and talk me out of my job!' Amber exclaimed, and then her shoulders slumped, the stress and strain of it all suddenly closing in on her, making her realise all at once how absolutely exhausted she was. 'I'm almost asleep standing up.'

'You should be in bed.' Never in her life had she seen a guy leap so fast for an escape route, or at least she thought that until Rocco lifted her up into his arms and carted her over to the divan and settled her down on it with pronounced care and absolutely none of his usual familiarities.

'Are you staying?' she asked in a small tense voice.

'Not if you don't want me.'

Her teeth gritted. 'Is this your bed?'

Rocco nodded slowly.

'OK…you can stay so I can nag at you until I fall asleep,' she muttered.

'I can live with that.'

Filching a rarely worn nightdress from her case, she headed into the bathroom. Her head felt as if it were spinning with the number of conflicting thoughts assailing her, but one emotion dominated. She loved him. It didn't stop her wanting to kick him but she couldn't bear to leave him alone with his guilty conscience. Regret was just eating him alive and furthermore, on a purely practical side, Rocco was telling her things that torture wouldn't have extracted from him eighteen months ago. If he wanted to talk more, she didn't want to miss out on a single syllable. So he had planned to surprise her with a house and an engagement ring? Rocco and his blasted surprises! If only she had known, she would've crashed into his office in a tank and pinned him down to make him listen to her eighteen months ago.

She crept into bed, wondering if the nightie was overkill, but she knew that taking it off would be noticed. She listened to him undress.

'How do you feel about getting married on Christmas Eve?'

Amber blinked and then came up over the edge of the duvet

to stare at the male ostensibly entranced in the shape of his own shirt buttons, but so tense she was anything but fooled. Her heart hit the Big Dipper and kept on hurtling higher. Well, he had his flaws *but*...

'Christmas Eve?' Amber echoed rather croakily. 'Well, I'm not doing anything else...'

'Like I said to you before, you won't regret it.'

It sounded like a blood oath. 'What about you?'

'I get you as my wife,' Rocco murmured, smooth as silk. 'I also get part-ownership on Freddy. Those facts will then become the only things in my life I don't have to feel bad about.'

'You're just killing me with your enthusiasm.'

'How much enthusiasm am I allowed to show?'

'Major moving on to maximum,' Amber muttered, leaning heavily on the encouragement angle. 'Fireworks, Fourth of July, whatever feels right.'

'Would you have married me eighteen months ago?'

She would have left a smoke trail in her haste to get to the church. 'Possibly...'

Rocco slid into bed. She was waiting on him mentioning love; she was praying on him mentioning love.

'You were such a workaholic then that we hardly saw each other,' Rocco remarked tautly, dimming the lights but not putting them out.

'It was such a boring job too—'

Rocco took her aback by hauling her across the bed into his arms and studying her with scorching dark golden eyes of disbelief. 'You put that *boring* job ahead of me every time!'

Amber winced, shimmied confidingly into the hard heat and muscularity of his big, powerful body and whispered softly, 'But I surrendered my wheelbarrow for you, didn't I?'

He captured her animated face between long brown fingers, gazing down into dancing green eyes that had miraculously lost the dulled look of exhaustion. 'Not without argument, *cara*.'

'I had Freddy's security to consider.' She shivered against him, drowning in the sexy depths of his stunning eyes.

'Of course...' Something cool in Rocco's agreement, a dry note, tugged anxious strings deep down in her mind, but then Rocco possessed her mouth with a raw and hungry sensual force that electrified her. He took precisely ten ruthless seconds to remove the nightdress.

'Are you angry with me?' Amber whispered, sensing a tension in him that troubled her and easing back with a furrowed brow.

'With myself...*only* with myself,' Rocco swore with roughened fervour, his spectacular gaze resting with an intensity she could feel but no longer read on her anxious face.

She edged back to him, weak not only with hunger but also with a desperate need for reassurance that everything was all right. It felt so much *more* than all right to her. She was so happy she could have cried. She didn't want him to be angry with himself. But he curved an exploring hand over the straining rosy bud crowning one pouting breast and, that fast, she was sucked down into a place where thinking was more than she could manage.

It was as though the stressful day had built up an incredibly urgent need in both of them. There was a wildness in Rocco, a wildness that was gloriously thrilling and fired her every response to fresh heights. He slid down over her quivering length, pausing to make passionate love to every promising curve and hollow he encountered in his path. Before very long, all she was remotely aware of was the thunderous crash of her own heartbeat, her breath sobbing in her throat and a level of sensation which seemed to transcend earthly existence.

'I want this to be amazing...' Rocco rasped.

She was half out of her mind with an intensity of pleasure at that point, which made it impossible to tell him that amazing did not *begin* to cover the excitement of what he was making her feel. Writhing with utterly mindless and tormented delight, she moaned his name like a mantra, clutched at his hair, grabbed his shoulders and surrendered to her own abandonment while being pleasured within an inch of her life.

'Amazing...' she managed when she could speak again but only just.

'It's not over yet,' Rocco husked in a tone of promise.

And if the beginning and the middle had been totally enthralling for her, the conclusion was an even more ecstatic and long-drawn-out affair. In the aftermath she was too weak to do anything but lie in his arms. She had a dazed sense of having seen, experienced and revisited paradise more than once and she was awash with tender love and wonderment that he was finally, actually and for ever hers.

That was the inopportune moment when Rocco shifted away from her and breathed flatly like a male to whom paradise was an utterly unknown place, 'At least I know you're not faking it now...'

I'm not going to say anything, screeched the alarm-bell voice inside her shaken head. She hadn't got the energy for a row, she told herself weakly, and she curved into a comfy pillow like a hampster burrowing into a hiding place. They could row *after* they got married.

CHAPTER TEN

AMBER focused on her own reflection in the cheval dressing mirror.

It was Christmas Eve and it was her wedding day and she was wearing the most divine dress she had ever seen or ever worn. The delicate gold-and-silver-embroidered boned bodice hugged her to the waist, where the full ivory rustling skirt flared out, overlaid at the back by an elaborate train with matching embroidery. She pointed her toes to see her satin shoes adorned with tulle roses, tipped up her chin the better to allow the light catch the superb contemporary gold and diamond tiara and the elegant short veil that hung in a flirty froth from the back of her head.

But it was no use! No matter how hard Amber tried to lose herself in bridal fervour, she had to emerge again to be confronted by an awful truth: Rocco *wasn't* happy! She was wilfully marrying a man who didn't love her, but who very much wanted to be a father to their son. Her nose tickled as she fought to hold back welling tears. It had honestly not occurred to her until after she had said yes to his marriage proposal that his most likely motivation had been sheer guilt and Freddy.

It had been days since Rocco had even kissed her—not since that very first night. The next day, she had returned from her shopping trip for her wedding outfit and a slight difference of opinion had resulted in her hot-headedly transferring her possessions into the guest room next to Freddy's.

She had kind of shot herself in the foot with that relocation: Rocco had neither come in search of her nor betrayed the slightest awareness of the reality that she had gone missing from his bed. Separate bedrooms and they weren't even married yet, she thought wretchedly. Just when she had believed that every cloud on her horizon had vanished, a brick-wall barrier had come up out of nowhere and divided them. Since then Rocco could not have made it clearer that Freddy was his biggest source of interest.

He had spent that whole day with Freddy while she'd been shopping. When she'd got back, Freddy had been in his bath. Rocco had been dive-bombing Freddy's toy boats with pretty much the same enjoyment that Freddy got from loads of noisy splashes and sound effects, but her entrance to the fun and frolics had cast a distinct dampener on the proceedings.

'Did you find a dress?' he asked with scrupulous politeness.

'Yes…it cost a fortune. Thanks,' she said with the semi-guilty, semi-euphoric response of a woman who had managed to locate her dream wedding gown, her dream veil and her dream shoes, not to mention a set of lingerie that had quite taken her breath away.

'Odd how being a kept woman within marriage doesn't seem to bother you quite the way it bothered you *before* I mentioned the wedding ring,' Rocco drawled in a black-velvet purr.

Screening her shaken and hurt eyes at that cutting comment, which she was absolutely defenceless against, Amber murmured, 'Would you like me to go and mow the lawn to justify my existence?'

'You picked me up wrong, *cara*…'

Like heck, she had misunderstood! So that was why she had shifted into a guest room but doing that had made it even easier for Rocco to distance himself from her. There he was surging home every evening to spend time with Freddy, perfectly charming and polite with her, but the instant Freddy had fallen asleep, Rocco had excused himself to work. It was as if they had already been married ninety years and he had nothing left to say to her!

Amber straightened her bowed shoulders, took a last longing, lingering look at her reflection in her dream wedding gown and faced facts. Nearly all week, she had refused to let go of her fantasy of becoming Rocco's wife. Hiding her head in the sand, she had shrunk from acknowledging that Rocco was showing as much enthusiasm for matrimony as the proverbial condemned man.

She could ring him on his mobile before he arrived at the church. Better a misfired wedding than the misery of a marriage that was a mistake, she told herself. Blinking back tears, Amber stabbed out his number and waited for Rocco to answer.

'Rocco? Where are you?'

'*En route* to the church. What's wrong?'

'I want to call it off,' Amber whispered.

'Call…what off?' Rocco breathed jerkily.

Amber gulped. 'I don't think we should go through with the wedding. You've been so unhappy for days—'

'And *this* is the magic cure? I'm a bloody sight *more* unhappy now!' Rocco launched down the line at her with incredulous force. 'You've got cold feet, that's all. Now pull yourself together. We're getting married today!'

'But you don't really want to marry me—'

'Where did you get that idea? I really, really, *really* want to marry you,' Rocco murmured intensely, changing both tack and volume. 'I want to be stalked by you every day for the rest of my life—'

'But you couldn't even stalk *me* as far as one of your own guest rooms!' A sob caught at Amber's voice.

'Cards on the table time,' Rocco muttered with fierce urgency. 'I somehow got the impression that you were only marrying me for Freddy's benefit—'

'Don't be stupid…' Amber winced and then confided in a small voice, 'Actually I was thinking the same thing about you.'

'Freddy's wonderful, but he's not so wonderful that I'd sentence myself to a lifetime with a woman I didn't want,' Rocco swore impressively.

'I also thought that maybe you were just marrying me because you felt guilty—'

'No, I think most guys run the other way if they feel *that* guilty. I can handle guilt, but I'm not at all sure I can handle not having you…'

Amber blossomed from a nervous wreck into a happy bride-to-be again. 'See you at the church—'

'You've made me really nervous now—'

'Well, you shouldn't have ignored me for so long in favour of Freddy,' Amber told him dulcetly.

Neville was waiting downstairs to accompany her. Opal had arrived with her husband early that morning to help Amber into her bridal regalia and had then gone on to the church in company with Freddy and Freddy's new nanny, a lovely friendly girl, whom Rocco had insisted on hiring to help Amber.

Amber negotiated the stairs with the housekeeper holding up her train. Her brother-in-law gave her a smiling appraisal. 'You look incredible, Amber. Rocco won't know what's hit him.'

Amber rather thought Rocco *would* know what had hit him after that emotional phone call they had shared. They were each as bad as the other, she reflected ruefully. Neither of them had shared their deepest fears over the past few days. She had been pretty tough on Rocco that first night in London. But she was really surprised that a male as confident as he was had entertained the lowering suspicion that she might only be marrying him for Freddy's benefit and for security. Somehow, she recognised, she had subconsciously assumed that Rocco *knew* she was still madly in love with him. Now she knew he *didn't* know and was amazingly subject to the same insecurities as she was. A sunny smile spread over her face at that acknowledgement.

The church was absolutely miles away, right outside London. Amber thought Rocco had picked a very inconvenient location but then she had had nothing to do with *any* of the arrangements: Rocco had assured her that he had everything organised. Feeling that he could at least have consulted her about her own wedding day, she had rigorously refused to ask questions.

The Rolls finally drew up outside a charming rural church surrounded by cars. As Amber got out her emergence and her progress into the church were minutely recorded by a busy bunch of men wielding all sorts of cameras. The press? she wondered in surprise. Then she looked down the aisle and saw Rocco waiting for her at the altar and all such minor musings evaporated. There he was, six feet four inches of devastatingly handsome masculinity, and her heart started racing. She might have generously offered him his freedom back, but she had never been so grateful to have an offer refused.

Stunning dark golden eyes scanned her, stilled and just stayed locked to her all the way down the aisle. It wasn't at all cool bridegroom behaviour, but Amber loved that poleaxed stare. He didn't have to speak: she knew he thought she looked spectacular. He reached for her hand at the altar. She was so happy that her eyes stung a little. The plain and simple words of the ceremony sounded beautiful to her. Freddy, however, let out an anguished wail at the sight of both his mother and his father disappearing out of view to sign the wedding register. Amber darted back to retrieve their anxious son from his nanny's knee and take him with them.

'You look incredibly gorgeous,' Rocco told her as he lifted Freddy from her arms to give him a consoling hug. Back where he felt he ought to be in the very centre of things, Freddy smiled.

Loads of photos were taken on the church steps and Rocco swept her off into the waiting limo as soon as he could.

Amber gave him a teasing look. 'Do you think you could tell me now where we're having our reception?'

'Wychwood House.'

A slight frown-line indented her brow. 'I've heard that name before somewhere.'

'Let me jog your memory.' A wolfish grin was now tugging at the corners of Rocco's expressive mouth. 'When we were together last year, do you remember the way you always used to devour the property sections of the Sunday newspapers?'

A slow tide of hot pink crept up over Amber's face, but she lifted her brows in apparent surprise. 'No…'

'Married an hour and already lying to me,' Rocco reproved with vibrant amusement. 'Did you think I didn't notice that while I was deep in the business news you were enjoying a covert thrill scanning the houses for sale?'

Feeling very much as though an embarrassing secret habit had been exposed, Amber bristled defensively. 'Well, just glancing through the property pages is not a crime, is it?'

'*Just glancing?*' Rocco flung his handsome head back and laughed out loud at that understatement. 'You were in seventh heaven rustling through those pages. So when you finally went to the lengths of removing an entire page from a newspaper, I knew it was a fair bet that you'd found your dream house.'

Just then, Amber recalled ripping out that particular page

while Rocco had been in the shower. A sudden, barely considered impulse after reading an interesting article about the history of a gorgeous country house that had been about to come on to the market.

'So after doing some investigation to find out which house it was, I bought it for you.'

'*Honestly?*' Amber was going off into shock. 'B-but I thought it was the house in London that you bought for us last year!'

'No, that was a much more recent acquisition. I bought Wychwood for you a week before we broke up.'

'But…' Amber was just transfixed with disbelief.

'I told you that I had a country estate,' Rocco reminded her gently.

Recalling the context in which that statement had been made and taken by her as a most unfunny joke on her gardening status, Amber swallowed with difficulty. By then the Rolls was already powering up an imposing winding drive that led through a long sweep of beautiful rolling parkland adorned by mature oak trees.

'Not all my surprises go wrong, tabbycat,' Rocco commented with the kind of rich self-satisfaction that she usually set out to squash flat in him.

However, as the magnificent Palladian mansion came into view round the next bend Amber was too dumbstruck to do anything other than nod agreement in slow motion.

'Although I have to confess that this particular surprise felt like it had gone *very* wrong when I got Wychwood without you included,' Rocco confided ruefully.

In normal mode, Amber would have told him that that was the direct result of his having dumped her and that he had deserved to have had his surprise backfire on him. But the truth was she was so thunderstruck by the sheer size of the house *and* the surprise, she was feeling generous.

Rocco lifted her out of the Rolls and up into his arms. It was just as well: she honestly didn't believe her legs would have held her up. 'Rocco...?'

She collided with dark golden eyes that filled her to over-flowing with joyful tenderness and what felt fearfully like adoration, so she didn't tell him she loved him, she said instead, 'I think you're totally wonderful.'

Was it her imagination or did he look a little disappointed?

'Absolutely fantastic...the most terrific husband in the world?' she added in a rush.

Evidently she finally struck the right note of appreciation because he took her mouth with hungry, plundering intensity. As excitement charged her every skin-cell, she realised just how miserably long a few days without Rocco's passion could feel.

'Incredibly sexy too,' she mumbled, coming up for air again as he carried her over the impressive threshold of Wych-wood House.

A towering Christmas tree festooned with ornaments and beautiful twinkling lights took pride of place in the wonderful reception hall where a log fire burned. 'Oh, my...' she whispered, appreciation growing by the second. 'Rocco, please, please tell me we're going to spend Christmas here.'

He smiled. 'The day after Boxing Day, we set off for warmer climes.'

All the photographers then sprang out from behind the tree to take loads more pictures of them and she tried not to let her jaw drop too obviously. 'Really conscientious, aren't they?' she whispered to Rocco when they had to stop to load more film.

'I told them I didn't want a single second of this day to go unrecorded.'

Freddy was belatedly fetched out of the Rolls where he had been abandoned because he was fast asleep. Reunited with his nanny when she arrived, he was borne upstairs to complete his nap in greater comfort and Rocco and Amber were free to greet their guests. Some of them she had met when she'd been seeing Rocco the previous year. Others were strangers. And then there were the Wintons: Harris coming as close to a grin when he wished her well as he was ever likely to come, and Kaye with her gutsy smile, not one whit perturbed by any memory of having warned Amber off Rocco only a week earlier.

Neville and Opal joined them at the top table in the elegant dining room where the caterers served a magnificent meal. Amber watched for Rocco getting that glazed look men usually got around Opal, but if he was susceptible he was very good at concealing it.

'My sister's very beautiful, isn't she?' Amber was reduced to fishing for an opinion when they were walking through to the ballroom where a band was playing.

'Do I get shot if I say no…or shot if I say yes?' Rocco teased.

Amber coloured hotly at his insight into her feelings.

Rocco curved an arm round her taut shoulders in a soothing gesture. 'She's lovely and very fond of you, but I have to confess that listening to her talk to you as if you are a very small and not very bright child is extremely irritating.'

Amber paled.

'Now what have I said? You know you rarely mention your family—'

She forced a rueful laugh. 'My parents were very clever, just like Opal—'

'Research scientists. I remember you telling me that.'

'By their standards I *wasn't* very bright. I'm average but they made me feel stupid,' Amber admitted reluctantly. 'I felt I was such a disappointment to them—'

'So that's why you always pushed yourself so hard. If your

parents had seen how hard you'd worked and how much you had achieved by the time I met you, they would have been hugely impressed,' Rocco swore vehemently.

'You sound like you really mean that, *but* I remember you offering me employment and behaving as if the job I had was nothing—'

'Give me a break.' Rocco laughed softly. The protective tenderness in his gaze warmed her like summer sunlight. 'All I was thinking of was being able to see more of you and you *were* wasted in the position you were in then.'

Amber stood up on tiptoe and whispered playfully, 'Go on, tell me more, tell me how bright I am—'

Rocco caught her to him with a strong arm, making her urgently aware of him and the glinting gold of his smouldering scrutiny. 'You picked me didn't you?'

'Is that really one of the brighter moves I've made?'

Rocco looked down into her animated face and murmured with ragged fervour, 'I hope so because I love you like crazy, *bella mia.*'

Amber stilled. 'Honestly?'

'Why are you looking so shocked?'

She linked her arms round his neck and sighed helplessly. 'You let me go, Rocco…you never came after me—'

A dark rise of colour had accentuated his fabulous cheekbones. 'I *did* come after you. It took me two months to get to that point. Two months of sleepless nights and hating every other woman because she wasn't you. I told myself I just wanted to confront you…which is pretty much what I told myself when I saw you with your wheelbarrow as well—'

'You *did* come after me?' Amber gasped in delight, finally willing to believe he might still truly love her. 'So why didn't you find me?'

'You'd moved out of your flat without leaving a forwarding address and I had no relatives or anyone else to contact,'

Rocco ground out in frustration. 'I even got a friend to run your Social Security number through a computer search system…that's illegal, but it didn't turn up anything helpful.'

'I forgive you for everything…I love you, I love you, I love you!' Amber told him, bouncing up and down on the spot, so intense was her happiness and excitement.

'For goodness' sake, Amber…remember where you are,' Opal's voice interposed in pained and mortified reproof.

'She's in her own home and I'm enjoying this tremendously, Opal. If you'll excuse us,' Rocco murmured with a brilliant smile as he whirled his ebullient bride onto the floor to open the dancing.

AT THREE IN the morning, Amber and Rocco came downstairs with Freddy to open some Christmas presents.

Freddy was in the best of good humour. It was Christmas Day and it was also his first birthday. He was truly aware of neither occasion but was enthralled by the big tree and all the twinkly lights and the shiny ornaments. He played with the card he was given and he played with the wrapping paper, watching while his parents struggled to get the elephant rocker out of its box, and then struggled even more on the discovery that it was only part-assembled. He sat in the rocker for about one minute before crawling off it again to head for the much more exciting box he wanted to explore.

'I think the rocker just bombed,' Rocco groaned. 'He's happier with the paper and the packaging.'

'As long as he's happy, who cares?' Amber said sunnily, entranced in watching the lights send fire glittering from the superb diamond engagement ring Rocco had slid onto her finger. 'I bet I'm the only bride for miles around who got an engagement ring *after* the wedding and it's really gorgeous!'

'Just arriving eighteen months late, tabbycat.' Rocco surveyed her with loving but amused eyes as she whooped over the matching eternity ring she had just unwrapped. 'That's for suffering all those weeks in hospital to have Freddy.'

'Well, perhaps it wasn't as bad as I made out…if I'd had you visiting, I'm sure I wouldn't have been feeling sorry for myself. Next time—'

'*Next* time? Are you kidding?' Rocco exclaimed in horror. 'Freddy's going to be an only child!'

As Freddy had crawled into the box and now couldn't get out of the box and was behaving very much as if the box were attacking him, Amber rescued him and put him back on the rocker. After that disturbing experience, the elephant's quieter charms were more appreciated.

'I'll be fine the next time,' Amber told him soothingly.

'I love Freddy, but I value your health more, *bella mia*.'

'Yes…you worship the ground I walk on,' Amber reminded him chattily as she measured the huge pile of presents still awaiting her and looked at Freddy and Rocco, especially Rocco. Rocco who was so incredibly romantic and passionate and hers now. Rocco winced. 'Did I say that?'

'And lots of other things too…you got quite carried away around midnight.' Confident as only a woman who knew she was loved could be, Amber gave him a glorious, wicked smile.

Rocco entwined his fingers round hers and hauled her back to him with possessive hands. 'You're a witch and I adore you—'

'I adore you too…so I didn't buy you the book on how to pleasure a woman in two hundred ways in case you thought I was dropping hints,' she said teasingly. 'I mean, I might die of exhaustion if I got any more pleasure. So I got you this instead. Merry Christmas, Rocco.'

Rocco unwrapped his miniature gold wheelbarrow and dealt her a vibrant grin of appreciation, which just turned her heart over. 'I'll keep it on my desk, *cara*.'

Freddy was slumped asleep over the elephant's head.

'You and Freddy are the best Christmas presents I have ever had,' Rocco confided with touching sincerity as he cradled his gently snoring son.

'Well, I did even better,' Amber pointed out, resting back beneath his other arm, blissfully content as she stared into the glowing embers of the fire. 'I got you, a fantastic wedding and this is going to be the most wonderful Christmas because it's our first together—'

Rocco urged her round to him and claimed her mouth in a sweet, delicious kiss that left her melting into his hard, muscular frame. 'Magical,' he groaned hungrily, and only Freddy's snuffly little complaint about being squashed got them back upstairs again.

* * * * *

A MARRIAGE PROPOSAL
FOR CHRISTMAS

Carole Mortimer

CHAPTER ONE

'I KNOW NO one is available to take my call at the moment, and no, I will not leave a message after the tone!' the man's voice snarled. 'I've already left four messages, and I'm sick of talking to this damned machine. I intend coming round there in person in the hopes that I can talk to a human being!'

Cally stood arrested in the doorway of the office as she heard the disembodied voice on the message her sister Pam was playing back on the answering machine. 'Not a dissatisfied customer, I hope?' She raised questioning brows as she came fully into the office and closed the door behind her, instantly shutting out the cold December wind blowing outside.

'Not yet.' Her sister looked up and smiled as she switched off the answering machine. 'So far he's just another person who seems to have forgotten that this is the season of peace and good will to all men.'

'I've always wondered what happened to "and all women" in that particular phrase,' Cally murmured as she slipped out of her thick outer coat, moving to hang it on the stand in the corner of the room. She appeared small and slim in the black business suit she wore, the thin green jumper beneath the jacket a perfect match for her eyes, long red hair loose about her shoulders.

Her sister, at twenty-eight the elder by three years, shrugged philosophically. 'Different century, darling,' she said dryly.

'You mean we were even less equal then than we are now?' Cally snapped irritably, moving to sit down behind the second desk in this cosily welcoming room that constituted the sisters' base for their business.

Pam chuckled. 'What's upset you this morning? Or should I say, who?' she corrected knowingly. 'Playboy of the West been keeping you awake all night again, has he?'

Cally raised auburn brows. 'Would you care to rephrase that?'

Pam's grin widened. 'Not particularly. But I will if it makes you happy,' she added teasingly as Cally's scowl deepened. 'Let's see.' She paused for thought. 'Has your neighbour been keeping you awake all hours of the day and night again with his noisy arrivals and departures in that gorgeous red vehicle that is just too glamorous to be called a mere car?'

'It's a Ferrari,' Cally supplied disgustedly. 'And that was at midnight last night. This morning—at six-thirty, would you believe?—it was a helicopter!' And she could still clearly remember being startled awake by the noise of its engines as it flew over the gatehouse where she lived, before landing on the lawn of the main house—where the 'Playboy of the West' lived!

'A helicopter.' Pam nodded, suitably impressed.

'It landed on the front lawn of the main house, continued to run its engines for ten minutes or so, and then flew off again. I was not amused, I can tell you,' Cassie growled, not willing, at this moment, to tell her sister just how unamused she had been—she was still too angry about the whole affair!

'Did he wake Lissa, too?' Pam looked concerned.

'No,' Cally allowed grudgingly, sure that her young daughter would sleep through an earthquake.

'Have you managed to meet Noel Carlton yet?' her sister asked eagerly.

Pam had been fascinated by the comings and goings of Cally's neighbour since he had moved into the main house almost a year ago. Cally didn't share the interest; she wished he would just take his Ferrari, and his helicopter, in fact, his whole over-the-top lifestyle, and go back to wherever it was he had come from!

The fact that he had flirted with her when she'd gone up to the house to complain about the noise a couple of months ago hadn't exactly endeared him to her, either. Especially as he hadn't followed up on the flirtation but had suddenly become coolly aloof! a little voice taunted inside her.

'No,' she fibbed. She felt guilty not telling Pam the truth, but couldn't face the grilling Pam would insist on giving her if she knew Cally had met the man twice now.

'Still think it was a good idea to move out to the "peace and quiet" of the country?' Pam teased as she saw Cally's frowning look.

Until Noel Carlton had moved in next door it had been a brilliant idea. The gatehouse she rented from the Parker Estate was just perfect for her and her young daughter, Lissa. Added to that, Lissa loved her new school, and was also able to indulge her interest in horse-riding at weekends. Even the forty-minute drive into work for Cally had been worth it just to see the happy smiles on her young daughter's face.

But Noel Carlton had moved in almost a year ago and since then it had all become a bit of a nightmare. Even complaints to the agent for the estate that she had arranged to rent the gatehouse from initially had not elicited any satisfaction.

Which was why she had paid Noel Carlton a visit herself two months ago. At that visit she had found the man absolutely charming, a fact he'd obviously picked up on as he had suggested they go out to dinner together some time to discuss the problem further.

To say she had been stunned by the invitation would be putting it mildly.

She had been disappointed when he hadn't bothered to call her, but had seemed to look through her the next time he'd seen her. And had continued to do so ever since.

Although, she recalled with a grimace, she hadn't exactly given him the opportunity to ignore her this morning!

Cally set her shoulders. 'It was an excellent idea,' she stated firmly. 'I'm determined that he will tire of country life before I do!'

Her sister chuckled, shaking her head. 'I wish you luck. I—uh-oh.' Her hazel-coloured gaze moved to the huge window that looked out on the busy high street from where they ran their business.

'What—?' Cally's attention was also caught by the grim-faced man striding determinedly past the window, the colour draining from her face as she realized he was coming here. 'It's him!' she squeaked breathlessly, at the same time coming sharply to her feet.

Pam turned back with a frown. 'What—?'

'It's him!' Cally repeated frantically.

'I—where are you going?' Pam demanded as Cally made a quick exit in the direction of the back room where they made hot drinks and kept the stationery.

'To make some coffee. I—get rid of him!' she pleaded before disappearing behind the open door.

But she made no effort to go and make coffee, or indeed anything else, as she heard the outer door open before being closed with suppressed violence. Nothing had changed there, then!

'Can I help you?' she heard Pam offer politely.

'I certainly hope so,' the man rasped.

Noel Carlton!

There was no doubt about it, Cally accepted with a wince after taking a surreptitious peek from behind the slightly ajar door and easily recognizing her nearest neighbour.

She couldn't mistake that handsomely chiselled face, or the dark hair he wore much longer than was fashionable. His suit, even from that brief glance, looked expensively tailored, as did the handmade black leather shoes.

Not that any of that mattered just now. There could be only one reason for this man turning up here: her comments this morning had obviously elicited some sort of response, after all!

'A human being at last,' he continued scathingly. 'You are a human being, aren't you?'

'Indeed I am,' Pam answered in her most soothing voice, always the calmer one of the two sisters—a fact Cally had always blamed on her own vibrantly red hair as opposed to Pam's more muted auburn. 'Would you be the gentleman who rang earlier?' she queried.

'Five times!' he confirmed indignantly.

Noel Carlton was the angry man on the answering machine?

'We don't actually open until nine o'clock, I'm afraid, Mr…?'

'Carlton,' he snapped.

'Mr Carlton,' Pam acknowledged smoothly—giving no indication of having recognized the name at all. 'I'm sorry there was no one here to take your calls earlier, but, as I said, we don't actually open the office until nine o'clock. However, I'm obviously more than happy to offer you any assistance that I can now.'

No, don't say that! Cally mentally tried to communicate with her sister. Noel Carlton was the last person either of them even wanted to talk to. Until they had consulted a lawyer, at any rate. Not that Cally thought she was even slightly in the wrong with her complaints, but that didn't mean that her neighbour saw it that way, too.

Cally took another peek around the door, just in time to see the man lowering his long length into the chair opposite Pam's desk, his back towards Cally now as she frantically tried to attract her sister's attention over one of his broad shoulders.

Pam shot her a questioning glance, obviously still none the wiser as to why Cally had disappeared so swiftly.

Cally quietly opened the door a little wider, raising her hands to make a movement as if she were holding the steering wheel of a car.

If anything Pam just looked even more perplexed!

Cally gave her sister a frustrated frown, pointing at Noel Carlton's broad back, then at herself, before repeating the action of holding a car's steering wheel.

Nothing.

Her sister looked completely puzzled now, at the same time staring at Cally as if she had gone slightly insane.

And maybe she had, Cally conceded heavily. She might have been extremely upset this morning, and told him exactly what she thought of him—but having Noel Carlton turn up at her place of work was the last response she had expected!

'The thing is that I need— Do I have your full attention… Mrs Davies?' Noel Carlton prompted, having paused briefly while he read the name on the front of the desk.

Pam broke her gaze away from Cally, a blush in her cheeks now. 'Of course you do, Mr— I'm sorry, what did you say your name was?' she encouraged in a slightly hushed voice, her eyes widening now with sudden recognition.

At last! Maybe there wouldn't be any need to hit her sister over the head with a book later, after all!

'Carlton,' he supplied again through clenched teeth. 'The thing is that I need— Mrs Davies?' he bit out impatiently as he obviously sensed her attention wandering again.

Not surprisingly really; Pam's gaze had returned to Cally as she stood behind him. The look in Pam's eyes was a mixture of recognition and excitement, tinged with wariness as to what he was actually doing here.

Cally had a pretty good idea as to the answer to the latter, although she hoped not to have to discuss that with her sister in front of her neighbour.

'What the—?' Noel Carlton, having followed Pam's gaze

and glanced behind him, stood up abruptly as he saw Cally standing there. 'You!' he accused.

Her.

And Noel Carlton looked no more pleased to see her again than she was to see him!

CHAPTER TWO

THE TWO OF THEM continued to stare at each other, Cally challengingly, Noel Carlton's expression now completely unreadable as he looked at her with those deep blue eyes.

In Cally's opinion, it wasn't fair that one man should be so good-looking. As well as that overlong hair being thick and darkly waving and his eyes being a beautiful deep cobalt-blue, his nose was straight and arrogant, his lips perfectly sculptured—the lower lip sensually fuller than the top—his jaw was square and determined, and his body tall and muscular, totally belying the thirty-five years or so that Cally guessed him to be. All that and rich too, Cally dismissed scathingly.

'Er—do you two know each other?' Pam was the one to break the chilly silence that had descended after Noel Carlton's initial outburst, her gaze accusing as she shot Cally a pointed glance.

Completely deserved, Cally accepted with an inner wince. But she simply hadn't had a chance yet to calm down enough to be able to rationally discuss the full events of this morning with her sister. Not that she thought Pam would be too impressed with that explanation, but it was the only one she had.

'No!'

'Yes.'

Noel Carlton and Cally spoke at the same time, Cally in the negative, Noel Carlton in the positive.

But if he thought having invited her out to dinner two months ago, and then promptly forgetting he had ever made the invitation, along with the argument this morning, gave him any right to claim an acquaintance with her then he was sadly mistaken; in fact, it was the opposite!

Pam gave the two of them a gleeful smile. 'Come on, now, which one is it?' she taunted.

'We most certainly do *not* know each other,' Cally answered before he even had chance to do so.

'Oh, come on, Cally,' Noel Carlton drawled, those deep blue eyes mocking now as he looked at her challengingly. 'That's not the impression I had earlier this morning.'

Cally's eyes widened indignantly, a blush creeping into her freckle-covered cheeks as Pam repeated, 'Earlier this morning, hmm?'

'Don't take any notice of him, Pam.' Cally glared at her infuriating neighbour. 'He's just trying to be clever!'

'And succeeding,' Pam pointed out. 'Dare one ask how it is the two of you happened to be together earlier this morning?' The look she gave Cally clearly said, You certainly didn't tell me that!

Cally drew in a sharp breath at her sister's speculative expression. 'It's really quite simple—'

'Oh, very,' Noel Carlton agreed mildly. He folded his arms across the width of his chest now as he looked at the two women. 'Tell me, are the two of you related? I seem to see a certain resemblance in the colouring and bone structure...'

'Sisters,' Cally supplied economically, not seeing what possible interest that could be to this man; if he had come here to cause trouble, then why didn't he just get on with it instead of standing there looking so damned irresistibly attractive?

Because he most certainly was! Cally found her pulse was beating rather faster than it should be, that blush having stayed in her cheeks as she became fully aware of his mere physical presence—mere? There was nothing 'mere' about this man!

Everything about him was overpowering, from the way he looked, to the way his height and size just dominated the room. And the people in it!

Well, they would see about that, Cally decided, giving herself a mental shake. Okay, so the man was good-looking and rich as Croesus, but that didn't mean that every woman he met had to fall down worshipping at his feet. Even if, that little voice taunted inside her again, her real anger towards him was based on the fact that he had never followed up on that dinner invitation…!

'Hmm, I should have guessed.' Noel Carlton gave Pam a smile warm enough to melt the flesh from her bones.

Something her elder sister welcomed, Cally realized disgustedly as she saw Pam return that smile and look at him from beneath lowered lashes.

Really, her sister had been happily married to Brian for the last eight years, had two little boys of school age, and yet here Pam was blushing like a schoolgirl herself just because Noel Carlton had smiled at her!

'I can't imagine why you should,' Cally dismissed. 'And while I appreciate that you went to some trouble to find me, I really have no intention of continuing our earlier conversation here.'

'That's very good,' he mocked, turning to smile at Pam once again. 'Your sister seems to be—the more emotional one of the two of you, shall we say? Has she always been that way?' he enquired.

'Always,' Palm confirmed, grinning at Cally's obvious discomfort at being discussed in this way. Her sister had patently decided it was the least Cally deserved after not telling her that she had actually met this man earlier this morning.

But there was a perfectly good reason why she hadn't told Pam about that meeting. In fact, there were several reasons. Firstly, losing her temper was never something she was particularly proud of. Secondly, even as she had been losing her temper with Noel Carlton she had found herself once more attracted to him. Thirdly, she had been able to tell by the warmth in his gaze that he returned the attraction…

'Hmm,' Noel Carlton murmured now appreciatively, at the same time giving Cally a look that it was impossible to see as anything else but a totally male assessment, taking in the rich redness of her long hair, the wide green eyes, her heart-shaped face dominated by those freckles, her determinedly raised chin, her slenderness in the black business suit, the long length of her legs.

Really, Cally thought crossly, did this man ever switch off his playboy mode?

'Could you just say what you want to say, Mr Carlton, and then leave?' she encouraged impatiently.

'Of course. I'm sure we're all busy people.'

'Nice of you to realize that,' she drawled.

'Cally,' Pam began warningly.

'Oh, don't be concerned, Pam,' she assured her sister lightly. 'Mr Carlton is perfectly well aware of my opinion of him!'

'Now, let me see…' Noel Carlton paused for dramatic effect. '"A rich, overindulged, totally selfish, egotistical idiot" was the phrase you used earlier, I believe. Did I miss anything out?' he asked, eyes openly laughing at her now.

'You know that you didn't!' Her cheeks were burning with indignation at the realisation that she had obviously amused him. And something else. It was that 'something else' that caused her to look away from him in some confusion.

She simply couldn't still find this man attractive! Oh, of course he was good-looking, but as far as she was concerned, after inviting her out and then not even bothering to call her, he had nothing else to recommend him, and she had no intention of being taken in by looks alone. That had already happened in her life once, and look what a disaster that had turned out to be…!

'Actually—' he glanced at the name on the badge attached to the lapel of her jacket '—Mrs Turner—'

'Miss,' Cally corrected. 'Miss Turner,' she enlarged almost defensively as he looked at her enquiringly, at the same time waiting for some cutting comment from him. One of the things she had thrown at him this morning in their heated exchange—well, to be honest, hers had been heated, Noel Carlton had looked as if not too much made him exert himself at that time of the morning!—had been that he had woken not only her up with the arrival and departure of that helicopter but her young daughter too. It wasn't true, of course. Lissa had still been fast asleep, but it had sounded good at the time.

His brows rose slightly before he spoke again, 'Miss Turner,' he acknowledged with an inclination of his head. 'Well, I hate to disappoint you, Miss Turner, but I'm afraid my being here today has absolutely nothing to do with you, and everything to do with the unfortunate predicament I find myself in.'

Cally blinked, staring at him in disbelief. Was he seriously expecting her to believe his coming to her workplace was just a coincidence?

'What predicament would that be, Mr Carlton?' Pam was the one to ask. 'I did detect a certain element of desperation in the telephone messages you left earlier,' she added sympathetically.

'Desperation!' He gave a huff of grim laughter. 'I'm beginning to wish I could just scrap Christmas altogether.'

'Bah, humbug,' Cally murmured tauntingly.

'Just call me Ebenezer,' Noel Carlton conceded. 'Not that I have anything against the present giving, or the decorations, or the fact that we get in more food and drink than we will ever be able to consume in two days—'

'Then what do you object to?' Cally queried with a puzzled smile. 'You seem to have got Christmas more or less covered there!'

'That's the problem—I haven't.' He sighed heavily. 'I don't object to any of it—I just haven't done any of it!' His voice started to rise in agitation. 'My parents and my two siblings are due to arrive from the States in two days' time, and I haven't done a damned thing towards providing them with the English Christmas they're all so looking forward to!'

'Ah,' Cally breathed as understanding slowly began to dawn. 'And you thought Celebrations may be able to do it for you?'

After all, it was what she and Pam did; arranged parties and weddings, and even Christmas, for people who were too busy, or just too disorganized, to be able to manage it for themselves, organizing decorations, food, drink, staff if they were needed—in fact anything a client needed to make the celebration a success.

The two sisters had started out quite small five years ago, working from Pam's home, as a way of them both earning some money, with the added bonus that they could arrange their jobs around the demands of their young children. During that five years they had built up a solid reputation, but unfortunately only locally, with other parents from school, or recommendation from them by word of mouth. And so they had discussed it with Pam's husband, and decided that, although it would be a struggle financially for a while, the only way for them to make a real success of the business— to eventually make money!—was to enlarge the business by moving into premises in town.

Something they had done only six months ago...

Cally just hadn't thought that Noel Carlton would be one of those disorganized people they were called in to help.

She smiled. 'Well, I'm really sorry about this, Mr Carlton...' the brightness of her tone telling him that she wasn't sorry at all '...but I'm afraid that we're fully booked this week—'

'Actually, we're not,' Pam admitted softly.

Cally turned sharply to her sister. 'What do you mean, we're not?'

Her sister gave a shrug. 'I haven't had chance to tell you

yet, but the Neilsons telephoned early this morning and left a message on the machine too.' She gave Noel a smile. 'Apparently they have had some sort of emergency in Sweden, have had to return home unexpectedly, and don't expect to return to England until after the New Year.'

'But I was due to go and put all the decorations up today! And what about all the food we have stored in the freezer?' Cally gasped her dismay, having been working exclusively on the Neilsons' Christmas for the last week. 'What are we supposed to do with all of that?' She groaned at the thought of all that work wasted.

And the fact that they weren't going to get paid!

'Excuse me,' Noel Carlton put in pointedly.

Cally shot him a narrow-eyed glare as she easily caught his meaning. 'Forget it,' she bit out, at the same time knowing that she and Pam couldn't afford to lose all the money they had expended on the Neilsons' Christmas; the deposit paid by the Neilsons wasn't refundable, but by the same token it in no way covered what had already been spent.

'But, Cally, it would seem to be the perfect solution to everyone's problems,' Pam reasoned, a worried frown furrowing her brow as she also thought of the money they were going to lose.

'This is my mother's first visit to England since she remarried and moved to America twenty years ago,' Noel Carlton argued persuasively. 'The last thing I want to do is disappoint her and my stepfather by not giving her the sort of Christmas she remembers.'

'Shouldn't you have thought of that earlier?' Cally frowned, not at all impressed by his attempt at emotional blackmail—even as she felt a faint stirring of concern for a woman she had never met.

The perfectly sculptured mouth firmed, his eyes narrowing to angry slits of dark blue. 'I did think of it. It's just—a series of—unexpected events have unfortunately made it impossible for me to complete my plans,' he explained.

'Oh, yes? And just what sort of "unexpected events" could a man like you—?'

'A man *like me*?' he interrupted in a softly, dangerous tone of voice.

'I think Mr Carlton has already told us as much of his predicament as we need to know, Cally,' her sister declared, standing up decisively. 'Mr Carlton has come here to ask for our help. Because of a last-minute cancellation, we are in a position to provide that help. I may be wrong, but I thought that was what we were in business for?' She gave Cally a pointed look.

They were. Of course they were. There was nothing more rewarding, after days, possibly weeks, of hard work, than to see the look of happiness on a client's face when their particular celebration passed off successfully because of Pam's and Cally's efforts. Cally just wasn't inclined to see that look on Noel Carlton's face. Unfortunately she could see by the stubborn set to Pam's mouth that her sister, quite rightly, was thinking of the overdraft on their bank account rather than whether or not Cally was comfortable with this commission.

'We still have the Neilsons' deposit,' she tried halfheartedly, knowing it wasn't enough. 'Besides, you're completely tied up at the moment with the arrangements for the Gregorys' wedding on Christmas Eve,' she reminded her sister hopefully.

'Yes, I am,' Pam confirmed, glancing down at her wristwatch. 'In fact, I have an appointment at the florist's in fifteen minutes,' she realized. 'But you, Cally, on the other hand, are totally free for the next three days.'

'I'm more than willing to pay extra, petrol money, whatever, if you will just agree to help me out,' Noel Carlton enticed.

'Bribery and corruption usually work, do they?' Cally snapped.

He grinned. 'Every time.'

'I thought so.' Cally gave a disgusted shake of her head.

'Cally!' Pam gasped reprovingly.

'Sorry,' she muttered, feeling as if she were swimming upstream—and rapidly losing the battle. Besides, a part of her knew that Pam was quite right to grasp this replacement commission with both hands. If only it weren't Noel Carlton's hands they were grasping!

'There's the added benefit that you'll be working close to home,' Noel Carlton encouraged, his smile one of false brightness when Cally gave him another frown for reminding her that he was her neighbour from hell. As if she needed any reminding of that!

But, in actual fact, it would be a benefit, more so than this man probably realized, if she agreed to arrange Christmas for him and his family.

She would be able to pick Lissa up from her sister's house much earlier in the day. Brian was looking after the children, school having finished for the Christmas holidays. It didn't happen very often that either Pam or herself couldn't care for the children during the holidays, but Christmas was such a busy time that it invariably ended with Lissa staying with her uncle Brian, a self-employed accountant who worked from home, for part of the Christmas holidays. Not that Lissa didn't enjoy being with her cousins, because she did, but it was a lot to expect Brian to cope with three children instead of two for long hours.

'I really do have to go now, so I'll leave you two to discuss it,' Pam stated briskly, moving to collect her outer coat. 'But, whatever the outcome, I do sincerely wish you a happy Christmas, Mr Carlton.' She gave him a warm smile.

In other words, Pam was leaving the decision completely

up to Cally as to whether or not they took pity on the man and agreed to work for him.

More to the point, her sister was leaving her with the knowledge that if she didn't agree to do this because of present—and past!—resentments towards Noel Carlton, then they probably wouldn't even have enough money in their bank account to cover their monthly rental on the shop premises.

Great.

Just great!

CHAPTER THREE

'I want you to know that I really do appreciate—'

'Fine,' Cally cut Noel off rudely, busy unloading the boxes of decorations from the boot of her car, not in the least mollified by the fact that her newest client had been waiting outside Parker Hall when she'd arrived ten minutes ago, with the obvious intention of helping her carry the boxes inside.

She hadn't wanted to do this job at all, but at the same time she was well aware of what Pam's reaction would be if she returned to the office and found that Cally had refused to help him after all. That, she told herself firmly, was the only reason she was here at all. That, and the thought of his poor mother's disappointment when she arrived to spend Christmas in England and found her son had done nothing about arranging it. No, she certainly wasn't doing this for Noel Carlton.

He straightened, arms folded across his chest as he gave her a considering look. 'Tell me, is that heavy?'

She frowned, looking at the box in her arms. 'Not particularly, no.'

'I wasn't referring to the box,' he drawled.

Cally blinked; she really didn't have the time to play word games with this man. In fact, she didn't have a lot of time at all, and would have preferred it if he hadn't been here! 'Then what were you referring to?' she asked distractedly.

'The monumental chip you have on your shoulder,' he said dryly. 'Can I take a guess at that having something to do with the fact that it's *Miss* Turner instead of *Mrs*?'

Cally stiffened. 'I beg your pardon?'

Noel Carlton drew in a deep breath. 'I said, does that monumental chip on your shoulder—?'

'I heard what you said,' she snapped.

He nodded unconcernedly. 'I thought that you did.'

She scowled at him. 'I was just giving you the opportunity to retract the question!'

He shrugged. 'An opportunity I have no intention of taking. Look, I really am sorry you were woken up by the helicopter this morning—'

'I can assure you, your insulting remark just now certainly hasn't helped the situation!' she assured him.

'I can see that.' He grimaced. 'Look, Cally—may I call you Cally?'

'I believe you just did.'

'And I'm Noel,' he told her unnecessarily, giving an impatient sigh as she looked unimpressed. 'Cally, I want you to know that Celebrations comes highly recommended—you organized my secretary's wedding last week,' he enlarged as she looked at him questioningly. 'Debra Hayes,' he supplied as she still looked blank.

'Oh, yes.' She smiled as she remembered the glowingly lovely bride she had spent months consulting with to make absolutely sure the elaborate wedding plans worked out successfully, that smile fading as she also remembered that Debra and her husband, Giles, were supposed to be honeymooning in Barbados right now. 'Exactly when did Debra recommend us to you?'

'I telephoned her last night, if you must know,' Noel Carlton revealed reluctantly. 'I was desperate, okay?' he added irritably as Cally raised incredulous brows.

She bit her lip in an effort to stop herself from laughing, finally giving up as she realized she was fighting a losing battle. 'I'm sure she and her new husband really appreciated that!' She chuckled gleefully.

Noel gave a rueful smile. 'I don't think Giles was best pleased.'

'Would you have been, in the circumstances?' Cally shook her head in disbelief as she continued to walk inside the house, depositing the box with the others in the huge hall at the bottom of the wide staircase. 'They're on their honeymoon, for goodness' sake!' She turned to grin.

'Yes. Well. I was desperate,' he muttered.

'So you already said.'

In actual fact, Cally had been slightly thrown off her guard when she'd arrived at Parker Hall and found Noel Carlton waiting for her, no longer wearing his business suit, shirt and tie, but dressed in faded denims and a rugby top that looked as if it might be a relic of his university days ten years or so ago. If anything, he looked more lethally attractive in these casual clothes than he had in his suit!

He raised a hand to sweep back that overlong dark hair. 'Ordinarily I could have asked Debra to help me out with this little problem—'

'Oh, so now it's a *little* problem, is it?' Cally teased.

It was Noel's turn to grin. 'It is now that you're here to help!'

'Don't expect miracles,' she warned. 'I'll do my best, but this is rather a big house.' She looked pointedly at the huge hallway they stood in, half a dozen doors leading off it, and this was only the ground floor; there were two more of them up the wide staircase.

Parker Hall was the old manor house to the local village of Axton, and had once housed the rich and influential family of Parker. But as with many of these old families, death duties and lack of interest in succeeding generations had almost brought about its ruin, the hall now rented out to whoever could pay the exorbitant fee being asked. Which Noel Carlton obviously could...

'As long as the Neilsons weren't going to eat smorgasbord

for Christmas, or something equally unsuitable, I really don't care!' he assured Cally now.

'You're in luck. The Neilsons intended having a traditional English Christmas as they were in this country—roast turkey and all the trimmings.'

'Great.' He smiled his satisfaction, that smile fading as another thought obviously occurred to him. 'Do you have any idea how to cook a turkey?' he asked tentatively.

Her eyes widened. 'Don't you? No, obviously not,' she accepted as he gave her a derisive look from those deep blue eyes. 'Well, I'm sure that your housekeeper will know— What?' she questioned sharply as he shook his head.

He grimaced. 'My housekeeper, Mrs McTavish, was the one who flew off to Scotland in the helicopter this morning; I'm not expecting her back until after the New Year.'

'Well, that wasn't very sensible of you, was it?'

'Sense had nothing to do with it.'

'You can say that again,' Cally muttered unsympathetically.

'Have you always been a know-it-all?'

She shrugged. 'Pretty much.'

'Well, it's very unbecoming in a beautiful woman—'

'Flattery will get you nowhere!' she told him, knowing even as she said it that her heart had given a little flutter at being called beautiful by this wildly attractive man.

Forget it, Cally, she instantly instructed herself. Remember, he was the one who asked a woman out to dinner and then forgot to follow up on the invitation by telephoning to make a definite date!

'I never for a moment thought that it would,' he assured her. 'But it isn't flattery when it happens to be the truth,' he added huskily.

Cally's breath was caught somewhere in her chest, even the air around them seeming to have become still as her gaze caught and held Noel's, blue clashing with green.

A pirate, that was what he reminded her of, Cally suddenly realized, with that dark flowing hair, eyes that smiled roguishly, his skin darkly tanned, his body lean but muscular, his smile sensual.

A pirate! she instantly scorned herself. Get a grip, Cally Turner.

'Fine.' She was deliberately dismissive, breaking their gaze as she turned away. 'As for the turkey, I'm sure your mother will know what to do with it when she arrives,' she said; after all, she was just putting up the decorations and providing the food. She had nothing to do with the how and why of what he chose to do with it after that!

His brow cleared. 'Of course she will. Why didn't I think of that?'

'Probably because you've been too busy disturbing Debra and Giles on their honeymoon, and sending your housekeeper away to Scotland in a helicopter,' Cally derided.

'For your information, young lady, I did not send Mrs McTavish away.' He totally ignored the jibe about his secretary. 'She fell down the stairs a couple of weeks ago and broke her arm. In the circumstances, she may as well go to Scotland and spend Christmas with her married daughter; keeping her here was a complete waste of her time and mine.'

'How considerate of you!'

His eyes narrowed to dark blue slits. 'You're determined to see the worst in me and my actions, aren't you?'

She gave him a falsely bright smile. 'Got it in one!'

He gave a heavy sigh. 'Look, Cally, there were—reasons, why I didn't—why I didn't follow through on that dinner invitation a couple of months ago. You see—'

'Did I mention anything about a dinner invitation?' she cut in quickly, her cheeks fiery red just at the mention of it.

'No, you didn't, but—'

'But nothing,' she interrupted a second time—she really didn't want to talk about that embarrassing incident.

He gave her a frowning look. 'You aren't even going to give me chance to explain?'

'No, I'm not—because there's nothing to explain!' She deliberately stood her ground as he took a step closer to her. 'Mr Carlton—'

'Noel,' he prompted softly, definitely standing much closer than was necessary. 'We're going to be pretty much thrown together for the next three days, so you may as well—'

'What?' Cally asked sharply, a sinking feeling in the pit of her stomach. 'But why are you going to be here? Don't you have work, an office, to go to?' she suggested desperately; spending hours, days, in this man's company had not been part of her agreement!

'Of course I have an office to go to. It just happens to be closed for the holidays.'

'But—but this morning!' she pounced frantically. 'You were dressed in a suit, obviously on your way somewhere—'

'I thought I might make more of an impression on the owners of Celebrations if I dressed in a suit and looked businesslike.'

'You had already made impression enough, I can assure you!' Cally snapped.

'So it would seem.' He shrugged. 'But in my defence, how was I to know that one of the owners was my own dear neighbour?'

Cally's eyes narrowed. 'I'm not your "own dear" anything.'

Once again he looked down at her with those dark, fathomless blue eyes. 'But you could be,' he murmured throatily.

She eyed him suspiciously. 'I thought I warned you about trying to flatter me?'

He arched dark brows. 'Was I flattering you?'

Too late Cally realized exactly how her last remark had sounded. Without thinking she retaliated. 'Correct me if I'm wrong, but I'm sure that Debra, during one of our many meetings to discuss her wedding, once mentioned the fact that her

boss—presumably you—was out to lunch with his fiancée?'
She smothered a gasp—having just made the connection between Debra and her boss, she now realized why Noel had
not followed up on his dinner invitation two months ago—
already having a fiancée was definitely reason enough!

The humour faded from his gaze, his expression hardening. 'Ex-fiancée,' he corrected her.

'Really?' Cally was not altogether sure she believed him.
'Look, are you going to help me unload the rest of the decorations, or just stand there looking ornamental yourself?'

He looked thoughtful. 'Do you talk to your other clients
in the way that you do me?' he asked slowly.

'No,' she came back pertly. 'It just seems to come naturally
where you're concerned.' She gave him another, meaning-
less smile before striding back outside to collect more boxes.

'Only because you have me at a disadvantage,' he guessed
shrewdly, having followed her outside to stand on the driveway beside her car.

Cally's grin widened. 'Is that what it is?'

'I should be careful about just how superior you feel, Cally
Turner,' he warned softly. 'It comes before a fall, you know.'

'I thought that was pride?' she challenged, eyes gleaming with humour.

'Same thing,' he assured her. 'You never know when you're
going to need a friendly neighbour, you know.'

Cally gave a scornful snort. 'I haven't needed him so far—
and I see absolutely no reason for that to change,' she added
firmly as he would have spoken.

'Please yourself.' He shrugged.

'I usually do,' she answered him dryly. 'Here.' She placed
a box of decorations into his arms. 'If you insist on hanging
around, then you really will have to make yourself useful!'
She turned her back on him as she sorted through the boot
of her car, picking up some of the things that had fallen out
of the boxes.

But she was nevertheless aware of him still standing behind her, of his gaze still on her as she leaned into the boot of the car, could almost feel it burning the back of her legs.

Finally, when she could stand it no longer, she straightened abruptly and turned to give him another verbal dressing down. Only to find herself looking at his back, he whistling softly to himself as he walked back into the house with that easy grace that reminded her of a big cat. A jaguar, perhaps. Or a panther.

Her breath left her in a sigh, the tension easing out of her now that he was no longer standing beside her.

These, she was perfectly sure, were going to be the longest three days of her life!

But at the same time she couldn't help but feel curious about his fiancée—ex-fiancée, she corrected slowly. Who had broken the engagement? Noel? Or the woman? And if so, why...?

CHAPTER FOUR

'YOU KNOW,' Cally said as she twisted herself round on the staircase to fix the bowers of holly around the banister, 'I'm not sure your Mrs McTavish was too good at her job even before she fell over and broke her arm.' She rubbed her dust-covered fingers together as she straightened to look at her handiwork.

'She wasn't,' Noel conceded with a grimace. 'But she was better than nothing.'

'I suppose,' Cally acknowledged distractedly, straightening the holly as it looked slightly out of line with the next piece down.

The two of them had started work on the hall first. Cally knew it was going to be first impressions that mattered, and that after their initial reaction Noel's family probably wouldn't take too much notice of the décor. It would be the food and the log-burning fire, that would please them after that.

But she really wasn't joking about Mrs McTavish's housework, and was glad she had returned to the gatehouse earlier to change into some of her old clothes before starting work; everywhere looked as if it could do with a good dust and polish. The old denims and loose cream shirt were better for working in than a skirt anyway, especially with Noel following her every move...

Cally nodded. 'Probably as well you whisked her away to Scotland for the holidays.'

Noel's eyes widened indignantly. 'You can say that, after the names you called me this morning?'

'Well...you could have scheduled her helicopter departure for a more convenient time,' she allowed ruefully.

In truth, she was slightly ashamed now of her outburst early this morning, knowing it had been the result of a broken night's sleep, and that ordinarily she would never have spoken to anyone in the way she had spoken to Noel.

He gave her a derisive look as he handed her another piece of holly. 'I'll try and remember that next time.'

'Thanks.' She grinned, adding the final touch to the bannister, then standing back to admire the results.

The front hall and staircase were transformed, a huge tree up and decorated downstairs, its lights blinking invitingly, a festive display of red and gold flowers on the table in the middle of the hallway, and real holly from the grounds acting as garlands up the stairs.

'So, what do you think?' She turned to smile at Noel.

'I think you've worked wonders in the last five hours.' He nodded his approval. 'I also think you need to take a shower or a bath; you even have a smudge of dirt on your nose!'

Cally attempted to wipe away the smudge. 'I'll take a shower when I get home.' Once she had picked Lissa up and collected a few groceries from the village store on the way back.

'I was suggesting you take one now.'

She looked sharply at Noel, finding only guileless innocence in his expression. 'No, thanks,' she responded dryly. 'I can wait.'

A mocking smile curved his lips. 'I'm not about to leap on you expectedly if you take a bath, Cally.'

She hadn't for a moment thought that he would, and the offer was tempting; she had seen the luxury of the Jacuzzi bath earlier when she'd gone to use the bathroom, couldn't imagine anything more decadent at this moment, covered in dust as she was. But she still had no intention of taking a bath in Noel Carlton's home.

'We'll never know, will we?' she teased.

'Spoilsport,' he taunted.

'My middle name.' She laughed. 'Well, I think that's enough for one day,' she added briskly. 'I'll be back bright and early in the morning to start on the sitting-room.'

'Exactly how bright and early?' Noel queried as he followed her down the stairs.

'Six-thirty do you?' Cally looked back at him, brows raised pointedly.

'Very funny.' He grinned his appreciation at her dig at him for this morning. 'I thought about nine o'clock?'

'Fine,' she agreed; it was the time she had in mind anyway, needing to take Lissa to Brian's first.

'You know, you can be quite accommodating—when you aren't calling me names!' Noel told her as he stood outside with her on the driveway.

'The remedy for that would appear to be—don't wake me up at six-thirty in the morning!' Cally came back lightly.

'Not a morning person, hmm?' he mused slowly. 'I'll have to remember that.'

Her eyes narrowed at the thought of the only sort of situation when that information would be of the least interest to him. 'I wouldn't bother,' she said. 'It's never likely to matter!'

He gave her a considering look, making Cally very conscious of that smudge of dirt she was sure was still on her nose, her hair tousled from their machinations earlier with the Christmas tree, and her shirt no longer being clean, either.

'Was he anything like me?' Noel finally asked softly.

She frowned in puzzlement. 'Was who anything like you?'

'Your daughter's father—hey, I didn't mean to startle you!' Noel reached out and took a firm hold of her arms as she would have recoiled from him and the question. 'Sorry,' he muttered repentantly. 'I shouldn't have asked.'

Cally could feel how the colour had drained from her

cheeks, her mouth feeling very dry too as she answered him. 'No, you shouldn't.'

'I just wondered if it was because I reminded you of him that you're so defensive with me.'

She gave him a tight smile. 'Believe me, I don't treat you differently from any other man!' The whole lot of them, apart from Brian, were only out for what they could get, as far as she was concerned. And the fact that Noel must have had a fiancée when he had invited her out two months ago certainly didn't make him any different!

He gave a heavy sigh. 'That's what I was afraid of.'

Her smile became genuine. 'I doubt that scares you too much, Noel.'

Those dark blue eyes looked into hers, seeming to see into the very depths of her being. 'You might be surprised,' he murmured. 'For instance, I was a little bowled over at the force of attraction I felt towards you two months ago.'

She swallowed hard. 'Obviously enough to forget you already had a fiancée!'

He gave an impatient shake of his head. 'I didn't have a fiancée then.'

Cally's eyes widened. 'You didn't…?' It must have been the shortest engagement in history. The shortest she had ever heard of, anyway!

'No,' he rasped. 'Look, could we just forget about my ex-fiancée?'

She frowned. 'It seems you already have…'

Cally was very conscious of the warmth of his hands on her arms, of the closeness of their bodies, of the soft warmth of his breath as it stirred the fiery tendrils of hair at her temples as she tried to break her gaze away from his, and failed.

'Cally…?' he questioned huskily.

Move, she instructed herself. Kick him in the shin. Do something to break this moment of intense intimacy!

But she couldn't seem to move, could only stand stiffly

immobile as Noel moved closer, his head bending, his lips claiming hers in a kiss of extreme tenderness.

If he had been rough, or in the least overpowering, Cally could have resisted him, but it was his tenderness that was her undoing, her arms moving up slowly to hold onto the width of his shoulders, her lips parting beneath his as his hands released her and his arms moved about the slenderness of her waist.

With the parting of her lips the kiss deepened, Cally groaning low in her throat as Noel moulded her body close to his, able to feel every hard contour, to know the sheer strength of him.

She knew that she had to stop this. Now!

She wrenched her mouth away from his. 'No!' she said in a strangled voice, her palms pushing against his chest until he released her. 'I'm here to decorate your house, Mr Carlton,' she insisted once he had reluctantly let her go. 'I have no intention of warming your bed as well!' She was breathing deeply in her agitation, at the same time aware that she was as much to blame as him for what had happened.

Because, despite what she might say to the contrary, she had been attracted to him for the last two months, too!

He had knocked her sideways at that first meeting. The strength of his body had been shown to such advantage in the faded denims and a loose tee shirt he'd seemed to have just pulled on over his nakedness to answer her knock on the door, and the tightness of his denims had certainly left nothing to the imagination. Although that certainly hadn't stopped Cally's imagination running riot just at the sight of him!

She had been surprised at her reaction to him; she hadn't felt attracted to any man since—since Michael. Which was, of course, the reason she had given Noel her telephone number so that he might call her and arrange a definite time for dinner.

Initially she had been disappointed when he hadn't telephoned. But as the days had passed without a call from him that disappointment had quickly been replaced by relief; she really did find him too attractive for her peace of mind.

He gave a wistful smile now. 'But we're nowhere near my bed, Cally.'

'And we aren't going to be, either,' she said as she pulled open her car door. 'It might be better if you don't help me tomorrow,' she added, determinedly avoiding the pull of that cobalt-blue gaze.

'Is that a request or an order?'

She raised her head to frown at him. 'I don't believe I'm in any sort of position to give you an order.' After all, she was working for him... 'But if you want me to finish the decorating and stocking up the freezer in time for your family's arrival, then I would suggest that you let me get on with my work.' She looked at him challengingly.

'That sounds suspiciously like a threat to me,' he said, his gaze narrowed now.

Cally tossed back the long length of her red hair. 'Not in the least,' she denied. 'I have my work to do, and I'm sure you must have yours.'

'Holidays, remember?' he taunted.

Her mouth twisted. 'I'm sure there must be a way you could make another million or two instead of just sitting around doing nothing for two weeks!'

He drew in a sharp breath, his jaw set and his gaze glacial now. 'You know, one day that chip is just going to get too heavy and it's going to crush you!'

She smiled without amusement. 'Then I would advise you to be well out of the way when it does.'

Noel gave a frustrated shake of his head. 'He must have been one hell of a louse!'

'Oh, he was,' she confirmed heavily, not even going to the trouble of trying to pretend she didn't know exactly whom he was talking about.

Cally was only too well aware that she treated men the way she did because of what had happened seven years ago, that it had been her disastrous relationship with Michael that had coloured all her dealings with other men since that time. Which was why it was so surprising that Noel had managed to get under her guard two months ago. It was also why she was so defensive with him now...

'A first class louse, in fact,' she added moodily.

Noel gave her a searching look. 'But without knowing him you wouldn't have your daughter,' he pointed out softly. 'And I'm sure, even from the little you've said about her, that you love her very much.'

'She's my life!' Cally admitted.

'Exactly.' He nodded.

Cally continued to look at him for several long seconds, surprised—and a little resentful too!—that he seemed to have latched onto the one thing that made thinking of her relationship with Michael bearable: Lissa.

She deliberately made her smile dismissive. 'Take my advice, Noel—forget the amateur psychology and stick to what you obviously do best!'

He raised an eyebrow. 'And what would that be?'

She gave a pointed look at their opulent surroundings before answering him. 'Making money?'

He gave a shake of his head. 'I don't own this place, Cally, I'm just renting it for a year.'

'With an option to buy at the end of that time,' she said knowingly. 'Oh, don't worry, Noel, I haven't been prying into your personal business,' she assured him as she saw the far from pleased expression on his face. 'The agent for the estate told me that little piece of information the first time I complained about the noise; as a way of trying to console me, I think.'

'Why didn't you just come and talk to me?' Noel demanded.

'I did,' she reminded him huskily.

He frowned. 'I really wish I could explain what happened two months ago—'

'There's really no need—' Cally began.

'Yes, there is,' he sighed. 'I just—'

'Could we please just forget about it?' Cally grimaced self-consciously.

'Can we?'

They would have to—if the next couple of days weren't going to turn out to be one long nightmare!

'Tell me about your family,' she changed the subject suddenly. 'They live in America, you said?'

He smiled wryly, seeming to accept for the moment that she really didn't want to talk about them. 'My sister and brother, Honey and Josh, at eighteen and twenty, are from my mother's second marriage. I suppose technically that makes them my half-brother and -sister.' He shrugged. 'But none of us have ever looked on the relationship that way. Honey certainly hates like a real sister!'

'We all do at eighteen.' Cally smiled, feeling a reluctant curiosity about his family now.

'You were probably pregnant with Lissa at eighteen,' he put in quietly.

Yes, she had been. Eighteen, pregnant, and scared. Scared most of all. There had never been any question in her mind as to whether or not she would keep the baby, only the worry as to whether or not she would be able to cope. But she had.

'Talking of Lissa...' she gave a pointed look at her wrist-watch '...I have to go and collect her from Pam's husband now.'

He nodded. 'I wondered how you organized that.'

'Did you?' Cally gave him a puzzled frown, wondering herself why he had given it a second thought.

Noel stepped back. 'I've kept you late enough.'

Cally blinked at this easy acquiescence to her departure

after what had seemed like deliberate delaying tactics minutes ago, but she got slowly into the car before driving off
with a brief wave of her hand.

It was only as she sped off down the driveway, the image
of Noel still in her driving mirror, that she realized the last
few minutes' conversation had completely driven her earlier
confusion, at being kissed by Noel, from her mind.

Deliberately so?

Probably, she acknowledged ruefully.

It had also prevented him making any reply to her request
that he not be at the house tomorrow while she was working,
she realized with a groan of frustration.

Again, deliberately so?

Definitely!

CHAPTER FIVE

PARKER HALL FELT very big, eerily so, without Noel Carlton's annoyingly provocative presence in it...

Cally had arrived promptly at the house at nine o'clock that morning, only to meet Noel going out of it, his car keys in his hand.

'Got to run,' he'd only had time to call out to her. 'See you later,' he'd added before roaring off in the Ferrari.

Well, it was a lot later now, the morning having passed, her packed lunch eaten, and most of the afternoon having passed too. All without sight or sound of another human being.

Was she complaining?

If she were honest?

Yes.

How on earth did Noel live alone in this huge house, every creak and groan of the floorboards contracting as the central heating system fired into life seeming to echo through its emptiness?

Not that Cally hadn't kept herself busy, because she had. The house had been polished and cleaned from top to bottom before she'd put up the tasteful decorations in the sitting-room, and another Christmas tree. She'd also draped more freshly picked holly along the top of the hearth, and put a match to the logs in the fireplace as a final nicety, pleased with the result as the flames crackled and burnt, filling the room with seasonal warmth and cheer.

But now she felt dusty and grimy from her Herculean efforts to turn this big old barn of a house into a warmly welcoming Christmas paradise, and was seriously tempted by the offer she hadn't taken up yesterday: that of soaking in that gigantic Jacuzzi bath!

It really was the most opulently luxurious bathroom she had ever seen in her life. The deep cream bath, which could have accommodated four people at once, took up the whole of one corner of the room. There were brown and cream tiles on the floor and on three of the walls, with a huge ornate mirror covering the fourth one. As for the cream towels on the heated rail, they looked softer and thicker than anything she had at home.

There was absolutely no competition between this and the bathroom in the gatehouse, where the white bath was old and stained, and the supply of hot water was erratic to say the least.

The hot water reached right up to her neck as she lay back in its scented depth, the bubbles tickling her nose as the Jacuzzi frothed the foam right to the top of the bath.

Heaven.

Absolute, unadulterated luxury.

Cally rested her head back on the side, her eyes closed as she imagined what it must be like to indulge like this every day. Not that she ever would, but she was going to enjoy it while she could!

'Oops!' exclaimed a deeply amused male voice.

Cally sat up with a startled cry, only to lie back down again as she realized the deep pink tips of her breasts were visible amongst the thick bubbles, the blush in her cheeks rising to meet that colour as she found herself staring across the bathroom at a man she knew she had never seen before!

Not that he looked in the least perturbed at the encounter—on the contrary, he was completely relaxed as he leant against the doorframe, blond brows raised as he grinned across the room at her. 'Well, well, Mama, and who's been lying in my bath?' he teased.

Cally continued to stare at him, having absolutely no idea who he was or what he was doing here, only knowing that she didn't appreciate the totally assessing male look in his sky-blue eyes.

'Tell me, do you have Noel in there with you?' he asked curiously.

'Don't be ridiculous,' Cally snapped as she found her voice at last, frowning across at him now, the bubbles decorously draped across her nakedness. She was not in the least reassured by the fact that he knew the owner of the house was called Noel, and was cross with herself for not thinking of locking all the doors before going upstairs for a bath.

He shrugged broad shoulders. 'Just a thought; you had such a sublimely happy look on your face when I came in!'

The blush deepened in her cheeks at his implication. 'Who are you? And what are you doing in here?' she demanded, knowing she would have remembered this man if she had ever seen him before. His hair was straw-blond, his face youthfully handsome, and he was tall and slim in faded denims and a heavy blue jumper.

'Shouldn't I be asking you that?' he taunted, making no effort to move.

'Would you mind leaving the bathroom so that I can get dressed?' she told him agitatedly.

He gave another shrug. 'Be my guest.'

'Go away!' Cally demanded, eyes sparkling like the emeralds they so resembled.

'Oh, but—'

'Josh? Josh, where are you?' called a pleasant female voice. 'I can't seem to— Oh!' A woman had come to stand in the doorway too now, still beautiful, despite obviously being aged somewhere in her late forties or early fifties. 'Hello.' She smiled warmly across at Cally. 'You must be Carol. Since Noel told us about you I've so been looking forward to meeting you!'

Cally was starting to feel as if this bathroom were in the middle of King's Cross railway station, the amount of people that just seemed to walk into it!

But she had also registered that the young man's name was Josh, which she remembered was also the name of Noel's younger brother. Now that she thought about it he did have a distinctive American accent—she had been too disturbed initially to notice! But if he was Josh, that probably meant the beautiful woman standing beside him was his and Noel's mother…!

That much Cally had managed to work out despite feeling more uncomfortable than she ever had in her life before. What she didn't understand was why Noel had bothered to tell his mother about the woman who was decorating his home for him. Or why his mother called her Carol, when no one had called her by her full name in years.

Although none of that really mattered just now. What did matter was getting out of this bath and back into her clothes, so that she did at least have some personal dignity left.

'Er—I'm afraid you've caught me at a complete disadvantage, so if the two of you wouldn't mind…?' she said.

'Oh, how silly of us,' Noel's mother realized self-disgustedly.

'Come along, Josh.' She grabbed hold of his arm as he would have continued to linger. 'Let's give Carol some privacy while she finishes her bath.'

Josh gave one last lingering glance in Cally's direction before reluctantly complying.

'I'll go down and make us all some tea, shall I?' his mother offered brightly.

'Thank you.' Cally nodded, just wanting the two of them to leave, breathing a sigh of relief when Noel's mother finally moved away, closing the door behind her.

Could it have been any worse? she groaned inwardly as she sank back down into the rapidly cooling bubbles. Yes, came the immediate answer; it could have been Noel who came home and found her in the bath instead of just his whole family!

Just his whole family...! Well, no, she had been spared his sister and stepfather coming to gawk at her in the bath, too!

The humour of the situation finally began to kick in, and a wry smile curved her lips. What a thing to have happened. Noel certainly hadn't mentioned, before he'd left in such a hurry this morning, that his family were going to arrive earlier than expected.

Which posed the question: where was Noel? He had been gone most of the day, and—

'Enjoying yourself?' he queried sarcastically.

Cally made a startled move to sit up, and then sank back down into the bubbles as she remembered what had happened the last time she'd done that, frowning across at Noel as he was the one now standing framed in the open doorway.

'Do none of your family ever knock before entering a bathroom?' She sighed.

He shrugged. 'Only when we expect someone else to be in there.' He straightened, moving further into the room, closing the bathroom door behind him. 'And none of us expected you to be in here,' he added dryly.

'What are you doing?' Cally eyed him suspiciously as he strolled over to sit on the side of the bath. 'Your family are downstairs—'

'I'm well aware of that.'

Her cheeks were burning with the embarrassment of having him so close to her when she was absolutely naked! 'Would you please go away?' she groaned awkwardly, feeling her hair starting to fall down from where she had loosely secured it on top of her head away from the dampness of the bubbles.

Noel looked down at her with deliberately guileless blue eyes. 'Is something bothering you, Cally?' he mocked even as he reached out a hand and scooped some of the bubbles up into his palm.

'Stop that!' Cally gasped, frantically splashing more bubbles up the bath towards her.

Not that there were as many as there had been when she'd started, the scented froth starting to disappear as the water cooled.

She closed her eyes. 'I can't believe this is happening to me!' she cried.

'Actually—' Noel grinned down at her wolfishly '—neither can I!'

Cally opened her eyes again to glare up at him. 'Opportunist!' she accused disgustedly.

He gave a shrug, scooping up another handful of bubbles. 'Come on, Cally, you have to admit, this is a pretty unusual situation!' he teased.

And of her own making, if she were honest. It should have occurred to her that Noel, at least, could walk back in at any moment and find her in the bath. Let alone almost every other member of his family!

She gave another embarrassed groan. 'Whatever must your mother think of me?'

'Actually,' Noel repeated, his expression now suddenly unreadable, 'I'm more disturbed by what my little brother thinks of you!'

Cally blinked, wincing slightly as Noel's mouth twisted humourlessly. 'And what was that?' she asked reluctantly.

'Do you want the full version or will the potted one do?'

'I believe the potted one will do!' she confirmed with a pained look, even the rapidly cooling water not bothering her too much now.

'Well, Josh thinks you're the most beautiful mermaid he's ever set eyes on!'

'Oh.' She grimaced.

'My mother, on the other hand—'

'Please!' she cried awkwardly. 'I feel badly enough about this as it is, without being told what your mother thinks of the hired help luxuriating in your bath!'

Noel gave her a considering look. 'It's worse than that, I'm afraid,' he told her softly.

Cally gave a shake of her head. 'It couldn't be!' She had no idea yet how she was going to get dressed, go downstairs, and face all of Noel's family after what had happened. Because she did have to face them, had to try and explain herself. Even if that explanation did sound a little lame!

'Oh, yes, it could.'

Cally gave him a suspicious look. 'What have you done?'

'Me?' His eyes widened incredulously. 'Cally, I'm not the one who was found cavorting about in the Jacuzzi—'

'I was not "cavorting",' she defended herself. 'I was just lying here minding my own business—'

'Paying court to half my family,' Noel interjected.

'Only because they walked into the bathroom unannounced!'

'I accept that, Cally.' He sighed. 'But, nevertheless, it's put us both in a very awkward position.'

Cally's heart sank, wondering whether his family wanted more than an apology from her for making free with their son's bathroom—like making a complaint against Celebrations!

It didn't matter that in the five years she and Pam had been running their company from home they hadn't received a single complaint; they had stepped out into the big time now, and something like this was enough to cause their pristine reputation considerable damage before they had even really begun.

'I'll explain—'

'It's too late for that, I'm afraid.' Noel stood up abruptly, starting to pace the bathroom, a dark frown furrowing his brow.

'Look, I'm sure that if I explain, and apologize, it isn't

going to be as bad as you're making out it is,' Cally pleaded, watching him worriedly as he paced up and down the small confines of the room. 'Your mother looked very nice,' she added hopefully.

In actual fact, his mother had looked very much like Noel himself; thick dark hair down to her shoulders, with warm blue eyes, her face a softer, prettier version of Noel's strong features.

'Oh, she is,' Noel confirmed. 'Very nice. She's also looking forward to being a grandmother some time in the near future.'

'Really?' Cally smiled. 'That will be nice.'

'You think?' Noel paused beside the bath, mocking humour lighting his eyes. 'Cally, I think you'll agree that, at this particular moment, you're very much a captive audience?'

She shifted self-consciously, wishing he wouldn't stand so close to her—especially when she was sure the previously frothy water was almost transparent by now! 'I'll agree that I'm not about to leap up and jump out of the bath while you're still in the room,' she conceded slowly, not sure where his remark was going.

He nodded. 'A captive audience.'

'Possibly,' she accepted warily.

'Did you notice earlier that my mother called you Carol?' he asked.

'Well, yes, I did notice that.' She frowned. 'But as it actually is my name, I just thought—' She broke off suddenly, staring up at Noel now. 'But you didn't know that, did you?' she realized.

He gave a wry smile. 'Not until just now, no.'

Several things began to click into place, things that had puzzled her earlier, but which could make perfect sense if—

'Noel, was you ex-fiancée named Carol, by any chance?' She gasped as a terrible realization started to take shape in her mind.

He gave her an admiring look. 'You really are a very astute young lady, aren't you?'

Astuteness had nothing to do with it. It was all so obvious when she thought of the lack of surprise on Josh's and his mother's faces when they'd found her taking a bath, and the way the older woman had said how much she had been looking forward to meeting her. She hadn't been referring to the woman decorating Noel's home at all, but to his fiancée!

Noel was right; this was so much worse than she had thought!

CHAPTER SIX

A KNOCK SOUNDED on the bathroom door. 'I'm sorry to interrupt, you two,' Josh called out cheerfully in a totally unrepentant voice, 'but Carol's sister is downstairs.'

Pam!

Could this situation get any worse if it tried? Cally groaned inwardly.

Not much, came the resounding answer. So far she had been caught lazing in a client's bath by his family, that family had mistakenly thought she was the fiancée of the eldest son, and in the middle of all that her practical no-nonsense older sister had to arrive.

'With Carol's adorable daughter Lissa,' Josh added as if on cue.

This time Cally shot up in the bath regardless of the fact that Noel was still in the room with her, reaching out to quickly pull one of the huge cream towels towards her as his gaze widened appreciatively on her nakedness.

'You didn't tell us about that one, big bro,' Josh said gleefully. 'Mama is downstairs absolutely drooling over Lissa right now,' he added for good measure, the sound of his laughter floating back to them as he walked off down the hallway.

'Going somewhere?' Noel taunted as Cally still hesitated about actually getting out of the bath.

'Well, of course I'm—Noel, you heard your brother; even as we speak, your family is probably welcoming Pam and Lissa into their midst!'

'Probably.' He nodded unconcernedly.

She looked at him warningly. 'Noel—'

'Cally,' he cut in firmly, straightening. 'As you seem to have deduced, we have something of a dilemma—'

'*I* don't have a dilemma,' she said heatedly, eyes flashing deeply green. '*You* do!'

'No.' He shook his head. 'As I see it, you're in this with me up to your beautiful neck. If you hadn't been lazing in the Jacuzzi, of course, then probably this mistake in identity wouldn't have occurred, but as it is…' He gave a fatalistic shrug.

'Will you stop going on about my being in the Jacuzzi?' Cally sighed frustratedly. 'You were the one who invited me to make use of the facility—'

'That was yesterday,' Noel reasoned. 'I would never have repeated the offer today, knowing that my family were about to swoop on me *en masse*—'

'You knew your family were arriving early?' Cally frowned. 'But if that's so, why did you just disappear for the day like that?'

'A misunderstanding about arrival times,' Noel dismissed carelessly.

Her gaze narrowed on his deliberately bland expression. 'You mean you got the time wrong?'

He gave a rueful grimace. 'Not only that—I got the wrong airport, too! For some reason I wasn't too attentive when my mother telephoned last night and told me the time and place of their arrival.' He gave Cally a pointed look. 'And so I've been waiting to meet the wrong aeroplane at Gatwick for the last five hours, and the family arrived at Heathrow three hours ago!'

Cally stared at him; surely Noel wasn't implying that she had anything to do with his inattentiveness to his mother last night…?

Noel shrugged again. 'It's easy to see why they thought you were Carol.'

It was perfectly obvious to Cally what had happened, and why—she just didn't know how they were going to get out of it without looking like absolute idiots.

'Why don't your family know of your broken engagement?' She pounced on the possible escape.

He looked pained. 'I hadn't got around to telling them yet—thought it was something I could just break to them gently over Christmas—'

'Oh, like "Here's your Christmas present, Mama, and by the way I'm not getting married any more"? Something like that, you mean?' Cally prompted disbelievingly.

'Well…maybe a little more subtle than that.' He smiled slightly.

She gave a disgusted shake of her head, very aware that she was still standing in the rapidly cooling bath water, and that goose-bumps were appearing on her flesh, despite the towel round her shoulders—she needed to get out of this bath right now!

'Of course,' Noel continued thoughtfully, 'now I would also have to tell her that the woman she found in my bath had never been my fiancée at all, that she was actually just the lady who came in to decorate the house for me.'

Cally drew in a deeply controlling breath. 'Could you just go out of the room for a few minutes while I get dressed?' she said evenly, exerting extreme control to stop herself from screaming hysterically, very aware of Pam and Lissa waiting for her down the stairs.

'Well, I could,' Noel answered conversationally. 'But as we haven't come anywhere near to reaching an agreement about this…misunderstanding, I think I had better just—'

'I think you had better just get out of here!' Her voice rose dangerously, her cheeks hot from anger now.

'Okay, okay.' He held up defensive hands. 'There's no need to get your—ah, but, of course, you aren't wearing any of those, are you? So they aren't likely to get into a twist, are they—?'

'Get *out*!' her voice went another couple of octaves higher, at the same time as she threw the wet sponge across the room at him.

Noel moved sideways, easily avoiding having the sponge hit him. The waterlogged article hit the far wall with a splat before sliding slowly down onto the floor. 'I suggest you wipe that up before you leave the room.' He grinned, opening the door. 'Otherwise the next person to use the room might slip and hurt themselves.'

'At this moment, if it happened to be you, I don't think I would care!' Cally assured him forcefully.

He tutted teasingly. 'I think I'll just pop down and talk with Pam and Lissa while you get dressed.'

'Don't you da—' Too late. Noel had already left the room, closing the door softly behind him.

Leaving Cally in a high state of agitation as she quickly hopped out of the bath and thankfully towelled herself dry, taking a brief moment to revel in finally setting warm.

But only a brief moment; who knew what further harm Noel could have done by the time she got downstairs?

'SHE'S ADORABLE.' NOEL'S mother came to stand by Cally as she stood transfixed in the doorway watching Noel and Lissa romping about the floor.

Lissa was a smaller version of herself. Cally had obviously always been biased when it came to her young daughter. Lissa's hair was more of a strawberry-blond than the red of her own, but otherwise the freckles and tiny features were all Cally.

She had prayed for that before Lissa was born, had inwardly dreaded having a mini version of Michael to look at every day. But once she'd held the totally defenceless Lissa in her arms for the first time, and looked down at the delicacy of her tiny face, she had known it wouldn't matter who or what she looked like; Lissa was hers, and she loved her.

But what held her so transfixed now was seeing Lissa playing so naturally with Noel, the two of them rolling over and over together on the carpeted floor while Josh, his sister Honey, and the man Cally guessed had to be Noel's stepfather, looked on indulgently, Pam nowhere to be seen.

Lissa obviously spent quite a bit of time at Pam's, enjoyed being with her uncle Brian, and loved the company of her two male cousins, but this was the first time Cally had really seen her daughter relate to an adult male in quite this way.

For a moment she felt an ache in her chest, brief uncertainty, as to whether she had done the right thing seven years ago in keeping Lissa's father in ignorance of his daughter's existence. She hadn't doubted the decision at the time, had believed that it had been the right one for everyone concerned, but looking at Lissa now, squealing with delight as Noel tickled her, she couldn't help wondering if it had been the right one for her daughter in the long term...

'Noel always did have a way with young children.' The woman at her side spoke softly as she watched her eldest son. 'He was wonderful with Josh and Honey when they were small too.' She smiled down at him indulgently before shifting that deep blue gaze back to Cally. 'It's the reason I was so happy when he told me the two of you were going to be married; he's going to make such a wonderful father. Of course—' she laughed softly '—I had no idea this was what he had in mind when he told me I was soon to be a grandmother!'

Cally reluctantly dragged her gaze away from her happily occupied daughter. 'Look, Mrs Carlt— No, it isn't Carlton, is it?' She became flustered as she seemed to be making one gaffe after another where this woman was concerned.

'It's Markham, but pleased do call me Hester,' the other woman invited warmly. 'And I understand from Noel that you prefer to be called Cally?'

'Yes,' she confirmed huskily. 'But about Lissa—'

'My dear, please don't feel you have to explain anything to any of us.' Hester frowned her concern as she put a reassuring hand on Cally's arm. 'I don't know how much Noel has told you, but I was alone with him until he was ten years old and I met and fell in love with Andrew.' She smiled across at her husband where he stood laughing at the antics on the carpet. 'He gave me back my faith in love and the permanence of marriage.'

Cally glanced across at the smiling man who stood so relaxed beside the fireplace watching his stepson, liking his easy smile, the warm glow in his brown eyes, the blond hair that had been inherited by both his children. Honey, Cally also noted, was a female version of Josh: tall and attractive, her blond hair worn long down her back, dressed like a typical teenager in denims and tee shirt.

'He looks very nice.' Cally turned back to Hester. 'It's just that—'

'Lissa doesn't know yet about you and Noel getting married,' the other woman finished gently. 'Yes, he told me that, too. But I really don't think it's going to be a problem, do you?' she added as Lissa giggled happily at being tickled by Noel.

No, Cally didn't think it would be a problem—if she and Noel really were going to be married. Which they weren't!

But Noel had certainly been busy confiding things to his mother in the few minutes it had taken Cally to dry herself and get dressed, seeming to have covered most of the questions they would probably have been asked by one member of his family or another.

Which was great for Noel. But not so great for her. Because she wasn't engaged to Noel, and had no intention of marrying him.

Chance would be a fine thing, a little voice inside her mocked.

Where on earth had that come from? Cally wondered dazedly.

After the disaster of her relationship with Michael, she had concentrated all her love and care on Lissa, on giving her the best that she could, consistently refusing any dates that came her way. In fact, she had become so adept at showing her lack of interest that, apart from Noel's invitation two months ago, she hadn't even been asked out on a date for the last two years!

So why was she even thinking that chance would be a fine thing?

Just because Noel Carlton, with his obvious wealth and playboy lifestyle, was like no one she had ever met before. Or was ever likely to meet again!

'Your sister had to leave, I'm afraid,' Hester commented. 'Something about getting back to the boys…?'

Cally smiled. 'Pam's husband, Brian, and their two little boys.' Although, if she knew anything about her big sister at all, Pam was going to be on the telephone later today wanting to know exactly what was going on!

'That's nice.' The older woman smiled. 'Families are important, aren't they?'

'Very,' Cally confirmed with perhaps a little more firmness than she had intended. 'At least, I think so,' she added less forcefully.

'I'm so glad you feel that way.' Hester nodded, linking her arm with Cally's. 'But then I should have known that Noel wouldn't choose to be with a woman who doesn't have the same values and interests as he does.'

Cally watched the man in question as he stood up, Lissa held in his arms. Obviously, despite her previous accusations about his not having bothered to be prepared for his family's arrival, his family was important to him, and there was no doubting that he did have a natural way with Lissa, and didn't mind in the least that his designer-label clothes were now slightly creased and rumpled. Perhaps he wasn't such a playboy, after all…?

'Mummy!' Lissa cried happily as she spotted her mother, reaching out her arms towards her. 'I've been having such fun.' She glowed excitedly, her smile revealing that she had recently lost one of her front baby teeth. But, if anything, it just made her more endearing.

'I can see that,' Cally murmured indulgently as she held her daughter in her arms, smiling up at her.

'And Noel says we're all going out for a meal together tonight,' Lissa told her ecstatically before turning to bestow a heart-melting smile on Noel as the benefactor of this unexpected treat.

Cally's smile faded somewhat as she felt something begin to tighten around her, trapping her in a situation that was rapidly spiralling out of her control.

Much as she knew Lissa would love to go, she knew it wasn't a good idea for them to go out with Noel's family for a meal, tonight or any other time, that the sooner Noel told his family the truth about his broken engagement, the better it would be for everyone.

'That sounds nice, darling,' she answered her daughter noncommittally. 'Noel, would you mind walking back to the gatehouse with us?' She turned to him, her gaze warning him against refusing. 'There are a couple of things we need to talk about,' she added determinedly as she saw Noel's younger brother give him a teasing grin at what must appear to be signs of domesticity.

'Of course,' Noel complied lightly as he moved to her side, at the same time shooting Josh a scathing glance. 'Don't say another word until we get outside,' he muttered for Cally's ears only.

'I have no intention of doing so,' she assured him with a pointed look at Lissa.

'I'm afraid it was my idea about going out this evening,'

Hester put in concernedly, obviously wondering if she had committed a *faux pas* of some kind. 'I do hope the two of you didn't have other plans? It's just that Noel says you've been working very hard to make everything so nice for us, that I thought it was the least we could do for you in return...?'

Cally felt the trap tightening even further, knowing she could hardly refuse to go out with them this evening when it was their way of saying thank you for all the hard work she had done on the house the last couple of days.

They couldn't possibly know that a cheque from Noel would more than compensate for that!

CHAPTER SEVEN

'OKAY, SO WHAT DO we do now?' Cally asked as she and Noel sat at her kitchen table a short time later drinking coffee, Lissa safely ensconced in front of the television for a few minutes with juice and biscuits.

Noel shrugged. 'Well, the general consensus seems to be that we're all going out for a meal later this evening—'

'That isn't what I meant, and you know it!' Cally cut in irritably. 'I like your family, Noel, they're nice—'

'Thank you.'

She sighed. 'I didn't say that included *you*!'

'No,' he accepted softly, bending towards her slightly. 'But you do like me, don't you?' he murmured huskily.

'No, I—yes,' she sighed in defeat as he raised sceptical dark brows at the vehemence of her denial. 'But I was actually referring to the fact that I don't like deceiving your family in this way—'

'Then let's not deceive them,' he suggested, getting up to go down on one knee in front of her on the tiled floor, taking one of her hands firmly in his. 'Cally Turner, will you marry me?'

Cally stared down at him in horror. 'Will you get up?' she instructed desperately, pulling her hand away from his, all the time casting worried glances in Lissa's direction as she sat only feet away from them in the sitting-room.

'Not until you give me an answer.' Noel remained on one knee.

Cally could feel the heat of confusion in her flushed cheeks. 'You look ridiculous,' she spluttered agitatedly.

'I know.' He grinned unconcernedly. 'But I intend staying this way until you give me an answer,' he assured her happily.

She looked at him speechlessly now, totally nonplussed by the unexpectedness of what he was doing.

But what if his proposal had been a real one…?

She would still have said no!

Wouldn't she…?

The problem was, she didn't know any more. Until yesterday she had thought her nearest neighbour to be an arrogant show-off, with his fast cars and helicopters arriving on the front lawn. An arrogant show-off who didn't make good on his invitations! But this last couple of days she had come to know what he was really like. And, if she were honest, she *did* like him!

Noel had shown her yesterday that he wasn't afraid of hard work. Had proved by his actions this last couple of days that he was a caring, considerate son. Had got down on the floor and played with Lissa as if he were six instead of in his mid-thirties. And as for the way he kissed…!

Cally shied away from remembering that, determined to think only of the fact that he wasn't really serious about this marriage proposal, that until recently he had actually been engaged to marry someone else.

She stood up abruptly, stepping round him to move to the far side of the small kitchen. 'My answer is no,' she said. 'And I think, the sooner you tell your family the truth, the better it will be for everyone.'

She could only feel relief as he got slowly to his feet, although she wasn't quite so sure about that emotion as he came to stand in front of her, so close she could feel the warmth emanating from his body.

She swallowed hard as she looked up at him. 'In the circumstances, I'm more than a little interested in knowing the truth myself,' she said huskily, pressing back into the work unit as far as she could go in an effort to put more distance between Noel's body and her own.

'What do you want to know?' He gave her a considering look, one hand moving up to cup the side of her face, his thumb moving lightly across her lips.

Cally's breath lodged somewhere in her throat as she desperately tried to resist the impulse to run her tongue across her lips where he had just touched, her gaze locked with his. 'Your fiancée,' she managed to speak gruffly.

His mouth tightened. 'Ex-fiancée,' he corrected, shaking his head. 'Have you ever thought that someone was something only to realize later on that you had made a terrible mistake and they weren't what you thought they were at all?'

She glanced across at Lissa as she sat enraptured in the cartoon showing on the television. 'Oh, yes,' she acknowledged ruefully.

Noel followed that glance. 'Lissa's father?'

Cally nodded. 'I—he—' She gave a deep sigh. 'I thought he was warm, caring, and single.'

'And?' Noel prompted softly, his gaze searching the paleness of her face.

'He was selfish, immature—and married!' She grimaced self-derisively, still able to remember her humiliation when Michael's wife had paid her a visit, hugely pregnant with their second child, to lay prior claim to him.

After that, as far as Cally had been concerned, Michael's wife had been welcome to him!

'Ah.' Noel nodded understandingly.

'And Carol?' she asked tentatively, amazed at how painful she still found it to talk of her own past disillusionment.

'Well, I thought she was warm, caring, and single, too,' Noel said dryly. 'It turned out that she was single, but it didn't take me too long to realize the warmth and caring were sadly lacking!' He gave a disgusted shake of his head.

'Long enough for you to become engaged to her,' Cally pointed out, relieved to have the conversation moved away from her own past misjudgement concerning someone's character.

'Hmm.' He frowned.

Cally gave him a considering look. 'Noel…?' She sensed there was something he wasn't saying.

He straightened, his hand falling away from her face. 'It's nothing,' he dismissed briskly.

That wasn't what Cally believed at all. She felt sure there was something he wasn't telling her about his engagement. Not that it was really any of her business—except that, as far as his family was concerned, she now seemed to be engaged to him herself!

'Is it really going to be that much of a problem for you and Lissa to come out to dinner with the family this evening?' Noel asked.

'Not a problem, no…' From what she had seen of his family, they were all very nice; she just didn't think it was a good idea to perpetrate this deception about her supposed engagement to Noel. 'But couldn't you just tell them the truth?' She sighed.

To her surprise, Noel grinned widely. 'Who knows, maybe if I delay doing that long enough, it will no longer be the truth!'

Cally frowned as she tried to follow his train of thought, her eyes widening incredulously as she realized exactly what he meant. 'I told you not to be ridiculous,' she snapped, not finding anything in the least funny about his proposal of marriage.

He shrugged. 'It seems like a pretty good idea to me.'

'That's because you're bordering on the insane,' Cally told him unsympathetically, clasping his shoulders to turn him firmly in the direction of the back door. 'Okay, we'll come out to dinner with all of you this evening,' she told him once he was standing outside the house, knowing that to do anything else would be a great disappointment to Lissa. And she tried never to disappoint her beloved daughter. 'But only on the condition that you tell your family the truth in the very near future!' she added sternly.

Noel's grin went from ear to ear, his eyes dark with approval. 'You really are a beautiful woman, Cally Turner!' he told her appreciatively before taking a determined step forward and kissing her forcefully on the lips.

She didn't know whether she was beautiful or not, Cally thought confusedly as the kiss continued and she melted into the hardness of his body, but she did know she was falling in love with this man. No—that she was already in love with him!

She pulled sharply back as this shocking realization hit her with the force of a physical blow, staring up at Noel as if she had never seen him before.

And maybe she hadn't. She had spent so long denying that she wanted any man in her life, that there could be a 'perfect' man for her out there, that she had almost missed seeing him at all!

Noel was everything she had ever wanted in a man, sure of himself, charming, caring, patient, funny. And the strange thing was, he seemed to find her equally fascinating.

'Cally?' he questioned huskily now.

She gave a shake of her head, pushing those thoughts very firmly from her mind. Because Noel was also very rich, very sophisticated—and, until recently, had been engaged to marry someone else!

'Nothing,' she dismissed quickly, stepping back into the house. 'What time do you expect to go out?'

Noel continued to look at her for long, timeless seconds, finally saying, 'I'll pick you and Lissa up in about an hour, if that's okay?'

'Fine,' Cally accepted shortly, moving back to firmly close the door in his face.

Which was when she realized just how much she was shaking, her legs feeling weak, her whole body trembling with—with what?

With the realization that she had fallen in love with a man who could never be hers!

CHAPTER EIGHT

'EVERYTHING ALL RIGHT?' Noel queried softly an hour or so later as they drove to the pub where they had decided to eat, Lissa safely strapped into the back seat. The rest of the family were following behind in the estate car they had hired for the duration of their stay.

'Fine,' Cally replied tersely—if you could call being given the third degree by your older sister for the last half an hour 'all right'!

Pam had been absolutely fascinated by the Markham family, even more so by what Cally had been doing upstairs with Noel when she had arrived at the house with Lissa earlier. Not that Cally intended satisfying her sister's curiosity about that!

She had no idea how to explain to Pam that for the moment she was trapped in a false engagement in an effort to try to salvage something of their company's reputation. Never mind her own!

'No Ferrari this evening?' Cally mocked in an effort to change the subject, although the Range Rover he drove now was very luxurious too.

'No room for Lissa. Actually, I'm thinking of getting rid of the Ferrari.'

Cally tensed warily. 'Why?'

Noel gave a shrug. 'It isn't exactly a family car, now, is it?'

Cally felt slightly breathless for a moment, quickly fighting down that feeling as she answered him mockingly. 'But then, you don't *exactly* have a family, do you?'

He gave her a sideways glance. 'That could easily change.'

'Not so easily as you might think,' she came back sharply—
and then wondered if she weren't just making a fool of herself;
Noel couldn't have been any more serious about that marriage
proposal earlier than his remarks were now.

He smiled. 'I've never minded fighting for what I want.'

And his gaze said he wanted her! But he couldn't be serious. Not really. This all had to be just a game to him.

She gave a dismissive shrug, deliberately turning away
from him to look out the window at the darkness beyond.

'Cally, just relax, hmm?' Noel reached out and briefly
squeezed her hand. 'Even if I do say so myself, my family
are all okay,' he added as she turned to look at him.

'I know that,' she answered brittlely.

He sighed. 'Then it must be me who's making you so nervous—'

'I'm not nervous!' she denied.

He touched her hand a second time, that light clasp remaining this time. 'Then why are you trembling?'

Was she? She hadn't been aware of it. But, yes, she was
trembling now that she thought about it. Not with nervous-
ness, she quickly realized, but with rising awareness of the
man seated at her side, the blood seeming to thrum through
her veins as her body responded to the closeness of his.

She had never wanted anyone, or anything, as much as she
wanted Noel Carlton!

'Cally!' he groaned as he must have seen some of that desire in her face.

She snatched her hand out of his grasp. 'I think your earlier insanity must be catching!'

'I certainly hope so.' He grinned.

Cally didn't know what she hoped any more. Her thoughts
were all chaotic, all the resolves she had made before leaving the house earlier this evening crumbling to ashes once
she was with Noel. Keep your distance, she had decided.
Don't respond to any of Noel's more intimate remarks, she

had instructed. Most of all, don't take any of what Noel said seriously.

Hah!

She wanted to launch herself into Noel's arms and forget the past, present, and future. She longed to respond to his every word. As for taking him seriously—she wished that she could!

Which was why it was probably just as well that they had arrived at the pub, all of them piling out of the cars to go inside, Cally finding herself seated next to Honey Markham on one side and Hester on the other. Lissa had very neatly placed herself between Josh and Andrew, both men paying court to her innocent charm.

Noel stood beside the table for several seconds, frowning, finally telling his brother to move up once he realized there simply wasn't any room for him on the padded bench seat next to Cally, scowling his displeasure across the table at his mother and sister.

Honey giggled softly next to Cally. 'My big brother has it bad, doesn't he?'

Cally swallowed hard, not sure she could keep up this subterfuge. 'Does he?'

'Oh, yes,' the beautiful teenager assured her smilingly. 'I always wondered what Noel would look like when he fell in love; now I know!'

Cally turned to give her a quizzical glance. 'And how does he look?'

Honey's grin widened. 'Pretty good, actually.' She gave her eldest brother a playful wink as he glanced her way, receiving a stony glare for her trouble. 'Incredible,' Honey murmured with a rueful shake of her head. 'Noel has always been super cool, you know,' she explained to Cally. 'But he isn't very cool about you, is he?' She grinned again.

Cool wasn't a word Cally would have used to describe either herself or Noel when they were together! Things were usually pretty heated between them, she had found, whether from temper or from passion.

'So when are the two of you thinking of getting married?' Honey prompted in a hushed voice after giving Lissa a brief look and establishing that she was totally engrossed in telling Andrew Markham about her school. 'I'll be nineteen in six months' time, and I always fancied being a bridesmaid while I was still a teenager,' she added happily.

'I—we haven't decided yet,' she answered evasively.

'Not too long, if I know Noel,' his sister predicted knowingly. 'It's pretty obvious he can't wait for the two of you to be married!' she said with another teasing glance at her eldest brother.

In fact, Noel's whole family seemed to be happy with the idea of the two of them marrying each other and bringing Lissa into the family too—so in a way it was a pity it was never going to happen.

In a way!

Cally was fast coming to the conclusion that she would be happy to be marrying Noel too, and couldn't seem to stop looking at him as he finally relaxed and engaged his mother in easy conversation. He really was the most gorgeous looking man she had ever seen, her fingers once more itching to touch the dark thickness of his hair, to experience again the feel of his lips on hers, to have his hands—

This had to stop!

How could she become aroused just from looking at him? Because she was aroused, her nipples hardening pertly beneath the jumper she wore, her thighs feeling warm.

'What would you like?'

She gave Noel a startled look as he leant across the table towards her, wondering if her longing could possibly have shown on her face. And if it had, what he was doing drawing attention to it in front of his family! 'What?'

'What would you like to eat?' he asked softly, the affectionate teasing in the deep blue of his eyes telling her that he had indeed seen that longing.

'Oh,' she gasped, picking up the menu that lay on the table in front of her. 'The chicken, please.' She chose the first thing she saw. 'Lissa will probably have the same. Er—if you'll excuse me, I need to go to the Ladies,' she added abruptly, knowing she needed to splash some cold water on her face. 'Lissa?' she prompted her daughter as she moved past Honey.

Lissa turned to give her a beaming smile. 'I'm fine, thank you, Mummy.'

'Would you like me to come with you?' Noel offered as she squeezed past his chair, the warmth of his gaze resting tantalizingly on her lips.

Almost like a caress, Cally acknowledged achingly, a melting sensation somewhere deep inside her. 'No, thank you,' she refused, moving hurriedly away.

This was awful, she groaned inwardly as she moved as quickly as she could through the crowded lounge bar to the Ladies situated in the adjoining room. She couldn't go on with this, she simply couldn't, was going to make a complete idiot of herself if she didn't—

'Cally? Cally Turner?'

She turned in the direction of that guardedly enquiring voice, staring blankly at the woman who had spoken to her, sure she had never seen the woman before. Nothing about her shoulder-length blond hair and attractively made-up face seemed in the least familiar.

And then a memory stirred, a deliberately long-buried memory, overlaying the gamine features in front of her with a slightly plumper face, short brown hair, and much fuller figure.

Jane Shaw…!

Michael's wife!

CHAPTER NINE

'IT IS CALLY, isn't it?' the other woman pressed. 'I don't know if you remember me, but—'

'I remember you,' she breathed hollowly, having felt her face pale as she stared at Jane Shaw with complete recognition.

How could she ever forget this woman? She had been the shatterer of Cally's dreams, but ultimately her salvation at the same time. As for what Cally represented to Jane Shaw...!

'Hey, I didn't mean to upset you.' The other woman frowned at her with concern. 'I just—perhaps I shouldn't have spoken to you.' She sighed regretfully. 'I—you're looking very well,' she concluded lamely.

So did Jane Shaw; now a slim, elegant, beautifully confident woman. She had been anything but that when Cally had last seen her: slow, cumbersome, with all the accompanying aches and pains that went with being seven months pregnant.

With Michael's second child.

Michael!

Was he here too? But a frantic look round in the general vicinity didn't show his presence anywhere near. Just as well; that would be just too much!

Cally turned back to the other woman, feeling completely flustered by this unexpected encounter with a woman she hadn't seen for almost seven years—and had hoped never to see again! 'What are you doing here?' she asked bluntly, too shaken to be polite.

'I live near here,' the other woman told her gently.

With Michael... How ironic that Cally should have moved out of the city to the country, only to find that Michael and his family had moved here too!

Cally shook her head, desperate to get away from this woman, and the humiliating memories she evoked. 'I really don't think—will you excuse me?' she said abruptly. 'I—I'm with some people, and—they'll wonder where I've got to.' She turned to leave, only to walk straight into the hardness of a chest that was completely familiar to her.

'Cally?' Noel reached up to clasp the tops of her arms as he steadied her, his gaze narrowed on the paleness of her face before he looked past her to Jane Shaw. 'A friend of yours?' he asked lightly.

A friend of hers! How wrong could he be? Cally wondered slightly hysterically!

'Jane Shaw.' The other woman held her hand out to Noel, her smile guarded as she glanced at Cally's stricken face.

'Noel Carlton,' he supplied slowly, briefly shaking that hand.

Jane Shaw's eyes widened fractionally as she looked at him. 'Of the communications network of the same name?'

'Yes,' he confirmed.

'And the international investment empire?' the other woman murmured appreciatively.

'That too.' Noel nodded.

Cally blinked, having had no idea herself what it was Noel did, or where his considerable wealth came from. But even she, someone who didn't keep up-to-date, had heard of the empire.

'But I prefer to think of myself as Cally's fiancé,' Noel continued, his arm moving possessively about the slenderness of Cally's waist as he came to stand beside her.

Cally could only gape up at him disbelievingly now; wasn't it taking this subterfuge a little far to introduce himself to a complete stranger in that manner? Not that she particularly minded where Jane Shaw was concerned; at least it showed the other woman that she hadn't simply curled up these last seven years and pined away for love of Michael.

Jane Shaw smiled at them both warmly. 'Congratulations! Well, I really must be getting back to my friends. It was nice seeing you again, Cally,' she added.

Cally didn't see how it could possibly be that, for either of them! But without increasing Noel's suspicions any more she could do little else but smile in agreement.

'Mummy, can I come with you, after all?' Lissa pranced up to them happily.

Cally looked at her daughter, then quickly back to Jane Shaw, swaying slightly as she saw the way the other woman was staring down at Lissa.

Was there something of Michael in Lissa, after all, a likeness that Cally couldn't see? Perhaps in the curve of her cheek? Or the set of her sometimes stubborn little chin?

Cally didn't think so, but then she was biased, thought her daughter the most beautiful child in the world—with not a single attribute of the man who had never known he had fathered her!

Jane Shaw's husband…

Not telling Michael of her own pregnancy hadn't been an easy decision to make when she'd discovered her condition seven years ago, but, as Cally's own relationship with him had been over anyway after the visit of his wife, to have told him of her own pregnancy would have ruined so many lives, not least Jane Shaw's own. There had also been the lives of Jane's child and unborn baby to consider.

No, Cally had decided, better to leave things as they were; after his deceit she had no longer loved or wanted Michael anyway, whereas Jane had seemed to have forgiven him for his relationship with Cally.

Although none of her reasoning then would help her now! Would Jane tell Michael she had seen Cally when she got home? Worse, would she mention that Cally had a little girl of six or so with her—?

'Mummy?' Lissa looked up at her again.

Who called her Mummy!

Cally broke her gaze away from Jane Shaw's questioning one to look down at her daughter reassuringly. 'Sorry, darling. Excuse us.' She smiled vaguely before taking hold of Lissa's hand and hurrying into the adjoining room, breathing a sigh of relief once she was away from Jane Shaw and her enquiring looks. Only the trembling of her legs told of the shock she had just received.

It was only as she stood outside the cubicle waiting for Lissa to come out that she realized she had left Jane Shaw and Noel alone together!

But surely Noel wouldn't— Even if he did, surely the woman wouldn't—

She closed her eyes, groaning inwardly as she imagined the conversation that could be taking place between Jane and Noel right this moment.

She certainly wasn't prepared to find a grim-faced Noel leaning on the wall outside waiting for her when she emerged into the noisy room with Lissa!

Cally looked at him searchingly as he straightened, but as he smiled down at Lissa it was impossible to tell anything from his expression. To know whether or not the other woman had told him that Cally had once had an affair with her husband and that he wasn't aware he had an illegitimate child!

'Ready for your dinner, young lady?' Noel teased Lissa as she slipped her hand into his.

'Yes, please.' Lissa beamed, walking along happily at his side.

Cally watched the two of them together with an ache in her heart. Why couldn't she have met someone like Noel seven years ago? Before Michael had broken her eighteen-year-old heart. Before she'd become disillusioned with men and love. Then perhaps Noel could have been Lissa's father, instead of a man Cally had grown to despise for his weakness and duplicity.

If only wishes were real.

Cally gave a rueful smile as she remembered her mother's teasing comment whenever she or Pam had wished for this or that when they were younger. She missed her mother. And her father. But they had both died in a car accident eight years ago.

Before Michael.

Before Lissa.

But how the two of them would have loved Lissa! Cally had absolutely no doubts about that. Never had. Had known that her parents would lament, for Cally's sake, the circumstances of Lissa's birth, but that they would have loved this grandchild as wholeheartedly as they would have loved Pam and Brian's children.

'Do you want to leave?'

Cally looked up dazedly at Noel's softly spoken question, suddenly aware of where they were, of Noel's family sitting at the table a short distance away, Lissa having already rejoined them. 'No,' she decided firmly. 'No, I'm fine,' she insisted, forcing a bright smile to her lips.

Noel looked down at her with narrowed blue eyes, the scepticism in that gaze telling her that he wasn't in the least convinced by that smile, that he knew something was seriously wrong. And that her meeting with Jane Shaw had something to do with it…

But unless the woman had told him about their history, Noel couldn't possibly guess the reason why, Cally acknowledged heavily. Who could…?

'Besides, the food's arriving,' she added lightly as two waitresses walked over to the table with four of the meals they had ordered. Although quite how Cally was going to eat after the shock she had just received…!

Noel continued to look down at her for long, timeless seconds, and then he gave a brief nod of his head. 'But the two of us are going to talk later,' he warned huskily.

She frowned her alarm. 'There's no need—'

'There's every need,' he rasped. 'Something is going on, and I want to know what it is!'

Cally raised auburn brows. 'And do you always get what you want?' she challenged dazedly, sure now that Jane Shaw hadn't told him the truth.

'Not always, no.' He gave her a look that was unmistakably pointed. 'But this time I don't intend taking no for an answer!' he added grimly.

'Really, Noel,' Cally taunted, her relief that Noel didn't know the truth making her feel almost light-hearted. Almost... 'There's no need to sound so serious!'

'Isn't there?' His expression remained grim.

'No,' she answered evenly.

Because whatever Jane Shaw chose to tell her husband, whatever Michael's reaction was to knowing he had another child, it would not affect Cally or Lissa.

She simply wouldn't allow it!

CHAPTER TEN

'THANK YOU, Noel, we had a really lovely evening,' Cally told him as he stopped the Range Rover outside the gatehouse a couple of hours later. 'Didn't we, Lissa?' she prompted her very tired daughter as she almost lay on the back seat.

'Lovely,' Lissa echoed in a very sleepy voice.

'I'll carry her inside for you,' Noel offered as he turned off the engine and swung out of the vehicle.

'There's no need!' Cally called after him, having hoped to escape into the house without Noel coming in with them, knowing, as he gave her a triumphant look as he lifted Lissa up into his arms, that she was going to be disappointed. 'Fine,' she accepted ruefully, getting out to unlock the door. 'First door on the right up the stairs,' she instructed as Noel stood in the hall with Lissa in his arms, following behind him as he walked up the stairs.

Lissa was so tired after her evening out that she was more than happy to just change into her nightgown, snuggling down under her duvet before turning over in bed and falling fast asleep.

Ordinarily Cally would have been pleased at her daughter's easy acquiescence in going to bed, but not tonight, not when Noel stood outside the bedroom waiting for her to go back downstairs...

No doubt Noel had decided it was time for them to 'talk later'!

Except that Cally still wasn't ready to do that. Wasn't sure that she ever would be!

Getting through the rest of the evening with his family had been strain enough, although it had been helped a little by the fact that Jane Shaw and her friends had left the pub about twenty minutes later, the other woman giving Cally a brief nod as she'd left.

But all in all it had been a dreadful evening, not even the continuing warmth and friendliness of Noel's family helping to alleviate that. How could it, when she was all too aware that it was because of the deceit of her fake engagement to Noel that they were behaving that way? Not that she thought the Markhams would have been unfriendly if the situation had been any different from what they thought, but the fact that they were treating her as a prospective daughter and sister-in-law made her feel very uncomfortable.

'Noel, tomorrow is Christmas Eve.' Cally turned to him decisively once they were in the privacy of her sitting-room. 'I won't keep up this deception to your family for any longer than that, so I would advise you to tell them the truth—'

'Whatever happened to, "Please, take a seat" or, "Can I get you a coffee?"' he cut in.

She gave him an irritated frown. 'Please, do take a seat,' she invited reluctantly, although he might be easier to talk to if he were no longer towering over her in this forceful way! 'But forget the coffee,' she told him heavily as he sat down in one of the armchairs. 'I have a very busy day tomorrow stocking up your freezer and refrigerator with food for over the Christmas period, so I would like to get to bed very shortly. Alone!' she added firmly as he raised questioning brows.

'Pity,' he murmured. 'So, who is Jane Shaw? And why did meeting her tonight upset you so much?' he asked shrewdly.

Cally stiffened. 'She's just—an old acquaintance,' she dismissed with deliberate unconcern, at the same time not quite able to meet Noel's searching gaze. 'But you're wrong, I wasn't in the least upset at meeting her—'

'Oh, yes, you were,' Noel said with certainty, blue gaze

narrowed piercingly. 'Don't lie to me, Cally,' he warned softly. 'I may be easygoing for the main part, but never take me for a fool!'

She never would have done that. The fact that he was the power behind the Carlton Empire was evidence enough of his shrewd business acumen, even if she wasn't already aware of the intelligence behind those deep blue eyes.

'I wasn't doing that,' she assured him before turning away to look down at the unlit fireplace, her thoughts racing as she tried to decide what to do for the best. 'But Jane Shaw is my business,' she told him as she looked up again, having made her decision. 'Not yours.' She looked at him with unblinking challenge.

Although looking at him was almost her undoing! She loved this man, knew it as surely as she loved Lissa, and the urge to tell him about Jane Shaw, to confide in him the entire truth about the past, was very tempting indeed. Cally had already told Noel that Michael had been a married man, but she hadn't admitted to Noel that she had kept Lissa a secret from Michael all these years. Cally wasn't sorry she had done so, but would Noel be horrified with her, thinking that Michael had a right to know his own child?

Also, how would Noel react to being told that Jane Shaw was the wife of the man Cally had been involved with seven years ago? Not only that, but she was the mother of Michael's legitimate children? Noel might say he understood that Cally, at eighteen, had just been young and stupid, but, having met Jane Shaw and seen how lovely she was, would his sympathies swing away from Cally and towards Jane Shaw?

Noel easily met the challenge in her gaze. 'And if I choose to make it *my* business?' he asked, giving every appearance of being relaxed as he sat in the armchair—while at the same time ready to pounce!

'Then of course I can't stop you.' She sighed. 'There's a possibility I shall be giving my notice in at the gatehouse after Christmas, anyway, so it really doesn't matter to me what you do.'

Until the words actually left her mouth, it hadn't even occurred to her that was what she intended doing! But as she said them she knew it was what she would have to do with Michael and his family living somewhere close enough for his wife to be in a local pub. Otherwise she was going to spend all of her time here looking over her shoulder, wondering if a simple trip to the local supermarket would bring a surprise meeting with Michael himself. Worse, she could have Lissa with her at the time!

Lissa!

She didn't want to move, knew Lissa was happy here, that it would mean changing schools and friends all over again. But what other choice did she have...?

Noel rose slowly to his feet, Cally backing away slightly as he took a step towards her. He came to an abrupt halt, his expression grim, his jaw set. 'When did you suddenly become frightened of me?' he growled.

When she realized she had fallen in love with him!

And it wasn't fear of Noel that had her backing away from him; it was fear of herself, of her feelings for him, of the way she simply melted in his arms every time he touched her. She had already made one disastrous mistake in her life, she didn't intend making another, even worse one, with Noel!

She straightened. 'I'm not frightened of you,' she declared.

'No?' He took another step towards her, his mouth twisting as she tensed even more.

Cally couldn't help that small tell-tale response, could feel her pulse rate quicken, her breathing shallow, her hands slowly clenching into fists at her sides—and knew there was nothing she could do to stop it.

'Noel, I've had a very busy day, have an even busier one coming up tomorrow, as I've already explained, and I'm really too tired to stand here and play power games with you.'

'I agree, you are.' He nodded, standing in front of her, one of his hands moving up to smooth the hair back from her cheek. 'I want to kiss you, Cally,' he told her huskily, his eyes darkly blue now.

'I know,' she whispered.

'I want to do more than kiss you,' Noel acknowledged hoarsely.

'I know that too!' Cally sighed weakly, unable to look away from his mesmerizing gaze. 'I just— Noel, I don't want to make any more mistakes in my life!' she told him achingly.

'And you think I would be a mistake?' he prompted gently.

'Yes! No! I simply don't know!' She shook her head, tears blurring her vision now.

His hands cradled both sides of her face as he forced her to look up at him. 'Do you trust me enough to believe me when I tell you I won't be a mistake?'

She blinked the tears away, feeling their dampness against her cheeks as she looked up at him searchingly. He looked so solidly sure, of himself, of her, of whatever feelings were between them, that Cally knew she wanted to believe him.

'Cally, I'm not going to hurt you. I would never hurt you!' One of his hands curved about her jaw as his thumb moved to caress her lips, his gaze fixed on their pouting invitation. 'I just want you so badly…!' He groaned before his head lowered and his mouth took fierce possession of hers.

Cally melted, her body melding perfectly with his, hard against soft as Noel crushed her to him, his arms tightening about her waist as his kiss deepened.

She clung to the broad width of his shoulders, giving a choked sob as she realized this might be the one and only time she would ever be in his arms like this.

She wanted him too. Wanted him so much she ached inside with the need of him.

She offered no resistance when he lifted her up in his arms and carried her over to the sofa, sitting down with her on his lap, all the time his lips sipping and tasting hers as he kissed her with ever-increasing hunger.

Cally moved slightly, lying on the sofa beside him now as he followed her down, her hands feverishly caressing his back, the heat between them rising to an almost unbearable degree.

Her back arched instinctively as he cupped her breast, the nipple already hard with arousal, and she gasped as she felt the caress of his thumb against that sensitive tip, heat like molten lava coursing through her body as she pressed herself closer against him.

Noel raised his head to look down into her flushed face, his eyes almost black with his own desire, holding her gaze as his fingers undid the buttons to her blouse before releasing the front fastening of her bra. Then he finally looked down at her nakedness, and a nerve pulsed rapidly in his tightly clenched jaw.

'Kiss me, Noel,' she moaned achingly, her fingers entwined in the dark thickness of his hair as she guided him down to her. 'Kiss me!'

His lips closed over one rosy tip, gently suckling as his tongue moved moistly against her, over and over again. Each gently pulling caress increased her pleasure, and the evidence of Noel's arousal throbbed hotly against her hips.

Cally's head rolled back on the cushion as she arched against him, feeling the increasing moistness between her thighs as Noel hotly pleasured her, wanting—oh, wanting!—so much more…! She simply couldn't—

'Mummy? Mummy, are you there?'

Cally jerked away from Noel as if a glass of cold water had suddenly been thrown over her, staring up dazedly into his grimly set face for several seconds as she tried to remember who she was—let alone where, and with whom!

'Mummy…?' Lissa voiced again, uncertainly this time.

Noel rolled away from Cally. 'You had better go to her,'

he acknowledged gruffly, sitting on the carpeted floor now as he kept his profile turned firmly away from her.

'Yes.' Cally swung her legs to the floor, already straightening her clothing even as she hurried up the stairs to see what had disturbed Lissa.

All the time knowing that her daughter couldn't be half as 'disturbed' as she was herself!

What had she been doing? How was letting Noel make love to her supposed to help the situation?

It didn't, she acknowledged with a choked sob, but she loved him so much, wanted him so much, that logic and caution had nothing to do with it when she was in his arms.

'Are you all right, Mummy?' Lissa queried sleepily as Cally entered her bedroom to sit on the side of the bed. 'You look upset.' She frowned.

Cally swallowed down the tears as her daughter's concern threatened to be her complete undoing. 'Never mind me,' she dismissed softly. 'Did you have a bad dream?'

'Not really. It's just that it's only one more day until Christmas!' she sheepishly explained her excitement.

Cally smiled emotionally, brought back down to earth as she looked at her beloved daughter. This was her reality, Lissa and the life they had together, and nothing—and no one— would ever be allowed to threaten that.

'I know, darling.' She smoothed Lissa's hair back from her brow. 'I wonder if Father Christmas will bring you everything that you asked for?' She thought of the bag of toys she had hidden away in the top of her wardrobe next door, the much-asked-for doll amongst their number.

Lissa's smile could hardly contain her excitement. 'I hope so.' She trembled.

'Right then, young lady, back to sleep,' Cally told her firmly as she stood up to straighten Lissa's duvet. 'Or Father Christmas will never come,' she warned teasingly.

Lissa looked up at her, entirely angelic in her sleepy,

tousled state. 'What have you asked Father Christmas for, Mummy?'

She drew in a sharp breath as she felt a shaft of pain through her chest, knowing that what she wanted for Christmas could never be hers. 'Some of that lovely foam bath I use,' she answered instead, knowing that Lissa had been out with Pam and bought her exactly that.

'Oh, goody!' Lissa grinned her pleasure. 'I'll go back to sleep now, Mummy,' she promised, snuggling back down with her much-loved teddy from baby days, closing her eyes to fall instantly back to sleep, it seemed.

The sleep of the young and innocent...

'Okay?' Noel prompted softly as Cally turned and found him standing in the doorway.

Cally had given a start of surprise as she'd turned and found him there, but hardened her resolve to leave here as she preceded him down the stairs; Lissa was just too precious to her to take any risks. Not that she thought Michael would particularly want his daughter, but he was bloody-minded enough to demand his paternal rights if he felt so inclined. And she had no intention of Lissa becoming an emotional pawn between herself and Michael—because the only loser in that would be Lissa herself!

Having Noel in her life could only complicate matters. Which meant that she had to leave him. Completely and for ever.

'You want me to leave now, don't you?' he guessed ruefully once the two of them were downstairs again.

Cally couldn't look at him—or the sofa where they had so nearly made love! 'I think that would be best.' She nodded.

'Cally—' Noel broke off, sighing his impatience. 'I'm not going to just disappear out of your life, you know.'

She did look up at him then, her expression one of scepticism. 'Aren't you?' she scorned, forcing herself to remember that it was only weeks ago this man had been engaged to marry someone else.

His mouth thinned. 'No,' he told her with certainty.

'We'll see.' She shrugged.

'Yes, we will, won't we?' He strode across the room, grasping her arm to turn her to face him, his eyes blazing deeply blue as he saw the challenge in her face. 'I'll see you tomorrow,' he finally bit out.

Cally nodded. 'I should be finished by lunchtime. The bill will be sent out to you—'

'Damn the bill!' he cut in harshly. 'Cally, I refuse to believe you're as cool towards me as you're pretending to be—damn it, I know you aren't!' he added, his smile grimly satisfied as he saw the colour that entered her cheeks at being reminded of the heated passion they had shared such a short time ago. 'Tomorrow,' he repeated, stepping back.

Tomorrow, or today, nothing would have changed; he would still be the rich 'Playboy of the West', and she would still be a single mother desperately trying to make ends meet.

And trying to keep Michael out of Lissa's life!

CHAPTER ELEVEN

'MICHAEL SHAW IS dead.'

Cally nearly fell into the chest freezer she had been stocking with all the food for Christmas at Parker Hall as she heard those words, the blood in her veins certainly becoming as cold as ice as she took in the full import of Noel's bald statement.

Michael was *dead...*?

She slowly reached up and pulled down the lid to the freezer, her shoulders tensing as if for a blow as she breathed deeply before turning to face Noel.

He stood in the doorway of the utility room, his face pale against the darkness of his hair, the expression in his eyes guarded as he looked across at her.

'Did you hear what I—?'

'Yes, I heard what you said!' Cally cut in sharply, a trembling beginning at her feet and spreading quickly up her whole body. She was shaking so badly now that she had to put out a hand on the top of the freezer to stop herself from falling. 'Are you sure?' she asked in a hushed voice.

'Oh, yes, I'm sure.' Noel nodded.

'But—I—how—?' Cally shook her head disbelievingly, barely aware of the sudden tears that fell hotly down her cheeks. 'I can't believe it!' she choked emotionally, before burying her face in her hands.

She had wished for a way to stop Michael from coming back into her own and Lissa's lives, had prayed for a solution to his presence nearby, one that wouldn't involve her uprooting Lissa again. But she would *never* have wished for Michael's death.

'Come on.' Noel spoke gently as he lightly grasped her shoulders and turned her into the main house. 'We'll go to my study,' he said gruffly, his arm about the slenderness of her waist as he guided her through the kitchen and down the hallway.

Cally was numb. Totally stunned at the thought of Michael actually being dead. She had hated him with a vengeance when she'd discovered his duplicity seven years ago, had hoped never to see him again after what he had done, but this—this was something she had never even thought of!

'Here, drink this.' Noel held a glass out to her once he had seated her in the armchair in front of the fire in the privacy of his study. 'It's brandy,' he explained as she looked up at him dazedly. 'For the shock.'

Oh, it was definitely a shock. Especially coming so quickly on the heels of the realization that Michael's family lived in the area somewhere.

But not Michael. Because he was dead.

Cally swallowed a little of the brandy, its fieriness melting some of the icy shock she felt inside. 'How can you be so sure? How do you know—?' She broke off, swallowing down the nausea that suddenly threatened to engulf her.

'Jane Shaw,' Noel told her economically. 'I went to see her this morning,' he explained as Cally looked at him frowningly.

Noel had been conspicuous in his absence when Cally had arrived at the house this morning. Honey had informed her, before she and the rest of the family had gone out shopping, that Noel had gone out on business but would be back later. But Cally had assumed that his absence might have had something to do with the way they had parted last night, rather than a real need to go out on business. It seemed she'd been wrong!

She moistened dry lips with the tip of her tongue. 'How did you know where to find her?'

Noel gave a dismissive shrug. 'I just did, okay?'

'No, it is *not* okay!' she snapped, eyes flashing her anger at the efforts he must have gone to to trace Jane Shaw. 'For one thing, you had no right to interfere. For another—'

'Despite everything, do you still love him?' Noel interjected swiftly.

Cally stared at him. Still love who—Michael…? Noel was asking her if she was still in love with *Michael?*

She had been eighteen when she'd met him, a student to his lecturer, had been bowled over, flattered, when he'd singled her out for his attention. But she wasn't sure she had ever been in love with Michael, and his flippant response to her discovering he was a married man, with no intention of their relationship ever being a serious one, had killed any infatuated feelings she might have had for him.

She certainly didn't love him now!

'Damn it, I think I need one of those!' Noel rasped at her continued silence, moving to the drinks tray to pour himself a glass of brandy, and then drinking it down in one swallow.

Cally looked at him, still bewildered, not really sure what to say to him. But it appeared she needn't say anything yet; Noel hadn't finished what he wanted to say!

'Thirty-six years it's taken me to find the woman I love and want to marry,' he ground out harshly. 'And she's in love with a man who has been dead for over a year!' He shook his head in self-derision. 'How stupid can I be?' he snarled. 'You—'

'Whoa,' Cally squeaked breathlessly. 'Could you go back a couple of sentences?'

'To where?' Noel rasped. 'To the fact that you're in love with—'

'No!' she cut in excitedly, getting slowly to her feet as she stared at him in disbelief. 'The bit about the woman you love and want to marry,' she prompted as he scowled at her.

'You.' He nodded impatiently. 'Cally, from what Jane Shaw told me of her ex-husband, the man was a womanizer and adulterer long before you even became involved with him. And he continued to be so until the day Jane Shaw left him three years later and took her children with her!' he added contemptuously.

'Jane left him…?' Cally repeated in shock.

'Three years after his relationship with you.' Noel nodded tersely. 'What is it, Cally? Thinking of all the time you could have been with him if you had known—?'

'Noel, shut up,' she gently interrupted him, crossing the room to stand in front of him, her gaze steady as she looked up at him. 'I don't love Michael, not now, not then,' she told him succinctly. 'I cried just now because—it was relief, Noel. Relief! I know it's selfish of me, but now I need never worry about him trying to take Lissa from me,' she said simply. 'I didn't know Michael was married when I met him, was flattered by his attention. I was only eighteen, Noel, I didn't even know what real love was at that age; I doubt that many people do. I do know that Michael could be vindictive, and that if he had learnt of Lissa's existence—!' She shook her head. 'I was worried you might think I should have told him about Lissa's birth.'

'You're saying he would have tried to make some sort of claim on her?' Noel guessed harshly. 'He would have had to come through me first!' he assured her grimly. 'And you made the decision you thought was best for you and Lissa. I would have supported you whatever had happened.'

Cally smiled. 'I didn't know what love was then—but I do now,' she said huskily, reaching up to tentatively touch the hardness of his jaw. 'Noel, you're the first, and only man I've ever loved,' she murmured, her breath catching in her throat as she waited for his response to her declaration.

He continued to look down at her unmovingly for several stunned moments, and then the frown cleared from his brow, his eyes blazing deeply blue as he reached out to grasp her arms. 'Do you really mean that?' he finally choked out.

Cally gave a radiant smile. 'Oh, yes.' She nodded with certainty.

'And you'll marry me?' he pushed forcefully.

Cally swallowed hard, not sure she could quite believe this was really happening. 'Lissa—'

'Already has me, and every other member of my family, firmly wrapped about her adorable little finger,' Noel assured her warmly. 'Any other reservations?'

Maybe one or two! But none of them really seemed to matter if Noel loved her and wanted to marry her! Except, perhaps one...

'What is it?' Noel asked concernedly as he saw her frown.

She drew in a deep breath before answering. 'Carol.'

'Hmm.' The frown settled back on his own brow at the mention of his ex-fiancée. 'That could be a little harder to explain...'

Cally blinked. 'Because you still love her?'

'No—because I never did.' He sighed. 'Cally, don't look at me like that!' He groaned as her eyes widened incredulously. 'The reason this is hard is because—even though I didn't love her, I don't want to be ungentlemanly.'

Cally thought back over the last few days, of Noel saying his mother was looking forward to being a grandmother soon, of Hester's own comments on the same subject—and everything became suddenly clear.

She looked up at Noel with shadowed eyes. 'You were going to marry her because you thought she was pregnant,' she said hollowly.

'Yes! No!' He gave a pained grimace. 'Yes...' he acknowledged heavily as she continued to look at him. 'That day two months ago, when I asked if you would have dinner with me, I knew then how attracted I was to you, but—by sheer coincidence Carol came to see me later that afternoon,' he recalled bleakly. 'She said she was pregnant. That the baby was mine. We had been involved, briefly, a few weeks earlier, so I had no reason to doubt her. I wasn't in love with her, but if the baby was mine... That's the reason I didn't call you as I had said I would.'

'Oh, Noel!' Cally sighed, moving forward to rest her cheek against the hardness of his chest, loving him more than ever; Noel had been going to do the honourable thing Michael would never have dreamt of doing in the same circumstances.

'She's the sister of an old school acquaintance.' He began to talk. 'We met quite accidentally, at a party, and once we both realized that I knew her brother Sean, we spent the rest of the evening together. He and I weren't close friends, you have to understand, but we knew each other enough for Carol and I to exchange anecdotes about schooldays.' He gave a humourless smile. 'We went out together for a couple of weeks, nothing serious—or so I thought!—just having fun. I'm not an angel, Cally—' he looked down at her openly '—but in my defence, I really thought that we both looked on our friendship in the same way.'

'Until she told you she was pregnant,' Cally stated evenly.

'Yes.'

'And was she?'

'No,' he bit out abruptly. 'She wanted a quick wedding. I wanted to wait until my family were over here for Christmas. I couldn't see what difference it made whether she was six weeks pregnant or ten.' He gave a shake of his head. 'Obviously it mattered to Carol—because she wasn't pregnant at all, had just decided, for some reason, that being my wife was what she wanted.'

Cally shook her head at his naïvety; Noel was rich, handsome and charming—but most of all rich. It was the oldest trick in the book, of course; Noel was just too sincere and up front himself to have seen it that way. But Cally certainly didn't think less of him for what had happened; in fact, she just loved him more!

'What happened next?' she enquired gently.

He drew in a harsh breath. 'I invited my family over for Christmas so that they could meet Carol. We would get a licence and be married at New Year. But Mrs McTavish fell over and broke her arm. For which I will be eternally grateful!' he added forcefully.

'I beg your pardon?' Cally gave a choked laugh as she raised her head to look up at him. 'What does Mrs McTavish have to do with anything?'

'Sounds incredible, doesn't it?' Noel allowed ruefully. 'But with Mrs. McTavish out of action, and my family due to arrive anyway—'

'It was left to Carol to arrange Christmas!' Cally realized knowingly. 'She didn't want to do it,' she guessed.

Noel's brow rose. 'Didn't want to do it. Had no intention of doing it. Didn't see why a man in my position couldn't get himself a new housekeeper. In fact, Carol didn't want to spend Christmas here at all, and fancied going to Canada skiing instead. Something that I didn't think was a good idea when she was pregnant. Her exact words when I insisted we stay here were, "If this is what being your wife is going to be like, being nothing more than a skivvy",' he mimicked, '"then I would rather not bother, thank you very much!"' He paused, his face pale now. 'For good measure, she admitted that there was no baby. There had never been a baby. And if she had her way, there never would be a baby!'

Cally closed her eyes as she could easily visualize his pain at being told these things. One thing she now knew about Noel—and which Carol had obviously realized too!— was that, despite what Cally had accused him of two days ago, he was very family oriented. He was also very aware of his responsibilities, and would have seen Carol's baby—his child—as his prime responsibility. Even if that had entailed marrying a woman he wasn't actually in love with.

Which made him so much more a better person than Michael could ever have been.

As if she had needed any convincing of that!

She smiled up at him indulgently. 'I can see, my love, that you need someone to look after you—possibly two someones,' she teased.

'You and Lissa?' he said hopefully.

'Me and Lissa.' She nodded.

'How do you think Lissa will react to that?' he voiced his concern. 'There's only been the two of you for so long.'

Cally smiled confidently. 'I think having you as her daddy is going to make the dolly she's been wanting for Christmas for so long fade into insignificance.'

Noel gave a relieved smile. 'And how about you?'

Her smile became mischievous. 'Well I don't want you as my daddy—'

'Idiot!' His arms closed about her possessively. 'How will you like having a husband?'

A husband. Something she had never, ever dreamt of having. Until Noel.

Her eyes glowed confidently as she looked up at him. 'As long as it's you, I'm going to love it!' she assured him.

'Oh, it's going to be me,' he said with certainty, holding her tightly against him. 'I love you, Cally Turner.'

'I love you too, Noel Carlton,' she responded emotionally.

What a wonderful, wonderful Christmas this was going to be, after all.

What a wonderful life they were going to have. Together…

* * * * *

A BRIDE FOR CHRISTMAS

Marion Lennox

CHAPTER ONE

'TELL me again why I've bought this wedding salon.' Guy Carver was approaching Sandpiper Bay with dismay. 'You didn't say this place was a hundred miles from nowhere.'

'You want to expand.' On the line from Manhattan, Guy's partner sounded unperturbed. 'Sandpiper Bay makes more sense than any other place in Australia. I told you...'

'You told me what?'

'It has the world's best surf,' Malcolm said patiently. 'It's surrounded by arguably the world's loveliest National Park, and half Hollywood owns property at Sandpiper Bay. Where are you now?'

'On the outskirts. It looks...'

'Don't judge until you see the town. Even my wife thinks Sandpiper Bay is great. She's furious you're doing the planning and not me.'

'As if *you* could plan a Carver Salon.'

'What's there to plan?' Malcolm demanded. 'Order a lake of ice-grey paint, give the widow a paintbrush and take a few days off.'

'I don't have time for a few days off,' Guy snapped, irritated by his partner's cheerfulness. 'I need to be back in New York on the twenty-sixth for the Film Conglomerate do.'

'We can handle Conglomerate with our hands tied. Spend Christmas on the beach.'

'Or not.' Christmas was a wasted day as far as Guy was concerned, and he had better things to do than surf. This year he'd timed this trip deliberately so he'd be flying home on Christmas Day. Christmas mid-air would get him as far away as was possible from useless sentiment.

He'd joined the coast road now, and he had to admit the place did look spectacular. Sandpiper Bay appeared to be a tiny coastal village bordering a shimmering sapphire sea, with rolling mountains beyond.

'So what am I looking for?' he demanded of Malcolm.

'A shopfront on the beachfront shopping strip. It's called Bridal Fluff.'

'Bridal Fluff?' He didn't explode. His voice just grew very calm. 'Did I hear right?'

'Sure did. The ex-owner's one Jenny Westmere. Widow. Apart from her dubious taste in naming her salon, she sounds competent. We've offered her twelve months' salary to make the transition easier.'

'There can't be a transition from Fluff to a Carver Bridal Salon,' he said grimly. 'I'll gut the place.'

He was turning into the main street now, and what he saw made him blanch. Bridal Fluff was indeed…fluff. The shop-front was pastel pink. The curtains in the windows looked like billowing white clouds, held back with pink and silver tassels. A Christmas tree stood in the window, festooned with pink and silver baubles, and a white fluffy angel smiling seraphically down on passers-by. The name of the shop was picked out in deeper pink, gold and silver. 'What the…?'

'Don't judge a book by its cover,' Malcolm said hastily, guessing what he was seeing. 'We don't need to give this woman any organisational role. We're just keeping her on the payroll to keep the locals happy. Every other salon we've acquired, the previous owner has been so chuffed to be associated with the Carver salon that the takeover's been a piece of cake. The bottom line is money. I've checked the books. I said it was a good buy and I meant it.'

'And if it's not…?'

'If it's not we'll just have to wear it.'

Malcolm had worked with Guy for years. Guy's reputation for dazzling event management left everyone he worked with stunned, but his personal reputation was for being aloof. Malcolm's cheerful nature, combined with a brash business acumen that matched Guy's, made them a formidable team. Together they'd built the Carver empire into the most lucrative events management chain in the world.

'No need to fret,' Malcolm was saying now, all breezy certainty. 'You and Mrs Westmere will get on like a house on fire.'

'Mrs Westmere?'

'Jennifer Westmere. I told you. The widow.'

'Great,' Guy muttered, pulling into a parking lot by the pink door. 'Middle-aged, frumpy and dressed in pink?'

'Nah,' Malcolm said, though he was starting to sound uneasy. 'The reports I have say she's young. Twenty-eight.'

'And I'm stuck with her?'

'The contract stipulates twelve months' employment.'

'I'll buy her out,' Guy said grimly. 'I should have stuck to Manhattan and Paris and London. I understand weddings there.'

'Then we'd miss out.' Malcolm cheered up again. 'Now you're expanding the Carver Salons worldwide, it's time we moved into Australia. Sandpiper Bay's more hip than Sydney or Melbourne. There's a huge buzz about the Carver Salons expanding. So go meet the lady with the pink fuzz. Make friends.'

'Not even close,' Guy muttered as pulled his car to a halt and finished the conversation. 'Friends? As if.'

JENNY WAS KNEELING on the floor and tackling about a hundred yards of hemline when he walked in. It was the fourth time she'd been around this hem. The dressmaker had thrown her hands up in horror, and now Jenny was left holding the baby. So to speak.

'I know it's not right,' the bride's mother was saying. 'We practised last night, and as she swept up the aisle I was sure the left side was longer than the right. Or was it the right longer than the left? Anyway, I knew you'd want to check. It has to be perfect.'

'Mmphf,' Jenny mumbled through pins, and then the door swung open.

Guy Carver.

This man's weddings were known throughout the world. *He* was known throughout the world. The phone call to Jenny offering to buy her premises had left her poleaxed.

'But why?' she'd stammered, and the man handling the deal for Guy had given her an honest answer.

'Eight of the ten most prestigious weddings in Australia have been held within ten miles of Sandpiper Bay in the last two years,' Malcolm had told her bluntly. 'There's a caveat on new businesses in what's essentially a historic commercial district. Setting up a business from scratch would be complex. Our people have checked your premises. Your building is big enough for us, and you already have a reputation for providing service. We'll do the rest. If you're at all interested, then we just need to settle on a price.'

She'd named a figure that had seemed crazy. Ten minutes later the deal had been sealed.

Jenny had replaced the receiver, stunned.

'It's more money than I ever dreamed possible,' she'd told her mother-in-law, and when Lorna had heard how much she'd gasped.

'That's wonderful. You'll be able to buy Henry whatever he needs.'

'I will.' Jenny smiled her delight. Even Lorna didn't know the depths of her despair at not being able to provide Henry with optimal medical treatment.

'But what will you do with yourself?'

'That's just it. They're offering me a job, doing what I'm

doing now, only on a salary. Twelve months' paid work, with the possibility of extending it. Holidays,' she said dreamily. 'Sick pay. Regular income with no bad debts.'

'And Guy Carver as your boss? Working with someone the glossies describe as one of the world's sexiest men?'

They'd grinned at each other like fools at that—a twenty-eight-year-old widow and her sixty-year-old mother-in-law letting their hormones have their head for one wonderful moment—and then they'd put their hormones away and thought seriously about what it entailed.

'Does he have any idea what he's letting himself in for?' Lorna had demanded. 'A country wedding salon…'

'It won't be a country salon for long. Currently the international jet-setters and the rich locals bring their own planners. Carver wants that business. I'm guessing most locals will stop being able to afford him.'

'Just like the rest of the businesses in this town,' Lorna said, grimacing.

'Sandpiper Bay's changing.'

'It's being taken over by the jet-set,' Lorna agreed. 'Every property within a twenty-mile radius is being snapped up at extraordinary prices by millionaires who spend two weeks of every year here.'

'We can't stop it.' Like Lorna, Jenny was ambivalent about the changes to their rural backwater, but there was little choice. 'The guy acting for Carver said if I didn't agree then they'd buy out the old haberdashery and set up in opposition. We'd be left with the brides that couldn't afford Guy.'

'Which would be most of our brides.'

'Right. I'd go under. As it is, my wealthy brides subsidise my poorer ones.'

'Which is why you're a lousy businesswoman.' Lorna gave her daughter-in-law a subdued smile. 'Like me.'

'Which is why I'm selling,' Jenny said firmly. 'We have no choice.'

So the arrangements had been fine. Sort of. Up until now it had been phone calls and official letters, with the business operating as normal. Only there was suddenly a lot more business, as people heard the news. Jenny was fielding phone calls now from as far away as California, from brides thrilled with the prospect of a Guy Carver wedding. She'd put them off, not clear when she'd officially be running Carver weddings, not really believing in the transition herself. But now the man himself was standing in the doorway.

'I'm looking for Jennifer Westmere,' he said, in a rich, gravelly voice, and Jenny's current bride gasped and pointed down.

'She's here.'

Jenny pushed aside a few acres of tulle and gave Guy a wave. 'Mmphf,' she said, and gestured to the pins in her mouth.

'I'm here on business,' he said enigmatically, and Shirley, the mother of the bride she was looking after, gave a sound that resembled a choking hen.

'You're Guy Carver. You're taking over this salon. Ooh, we're so excited.'

Guy stilled. Uh-oh, Jenny thought. One of the stipulations in the contract was that this takeover be kept quiet until the salon had been transformed to Carver requirements. But that hadn't been stipulated until the third phone call, and in the interim Lorna had managed to spread the news across Sandpiper Bay.

There was nothing she could do about that now. She watched as Guy sat, crossing one elegantly shod foot over the other. 'Carry on. I'll watch,' he said, his voice expressionless.

Great. Jenny went back to pinning, her mind whirling.

The man was seriously…wow! He was tall and dark, almost Mediterranean-looking, she thought, with the sleekly handsome demeanour of a European playboy. Not that she knew many European playboys—to be honest, she didn't know a single one—but she imagined the species to have just those dark and brooding good looks. He looked almost hawk-like, she decided, and she also decided that the photographs she'd seen in celebrity magazines didn't do him justice. His magnificently cut suit and his gorgeous silk tie screamed serious money.

Actually, everything about him screamed serious money.

There was a Ferrari parked outside her front window.

Guy Carver was sitting in her salon.

Was he annoyed about the lack of confidentiality? Was he annoyed enough to call the deal off?

'What's the problem with the dress?' Guy asked in a conversational tone, and she mmphfed again and waved a hand apologetically to the bride's mother.

'The hem's crooked,' Shirley Grubb told him, beaming and preparing to be voluble. 'Kylie's not getting married in a crooked dress.'

'When's the wedding?'

'Next Thursday.' Shirley looked smug. 'I know two days before Christmas is cutting it fine. We were so lucky to get the church. It's just this dratted dress that's holding us up.'

'When was the dress ordered?'

'Oh, she's had it for years,' Shirley told him, ready to be friendly. 'When Kylie turned sixteen I said we'll buy your wedding dress now, while your father's still working and while Jenny's here to organise it. No matter that you don't have a fella yet. Just don't put on too much weight. That was four years ago, and now we can finally use it.'

'Um…right,' Guy said mildly. 'When's the baby due?'

'Mid-January,' Shirley said, and beamed some more. 'Aren't we lucky we got the dress made? When we ordered it I told Jenny to leave heaps to spare at the hem. I was six months gone with Kylie before my old man did the right thing, and here's Kylie got her fella the same way. Hot-blooded, we are,' she said, preening. 'It's in the genes.'

Guy appeared to be focussing on the tip of one of his glossy shoes. Wow, Jenny thought. Guy Carver chatting to Mrs Grubb. Has he any idea what he's getting into?

She went on pinning. It gave her breathing space, she thought. So much tulle…

'Why did you choose Bridal Fluff to organise your wedding?' Guy asked conversationally, and Jenny winced. She just knew what Shirley would say, and here it came.

'Lorna—that's Jenny's mother-in-law—and me went to school together. Lorna won't charge me.'

Ouch. This technically wasn't her salon any more, Jenny thought. Nor was it Lorna's. It belonged to Guy.

'So this arrangement was made a long time ago?'

'When we were girls. Lorna always said she'd plan my wedding, and any of my kids' weddings and any grandkids' weddings, and when I rang up last month she said sure.'

'Lorna isn't planning your wedding,' Guy said mildly. 'It seems Jenny is. And Jenny works for me.'

For the first time Shirley seemed unsure. Her mouth opened, and failed to shut again.

'You mean,' she said at last, 'that we have to pay?'

It was time to enter this conversation. Jenny carefully removed the remaining pins and set them into her pin box.

'Any arrangements I made before Mr Carver purchased the business will be honoured,' she said. 'I'll take care of Kylie's wedding.'

'And the rest of them?' Shirley looked affronted.

'Maybe in my own time,' Jenny said. 'Not from this salon.'

'Well…' Shirley was about to start a war, Jenny thought, and Shirley's wars were legion.

'Leave it, Ma.' For the first time Kylie spoke up. She was a pale, timid young bride, and only the fact that her prospective husband was even more timid than his fiancée—and totally besotted—made Jenny feel okay about the wedding. But now Kylie had a flush to her cheeks, and she turned to

Guy as if she was trying to dredge up the courage to ask him something important. 'Mr Carver...?'

'Yes?' Guy was staring down at Jenny—who was meeting his look and holding it with a hint of defiance. Things were about to change in her life because of this man, and she wasn't sure that she liked it.

'When did you buy Bridal Fluff?' Kylie asked, and Guy turned and gazed at the bride.

It wasn't a great look, Jenny thought ruefully. The first of her brides that Guy was seeing was a waif of a bride in a vast sea of tulle. Her dress had been made when she'd had a size eight waist. It had been close fitting then. Now two strips of satin had been sewn into the waist to accommodate her advanced pregnancy. Jenny had attached a loose-fitting lace camisole to disguise the bulge a little, but it was no small bulge. The fact that the bulge kept changing meant that the hemline kept changing as well.

As well as that, Kylie's mother had definite ideas on what a bride should look like—which was a vision in every decorative piece of lacework she could think of. The veil even had tiny cupid motifs hand-sewn onto the netting. Seeing the veil turned into a train, Jenny estimated Guy was looking at approximately eight hundred cupids.

This was not one of her most elegant brides.

'Do you officially own this place yet?' Kylie asked, and Guy nodded, with what appeared to be reluctance.

'Yes.'

'Then I'm a Carver Bride,' Kylie said, suddenly ecstatic. She held her hands together in reverence. 'Like in those glossy magazines we buy, Ma. I'm the first Australian Carver bride. I reckon we ought to phone some reporters.'

'No,' Guy snapped, rising and looking at Kylie in distaste. 'You're not a Carver Bride. You are Mrs Westmere's responsibility. My takeover was supposed to be confidential, and the name-change won't happen yet. There'll be no Carver

Brides until my people are here and we can get rid of this…' he gazed around the salon with distaste '…this fluff.'

HAD HE MADE a mistake? Guy watched as the hem-marking continued. 'It's a small place,' Malcolm had told him. 'The council has the power to make all sorts of complications, like refusing our requests to expand the building. We need to keep the locals on our side. Make an effort, Guy.'

Maybe he hadn't made an effort. But really… Kylie, a Carver Bride? Some things were unthinkable. And what had happened to the confidentiality clause? It could be a disaster.

He waited on, ignored by the Grubbs, which suited him. Finally the hem was finished, and Kylie and her mother sailed off down the street to spread the news. Indignation was oozing from every pore.

They might be indignant, but so was he.

'I understood this takeover was to be kept quiet,' he said, in a voice that would have had his secretary shaking. Cool, low and carefully neutral.

It didn't have Jenny quaking. 'Your accountant, or whoever he is, should have said that earlier. My mother-in-law had ten minutes between offer and acceptance where that stipulation wasn't known. Ten minutes can mean a lot of gossip in Sandpiper Bay.'

'It means I can call the contract off.'

'Fine,' she said and tilted her chin. 'Go ahead.'

He was taken aback. She should be apologising. He'd come all the way here to find the terms of the contract had been breached, and all she was saying was take it or leave it.

He'd come a long way. Maybe it didn't matter so much. If he worked hard to get the place sleek before anyone important saw it…

That meant he also had to get rid of unsuitable clients. Fast. Clients like the Grubbs had no place in a salon such as this.

'Why the hell did you take that pair on?' he demanded of

Jenny, watching through the pink-tinged window as Shirley tugged her daughter into the butcher shop next door.

Jenny was still on the floor, gathering pins. When she answered, her voice was carefully dispassionate. 'It's obvious, isn't it? They're local, and I'm the local bridal salon.'

'They'll do your reputation no good at all. And as for you being the local bridal salon… We have a contract. Unless I walk away, you're no longer in charge. And you won't be doing weddings like this.'

'Right.' Jenny sat back on her heels and eyed him with disfavour. 'So the Pregnant-with-Tulle-and-Cupids isn't a Carver look?'

He choked. She eyed him with suspicion, and then decided to smile. 'Great,' she said. 'That's the first positive I've seen. I hoped you'd have a sense of humour.'

He collected himself. 'I haven't.'

'Yes, you have. I can see it. It's a pity it seems the *only* good thing I've seen.' She went back to gathering pins.

His jaw dropped. She was criticising him, he thought, astonished. She was on his staff. Criticism was unthinkable.

He tried to remember when he'd last heard criticism from his staff—and couldn't.

'You realise things are going to have to change around here?' he said cautiously. 'There'll be less fluff, for a start.'

She thought about that as she kept sorting pins, and suddenly she smiled. Which threw him all over again. It was an amazing smile, he decided, feeling more than a little confounded. Somewhere his vision of the Widow Westmere was being supplanted by this girl called Jenny. This woman? Okay, a woman. Her body was slim and lithe. Her glossy brown curls were cut in a pert, elfin haircut, which, combined with her informal jeans, her T-shirt and the smattering of freckles on her nose, made her look about fourteen.

But she wasn't fourteen. There were lines around her eyes, soft lines of laughter—but more. There was that look at the back of her eyes that said she'd seen a lot. There was not a trace of fluff about her.

This woman was a widow. There had to be some tragedy…

He didn't need to know, he told himself. She was here for twelve months to smooth the transition. Her leaving after that would be marked with a card of personal regret. When his secretary put those cards before him to sign he could hardly ever put a face to the name.

He liked it like that. He'd gone to a lot of trouble so it was like that.

He gazed around the shop, searching for something to distract him. Luckily there was plenty of distraction on offer.

'Three Christmas trees?' he said cautiously, and Jenny nodded, whatever had amused her obviously disappearing, the edge of anger creeping back.

'Lorna put up the big one in the window. She organises it halfway through November and it drives me nuts. Pine needles everywhere. The one in the entrance is a gift from Kylie's fiancé—he works in a timber yard and came in with it over his shoulder, looking really pleased with himself. Then the guys at Ben's work brought me one. How could I refuse any of them?'

'Ben?'

'My husband,' she said, and there was that in her voice that precluded questions.

'So…' he said, moving on, as she clearly intended him to do. 'We have three fully decorated Christmas trees, two mannequins in full bridal regalia and one groom in what looks a pretty down-at-heel dinner suit. Plus Christmas decorations.'

'They're not Christmas decorations,' she said tightly as he gestured with distaste to the harlequin light-ball hanging in the centre of the room and the silver and gold streamers running from the ball to the outer walls. 'The ball and streamers are here all year round.'

'You're kidding?'

'Nope,' she said, with a hint of defiance. 'We run the most garishly decorated bridal salon in the southern hemisphere. Our brides love it.'

'Carver Brides won't.'

She nodded. 'You've made that plain. It wasn't kind—to swat Kylie and Shirley like that.'

'If anyone publishes pictures of Kylie as a Carver Bride…'

'They won't. They might be provincial, but they're not stupid.'

'They sound stupid. What the hell was Malcolm about, buying this place?' Guy demanded, and Jenny's face stilled.

'You don't like it?'

'It's a backwater. Sure, it's scenic…'

'Do you know the average income of our locals?'

'What has that to do with it?'

'A lot, I imagine,' she said. 'There's two types of business in this town. First there are the businesses that provide for the original inhabitants. The likes of Shirley and Kylie. Those who you consider stupid. Then there are those that cater for the elite. We have no less than twenty helicopter pads in the shire. Millionaires, billionaires—we have them all. In your terms, not a stupid person in sight. The town has a historic overlay and a twenty-acre subdivision limit, so development is just about non-existent. In the last ten years every place coming onto the market has been snapped up by squillionaires. You know that, or you wouldn't have bought here.' She hesitated. 'You really want to get rid of the likes of Kylie?'

'I didn't want to imply all the locals are stupid. But if Kylie can't afford me…'

'She won't be able to afford me. None of the real locals will. Why do you want me to stay on?'

'To ease the transition.'

'There won't *be* a transition. You've just told Kylie there won't be Carver Brides until your people are here. I thought… according to the contract…I'd be one of *your* people.'

He might as well say it like it was. 'You won't have any authority.'

Any last hint of a smile completely disappeared at that. 'So the offer to employ me for a year was window-dressing to make me feel good about you guys taking over?'

'I can't employ you if you seriously like...' he stared around him in distaste '...fluff.'

'The fluff's Lorna's.'

'Lorna?'

'Lorna's my mother-in-law,' she said. She was speaking calmly, but he could see she was holding herself tightly on rein. 'Lorna set this salon up forty years ago. She had a stroke eight years ago, and advertised for an assistant. I got the job and met Ben. Now it's my business, but Lorna still puts in her oar. Lorna's been incredibly good to me. If she wants pink, and the locals like pink, I don't see why she can't have it.'

'Carver Salons are sleek and minimalist.'

'Of course they are. So you're here to toss the fluff?'

'I'll do the preliminaries,' he told her. 'That's why I've come—to decide what needs to be done. By the look of it, we'll start from scratch. We'll gut the place. My staff will take over the rebuilding, and everything that comes after.'

'But you'll still employ me?'

'We envisage a smooth transition.'

'You're employing me for local colour?'

'I didn't say that.'

'You didn't have to. I can't see me fitting the image of a Carver Salon consultant.'

'Have you ever met a Carver Salon consultant?'

'As it happens, I have,' she said, almost defiantly. 'A year ago I had a...well, I needed a holiday, and my parents-in-law sent me to Paris. I wandered through your salon, just to see how the other half live. Only of course I wasn't up to standard. I hadn't been in the salon for two minutes before I was asked to leave.'

'If my staff thought you were possible opposition, then...'

'Now, that's the funny thing,' she said. She'd risen and moved over to one of the Christmas trees. The angel on top was askew and she started carefully to adjust it. Then she began to check the lights, twisting each bulb in turn, taking her attention from him. 'They didn't even ask why I was there,' she said over her shoulder. 'I could have been there to talk about my wedding. I could have been there to make enquiries about anything at all. But I was wearing jeans and a T-shirt, and carrying a small backpack Lorna had given me.' She gave a rueful smile. 'The backpack was pink. Anyway, they obviously sorted me as a type they didn't want. They asked me to leave, and suddenly there was a security guard propelling me onto the pavement.' She shrugged. 'Given my opinion of Carver Salons, I should have told you to take your very kind offer to buy this salon and stick it. But of course it's a very generous offer, and I need the money and the thought of me being in opposition to you is ridiculous.'

There was a moment's silence then. Guy thought about his Paris staff. They were the best. They ran weddings that were the talk of the world.

They'd kicked this woman out. She must have been humiliated.

Maybe he needed to be a bit more hands-on.

He didn't like to be hands-on.

He thought suddenly of the first wedding he'd planned. He'd been home from college, where he'd been studying law—a career his parents had thought eminently suitable but which bored him stupid. Christa—the girl he'd been dating since both their mothers had organised them to their first prom—had been managing his social life, and that had bored him, too. Then Christa's sister had announced her engagement to someone both families thought entirely unsuitable.

Louise had wept on Guy's shoulder. Without parental support, and with no money of her own, she'd been doomed to have a civil ceremony and go without the party she'd longed for.

Intrigued, Guy had set to work. He'd painted cardboard until his hands were sore, transforming a small local hall into a venue that looked like a SoHo streetscape. He'd organised the local hotdog vendor to set up in a corner. The pretzel seller had come as well—and why wouldn't he have? An inside venue in the middle of a hot August had been a welcome change. Guy had built and painted a bar, made of plywood, but it had looked fantastic. Guests had had to pay normal price for hot dogs and pretzels and beer, but the wealthy guests had been intrigued rather than offended. He'd persuaded buskers to come, including a rap dancer with a hat out for offerings. He'd been hands-on every step of the way, and he'd loved it.

The bride had been ecstatic. Christa and Guy's mother had been less so. But when Guy had been approached the following week to do another wedding, and another, they'd been forced to stand by as Guy's career took off in another direction.

He remembered the family horror—his fledgling company had had to fly by the seat of its pants, and to risk money was unthinkable. Christa had been beside herself with rage. But he'd kept on. It had been fun, and he'd never known what fun was until he'd thrown aside the mantle of family responsibility.

When had he stopped having fun?

He could hardly remember. All he knew was that after Christa had been killed it had become his refuge—organising vast numbers of people in glittering social events that held no personal attachment at all.

His firm had grown, so he was now no longer hands-on. He employed hundreds—staff handpicked for their artistic and business acumen.

Would they have kicked this woman out on the street? He

didn't know, and maybe he shouldn't care as long as they did their job well. But now he thought back to that first wedding, and remembered Louise's joy. He looked at Jenny, her face a trifle flushed and more than a trifle defiant, and he thought, Hell, she must have been demoralised.

What had she said?

A year ago I had a...well, I needed a holiday, and my parents-in-law sent me to Paris.

She'd had a what? A breakdown? What had happened to the husband?

'I'm sorry,' he said.

'It wasn't your fault.'

It was, though, he thought grimly. He took the credit for Carver weddings. He took responsibility for his staff.

'You don't really want to employ me,' she said. 'Do you?'

'I'd rather this place was kept open for business during transition. I had hoped to keep the acquisition quiet until I got my staff in place, but now it's got out... It's unfortunate, but nothing we can't handle. I want the place open for queries and future bookings. You need to be the front person. I'll give you a pricing structure so you can give brides an idea of what we offer. Run the weddings you have now under...' He hesitated, then said, without bothering to hide his disdain, 'Under Bridal Fluff. New bookings will be under Carver Salon.'

'New bookings will be expensive?'

'We're exclusive.'

'You don't need to tell me that.' She grimaced, and he was aware of a stab of...regret?

Once upon a time he'd tried to make his functions wonderful because they created joy. He hadn't heard of the concept of *exclusive*. He'd lived on a shoestring.

He'd learned the hard way that was nonsense. That last day with Christa... 'If you loved me you'd keep doing law. Your father's expecting you to take over the family firm. Your mother's scared you're gay. Guy, you play with paints.

Paints! And me... How do you think I feel being engaged to
a *wedding planner*?'

She'd said the words with such scorn. Then, two hours
later, she was dead. If she'd lived he was under no illusion that
their relationship would have been over, but he knew that his
life decision had killed her. And his father... His father had
heard of Christa's death and it had been as if he'd said goodbye to the son he'd now never have. A wedding planner...
Two days later he'd had a stroke, and he'd never recovered.

Guy hadn't gone back to law. He'd known he'd be good at
this, but right there and then he'd vowed that he'd be a cor-
porate success. Their deaths had been crazy and unnecessary. No one was going to throw *wedding planner* at him as
a term of derision.

He worked hard. He kept to himself. He made money and
he carefully didn't *know* people. His life decisions would
never hurt anyone again.

He had become exclusive.

The telephone cut the stillness, and he welcomed it. He
motioned Jenny to answer, then picked up a catalogue to flick
through while she spoke.

Here were Bridal Fluff weddings over the past few years,
catalogued down to the last ghastly feather.

He flicked through. And paused.

One bridal couple smiled out from the pages, dressed like
a pair from the set of *Cabaret*. He looked more closely, taking in details of the setting.

The whole theme was *Cabaret*.

It was actually rather good. It'd be good even as a Carver
Wedding.

He flicked through a bit more. Fluff, fluff... But every
now and then something different.

There were just a few weddings in here that showed tal-
ent. He glanced up at Jenny, and she was smiling and mak-

ing hand signals. A second phone lay on the reception desk.
She was motioning to him to lift it.

He lifted it and listened.

'…be there for Christmas. About three hundred people.
Barret's pulled strings and found someone who'll marry them,
so you don't need to worry about the licence. All we need you
to do is to turn a Christmas feast into a wedding feast. I'll outline details in my fax. The most important thing is that Anna
needs a wedding gown, and she's caught up on location until
she gets on the plane. But she trusts Carver implicitly. If he
approves it, it'll be fine. There'll be six bridesmaids and six
groomsmen. I'll fax through sizes. Anna's only stipulation is
that she'd like a traditional wedding—the same as she saw at
home when she was a little girl.' The woman hesitated. 'She
said something about pink tulle.'

'Oh, we can do pink tulle,' Jenny told her, sounding chirpy
and still smiling. 'Mr Carver's good at pink tulle.'

Guy stared at Jenny, astounded.

'You've been really lucky,' Jenny continued, ignoring
Guy's astonishment. 'Mr Carver had stipulated there'd be
no weddings from this salon until his people were in place.
But as luck would have it Mr Carver himself arrived here
this afternoon. I regret I personally won't be involved, but I
know I'm leaving you in good hands. Sure, it's fine that you
put out a press release. If you could fax us a copy it'll let us
see exactly what tone we need to set. The figure per head is
perfectly acceptable. Goodbye.'

And she replaced the receiver with a definite click.

Guy stared at her. Jenny stared straight back, still smiling. Her chin jutted out just a little, and she held his gaze
and didn't break.

'What the hell have you done?' he demanded, and she
smiled some more, a tight, strained smile that didn't reach
her eyes.

'I just quit.'

'You quit?'

'The contract says my continued employment is optional. If I wish to leave at any time then I can. I know it was put there as a sop, so I'm letting you off the hook. I'm walking out now. Any remaining Bridal Fluff brides will be looked after by me from home. The salon's yours.'

'But you've just booked a wedding.'

'I have. It sounds just your style.'

'What wedding?'

'You were on the phone. Didn't you hear?'

'I heard nothing. Only Barret and Anna...' He paused as an appalling thought hit. 'Barret and Anna? You don't mean...'

'Barret and Anna,' she agreed, smiling benignly. 'Surely you of all people know Barret and Anna? Barret's just won... is it his second Oscar or his third? And Anna's on the front cover of this month's *Glamour*.'

'They're getting married?' he said stupidly, and she nodded. She walked over to the desk and picked up her handbag. It was of ancient leather, he noticed, his mind settling on details as if they were important. It looked as if it was falling apart.

'On Christmas Day,' she said, following his gaze to her handbag, flushing, and putting it behind her. 'That gives you ten days to organise it. I'll send my father-in-law to clear the store of my gear. We'll have it out of here by tomorrow night, so you'll have a clear run. You'll need it,' she said thoughtfully. 'Three hundred people in ten days...'

'What the...?'

'It's a very good idea,' she said. 'You know Anna's a local girl? She's hardly been home for twenty years, and by local I mean Sydney, but she bought a property here two years back. She and Barret flew in here after *Amazon Trek* for a break, and the town went nuts. It seems they were planning a Christmas party, but suddenly they've decided it would be an excellent time to get married. Only nothing's organised.

A blank canvas, Mr Carver, just how you like it. So now you have your very first Australian Carver Bride raring to go. Three hundred guests on Christmas Day.' She smiled some more. 'Ten days. You'll be very busy. But me... I have a little boy, who'll have Christmas with his mummy. Which is just as the world should be. Now me and my disreputable handbag will take ourselves out of your life. Good luck, Mr Carver. And goodbye.'

CHAPTER TWO

THIS was no drama. Guy watched her go with mixed feelings. There was a part of him that felt a strange lurch that she should walk away, and it had nothing to do with the bombshell she'd thrown at him. As usual, though, he attempted to shove personal thoughts aside and slip back into business mode.

It was difficult to shove the vision of Jenny away. The way she'd carried her handbag...

Barret and Anna. He had to think.

Barret Travers and Anna Price had a hugely powerful media presence. With Barret in a movie, an immediate box office hit was assured, and Anna's profile was almost the same. Their impending wedding would turn the eyes of the world right here.

To what? He couldn't put on a huge, media-circus-type wedding with this much notice. The booking was only five minutes old. He had to cancel, and fast.

That shouldn't be a problem. He'd phone Malcolm and get contact details straight away. But before he could lift his phone the fax machine on Jenny's desk hummed into life. Bemused, he watched the feed-out, recognising it for what it was. A press release.

'Barret and Anna to Wed!' the caption blared. 'Wedding to be in Sandpiper Bay, Australia. Guy Carver's first Australian wedding.'

They'd had it planned before they'd contacted Jenny, he thought. They'd had this press release ready to go.

Why? What could possibly add *more* media hype to this pair?

Carver's first Australian wedding. Guy thought about it, and his heart sank.

Anna had been pilloried in the press for her bad taste. Of course she'd want pink tulle, he thought. Pink tulle would be right in her league.

How to get pink tulle but still be thought cool by the cognoscenti?

Have a Carver wedding.

He had to cancel.

He stared down at the press release. Specifically at the tiny *cc*...

This was not a press release sent early just as confirmation to him. This was a press release which was simultaneously being read by every media outlet in the western world.

They'd been expecting his yes as perfunctory. Jenny had given them their yes, and they'd told the world.

If he pulled out now...

Carver Event Management pulling out would be news. People knew he was in Australia. Jenny had just confirmed it. So why couldn't he organise the wedding? No matter how carefully he explained it, Anna would take his refusal as a personal slight, and the world's press would agree.

Which meant problems for Anna.

The paparazzi spent their life reporting on Anna—and Barret. Barret was a loud-mouthed boor, but he was number one at the box office. In contrast, Anna was struggling a little. A few months ago she'd spent time in drug rehab. and the press had had a field-day. Her life seemed to be together now, but the media still wavered between idolatry and ridicule.

If they knew he'd knocked her back—*International Events Organiser Guy Carver Refuses Anna/Barret Wedding*—the world's press would say it served her right. They'd say she'd got what she deserved and the balance might well tip on the side of ridicule.

Which she didn't deserve.

Damn, he didn't get emotionally involved. He didn't.

He was. Right up to his neck.

He thumped the desk with his fist, and a fluffy stuffed dog, endowed for some reason with a disembodied head, started nodding in furious agreement. He stared down at the stupid creature and came close to throwing it through the pink-tinged windows.

Jenny was outside the window.

Over the road was the beach. A group of teenagers were clustered by the side of the road, leaning on their surfboards and chatting to Jenny. She was laughing at something one of them said.

She looked...free.

'Of course she looks free. You've just sacked her.'

Except he hadn't. She'd walked out on him. The thought was astonishing.

Focus on this wedding. How long did he have? Ten days?

The idea was ridiculous. He went through his top people in his head, trying to figure who could come.

No one could come. Everyone held parties at Christmas. And every event he had in his mental diary was major. There'd be repercussions if he pulled anyone out.

For a wedding like this, at this short notice, he needed local people. He needed...Jenny.

She was climbing into an ancient Ford, a wagon that looked more battered than the decrepit vehicles the surfers were using. While he watched, she backed out of the parking spot, then headed right. Her wagon passed the teenagers and did a backfire that made everyone jump.

'She'd be hopeless,' he told no one in particular, and no one in particular was interested.

'I can't ask her.'

No one was interested in that, either.

He stared at the fax again and swore. 'Do I care if the wonderful Anna's career goes down the toilet?'

He did, he thought. Damn, he did. Two months ago he'd catered for a sensational Hollywood ball. Anyone who was anyone had been present. He recalled a very drunken producer hitting on Anna. When she'd knocked him back he'd lifted her soda water, sniffed it, and thrown it away in disgust.

'Once a tart, always a tart, love,' he'd drawled at her. 'You're not such a good little actress that you can pretend to be something you're not for ever.'

Guy had intervened then, handing Anna another soda water, giving her a slight push away and deflecting the creep who'd insulted her by showing signs of investing in his latest project. But he'd seen Anna's white face, pretence stripped, and he'd also seen how she'd stared into the soda water, taken a deep breath, and then deliberately started to drink it. To change your life took guts—who should know that better than him?

If Anna wanted him to cater for her wedding then he would.

'Even if it does mean I have to go on bended knee to the Widow Westmere.'

JENNY PULLED INTO the front yard of her parents-in-law's farm, switched off the ignition, took a few deep breaths—how to explain all this to Lorna and Jack?—and a car pulled in behind her.

A Ferrari.

Ferrari engines were unmistakable. What are the chances of someone else with a Ferrari pulling into my yard? she thought, and decided she ought to head inside fast, close the door and not even look out to see whether Mr Guy Hotshot Carver was on her property.

'Mrs Westmere,' he called, and the moment was lost. She

sighed, leant back on her battered wagon with careful insouciance—and folded her arms.

'What?'

'I'd like to talk to you about your contract.'

'It's clear,' she said, trying to be brusque. 'I have the right to work for you for a year, and I also have the right to walk away any time I like. Your business manager seemed to think I'd be jumping all over myself to stay, but the obligation is on your side; not mine.'

'I'd like you to stay.'

'Nah.' She should be chewing gum, she decided. She didn't have the insouciance quite right. 'You're pleased to be shot of me.' Then she broke a bit—she couldn't quite suppress the mischief. 'Or you were until I landed you with the wedding of the century. You're going to have to cancel on the biggest wedding we've seen in this place. What a shame.'

'I can't cancel.'

'Come on. You can afford to lose one wedding. All that hurts is your pride. And pride doesn't matter to you. Just look what you did to Kylie.'

'I—'

'Is that you, Jenny?' Jack's voice interrupted, and Jenny hauled herself away from the wagon and abandoned the insouciance.

'I need to go inside. You need to go…wherever rich entrepreneurs go when they're not messing with this town. See you later.'

'Do you have someone out there?' Jack called.

'Jenny, I need to talk to you.'

'Mrs Westmere,' she flashed. 'It's Mrs Westmere, unless I can call you Guy.'

'Of course you can call me Guy.'

'Bring your visitor in, Jenny.'

'Go away,' she said.

'I need you.'

'You don't need anyone. You come waltzing into town in your flash car...'

'It's borrowed from a friend.'

'You *borrowed* a Ferrari?' she demanded incredulously. 'Someone just tossed you the keys of a Ferrari and said, "Have it for a few days." Like he has one Ferrari for normal use and another to lend to friends.'

'His other car's an Aston Martin,' he said apologetically. 'And his wife drives a Jag.'

'I *so* much don't need this conversation.' She made to turn into the house, but he stepped forward and caught her shoulders. The action should have made her angry—and at one level it did—but then there was this other part of her...

He really was a ludicrously attractive male, she thought. She wasn't the least bit afraid of him. Well, why should she be when she had Lorna and Jack just through the screen door? But there was more than that. His grip felt somehow...okay.

It wasn't the least bit okay. This was those damned hormones working again, she thought. She'd been a widow for too long.

But she had protection—against hormones as well as against marauding males. She hadn't answered Jack, and Jack and Lorna had grown worried. Now the front screen slammed back and Jack was on the veranda. Jack was a wiry little man in his late seventies, tough as nails and belligerent to go with it. He was crippled with arthritis, but he didn't let that stop him.

'Who's this?' he growled, before Jenny could say a word. He stalked stiffly down the veranda, trying to disguise the limp from his gammy hip, trying to act as if he was going to lift over six feet of Guy Carver and hurl him off the property.

Guy dropped his hands from Jenny's shoulders. He didn't step away, though. He stood a foot away from her, his eyes filled with quizzical laughter.

'You have a security system?'

'I surely do,' she answered, taking a grip of her wandering hormones and turning to face her in-laws. 'Jack, Lorna— this is Guy Carver.'

Lorna was out on the veranda now. She'd pushed her wheelchair though the doorway, rolling to the edge of the ramp but no further. Lorna had once been a blousy, buxom blonde. Her hair was still determinedly blonde, and her eyes were still pretty and blue, but a stroke had withered one side of her body. One side of her face had very little movement and her speech was careful and stilted.

'Mr Carver,' she managed.

'He says we can call him Guy.'

'Why are you manhandling my daughter-in-law?' Jack barked, and the lurking laughter behind Guy's eyes was unmistakable.

'I was just turning her in the right direction. Towards you.'

'It's okay, Jack,' Jenny told him. 'Mr...Guy's just leaving.'

'Look at the car,' Lorna said, suddenly distracted. 'What is that?'

'A Ferrari,' Guy said, bemused, and at that the screen door swung open again.

'Don't come out, Henry,' Jenny said quickly, but it was too late. Henry was already on the veranda.

She winced. She badly didn't want Guy to see Henry. He'd already shown himself to be insensitive. How much damage could he do now?

For the crash that had killed his father had left Henry so badly burned that for a while they'd thought he might not live. The six-year-old was slowly recovering, but the scars on the right side of his face were only a tiny indication of the scars elsewhere. His chest and his right leg bore a mass of scarring, and he was facing skin graft after skin graft as he grew.

Henry should be a freckle-faced kid facing life with mischief and optimism. There were signs now that he could be again, but the scars ran deep. His thatch of deep brown curls stopped cruelly where the scarring began, just above his right ear. His brown eyes were alive and interested—thank God his sight had been untouched—but he'd lost so much weight he looked almost anorexic compared to most six-year-olds. His right leg was still not bearing weight, and he used crutches. His freckles stood out starkly on his too pale skin. Standing on the veranda in his over-big pyjamas—Lorna was sure he'd have a growth spurt any minute, and she sewed accordingly—he looked a real waif. The surgeons said that in time they'd have his face so normal that, as he matured, people would think of him as manly and rugged, but that time was a long way off from now.

'I want to see the car,' Henry said.

She held her breath, waiting for Guy to respond. If she had her druthers Jenny would keep her private life absolutely to herself. A private person at the best of times, these last two years had been hell. She'd been forced to depend on so many people. The locals had been wonderful, but now she was finally starting to regain some control of her shattered life, and the look of immediate sympathy flashing into Guy Carver's eyes made her want to hit him.

What's wrong with your little boy...?

How many times had that been flung at her since Henry had recovered enough to be outside the house? It was never the locals—they all knew, and had more sense than to ask about his progress in front of him. But the squillionaires who arrived for a week or two were appalling, and she wanted to be shot of the lot of them.

Maybe now she'd sold the business she could move, she thought. She could get a great place if she was prepared to go inland a little. But Jack and Lorna had lived here all their lives. She and Henry were all they had.

She couldn't leave.

So now she flinched, waiting for Guy to say something like

they all did. *What's wrong?* or, *Gee, what happened to your kid? Why is he so scarred?* Or worse, *Oh, you poor little boy...*

But Guy said nothing. He had his face under control again, and the shock and sympathy were gone. Instead he glanced at the Ferrari with affection. 'It's a 2002 Modena 360 F1,' he told Henry, man to man.

'It's ace,' Henry whispered, and something in Guy's face moved. Something...changed.

'If it's okay with your mother, would you like a ride?'

Henry's small body became perfectly still. Rigid. As if steeling himself for a blow.

'I... Mum...?'

'You're kidding,' she said to Guy.

'I don't kid,' he said, and his voice had changed, too. It had softened. 'I mean it. I'm assuming this is your son?'

'Yes, but...'

'I'm Guy,' he told Henry. 'And you are...?'

'Henry,' said Henry. 'Is this your car?'

'It's borrowed.'

'Do you have a car like this?'

'I have a Lamborghini back in New York.'

'Wow,' Henry breathed, and looked desperately at his mother. 'Is it okay if I take a ride with him?'

'It's dinnertime.'

'Dinner can wait,' Jack growled. Jenny's father-in-law was looking at the car with an awe that matched his grandson's. 'If anyone offered me a ride in such a car I'd wait for dinner 'til breakfast.'

'You're next in the queue,' Guy said, and grinned. 'I'd take you all at once,' he added apologetically, 'but it's hard to squeeze three people in these babies. Jenny, you can go third.'

'I don't want to go.'

'Is it okay if I take Henry?'

'Of course it's okay,' Jack snapped, as if astounded that anyone could ask that question. 'Isn't it, girl?'

'Fine,' she said, defeated, and Henry let out a war-whoop that could be heard back in Main Street. Then he paused.

'You don't mean just sit in it?'

'Of course not.'

'Can we go out on the coast road?' Henry asked, eyeing his mother as if she'd grown two heads. *Never go with strangers...* Her consent meant she knew this guy and trusted him. His mother had a friend with a Ferrari. She could see she'd just raised herself in his estimation by about a mile. 'The coast road winds round cliffs. With this car...it'll go like it's on rails.'

'You won't go fast?' She knew her voice was suddenly tight, but she couldn't help it.

'We won't go fast,' Guy told her, and there was that tone in his voice that said he understood.

How could he understand?

The remembrance of his hands on her shoulders slipped back into her mind. Which was dumb.

'Henry's in his pyjamas,' she said, too quickly, but suddenly that was how she felt. As if everything was too quick. 'Does he need to change?'

'No one notices who's in a Ferrari,' Guy told her. 'They only notice the Ferrari. If you're in a Ferrari you can wear what you d— Whatever you like. You're cool by association. Are you ready, Henry?'

'Yeah,' Henry breathed, and tossed aside his crutches and looked to his mother for help to go down the ramp. 'Yeah, I am.'

'HE SEEMS LOVELY.'

'He's not.' Back inside, Jenny was trying to explain the extraordinary turn of events to her in-laws. 'He won't do Kylie's wedding. She's not good enough to be a Carver Bride.'

'Kylie is a bit...' Lorna said, and Jenny glowered and tossed tea into the pot with unnecessary force.

'Don't you come down on his side. Kylie and Shirley were great to us.'

They had been. All of those dreary months when Jenny had needed to be in the hospital—for three awful weeks Henry had not been expected to live—Kylie and Shirley and a host of other locals had run this little farm, had ferried Lorna and Jack wherever they'd wanted to go, had filled the freezer with enough casseroles to feed an army for years, had even taken over the organisation of local weddings. The town had been wonderful, and Jenny wasn't about to turn her back on them now.

'I know they're fabulous,' Lorna told her. 'And of course I promised we'd do Kylie's wedding. But they won't hold us to more than that. I was just so upset. With Ben dead, and we thought we'd lose Henry...'

'You would have promised the world,' Jenny said. 'Shirley knows that. She tried it on with Guy this afternoon—and why wouldn't you? But I will do Kylie's wedding for cost, and Guy can't stop me. I'll just organise it from here.'

'And the rest?'

'He can have the society weddings. I don't want them.'

'They're the only ones that make us money.'

'We'll survive. He paid heaps for the business—more than its worth. But I don't want Guy Carver as my boss.'

'There'd be worse bosses,' Jack said, and Jenny sighed.

'Just because the man has a Ferrari...'

'What's he driving Henry for?'

'To wheedle his way into getting me to work for him,' she snapped. 'The man's a born wheedler. I can see it.'

'He doesn't look like a wheedler to me,' Lorna said. She'd been laying plates on the table, but now she stilled her wheelchair and turned to face her daughter-in-law. 'Jenny, it's been two years. We know you loved Ben, but maybe it's time you moved on?'

'What are you talking about?'

'He looks quite a catch,' Jack said, crossing to the door to look—hopefully—out. With a bit of luck there'd be time for a ride for him before dinner was on the table. 'A Lamborghini at home, eh?'

'You think I should jump him because he owns a Lamborghini?' Jenny asked incredulously, and Jack had the grace to look a bit shamefaced.

'I just meant…'

'He just meant don't look a gift horse in the mouth,' Lorna said decisively. 'I'm asking the man to tea.'

'You can't.'

'Watch me,' Lorna said, plonking a fifth plate on the table. 'I just know the nice man will stay.'

THE NIGHT WAS interminable. Jenny couldn't believe he'd accepted Lorna's invitation. She couldn't believe he was sitting at her dining table with every appearance of complacency.

This was a man international jet-setters regarded as ultra-cool—the epitome of good taste. If they saw him now…

For a start he'd walked in the front door without even appearing to notice Lorna and Jack's decorations. The Christmas after Ben had been killed, when Henry's life had hung by a precarious thread, Lorna had decreed Christmas was off. 'It doesn't mean anything,' she'd declared. 'I'm tossing all my decorations.'

Twelve months later she'd rather shamefacedly hauled out her non-tossed decorations. Jack and Jenny had been desultorily watching television, with Henry on the sofa nearby. They'd been miserable, but they'd fallen on the decorations like long-lost friends. That night had been the first night when ghosts and fear and sadness hadn't hung over the house, and this year Henry had demanded his grandparents start sorting the decorations on the first day of November.

So there was a reason why the decorations were just ever so slightly over the top, Jenny conceded. She'd hauled Henry's chair close beside her. He was leaning on her, still lit up after his ride in Guy's wonderful car. He was tired now, but Jenny thought there'd be trouble if she tried to send him to bed. Lorna and Jack were chatting to Guy as if they were entertaining an old friend, and Henry was soaking in every word.

He had a new superhero.

As for Jenny…Jenny was trying to block out the flashing lights from the real-sized sled in the front yard. The house and the yard were chock-full of Christmas kitsch. She loved every last fluffy pink angel, she decided defensively, trying not to wonder what he was thinking of her. If Guy didn't like them, then he could leave.

Guy Carver would be a minimalist, Jenny thought, watching Lorna ladle gravy over his roast beef and Jack handing him the vast casserole of cauliflower cheese. He'd like one svelte silhouette of a nativity scene in a cool grey window.

Jenny could count five nativity scenes from where she was sitting.

'The decorations are wonderful, Mrs Westmere,' Guy told Lorna, and Jenny cast him a look of deep suspicion as Lorna practically purred.

'Jenny thinks maybe the front yard is a bit over the top.'

'How could you, Jenny?' Guy said, and cast reproachful eyes at her.

She choked.

'Are you staying until Christmas?' Jack asked, and Guy said he wasn't sure.

'Why I'm asking,' said Jack, obviously searching for courage, 'is that every year Santa comes to Sandpiper Bay.'

'If you're asking me to wear a Santa suit…' Guy said, suddenly sounding fearful, and Jenny looked at Guy's Mediterranean good looks and thought, *Yeah, right. Santa—I don't think so.* 'Then, no.'

'No, no,' Jack assured him. 'We have a very fine Santa. Bill went to a training course in Sydney and everything. But the thing is that every Christmas morning Santa drives through the town tossing lollies—'

'From the fire truck,' Henry interrupted, which just about astounded Jenny all by itself. Normally when visitors came Henry was seen but not heard. Henry had been a happy, cheerful four-year-old when his father's car had collided head-on with a kid spaced out of his brain on cocaine. Now Henry's world was limited to hospital visits, physiotherapy clinics and his grandparents' farm. For Henry to go with Guy tonight had been astonishing, and the fact that he was chirping away like a butcher's magpie now was even more so.

'See, there's the problem,' Jack explained, growing earnest. 'The problem with Christmas in Australia is that it's at the height of summer. In summer there's fires. Last year the fire truck got called away. One minute Santa was up top, handing out lollies, the next he was standing in the middle of Main Street with a half-empty Santa sack while the fire truck screamed off into the distance to someone's burning haystack.'

'Goodness,' Guy said faintly; *Goodness*, Jenny thought, suddenly realising where this was going.

'Now, if you were here, young man, in your Ferrari...'

'Santa could use your Ferrari,' Henry said, suddenly wide-eyed. 'Cool. Course it's not the *real* Santa,' he explained, while Guy looked as if he was trying to figure how he could escape. 'He's a Santa's helper. Mum told me that last year. I sat in the back of our car and the fire engine came right up and Santa gave me three lollies.'

'That was before it was called away,' Jenny said, trying not to get teary. Too late—she was teary. Dratted tears. She blinked them away, but not before Guy had seen. She knew he'd seen. He had hawk-like eyes that could see everything.

'Mr Carver's going home before Christmas,' she told Henry, feeling desperate. 'Aren't you, Mr Carver?'

'I'm not sure,' Guy told her. 'And the name is Guy.'

'You're not seriously thinking of doing the Anna/Barret party?'

'I'd need help.'

'A party?' Lorna intercepted, bright-eyed. 'What sort of party?'

'Anna and Barret's wedding.'

'Anna and Barret…' Lorna paused, confused, and then confusion gave way to awe. 'You don't mean *Anna and Barret*?'

'I mean Anna and Barret.'

'They're getting married? Here?'

'If we can cater. If your daughter-in-law will come back as a member of my staff.'

'Jenny,' Lorna said, eyes shining. 'How wonderful.'

'It's not,' Jenny said. 'He won't do Kylie's wedding.'

'We can do Kylie's wedding,' Guy said.

She eyed him with disbelief. 'As a Carver Wedding?'

'I don't think—'

'Ha!'

'She wouldn't like my style of wedding.'

'Anna wants pink tulle. Surely you give the clients what they want?'

'If it fits into my—'

'That is such an arrogant—'

'Will you two stop it?' Lorna said, stuttering in an attempt to get this sorted. 'Jenny, you need to help him.'

'I don't.'

'As a matter of interest,' Guy said calmly, '*could* you help me if you wanted to?'

'Do what?' she said, trying to disguise a child-like glower. But he saw it and his lips twitched. No wonder the glossies described him in glowing terms, Jenny thought. Until now she'd wondered how the head of what was essentially a ca-tering company had become someone that the gossip columnists described as hot property. Now she knew. Guy would just have to look at you with those eyes, that held laughter...

The man was seriously sexy.

'Do you have the resources to run a wedding for three hundred on Christmas Day?' he asked, and she had to make a sharp attempt to haul her hormones into line. 'Are we arguing about something that's an impossibility?'

'It's not impossible,' she said, and then thought maybe she shouldn't have admitted it.

'Why is it not impossible?'

'Anna says she wants pink tulle?'

'So?' The laughter was gone now, and she could see why he was also described as one of the world's best businessmen. She could see the intelligence...the focus.

'So we could give her a country wedding. Kylie-style. It would be so unexpected that she'd love it.'

'We could put on a country dance,' Jack contributed. 'It's great weather this time of year. Haul some hay bales out into the paddock for seats, some more for a bar, and shove a keg on the back of the truck.'

'Keg?' Guy asked faintly.

'Fosters,' Jack told him. 'Gotta be Fosters.'

'He means beer,' Jenny told him, putting him out of his misery. 'I don't think this crowd would be happy with only beer.'

'Drink's the least of my problems.'

'So what's your problem?'

'Finding clothes for the wedding party in ten days. Sourcing food. Finding staff to wait on tables and clear up afterwards.'

'Piece of cake,' Jenny said, and then thought that was stupid. What was she letting herself in for?

'How is it a piece of cake?'

'Make Kylie's wedding the first Australian Carver Wedding and I'll tell you.'

'Kylie doesn't want a Carver Wedding.'

'You're making huge assumptions here,' she flashed, and Henry stirred and looked up at his mother in surprise. Lorna shifted her wheelchair sideways so she could take his weight, and he moved his allegiance to his grandmother. As if he wasn't quite sure who his mother was any more. 'What's the difference between Anna and Kylie?' she demanded. 'Career choice and money. Nothing more. Kylie's got herself pregnant, but Anna ended up in drug rehab. Two kids getting married. Kylie does want a Carver Wedding, and she asked first.'

'You'd seriously make me—'

'No one's making you do anything,' she told him. 'Including staying at our dinner table.'

'You're telling me to leave?'

'I don't like what money does to people.'

'The man hasn't finished his dinner yet,' Jack protested. 'Have a heart.'

'It's a bit rude to invite him to eat and put him out,' Lorna added, looking curiously at Jenny.

'Jenny's just itching for a fight,' Jack told Lorna, speaking across the table as if no one else was there. 'Dunno what's got into her, really.'

'It's hormones,' Lorna decided. 'You have a nice cup of tea, Jen.'

'Lorna…'

'She could do the wedding if she wanted to,' Lorna said, turning to Guy. 'She's the cleverest lass. I used to run the salon, making dresses for locals and organising caterers for out-of-towners. Only then the out-of-towners grew to so many that I had to employ Jenny. It was the best thing I ever did. Her mum didn't have any money, and her dad lit out early, so there wasn't enough to send Jenny to anywhere like university. She took on an apprenticeship with me. She's transformed the business. She's just…'

'Lorna!' Jenny said, almost yelling. 'Will you cut it out? Mr Carver doesn't want to know about me.'

'Yes, I do,' he said mildly. 'I need to persuade you to use some of your skills on my behalf. Where could you get caterers on Christmas Day?'

'I don't—'

'You tell him, lass,' Jack said. 'Don't hide your light under a bushel.'

She stared wildly round, but they were all watching her expectantly. Even Henry.

'This town is full of retirees,' she said at last, trying desperately to get her voice under control. 'Most of them have a very quiet Christmas. If we had all the food planned the day before—if we settled on country fare that all the women round here can cook—if Anna settled for a late wedding and if we told the locals that they could come to the dance afterwards—there'd be queues to work for us.'

'Locals come to the *ceremony*?' he said, incredulous.

'Not the ceremony. The idea would be that there'd be a huge party afterwards, with workers welcome. Think of the publicity for Anna and Barret. If you got onto that nice PR person I talked to this afternoon...'

Guy stared at her, poleaxed. 'It might...'

'It might well work,' she said. 'She's not squeaky clean, our Anna, and this would be great publicity.'

'You know about Anna's past?'

'The world knows about Anna's past. This wedding will be great for her.'

'It would,' he agreed, and suddenly Jenny's eyes narrowed.

'That's why you're thinking of doing it,' she said softly, on a note of discovery, thinking it through as she spoke. 'I couldn't understand...' But suddenly she did, seeing clearly where her impetuous nature had landed Guy. 'The Carver empire doesn't need this wedding, but Anna needs the Carver emporium.' She bit her lip. 'I should have thought about that when I was contacted. Oh, heck. I was angry with you, and I didn't think.'

To say Guy was bewildered was an understatement. That Jenny was sensitive enough to see connotations that he'd only figured because he moved in those circles....

His estimation of the woman in front of him was changing by the minute. Gorgeous, smart, funny...

He didn't do gorgeous, smart and funny. He didn't do complications.

He rose, so sharply that he had to make a grab to catch his chair before it toppled. 'I need to go.'

'You haven't had coffee,' Lorna said mildly, but he didn't hear. He was watching Jenny.

'You agree to staying on my payroll until Christmas?'

'Can Kylie have a Carver Wedding?'

'Yes,' he said, against the ropes and knowing it.

She hesitated, but then gave a rueful smile. 'Okay, then. I've never worked for a boss before.'

'What about me?' Lorna said, indignant, and Jenny grinned.

'That's different. I walked into your shop for the interview and Ben was there. I was family from that minute on.'

'You were, too,' Lorna said, and reached over and squeezed her hand.

Family.

Something knotted in Guy's gut that he didn't want to know about. He backed to the door.

'Where are you staying, young man?' Jack asked.

'My secretary booked a place for me. Braeside?'

'You been there yet?'

'No. I—'

'You'll never find it,' Jack said with grim satisfaction. 'It's up back of town, by the river. Tourists get lost there all the time.' It seemed a source of satisfaction. Jack was looking at him with what seemed to be enjoyment.

'I have directions.'

'I've seen the directions they use. You'll be driving through the mountains 'til dawn. Jenny'll have to take you.'

Jenny stilled. Then she nodded, as if she agreed. 'You will get lost. I'll drive there, and you can follow me.'

'What fun is that?' Jack demanded. 'You haven't had a drive in his Ferrari. I've got a better idea. You drive him home in his Ferrari and then bring it back here. Then pick him up on the way to work tomorrow morning.'

'I can't drive a Ferrari,' Jenny said, astonished.

'Course you can,' Jack said roundly. 'If you can make your ancient bucket of bolts work, you can make anything work. Her wagon's held together with string,' he told Guy. 'She ought to buy another, but she's putting every cent she owns into a fund for Henry's schooling.' His face clouded a little. 'There's been a few costs over the last couple of years we hadn't counted on.'

Of course, Guy thought, his eyes moving to Henry's face. The little boy's face was perfect on one side, but on the other were scars—lots of scars.

'I can't drive a Ferrari,' Jenny said again, and he forced himself to think logically. Which was hard when his emotions were stirring in all sorts of directions.

'Yes, you can,' he said, and managed a smile that he hoped was casual.

'There you go, then,' Lorna said, triumphant. 'Jack and me will put Henry to bed. Henry, your mother is going to have a drive in the lovely car. Isn't that great?'

'Ace,' said Henry.

CHAPTER THREE

It FELT weird, Jenny thought as they walked across the yard towards his car. It was almost dark. She should be reading her son his bedtime story.

She shouldn't be climbing into a Ferrari.

'You drive,' Guy said, and tossed her the keys.

'This is a bad idea,' she muttered. 'This is a borrowed car. Surely your friend wouldn't agree to me using it?'

'If you crash it I'll buy him another.'

The idea made her stop in her tracks. 'You're kidding.'

'Why would I kid?'

'I don't want to go with you,' she said, and it was his turn to pause and stare.

'You have ethical objections to money?'

'No, I...'

'You should be charging Kylie. There's no need for you to be broke.'

'Isn't there?' she snapped, and glared.

'Giving your services for free is noble, but...'

'You have no idea, do you? This community...we're here for each other. We do what has to be done, and asking for payment—'

'Your career is a bridal planner. Selling yourself short is stupid.'

'When Ben was killed, Henry was injured, and he had to spend months in a burns unit in the city,' she snapped. 'Jack has macular degeneration—his eyesight's not what it should be—and Lorna hasn't driven since her stroke. Shirley Grubb was one of a team who took it in turns to drive Jack and Lorna down to see us. Twice a week for nearly six months. Every other day they drove Lorna into the bridal salon and someone stayed with her all the time. The business stayed open. There were casseroles—you can't believe how many casseroles. And you know what? Not a single person charged us. Did they sell themselves short, Mr Carver?'

'Guy,' he said automatically, and opened the driver's door of the Ferrari. 'Get in.'

'I'm not driving.'

'You are driving. You need to bring it home yourself, so you can try it out now.'

'We can take my wagon.'

'Your wagon backfires. Backfiring offends me. And I have no intention of being lost in these mountains for want of a little resolution on your part. Get in and drive.'

IT WAS SUCH a different driving experience that she felt... unreal.

The road up to Braeside was lovely. It followed the cliffs for a mile out of town, and the big car swept around the curves with a whine of delight. By the time the road veered inland, following the river, she had its measure, and was glorying in being in control of the most magnificent piece of machinery she'd ever seen.

'Nice, huh?' Guy said, five minutes into the drive, and she flashed him a guilty look. She'd been so absorbed in her driving that she'd almost forgotten he was there. Almost.

'It's fantastic.'

'You get this wedding working for me and you can keep it.'

She almost crashed. She took a deep breath, straightened the wheel, and tried to remember where she was.

'Don't be ridiculous.'

'I'm not being ridiculous. I'll merely pay my friend out. It's not like it's a new car.'

'It's not like it's a new car,' she said, mocking. 'No, thank you, Mr Carver. My salary is stipulated in the contract. I'll take that, but that's all. I'd be obliged to you for ever, and I've had obligations up to my neck. So leave it.'

He left it. There were another few moments of silence while Jenny negotiated a few more curves. It was so wonderful that she could almost block Guy out—and his preposterous offer.

'Feels great, doesn't it?' he said, and she was forced to smile.

'It's magic.'

'Yet you don't want it?'

'I couldn't afford the trip to Sydney to get this serviced,' she told him. 'Much less the service itself. Leave it alone.'

'I'm not used to having my gifts knocked back.'

'Get used to it.'

'Jenny…'

'I'm not for sale, Guy,' she said roughly. 'And don't interfere with my life. I intend to do these two weddings and then get out of your business for ever. You'll go back to Manhattan and live your glamorous life, a thousand miles from mine—'

'What do you know about my life?' he said, startled, and she screwed up her nose in rueful mockery.

'I've spent the last two years in doctors' waiting rooms.'

'So?'

'So I reckon I've read every issue of *Celebrity* magazine that's ever been printed. With you being rich and influential, and associated with every celebrity bash worthy of the name, your life is fair game. I know how rich you are. I know you don't like oysters and you never wear navy suits. I also know you were in a car crash with your childhood sweetheart about fifteen years ago. Her father and your father were partners. She'd been at your parents' company Christmas dinner alone, and then she'd collected you from some celebrity bash you'd been organising. She was killed outright. Your parents disowned you then. They said she'd been drinking because she was angry. They said if you'd stayed in the family law firm like you were supposed to it would never have happened. And you... The glossies say you're still grieving for your lost love. Are you?'

'No,' he said, stunned.

'I hope you're not.' She took a deep breath, deciding whether to be personal or not. What the heck? 'It's hard,' she confided. 'Ben's only been dead for two years, but you know, my photographs of Ben are starting to be clearer than the image I hold in my head. I hate that. Are you better at it than me? Can you remember...what was her name? Or do you only remember photographs?'

'It was Christa,' he said, in a goaded voice. 'I can't imagine why you'd be interested enough to read about us.'

'I wasn't very,' she admitted. 'It was just something to read in the waiting room—something to take my mind off what was happening to Henry. But I remember thinking it was crazy, wearing the willow for someone for fifteen years.'

'So how long do *you* intend to wear the willow for Ben?'

'I'm not.'

'You're living with his parents.'

'That's because they've become my parents,' she said. 'Sometimes I wonder whether I fell in love with Ben himself or if I fell in love with the whole concept of family. Like you tonight, looking round the dining table and looking...hungry.'

'I didn't,' he said, revolted. 'Can we leave it with the inquisition?'

'Sure,' she said, and she thought maybe she had pushed it too far. This man was supposed to be her boss. She should be being a bit deferential. Subservient.

He didn't make her feel subservient. He made her feel...

She didn't understand how he made her feel. She tried to conjure Ben up in her mind. Kind, gentle Ben, who'd loved her so well.

'It's tough,' he said into the stillness, and she wondered what he was talking about. 'The first Christmas was the worst, but it's still bad,' he added, and she knew he knew.

'It's okay.'

'But it's tough.'

'I've got thirteen years before I catch up to you in the mourning stakes,' she snapped, and turned the car into the front yard of Braeside. 'Here's your guesthouse.'

It was a fabulous spot, Guy thought, staring around with appreciation. The moon was glinting through bushland to the river beyond, hanging low in the eastern sky over the distant sea. The guesthouse was a sprawling weatherboard home, with vast verandas all around.

'I've heard it's sumptuous,' Jenny said, climbing out of the car to stretch her legs.

'You've never been inside?'

'The likes of me? I'd be shown out by security guards.'

'I'm sorry about Paris.'

'I shouldn't have told you about Paris.' She hesitated while he hauled his gear from the trunk. 'Are you serious about me driving this thing home? You realise it'll be parked near chooks.'

'Chooks?'

'Feathery things that lay eggs.'

'Park it as far away as possible,' Guy said, sounding nervous.

'Okay. I was just teasing. I might even find a tarpaulin. I'll collect you tomorrow at nine, then. With or without chook poo.'

'Fine,' he said. He turned away. But then he hesitated.

'Thank you for tonight,' he said. 'And we really will give Kylie a great wedding.'

'I know we will.' She trusted him, she thought. She wasn't sure why, but she did.

But suddenly she didn't trust herself.

She should get into the driver's seat, she told herself. Guy needed to walk away.

But then…and why, she didn't know…it was as if things changed. The night changed.

'Jenny?' he said uncertainly.

'I know,' she said, but she didn't know anything. Except that he was going to kiss her and she was going to let him.

She could have pulled back. He was just as uncertain as she was—or maybe he was just as certain.

He dropped his holdall. Moving very slowly, he reached out and caught her hands, tugging her towards him. She allowed herself to be tugged. Maybe she didn't need his propulsion.

'Thank you for dinner,' he said, and she thought, *He's making this seem like a fleeting kiss of courtesy.* Though both of them knew it was no such thing.

'You're welcome,' she whispered.

His lips brushed hers, a feather touch—a question and not an answer.

'You're very welcome,' she said again as he drew back—and suddenly she was being kissed properly, thoroughly, wonderfully.

She'd forgotten…or maybe she'd never known this heat. This feeling of melting into a man and losing control, just like that. There was warmth spreading throughout her limbs. A lovely, languorous warmth that had her feeling that her world was changing, right there and then, and it could never be the same again.

She kissed him back, demanding as much as he was demanding of her. Tasting him. Savouring the feel of his wonderful male body under her hands. Guy Carver…

Guy Carver.

This was crazy.

She, Jenny Westmere, mother of Henry, wife of Ben… To kiss this man…

She was out of her mind. Panicked, she shoved her hands between her breast and his chest, pushing him away.

He released her at once. He tried to take her hands but she'd have none of it. She was three feet away from him now. Four.

'No.'

'No?' His eyes were gently questioning. Not laughing. She couldn't have borne it if he was laughing. 'No, Jenny?'

'I only kiss my husband,' she said, and the words made perfect sense to her, even if they didn't to him.

But it appeared he understood. 'You're not being unfaithful, Jenny. It was only a kiss.'

Only a kiss? Then why was her world spinning?

'I'm not some easy country hick…'

'I never thought you were.'

'You're here until Christmas. Will we see you again after that?'

'Probably not.'

'We're ships passing in the night.' She took a deep breath and steadied. 'So maybe we'd better do just that—pass.'

'I'm not into relationships,' he said, not even smiling. 'I'm not about to mess with your tidy life.'

'My life's not very tidy,' she confessed. 'But thank you. Now…I think I'd better go home.'

'You're brave enough to drive the Ferrari by yourself?'

'Something tells me it'd be far more dangerous to stay here with you,' she muttered. 'But I'll pick you up in the morning. As long as you promise not to kiss me again.'

'You want me to promise?'

'Yes, I do,' she said, and if her voice sounded desperate she couldn't help it.

'I won't kiss you again. I know a mistake when I see one.'

'I'm a mistake?'

'Absolutely,' he told her. 'This whole place is a mistake. I should leave now.'

ONLY OF COURSE he didn't. He couldn't. He booked into the fantastic guesthouse he'd been delivered to. He rang Malcolm in New York and confirmed that there was no one who could get here on short notice to take over organisation.

'Scooping the Barret and Anna wedding is fabulous, though.' Malcolm was chortling. 'Every bride in Australia will want you after this. It's just as well you're there to do it hands-on. You'll use the local staff? Great. Make sure you don't mess up.'

The local staff? Guy thought of what he had to build on— Jenny and, by the sound of it, a crew of geriatrics—and he almost groaned.

'It's the best publicity we could think of,' Malcolm said jovially. 'I'll manage the Film Conglomerate do. We're fine.'

Only they weren't. Or he wasn't. Guy lay in the sumptuous four-poster bed that night, listening to owls in the bushland outside, and wondered what he was getting into.

He didn't know, and he didn't want to find out.

AND FIVE MILES away Jenny was feeling exactly the same.

When she got back to the farmhouse Henry was asleep and Lorna and Jack were filling hot water bottles from the kitchen kettle.

'Did you have a nice ride, dear?' Lorna asked, and for the life of her Jenny couldn't keep her face under control. Lorna watched her daughter-in-law, her eyes twinkling.

'He seems very…personable,' she said, speaking to no one in particular, and Jenny knew her mother-in-law was getting ideas which were ridiculous.

They *were* ridiculous.

She scowled at her in-laws and went to bed. But not to sleep. She stared at the ceiling for hours, and then flicked on the lamp and stared at the picture on her bedside table. Her lovely Ben, who'd brought her into this wonderful family, who'd given her Henry.

'I love you, Ben,' she whispered, but he didn't answer. If he was here he'd just smile and then hug her.

She ached to be hugged.

By Ben?

'Yes, by Ben,' she told the night. 'Guy Carver has been here for less than twenty-four hours. He's an international jet-setter with megabucks. He kissed me tonight because I'll bet that's what international jet-setters do. He's your boss, Jennifer Westmere. You need to maintain a dignified employer-employee relationship. Don't stuff it up. And don't let him kiss you again.

'He won't want to.

'He might.'

She wasn't sure who she was arguing with. If anyone could hear they'd think she was crazy.

'Ben,' she whispered, and lifted the frame from the bed-side table and kissed it.

She turned off the lamp and remembered the kiss.

Not Ben's kiss.

The kiss of Guy Carver.

CHAPTER FOUR

JENNY arrived at Guy's guesthouse the next morning wearing clothing that said very clearly she was there to work. Plain white shirt, knee-length skirt, plain sandals. Guy emerged dressed in fawn chinos, a lovely soft green polo shirt with a tiny white yacht embroidered on the chest—Jenny bet it had to be the logo of the world's most exclusive yacht club—and faded loafers. He looked at what Jenny was wearing and stopped dead.

'The Carver corporation has a dress code,' he said.

'What's wrong with this?'

'It's frumpy.' It was, too. In fact, Jenny had worked quite hard to find it. There'd been an international lawn-bowls meet in Sandpiper Bay two years ago, and she'd helped organise the catering. The dress code for that had meant she'd had to go out and buy this sophisticated little outfit, and she hadn't worn it since.

'It's my usual work wear,' she lied. 'Yesterday I was too casual.'

'We were both too casual,' he agreed, and she blushed.

Right. Get on with it.

'So where do you want to start?'

'I've come here to plan the refurbishment of the salon.'

'That's important. But there's the little manner of two weddings…'

'Leave the planning to me,' he said, and she subsided into what she hoped was dignified silence. She was this man's employee.

He'd kissed her. She should forget all about that kiss. She should...

Let's not aim at the stars here, she told herself. Let's just be a good little employee and put the memory of that kiss on the backburner.

But not very far back.

HE WAS OUT of his depth.

They'd purchased three salons so far in this round of expansion. In each of those, Guy had visited early, taken note of the features of the building as they were, then brought his notes back to his cool grey office in Manhattan and drawn them up as he'd like them to be. With plans prepared, he'd sent a team of professionals to do his bidding, and six months later they'd opened as a Carver Salon.

Now, thanks to Lorna's indiscretion, the Carver name would be used before he could leave his imprint.

He had to get rid of the fluff, and fast. Instead of sitting down, calmly planning for the future, he was trying to figure how he could get this place clear so if the media arrived to see the latest Carver Salon they'd see something worthy of the name. How to transform fluff to elegance in a week?

And how to ignore Jenny, sitting silently at her desk? She sat with her hands folded in front of her, a good little employee, waiting for instructions.

What was it about this woman that unnerved him?

Why was she so different?

He didn't do relationships. He didn't...

'Phone Kylie,' he said at last, goaded. 'Tell her she's having a Carver Wedding.'

'I already have,' she said meekly.

He was out of his depth. He needed help here.

'I need your assistance,' he snapped, and she nodded, ready to be helpful.

'Yes, sir.'

'Jenny...'

'Sir?'

'Will you cut it out?'

'Cut what out?'

'I don't know where the hell to start,' he confessed, and watched as she struggled to keep the expression on her face subservient.

'You're asking for my input?'

'I want some solid help here,' he told her. 'I assume you're not just the girl who mans the desk? You've been running this place on your own since Lorna's stroke.'

'But you're in charge. I'm waiting for orders.'

'We need to get a dumpster,' he said in exasperation. 'Something to get rid of this lot.'

'You have two weddings to organise before Christmas and you're planning to redecorate the salon?' she said cautiously.

'Right.' She lifted the phone. 'I'll order a dumpster.'

'Dresses,' he said, in increasing frustration. 'We need to organise a wedding dress and attendants' outfits.'

'They might take some time,' Jenny said, and started dialling.

He lifted the phone from her hand and crashed it down onto the cradle.

'If I don't get some solid help here I'll—'

'Sack me?' she said, and smiled.

Damn the woman. He knew she was competent. He wanted to take her shoulders and shake her.

He wanted to kiss her.

That thought wasn't helping things at all. His normally cool, calculating mind was clouded, and it was clouded because this woman was looking up at him with a strange, enigmatic smile.

This woman who was as far from his life as any woman he'd ever met. This woman who was up to her neck in emotional entanglements.

His employee.

He took a deep breath, turned, and paced the salon a couple of times, trying to clear his head. He knocked one of the bridal mannequins and spent a couple of minutes righting it.

He turned to Jenny and she was watching him, her eyes interested, her head to one side like an inquisitive sparrow.

Forget she's a woman, he told himself. And forget she's an employee. Let's get this onto some sort of even keel.

'Jenny, I'm out of my depth here,' he told her. 'I don't know where to start.'

She stilled. The faint smile on her face faded. He'd shocked her, he thought. Whatever she'd been expecting it hadn't been that.

There was a long silence.

She could keep up the play-acting, he thought. And she was definitely considering it. The role of subservient employee was a defence. He watched as indecision played on her face. Finally she broke. Her face was incredibly expressive, he thought. He saw the exact moment she put away the play-acting and decided to be up-front.

'Two weddings,' she said. 'The biggest problem is the dresses. We need to get things moving. There are three local women with the capacity to sew fast and well.'

'Contact them.'

'No.' She shook her head. 'They're all up to their ears in Christmas preparations.'

'Then what—?'

'There are a couple of oldies I know who love babysitting,' she said. 'They have very quiet Christmases, so they may be prepared to help. Jonas Bucket had an accident at work some years ago and is confined to a wheelchair. He loves Christmas cooking. So if I...'

'What are you talking about?' He was lost.

'Mary, Sarah and Leanne are my seamstresses,' she said patiently. 'Mary and Sarah have small kids, and Leanne's having eighteen people for Christmas dinner. If I ask them to sew for me they'll say no. But if I say I've already organised childminding and cooking and house-cleaning—and someone to set Leanne's table—then they'll jump at the chance to escape by sewing. Now...'

'Now what?' he said, stunned.

'You're the boss,' she said, 'but if I were you I'd sit down and write the menu for the Barret and Anna wedding. We need to get the food ordered right away. They've elected to do a Christmas theme, so we'll keep it like that. Roast turkey and all the trimmings.'

'For a sophisticated—?'

'She *did* say pink tulle,' Jenny said, though she sounded a bit less certain of her ground.

'So she did,' Guy said, thinking fast, and then looked up as the doorbell tinkled.

It was Kylie. She was dressed in pregnancy overalls with a white T-shirt underneath. With her face flushed with either nerves or excitement, and her blonde curls tied up in two pigtails, Guy decided she looked like one of those Russian Mazurka dolls. If you pushed her she'd topple over and then spring right up.

'Hi, Kylie,' Jenny said, and Guy winced. This woman was a client. His first Australian Carver Wedding...

'Mum just rang me,' Kylie said, with a nervous look aside at Guy. 'She says Mr Carver's agreed to do my wedding.'

'He has,' Jenny said. 'But there's no need to change your plans. We'll do your wedding exactly as we've planned it.'

'No,' said Kylie.

There was a moment's silence. 'No?' Jenny said at last, cautiously, and received a furious shake of her head in reply. 'You don't want a wedding?'

'Of course I want a wedding,' Kylie said. 'Me and Daryl are really excited. But...'

'But what?' Jenny asked.

'It's *Mum's* wedding,' she burst out. 'And Daryl's mum's. They've been at us for ever to get married, and of course we want to, but we didn't want this. We thought maybe we'd just have the baby and then go somewhere afterwards and get married quietly. But from the minute we told them we were expecting they've been at us and at us, until finally we cracked. And that dress... Mum had you make it for me when I was sixteen. She chose it. Not me. Every week since then Mum gets it out and pats it. Do you know how much I hate it?'

'No,' Jenny said, stunned.

'I can't tell you,' Kylie declared. 'But I loathe it. I would have gone along with it. Fine, I said to Daryl, whatever makes them happy. But when Mum rang and said I could have a Carver Wedding I thought suddenly, *A Carver Wedding!* I could maybe have it like I want. Elegant. Sleek. Sophisticated. Something so when our kids grow up they'll look at our wedding photos and think, Wow, just for a bit our parents weren't assistants in a butcher's shop. If you knew how much I hate pink tulle...'

'Your six bridesmaids are in pink tulle,' Jenny murmured.

'Exactly.' Kylie's colour was almost beetroot as she desperately tried to explain herself. 'It was bad enough when I was skinny, but now I'll look like a wall of cupids coming down the aisle, with a sea of pink tulle coming after.' She turned to Guy. 'They say in the fashion magazines that you can perform miracles. Get me out of cupids and pink tulle. Please.'

There was a deathly hush.

'We can't,' Jenny said at last. 'Kylie, the dresses are finished. There's less than a week to your wedding, and we have another enormous wedding to cater for on Christmas Day.'

The passion went out of Kylie like air out of a pricked balloon, and defeat took its place in an instant. She'd expected this, Guy thought. Her request had been one last stand, but defeat had been expected.

'That'll be for someone rich, I'll bet,' Kylie said, but it

wasn't said in anger. It was said as a fact, and there was a wealth of resignation in her voice. 'Someone who can afford any wedding she wants and who has enough guts to stand up for it.'

Guy looked suddenly at the girl's hands. They were scrubbed almost raw. There were jagged scars on two fingers.

'You work in a butcher's shop, Kylie?' he asked her, and Kylie bit her lip.

'Yeah. Morris's butchers next door. That's why I could come so quickly. But I should be back there now.'

'You'll work there after you're married?'

'Course I will,' she said. 'It's Daryl's dad's shop, and there's no way we can afford for me to stay home. We're having a week's honeymoon staying at Daryl's auntie's place. I'll have another week off when the baby's born. Then we'll set up a cot in the back.' She shook her head. 'Sorry. It was dumb to ask. I gotta get back.'

She sounded totally resigned, Guy thought. Accepting.

Jenny was watching him.

What had Kylie said when she first arrived? *They say in the fashion magazines that you can perform miracles.*

He couldn't perform miracles. Of course he couldn't. But...

'Anna wants pink tulle,' he said slowly, and Jenny nodded. She seemed...cautious.

'That's no problem. We can order more.'

'But Anna will be more than happy with a kitsch wedding,' he continued, thinking it through as he spoke. 'From the sound of the fax they sent me, kitsch is exactly what she wants. And Anna has six bridesmaids.'

'So?'

'So we swap,' he said, and his organisational mode slipped back into place, just like that.

Jenny's presence—Jenny herself—had somehow thrown him off course. He'd been feeling out of control since yesterday, but suddenly now he'd slipped back behind the wheel, knowing exactly where he was going.

'We'll take Kylie's wedding dress and bridesmaids' dresses and we'll alter them to fit Anna and her followers,' he said. 'Jenny, you said you have three dressmakers ready to go? Let's get the measurements and get them started. Kylie, your bridesmaids...'

'Mmm?' She was staring, open-mouthed. 'What's kitsch?' she said.

'What your wedding was, and what it won't be any more,' he said. 'My alternative bride and her friends will think it's fun. It's fun when you're not forced into it. Do your bridesmaids all have little black dresses? The sort of thing you wear when you want to be elegant?'

'Course,' Kylie whispered, not seeing where he was going. 'I mean, everyone has to have a black dress. For when you dunno what else to wear.'

'Would they be upset to lose the pink tulle?'

'You have to be kidding. They hate pink tulle as much as I do. Two of them are my sisters, and three of them are Daryl's sisters, so they have to do what our mums say. The other one's my best friend, and Doreen says the pink tulle makes her look like a Kewpie doll.'

'Right,' Guy said. 'Let's go for an elegant Christmas theme. Deep crimson and a rich, dark green.'

'Seven dresses?' Jenny said faintly.

'Six bridesmaids in their lovely black dresses. It means they won't have to spend a cent, and they'll have already chosen something that looks great on them. There'll be no one-style-suits-all disasters. They'll wear their hair sleek and elegant—up if it's long, in sophisticated chignons, or if it's short I'll arrange really good cuts. I'll do it myself if need be. Black strappy shoes. The only colour about them will be a beautiful crimson and green corsage. That'll bring in a tiny Christmas theme, which seems appropriate at this time of the year. I'll get onto a Sydney florist this afternoon and organise the best.'

'What about me?' Kylie whispered. 'And the men?'

'Gangster-style suits and hats,' Guy decreed. 'We'll hire them from Sydney or fly them from New York. What do you think?'

'Gangsters?' Kylie said, the beginnings of anticipation curving the sides of her mouth into a smile. 'Hats and braces and white shoes?'

'You've got it.'

'Daryl will love it.'

Guy smiled. 'Great. And you…' He looked at Kylie for a long minute while Jenny watched in dumbfounded silence. 'Kylie, let's not try to disguise your pregnancy. Let's be proud of it. I'm thinking pure white shot silk—Jenny, can we get shot silk?'

'Sure,' Jenny said, dazed.

'A really simple dress,' Guy said. 'Shoestring straps and a low sweetheart neckline that accentuates those gorgeous breasts.' Kylie started to blush, but he wasn't distracted. He'd grabbed the pad beside the phone and was sketching. 'Like this. Practically bare to the breasts. Softly curving into your waist, accentuating the swell of pregnancy, curving in again, and then falling with a side slit from your thigh to your ankles. I bet you have great legs.'

Kylie was staring at the sketch, entranced. 'Daryl says…' She subsided. 'Yeah,' she whispered. 'My legs are…okay.' The sketch was growing under Guy's hands and she couldn't stop watching. 'Wow. That even looks like me. What are you doing to my hair?'

'Piling it up in a thousand tiny curls on top of your head,' he said. 'The simplicity of your bridesmaids' hair will accentuate yours. We'll thread the same crimson and green though your hair—just a little. You'll carry a tiny bouquet of fern and crimson rosebuds. And if you want…'

'Wh-what?' she stammered.

'We'll thread tiny silver imitation pistols through the ribbon of your bouquet. You're a gangster's moll. This is a shotgun wedding and you've got your man.'

Kylie stared. Jenny stared. Then, as one, they burst out laughing.

'My mum will hate it,' Kylie said when she finally recovered.

'It's a Carver Wedding. Take it or leave it.'

'Oh, I'll take it,' Kylie whispered, smiling now through the beginning of unshed tears. 'Yes, please.'

'YOU'RE A MAGICIAN.' Kylie had left them to spread her news. Guy was left with Jenny, who was staring at him as if he'd grown two heads.

'I'm no magician,' he said, but he was aware of a tinge of pleasure. It was a pleasure he hadn't felt for a long time. And...was there also a tinge of excitement? He wanted to do this well, he thought, and when he tried to figure out why he knew that it had little to do with the reputation of the Carver empire. It was all to do with making Jenny smile.

And he had made her smile. She was definitely smiling.

'I need to organise cars,' he said, trying to move on.

'There are limousines booked.'

'Limousines won't do. Transfer that booking to Anna's, if you can. For Kylie we need to get Buicks, or something similar. We'll take the theme right through.'

'We'll never get them locally.'

'I'll try Sydney.'

'Kylie can't afford—'

'We'll cover the cost ourselves,' he said. 'As the first Australian Carver Wedding, it'll more than pay for itself in publicity. As for dress, we've done gangster-type weddings in my other salons, so gear shouldn't be a problem. I'll fly in costumes for the waiting staff.' He paused. 'I assume you have staff booked?'

'Of course I have staff booked,' she said, incensed. 'This wedding is planned down to the last pew ribbon.'

'We'll use some of those resources for the Anna and Barret wedding. We'll design the wedding for Kylie from scratch, and use the basis of Kylie's for Anna's. It'll work. I'll need to paint sets for the gangster setting. I'll see if we can get a smoke machine from Sydney.'

'A smoke machine…'

'It creates the haze without the health risk. I should have everyone smoking either cigars or Gauloise, but I'll bet you have laws preventing it.'

'We do.'

'There you go, then. A smoke machine it is. Now, let's look at these dresses and see if any of them might fit without alterations.'

'You're good,' she said, on a note of discovery, and Guy stopped making lists and glanced up at her.

'You're surprised?'

'You said you could even cut hair?'

'There's nothing I haven't been landed with in the years I've been building this business. I know my stuff, Jenny. I wouldn't be here if I didn't.' He smiled at her look of scepticism. 'You don't need to worry,' he said softly. 'We'll look after Kylie. The first Australian Carver Wedding will go off with a bang.'

'It surely will,' she said, awed, and then suddenly, as if she couldn't help herself, she slipped out from behind the counter, took two steps forward and kissed him.

It was nothing like the kiss they'd shared last night. It was a kiss of gratitude, nothing more, and why it had the capacity to make him feel as if his feet weren't quite on the ground he couldn't say.

'You're making Kylie happy,' she said softly. 'Thank you.'

'Think nothing of it,' he said, or he tried to say it, but the words weren't quite there. He was staring at Jenny as if…

He didn't know what.

This wasn't the type of woman that attracted him.

He hadn't exactly been celibate since Christa had died. What had Jenny said? *It was crazy, wearing the willow for someone for fifteen years.* He hadn't. Or maybe he had, but only in the sense that he never got emotionally involved. Where relationships went he used his head and not his heart. It did his firm's reputation good if he was seen with A-listers on his arm. He chose glamorous women who could make him laugh, but who knew commitment was neither wanted nor expected.

But Jenny…

She was dressed like a prim secretary. Like a repressed old maid. Like something she wasn't. He knew she wasn't. Because otherwise why would his body be screaming that it wanted this woman—*he* wanted this woman?

She was a complication, he told himself desperately, and he'd spent his entire adult life making sure that he had as few complications in his life as possible.

'I need to go check the facilities at Anna's property,' he said, and if he sounded brusque he couldn't help it.

She grabbed her bag. 'It's in the hills, north of town.'

'I'll find it,' he said, and she hesitated and then put her bag down again.

'You want me to stay here?'

'Yes.'

'Fine.' Back to being subservient. 'I'll make lists of what's needed.' She hesitated. 'That is, if you want me to?'

'I want you to.'

'Fine.'

What was it between them? What was this…thing? It felt like some sort of magnetic charge, with both of them hauling away from it.

'Fine,' he repeated, and he left—but some important part of him stayed behind. And he couldn't for the life of him think what it was.

CHAPTER FIVE

THEY worked brilliantly as a team—apart.

For the next few days plans for the two weddings proceeded as swiftly as for any function Guy had organised in Manhattan. Most of it was down to Jenny. Guy just had to hint at a suggestion and she had it organised. She seemed to know every last person in a twenty-mile radius of Sandpiper Bay. He needed oysters? She knew the couple who leased the best oyster beds. He wanted lobsters? She knew the fisherman. Fantastic greens? Her husband's best friend had a hydroponic set-up where they could get wonderful produce straight from the grower.

Jenny wrote out a menu for Anna's wedding, and when Guy read it he grinned. It was inspired. Yabbies, prawns, oysters, lobsters, scallops—seafood to die for, and all in enough quantities to make their overseas guests drool. After the main courses the menu became even more Australian—pavlovas with strawberries and cream, lamingtons, ginger fluff sponges, chocolate éclairs, vanilla slices, lashings of home-made berry ice-cream, bowls and bowls of fresh berries...

Guy thought of how much this would cost in New York, and then he looked at the figures Jenny had prepared and blinked—and then he thought he'd charge New York prices anyway. It would mean he could put more into Kylie's wedding. He could employ a really excellent band...

But this was all discussed by phone. Guy had left Sandpiper Bay to make a sweep of Sydney suppliers. The time away let him clear his head. In truth, the day he'd tried to find

Anna's property he'd become thoroughly lost. He'd got back to the salon flustered and late, and Jenny had merely raised her brows in gentle mockery and not said a word. She'd known very well what had happened, he thought, and he didn't like it. He didn't like it that she could read him.

So he'd gone to Sydney. He wasn't escaping, he thought. It was merely that things needed to be organised in Sydney.

On Monday, three days before Kylie's wedding, five days before Christmas, he returned.

The beach was crowded—summer was at its peak and there were surfing-types everywhere.

Bridal Fluff was closed.

What had he expected? he asked himself. Jenny had told him things were going well. And besides, he didn't want to see her.

Did he?

He let himself into Bridal Fluff. There was a typed list on the desk, of everything that had to be done for the two weddings, with a neat tick beside everything that had been done.

She was good.

He didn't want to think about how good she was.

He drove back to his guesthouse, dumped his gear and made his way disconsolately down to the lobby. He needed something to do. Anything. Even if it was just to stop him thinking about Jenny.

Especially if it was to make him stop thinking about Jenny.

'You should go to the beach,' the guesthouse proprietor told him. 'It's a wonderful day for a swim.'

'I need to—' he started, and then thought, No, he didn't need to do anything. 'The beach looks crowded.'

'That's just the front beach,' his host told him. 'There's no need to be crowded at Sandpiper Bay. All the kids go to the front beach. They say the surfing's better there, but in truth it's just become the place to be seen. And being so near Christmas there'll be lots of out-of-towners coming for picnics. Family parties and such. If you want a quiet beach, I can draw you a map showing you Nautilus Cove, which has to be one of the most perfect swimming places in Australia.'

So ten minutes later he was in the car, heading south for a swim.

There were two cars at the side of the road when he pulled up—expensive off-roaders—and he was paranoid enough to be thankful they weren't Jenny's. 'There might be a couple of locals there,' he'd been told. 'But they won't mind sharing.'

Actually, *he* did mind sharing, but it was a bit much to expect to have the beach to himself. And two cars hardly made a crowd.

There were a few empty beer cans by the side of the road. That gave him pause for a moment. In this environmentally friendly shire, roadside litter was cleared almost as soon as it happened. Were the owners of the off-roaders drinking?

No matter. He could handle himself. He just wanted a quick swim. He tossed his towel over his shoulders and strode beachwards. As he topped the sand hill, the cove stretched out before him, breathtakingly beautiful. Golden sand, gentle surf, sapphire sea. There was a group of youths at the far end of the beach—the off-roaders' occupants? Surely not, he thought, frowning. They looked too young to be driving such expensive cars. Someone was yelling. It looked a small but intimidating group of youths. Drunken teenagers showing off to each other?

He didn't want trouble, and they looked like trouble. He'd find another beach.

But then he hesitated. A figure broke from the group. Someone shoved and the figure stumbled. There was raucous laughter, cruel and jeering.

Someone was in trouble. They were a few hundred yards from him, and it was hard to see. But then... He focussed. It was a woman, he thought, and the woman seemed to be carrying a child. She took a few more steps towards him.

Jenny.

She was trudging through the soft sand, carrying Henry. Henry was clinging to her, his face buried in her shoulder, as the taunts followed them.

'Get the hell off our beach!' they yelled. 'Take your deformed kid with you.' A beer can hurtled through the air. It didn't hit Jenny, but it hadn't landed before Guy was hurtling down the slope as if the hounds of hell were after him.

Jenny.

She was carrying a bag which looked a load in itself. She was concentrating on putting one foot in front of another, making sure she kept her balance in the soft sand. She didn't see him approach, every fibre of her being concentrating on getting off the beach—fast.

He reached her and put out his hands and stopped her. She flinched backwards.

'Jenny.'

She looked up at him, her face pale and gaunt, but as she saw who it was relief washed over her. She almost sagged. 'G…Guy. Get us out of here,' she stammered.

Another beer can headed in their direction. 'You're not moving fast enough,' someone yelled from the group. 'Hey, mister, keep away from them. The kid's a mutant.'

'Go,' Guy said urgently, and put his body between her and the barrage of cans and foul language. If he could have picked her up and carried her he would have, but picking up Jenny and Henry *and* their gear was a bit much even for someone with superhero aspirations. 'Go on up to the road,' he told her. 'Get to my car and wait for me.'

'But—'

'Go.' He tugged his cellphone from his belt. 'It's 000 for emergency here, isn't it?'

'Yes, but—'

'Go.'

She went. She didn't have a choice.

He stood his ground and dialled, and two seconds later he had a response. He stood facing the teenagers and spoke into the phone, loudly and firmly. Loud enough for them to hear.

'There's a group of what looks like under-aged drinkers on Nautilus Cove,' he told the officer who'd answered his call. 'I'm guessing they've been driving drunk, and none of them look old enough to hold a driving licence. Their cars look expensive. The kids' average age is about sixteen, so I'm guessing the cars are stolen. They're throwing beer cans at a woman and child on the beach. It's ugly.'

'We'll have someone there in minutes, sir,' the operator said. 'Can you stay on the line?'

'Sure. You'll hear everything that goes on.' Ten or eleven youths were staring at him now, with the uncertainty that stemmed from being drunk and out of control and seeing someone acting *in* control. They could turn on him, he thought, but he had a window of opportunity to stop that happening. They didn't know who he was, he sounded authoritative, and they were too drunk to act fast.

'If those cars are stolen,' he said, loudly but calmly, 'then you all have a major problem. The police are on their way. You can stay and get arrested, or you can go now.'

They stared at him in silence, drunk and still aggressive, but obviously trying to think. One took a menacing step forward.

Guy didn't budge. His face stayed impassive. 'The road into this beach is a one-lane track,' he said, conversationally, as though informing them of something important they should have remembered. 'If you try and drive out, you'll meet the police coming in. They'll block your way.'

There was a further uneasy silence. Then, 'Hey, Jake, I'm off.' One of the kids at the back of the group sounded suddenly scared. 'It's my old man's car. If I'm found in it I'll be grounded for years. As far as I'm concerned *you* pinched it. Not me.' He turned and stumbled away, half-running, half-walking, heading northwards along the beach. Around the headland were more beaches and bushland, where maybe he could hide himself and then head home to be innocent when his father found the car missing.

'Geez, Jake, my old man'll do the same,' another said, already backing and starting to run. 'Mac—wait up.'

'But you guys've got the keys,' Jake yelled, and hurled another can after his retreating mates.

Some of the other kids were backing away now. Half seemed inclined to stay with Jake. The others seemed inclined to run.

'We're on our way,' the policeman said on the other end of the phone line, and Guy nodded and held the phone helpfully out towards the kids.

'The police are on their way. This officer says so. He'd like to talk to you. Jake?'

'Go to hell,' Jake yelled.

'Is that Jake Marny?' the officer asked.

'I'll ask him,' Guy said, and held out the phone again. 'He says are you Jake Marny?'

'Geez—he knows us. The cops know us,' one of the kids yelled, panic supplanting aggression in an instant. And that was enough for them all. They were stumbling away, heading after the first two boys. For a long moment Jake stared at Guy, murder in his eyes, but it was the drink, Guy thought. Underneath, Jake was nothing but a belligerent kid—and a kid alone now, as his friends deserted him. He picked up another can and hurled it, but he didn't have his heart in it.

'What will you do, Jake?' Guy said, and Jake turned and found all his mates had gone without him.

He turned and ran.

The police arrived before Guy had made it up to where he'd parked his car. He told them what had happened, briefly and succinctly, and left them to it. They'd radioed in the registrations of the cars as soon as they saw them. They knew the kids.

'You'll take care of Mrs Westmere and Henry?' they asked.

'Sure,' he told them, and headed up the track to find them.

They'd reached his car. Jenny was leaning back on the bonnet, still hugging Henry, her face buried in his hair.

'Jenny?'

She looked up, and he saw that her face was rigid with tension and with anger. She was fighting back tears.

The little boy was huddled against her, and clinging. His body language was despairing.

Guy had never had anything much to do with children. He'd met Malcolm's kids, beautifully dressed and with precocious social manners. He was godparent to their youngest, and sometimes he even took them gifts.

'Thank Mr Carver,' their father would say, and the appropriate child would smile.

'Thank you, Mr Carver. This is a cool present.'

They were well-trained, well-adjusted kids, with two solid parents and all the advantages in the world.

But this mite… He was too thin. He was wearing some sort of elastic wrap on one of his legs and around his chest. His face was scarred and it was creased with crying. But now he faced Guy with the same sort of determination Guy saw in his mother. He wouldn't show the world he was upset. He blinked back tears and gulped.

Guy's heart twisted. This had nothing to do with how he felt about Jenny. Here was a whole host of other emotions.

He didn't get involved.

Too late. He looked from Jenny's face to Henry's and back again, and he was so involved he knew that from this minute on nothing would be the same again.

'Tell me what happened,' he said, and something about his voice made Jenny's face change. Her defences slipped a little.

'We were going to have a picnic,' she whispered, and he

reached forward and took the basket from her grasp. It suddenly seemed to be unbearably heavy. He would have liked to take Henry, too, but Henry was clinging to his mother as if he'd never let go. 'Jack's been delivering Christmas presents. He dropped us off at one, and was going to pick us up at three. But...'

'But?'

'But I reckoned without Henry's scarring,' she whispered. 'Those kids... They arrived about fifteen minutes after we did. They were dreadful—weren't they, Henry?'

'What happened?'

Jenny shook her head, but Henry, surprisingly, took over. 'We had a ball,' he said. 'Mummy threw it to me and I missed it, and it rolled along the beach and ended up near one of the men's beer cans. When I went to get it he said I was deformed. He said, "Get lost, you ugly, deformed little s..."'

Henry's words were spoken almost exactly as he'd heard them. Guy heard the vindictiveness in the child's bleak recital, and he flinched. He tried to find his voice but it wasn't there. There weren't words.

He wanted to—

'Don't,' Jenny whispered, and he knew she was reading the primitive desire that was starting to build—to launch himself back down the beach and punch Jake and his mates until they bled.

It would achieve...nothing. And the police were there. They'd be taken care of.

'Why do you think they said that?' he said at last. He didn't recognise his voice. He didn't recognise his feelings. Dumb fury and more...

'I don't know,' Henry whispered.

'I don't know, either.' He was fighting desperately for the right words here. For any words at all. 'It surely isn't because you're deformed, Henry. You're wearing an elastic bandage and you have a couple of manly scars. That doesn't make you deformed.'

'The boy kicked me.'

'He was probably jealous,' Guy said, swallowing his anger with a huge effort.

He set Jenny's picnic basket on the ground and hauled it open, inspecting its contents with a critical eye. It gave him something to do. Independent or not, afraid of relationships or not, he wanted to hug them and hold them close, but he knew they'd accept no such gesture. And such a gesture wouldn't help. Nor would violence. He had to come up with something better.

'I thought so,' he said, feeling his way. 'There's pink lemonade in here. And *great* food. They only had beer. Jealousy makes people say funny things. Do you think that's it?'

'I don't know,' Henry said, staring down at the pink lemonade. 'That's silly.'

'Not as silly as calling you names.' Guy took a deep breath and turned his back to them both. 'When people have been angry about things they've called *me* names, too. A lady burst into tears at a swimming pool once. She called me a poor thing. She was stupid. I'm not a poor thing at all. Take a look at this.'

He tugged his shirt over his head, baring his back. They'd be seeing the myriad of scars running down the left side of his body. He heard Jenny's intake of breath and he winced. The last thing he wanted was sympathy, but this was the only thing he could think of to do.

His scars were a bleak reminder of the night Christa had been killed. She'd been speeding in her father's Maserati and she had been furious. 'Why can't you be a lawyer?' she'd screamed. 'I refuse to be married to some dope who organises tinpot weddings and doesn't have any money to even pay for a decent car. You drive a van with a wedding logo on it. I'll be damned if I'm ever seen in it.'

She'd slammed her foot on the accelerator, making the point that the van he drove could never be as fast as this. Guy could still see the truck in front of them, the driver's face frozen in horror as their car slid on black ice, over to the wrong side of the road, straight into him. They'd hit almost broadside, killing Christa instantly and throwing shards of splintering metal into his side.

He'd learned not to hate his scars, but until now he'd never been grateful.

'Would you call *me* deformed?' he asked Henry, his tone carefully neutral.

'You've been cut,' Henry whispered.

'And you've been burned. Most people start out as babies with no marks on them, but as interesting things happen they get marked. We all get marked from life. Somewhere I read that the native people in Australia deliberately make scars on their chests to show they're grown up. I think the more marks you have on you, the more interesting you become.' He smiled at the little boy, searching for a response. 'So you and me, Henry…we're really interesting. And drunk people, stupid people, get jealous. Or sad that they're not mature. Those guys on the beach were stupid kids who'd drunk too much. They'll be sick soon, and they'll go to sleep and wake up with a headache, and then they'll know they've been dumb and they've been wrong. But meanwhile we should enjoy our day.'

Enough. He'd made his point. Now he needed to lighten up. 'Hey, there's more here than pink lemonade,' he said, turning back to the basket. 'Do you have enough picnic for me, too?'

'Yes,' said Henry.

Jenny was doing a lot of silent blinking.

He glanced back to the beach, where a couple of the youths had been caught before they'd disappeared round the headland. He could see glimpses of them though the trees—police and kids. The kids were gesticulating wildly after their mates.

They needed to leave here, he thought. He didn't want any

more invective as the police brought the kids up to the cars. 'Are there any more beaches around here, Jenny?' he asked.

'There's another cove about a mile south,' she managed, in a voice that was none too steady. 'But…we haven't got a car.'

'So it's the Ferrari,' Guy said, and grinned. 'Three people and a picnic basket in a Ferrari? We need to squash. And we need to leave now, before we have police watching. I think what I intend to do might be just a little illegal. But desperate times call for desperate measures.'

'Everyone in your car?' Henry said, brightening immediately. 'Now?'

'Absolutely now,' Guy said, with a lot more certainty than he was feeling. 'Let's go.'

So INDEPENDENT, ALOOF Guy Carver had a family picnic. Jenny couldn't believe it. She'd seen this man in celebrity magazines. She'd never dreamed he could be…human.

But human he was. From squashing them all into his Ferrari, from helping her to put on suncream, from making sand bombs…

He was more than human. She thought of the gift he'd given Henry by showing him his scarred back and the tears kept welling. Such a gift was beyond value. Henry had been given back his pride.

But she couldn't say anything. Guy was acting as if the whole ugly incident hadn't happened, and so must she.

They ate lunch, and Henry chattered about anything and everything, a contented six-year-old having a blissful day out with a man who drove a Ferrari and had life scars. What a hero. She watched as Guy spoke to him man to man, and her son's dreadful day disappeared to nothing and hero-worship took its place.

She didn't blame Henry. She was getting pretty close to hero-worship herself.

Guy lent her his cellphone. She contacted Jack to tell him

Guy would be bringing them home, so not to worry about collecting them. Then they spent a couple of hours in the shallows, teaching Henry to float. The little boy hadn't spent much time in the water since his accident and he was nervous. Up until now Jenny hadn't persuaded him to put his face under water, but he'd do anything Guy asked. By mid-afternoon he was floating, kicking his scarred little legs, taking a brief gasp of air and floating again.

'I'm swimming,' he gasped, exultant, lit with happiness, and Jenny had to do a whole heap of blinking all over again.

Finally he was exhausted. Guy carried him up the beach and towelled him dry while Jenny packed the picnic gear. They loaded everything once more into the Ferrari, and Guy drove home with Henry's legs on his knee, picnic gear covering Jenny and a liberal supply of sand coating everything.

'Every Ferrari should look like this,' Jenny said, squashed and happy. 'It's perfect.'

'It is,' Guy said, and smiled at her, and Jenny felt her heart flip and flip again.

She was so close...

Don't, she told herself fiercely. This man is not of your world. He is nothing to do with you. He just happens to be wonderful right now.

But not tomorrow?

Then they were pulling into the farm and Jack was limping down the steps to greet them, looking worried.

'There's been news about trouble with some kids on the beach,' Jack growled. 'Jenny, the police rang and say they want a statement from you. What happened? What's wrong?'

'Nothing's wrong,' Jenny said quickly. 'Something's right. Mr Carver taught Henry to swim.'

'I can swim, Grandpa,' Henry said sleepily. 'I can really, really swim, and Mr Carver says one day I'll be a champion.'

'You're a champion already,' Jack said gruffly, and lifted his grandson out of the car. He looked from Jenny to Guy, and then looked at his little grandson. His mouth twisted. Maybe the police had told him what had happened, Jenny thought, but he had the sense to let it go.

'Mother, Mr Carver's taught our Henry to swim,' Jack boomed, and Lorna waved her delight from the veranda.

'How wonderful. Mr Carver, what are you doing for Christmas?'

'It's Guy,' Guy said. 'And we're putting on a wedding on Christmas Day.'

'But not until late,' Lorna called. 'Christmas dinner's always at midday. You're to come to us. Now, no argument. A place will be laid.'

'You're coming for Christmas?' Henry said sleepily, and Jenny watched Guy's face as he stared at Henry.

He was fighting something, Jenny thought. And he was… losing?

'I'll come,' he said. 'If I can get all the arrangements in place…I'll be here.'

'HE'S LOVELY.' LATE that night Jenny was sitting on the veranda with her mother-in-law, watching the stars over the distant ocean and listening to the soft clicking of Lorna's knitting needles.

'Guy?'

'Of course Guy,' Lorna said, and smiled. 'Jenny, he's just what you need.'

'I don't need anyone.'

'Of course you do,' Lorna said equitably. 'You're a lovely, healthy young woman. You've lost Ben, and that's dreadful, but Ben would be the first one to say you shouldn't spend the rest of your life grieving.'

'I could never leave you,' Jenny said, and Lorna looked at her face and saw the emotions working there.

'So you *are* feeling…?'

'Of course I'm feeling,' Jenny burst out. 'He's gorgeous,

and I'd have to be non-human not to feel that. But he can have any woman he wants. He's a squillionaire. As soon as this wedding's over he'll go back to his life in New York.'

'And if he asked you to go with him?'

'He won't.'

'Jenny...'

'He won't,' she said definitely. 'And even if the impossible happened and he did, do you think I could take Henry away from all this? There's no way, and you know it.' She gave herself a mental shake and managed a grin. 'Okay, he's gorgeous, and if he happened to kiss me again...'

'He *kissed* you?' Lorna squeaked, and Jenny's grin firmed.

'There's things that even you don't know, Lorna Westmere. It's true I find him enormously attractive, and the memory of Ben won't hold me back. But it's only for a few days and then it'll be over.'

GUY SPENT MUCH of that night awake. Thinking of Christa.

Thinking of Jenny.

He'd loved Christa, he thought. He remembered the bleakness, the guilt, the horror of those weeks after she'd been killed, but in contrast... He remembered the joy of Christa's life, how she'd made him laugh, how when she'd agreed to marry him he'd felt like the luckiest man in the world.

But then things had changed. She'd hated his new career. There'd been fight after fight. The relationship had soured to the point where if she hadn't been killed it would have been over.

He'd thought he'd been in love and he'd been wrong, and such a fundamental mistake had stayed with him ever since. Hell, if he could be so wrong about someone he'd believed he loved so much, how could he ever commit again?

He couldn't.

'So what the hell are you thinking of now?' he demanded of himself aloud, and there was only one answer.

'You're thinking she's gorgeous. You're thinking that she's been through hell and her little boy needs someone and...

'You're thinking of *marrying*?' It was an incredulous demand into the darkness. 'You're thinking of taking them *home*?'

Why not?

The idea was so far out of left field that he almost laughed. But...

But.

It wouldn't mess with my life, he told himself. She'd come back to New York. We'd get the best medical attention for those scars. Henry could go to school. Jenny could work in the company.

And live with you?

Of course live with me, he told his alter ego, letting the picture of domestic bliss build. I have a huge apartment. There's room to spare. Henry could have his own wing, and Jenny and I...

There was the nub of the matter. Jenny and I.

Jenny. Jenny as she'd been today, dressed only in a bikini, all womanly curves, defending her son, defiant, taking on all comers. Jenny squashed into his Ferrari, giggling with her son, meeting his eyes over Henry's head and sharing his laughter.

Jenny.

You haven't even slept with the woman, he told himself, and he sounded desperate, even to himself. How do you know you want her every night for the rest of your life?

Because I do, he thought, suddenly sure.

It was crazy. It was way too fast. But the thought of Jenny in his bed was suddenly immeasurably enticing.

It's too soon, he told himself, his heart for once agreeing with his head. The way you're feeling... It might just be sympathy.

It's not sympathy and you know it.

It might be. You thought you loved Christa.

You wouldn't be committing in the same way, he told himself. You can stay independent. What's the harm? If it doesn't work, what do you have to lose?

Nothing if you stay independent.

Can you stay independent?

Maybe. I can try.

CHAPTER SIX

KYLIE's wedding took place two days before Christmas, and it was more than Kylie and Daryl had ever dreamed of.

Kylie moved though her wedding day in a blissful whirl. She looked totally in love with her wedding—and totally in love with her man. Daryl, too, looked as if all his dreams had come true. He had the woman he loved, and he had a wedding ceremony that would be the talk of the district for years.

For it was a true Carver Wedding.

The man had brilliance, Jenny thought, gazing round the transformed hall where the reception was being held. It was no longer a hall. Instead it was a smoky gambling den, straight out of the nineteen-twenties. Guy had spent the last few days painting sets, organising props, training a couple of acting students he'd flown in from Sydney, throwing himself into this wedding as if it was a vastly publicised celebrity wedding instead of the wedding of two butcher's assistants with no profit to be made at all.

His work was worth it for the sheer pleasure it gave, Jenny decided. It was fantastic. As every guest arrived they gasped in wonder, joining instantly into the pleasure of make-believe mingled with a true-love wedding. The press, arriving to see the first Carver Wedding in Australia, were hauled right into the theme, being directed to point their cameras at the groom's right side and make him look good or they'd be wearing concrete shoes before they knew what had hit them.

The photographers didn't know where to point their cameras next. Even Shirley Grubb abandoned her need for pink tulle and embraced the theme with enthusiasm.

'Oh, Jenny… I've been dreaming of this wedding since Kylie was born, and I so wanted everything to be right,' she confided towards the end of the evening. 'I was so upset when Kylie told me she wasn't doing it my way. But now… My two sisters are here. Their daughters had flash weddings in Sydney—no money spared—and you know what? They're *jealous*. They're jealous of their little sister who married Fred Grubb and never has any money to her name.' She hugged Jenny, and there were tears slipping down her face. 'He's fabulous,' she whispered. 'You're so lucky.'

Guy was fabulous? Jenny was lucky? Jenny examined the comment from all sides, then decided to ignore it and hand out a few more drinks.

She couldn't quite ignore it.

Guy was everywhere, working hands-on, making sure the event went without a hitch. He was dressed as a bodyguard, armed and dangerous, his slicked-down hair making his face look somehow menacing, his mock pistols too obvious, moving among the crowd, making amiable if-you-don't-have-a-good-time-I'll-punch-your-lights-out comments—sure his wedding couple were safe.

I'd think *I* was safe if I had him for a bodyguard, too, Jenny thought while she dispensed drinks. But she shoved the notion aside and went to make sure the cake, an overblown affair, adorned with a miniature gangster and his bride driving away in their fancy car—*where had Guy found these props?*—was ready for cutting.

She put the thought of Guy to one side.

But she stayed achingly aware of him.

And Guy…?

He moved through the wedding with his customary efficiency, ensuring each and every guest took home memories to cherish. Whether it was adroit flirting with the brides-maids, bullying Uncle Ern to take Cousin Cecilia onto the dance floor, or removing the third glass of champagne from fifteen-year-old Bert's grasp and replacing it with cola. 'That stuff is a lady's drink—I never touch it,' he told the kid, who gazed at Guy in suspicion and then decided that maybe cola really was okay. Wherever there was a need, there he was.

But at any given moment Guy knew Jenny's whereabouts. She was dressed in a pert maid's uniform, doing the same as him, working the crowd. He watched her laughter and her affection for these people. He watched as people responded to her with affection, and the more he saw of her the more his mind had to dwell on.

Jenny.

The night wore on. The crowd started to thin.

His awareness of Jenny built.

And the crazy idea from the night after the beach incident became louder and louder in his head. *You're thinking of marrying?*

Yes. Yes, he was.

He couldn't stay independent without her, he thought. It was a dumb notion, but maybe if he married her and kept her safe he could get her out of his system?

Or not. Whatever.

You're thinking of marrying.

JENNY HAD NO time to talk to Guy until Daryl and Kylie had driven away, their found-for-the-occasion Buick trailing a suitable clattering of ancient shoes and tin cans. The guests dispersed with reluctance, the crew cleared the mess, and Jenny was left with Guy.

'That was fantastic,' she told him as they emerged into the warm night air, glad to be free of the fog inside. 'It was the *best* wedding.'

'It was, wasn't it?' Guy said. He flicked a switch and the

lights of the hall disappeared. They were left in darkness, their two cars standing in solitary state in the abandoned car park. 'I'd forgotten how much fun it was to be hands-on.'

'I loved it.' She sighed in exhausted pleasure. 'There's no nicer thing than a truly happy wedding.'

'No,' he said, and paused.

It was one a.m. It was time she was home, Jenny thought ruefully. Henry would be awake at six, and the next day was huge. There was still planning to do for Anna and Barret's wedding, and Christmas was in two days' time.

Christmas…

Christmas without Ben was awful. She'd hated the last two Christmases. But now…things had changed, she thought, and she wasn't sure how. All she knew was that in the last few days she'd changed. She was no longer dreading Christmas.

Because of this man?

Maybe, but he didn't have to know it, she thought. He'd set something free in her that she hadn't known was imprisoned. She felt light and happy and young.

Whoa. This man was dangerous, she decided. Happy and young or not, she was Henry's mother, and she needed to go home to bed.

'Goodnight, Guy,' she said, and turned away, but his hands came out and caught her shoulders, turning her back to face him.

'Jenny…'

'Mmm?' She had to stay cool, she told herself. She mustn't let him see that just by touching him he could…he could…

He kissed her.

She let him kiss her. How could she not? It was a lovely, languorous kiss, a kiss to melt into, a kiss to lose yourself in. He was so big and dangerous and warm and safe and wonderful…

These were crazy thoughts. *She* was crazy, she decided,

as the kiss went on and her entire being was consumed with the feel of him, the thought of him. Guy…

It was a magic end to a magic evening—to be kissed by Guy. Her life had been barren for too long. To have this man's hands hold her, to have this magic sensation drifting through her… It was wondrous.

The kiss went on and on, and she took as much as she gave. It was a healing, she thought as she savoured the feel of him. It was a lovely way to end her mourning.

And at some deep, primeval level she knew it was more than that. There was no thought of Ben as she kissed him, but as he pulled away at last she caught at the ragged ends of her self-control and told herself that of course this was because of Ben. She was a widow, and now she was re-emerging to the outside world. This was nothing more than a reawakening. So she sighed with absolute pleasure as he broke the contact, as he held her at arms' length and smiled down at her in the moonlight. She sighed with pleasure and tried to hold back the regret that the kiss was at an end. And she tried to think of Ben.

'You're beautiful,' he said, and she managed to smile back.

'You're not bad yourself, buster,' she whispered. 'Though I'm not sure I go for the hair oil.'

'I'm serious,' he told her.

Her smile faded and she looked up at him, wondering.

'Serious?'

'I want to ask you something.'

She didn't want to talk. She so wanted to kiss him again. She desperately wanted to kiss him again. But… She was a sensible woman. She had to move on.

'About Barret and Anna's wedding?' she asked. 'Can it wait until tomorrow? I'm really tired.'

'Jenny, I wondered if you'd be interested in marrying me.'

She stilled. The words seemed to echo over and over in the stillness. Marrying…?

He's gone mad, Jenny thought at last. The romance of to-night must have gone to his head.

'I beg your pardon?' she whispered, and he raked his fingers through his hair—then remembered the oil slick. He stared down at his oily fingers with a rueful smile.

'Urk. I've made a mess of that.'

'Of what?'

'Of my proposal.' He took a too-big handkerchief from his breast pocket and carefully wiped his fingers clean. 'I haven't had that much practice, you see. I didn't mean to do it.'

'Then why did you?' She was having trouble making her voice work. She was having trouble making *anything* work.

'I could make you safe,' he said, and she looked up at Guy's earnest face, at his mock pistols and his slicked-down hair, and suddenly, irresistibly, maybe even hysterically, she started to laugh.

'What?' he said, sounding offended, and she bit back her bubble of laughter and tried to be serious. Or tried to be light-hearted. Or something.

'I don't need a bodyguard,' she told him. 'But it was a very nice offer. Thank you.'

'I'm not offering you a bodyguard. I'm offering you a husband.'

She stilled at that, her laughter fading. It wasn't a joke, then. He was…serious?

He was asking her to marry him?

The idea was so preposterous that she almost choked.

'I'm already married,' she said, before she could stop herself, and she watched as his face changed.

'What—?'

'I'm married to Ben,' she said stupidly.

'Ben was killed two years ago.'

'Yes, but…' She took a deep breath, searching for… Searching for she didn't know what.

'I can't remember him properly,' she said inconsequentially. 'I can't remember the way he held me. I can't—'

'Jenny, it's natural.'

Was it? She felt her heart clench with a well-remembered pain. Ben was dead. Move on, people said. Her own mother-in-law... Let Ben go. And she had tonight. For the first time she had. But to have this moment become a decision about the rest of her life...

Ben, her heart screamed. Ben. I'm not ready to let you go.

'He's my husband,' she whispered. 'He's in my heart. I thought you at least would know that.'

Guy stood, gazing down at her in the silence.

'I do know that.'

'Then why...?'

'You make me feel different.'

'You make me feel different, too,' she said, and she put her hand up to his face and cupped the curve of his jaw. The feeling she had then...it was indescribable. Say yes, her heart screamed. Say yes before he changes his mind.

'I can't do it,' she whispered. 'You must see it's impossible.'

'Why is it impossible?'

'Henry...'

'Henry would come with us,' he said strongly, taking her hands in his, trying to make her see where his thoughts had taken him. 'You can't tell me he's getting optimal medical treatment here. The world's best doctors are in New York.'

She stilled. 'You'd take us both to New York?'

'Of course.'

'But our home is here.'

'I have a massive apartment in Manhattan. You can see the Statue of Liberty from—'

'Our home is here.' Her voice was flat, without inflexion, and suddenly desperately weary. 'Do you think I could leave Lorna?'

'Lorna has Jack.'

'She does. And she has me. And she has Henry. We're family, Guy.'

'You don't need family.'

'At Christmas?' she whispered. 'You're saying that two days before Christmas? That I don't need a family?'

'Hell, Jenny…'

'This is ridiculous,' she said, trying hard to be strong. 'We hardly know each other.'

'And yet you feel what I'm feeling.'

'I don't.'

'Jenny,' he said, and the hands holding her shoulders suddenly firmed. 'You're lying.'

Of course she was lying. Whatever he was feeling she was feeling, too. Multiplied by about a thousand. He drew her into him, his lips met hers, and she felt… She felt…

Heat.

The word slammed in her mind as the sensation slammed through her. Heat. A conflagration that was all-consuming, starting from her lips and flooding through the rest of her. As if she was dry tinder and a match had been held to the all-too-ready fuel.

She wanted him with every inch of her being. Her lips opened under his. She welcomed him with joy. Her hands came around his chest and tugged him closer.

Guy.

The kiss went on and on. Neither could stop it. Why should they?

Guy had asked her to marry him. This man who was holding her, who was making her feel as if life itself could start now…

Guy.

He was her employer.

The thought slammed into her mind and somehow it steadied her. The thought had her remembering that her feet were planted on Sandpiper Bay ground—and had to stay that way.

Somehow she tugged back, and Guy gazed down at her in the moonlight, concerned.

'What is it, sweetheart?'

What right did he have to call her sweetheart? She loved it, she decided. But…she couldn't.

'Guy, leave it,' she demanded, and he let her take a further step back. The fact that her body was screaming to remain in his hold had to be ignored. It *must* be.

'What's wrong?'

'If you weren't my boss I'd slap your face,' she managed.

'Why?'

'For taking liberties.'

'You want to be kissed.'

'I don't.'

'You do.' He was teasing her with his eyes. He was smiling down at her. And there was such…love?

She was imagining it. Love? No.

She was married to Ben.

'I still love Ben,' she said, and tilted her chin.

'Maybe I still love Christa. But it's memories that we love, and memories make cold bedfellows.'

'You want me in bed?' She'd started to shake, and it wasn't from cold. Bed with this man… Bed with Guy…

'A man would have to be inhuman not to want you in his bed.'

She could do it, she thought. She could just step forward into this man's invitation and let her life be taken over.

She could be Guy Carver's wife.

The thought scared her witless. She steadied, trying desperately to see his invitation for what it was.

For some reason he wanted her. Well, maybe that wasn't so strange. Because she wanted him, too.

But he was a billionaire, and he lived in New York in a massive apartment. Henry would have the best doctors, and she… She…

She'd be Guy Carver's wife.

It seemed so ridiculous that she almost laughed. Almost.

'You don't even know me,' she whispered. 'You don't know Henry.'

'I know that I want you.'

'But I…' She tilted her chin again and met his gaze, knowing what had to be said and knowing she had to say it. 'Guy, I want family.'

'I'm offering—'

'Your name. Your millions. It's a fantastic offer.' She managed a rueful smile. 'There's probably thousands of women who'd jump at what you're offering. And if I was alone maybe I could make a go of it. You're saying we're sexually attracted, and we definitely are, but that's not enough to build a marriage. I'm Cinderella and you're Prince Charming, but I have a feeling that marriage for Cinders had its downside.'

'I've never heard any fairytale where they divorce,' he said, startled, but she refused to smile.

'No,' she said thoughtfully. 'But being all alone in his castle, with everyone knowing she'd come from rags to riches… she'd have to be grateful for ever. And if she'd had a son, then that little boy might feel the same and resent it.'

'You're flying off at tangents,' he said, half laughing, and she grimaced.

'I am,' she said softly. 'But I'm thinking forward. You see, I must. I have a future, but it's inextricably tied up with Henry's future, and Lorna's and Jack's and this little town.' Her chin tilted some more. 'When I first came here I was needful,' she told him. 'This little town made me happy, and I'll not walk away because you make me feel wonderful.'

'I make you feel wonderful?' he demanded, pouncing on her words, and she felt a stab of sudden anger.

'Of course,' she said scornfully. 'But you've jumped in at the deep end. You've figured for some reason that you want me, and the easiest way to have me is to install me in Man-

hattan and have me in the pieces of time you have left over
from the rest of your life.'

'What's wrong with that?'

He couldn't see?

She had to be grown-up for the pair of them, she thought
miserably. She had to be sensible. Her heart had to be ignored. She was a married woman with a son to care for. With
responsibilities. With Christmas in two days and she hadn't
even made her mince pies.

'If you don't know then I can't teach you,' she said. She
took a deep breath, leaned forward and kissed him lightly on
the lips. A feather kiss that was over before he could react.
Then she stepped back and felt for the handle of her wagon
door. She slid in, still looking at him.

'Thank you for the proposal,' she whispered. 'It was…
magic. But you're my boss, Guy, and that's the way it has to
stay. Now I'm going home. To my family. I have Christmas
to organise.'

HE'D MADE A proper hash of that.

How could he go home to sleep? He couldn't. So he made
his way to the little beach where he and Jenny and Henry had
swum only days before.

Family.

What was she asking him to do? Take Lorna and Jack as
well as Henry back to New York with him?

No. She wasn't asking anything of him, he thought. She
was simply looking at his offer in surprise and rejecting it
out of hand.

It wasn't a ridiculous offer. He'd made it to no other woman
but Christa.

Christa would have been happy with what he was offering Jenny, he thought. He could have provided everything
she'd needed. She would have been able to do whatever she'd
wanted.

Jenny wasn't Christa.

Christa had been easier. He'd known what Christa had wanted. She'd wanted what their parents wanted: prestige and money.

He had that. He was offering it to Jenny, and she'd knocked it back. What else did he have to offer her?

Nothing.

So move on, he told himself. You offered to marry her because you felt sorry for her.

Was that right?

No. It was much more. He wanted Jenny in his bed.

So it's sympathy and sex. You can find sex elsewhere. She doesn't want the sympathy. You've made your offer and it's been rejected. So move on.

Back to thinking of Jenny as an employee?

She wasn't the least like an employee.

She was just…Jenny.

CHAPTER SEVEN

THE next day was frantic. Barret and Anna and entourage arrived, and had to be taken through the arrangements. Then the arrangements had to be tweaked so bride and groom were happy, and those tweaks weren't insubstantial. Guy, who'd worked with both Barret and Anna before, did the front work while Jenny stayed in the background.

Last night might not have happened. She was briskly efficient and very, very capable.

'There's an extra bridesmaid? Get her here by two this afternoon and we'll fit her out. We have half a ton of pink tulle, and our seamstresses are enjoying themselves.'

'Anna doesn't like the wedding cake? No, that's okay. We'll soak it in brandy and call it Christmas pudding for the party afterwards. I can get a couple of ladies onto sponge cakes now. Have her draw up details of decorations.'

'Gifts for the bridesmaids? Pearls? Yes, it's too late to get seven identical necklaces locally, but I can contact a jeweller in Sydney and have them couriered.'

She reassured him every time he called her, and after every call he felt about ten years old and as if she was his schoolteacher.

That was the tone she was taking, he thought. Cool, distant and bossy.

She was also never there. Every time he found an opportunity to visit the shop she was somewhere else.

'She hasn't finished her Christmas shopping,' one of the sewing ladies told him.

The three women seemed to be having a wonderful time, sitting in the back room with a vat of coffee and half a ton of chocolate biscuits, their fingers flying. 'I think she's gone to find a present for Lorna.'

'Hush!' Guy turned to the shop's entrance to see Jack pushing Lorna's wheelchair inside. 'I don't like knowing my presents before Christmas Day,' Lorna called. 'So if you know, don't tell. Guy, I'm pleased we found you.'

'I'm busy,' he said, and then thought maybe he shouldn't be that blunt. Jenny obviously loved this woman. It was just... Lorna was part of the family thing that was threatening to engulf him.

'I won't hold you up,' Lorna replied, her voice holding a hint of reproof. 'And I'm not asking any favours, so you can stop looking like that. We just called to remind you that you're doing the Santa run in your Ferrari tomorrow. You need to be at our place at nine. Henry's really looking forward to it.'

Hell, he'd forgotten. He'd also forgotten Henry's face when he'd thought it might happen.

But...

Why not ignore a few buts here? he told himself. He could do this. It didn't mean getting emotionally involved—or any more emotionally involved than he already was.

Okay, he'd do it, and then he'd walk away. He'd moved his return flight to the day after Christmas. His escape route was organised.

How could you ask a woman to marry you and then look forward to getting back to your own life?

He was having an internal conversation, watched by Lorna and Jack and three seamstresses, but the conversation went on regardless.

Easy, he told himself. I didn't ask to join her life. I asked if she'd join mine.

No wonder she refused you.

'Fine,' he managed, and if he sounded ungracious he couldn't help himself. 'I'll be there.'

'Great,' Jack said warmly. 'We'll hang up a stocking for you.'

'A stocking?'

'Wait and see,' Lorna said. 'Our Santa does the best stockings.'

'HE'S STILL COMING for Christmas dinner?'

'Of course he is. He promised. And he's coming at nine for stockings. He's cute,' Lorna told her daughter-in-law. 'He drives a wonderful car. Henry thinks he's the ant's pants.'

'Guy Carver is not the ant's pants. He is an American billionaire who happens to be my boss…'

'I'm sewing him a stocking.'

'Lorna, he *can't* have a stocking.'

'Everyone in the whole world needs a stocking. Now, what will Santa put in it?'

CHAPTER EIGHT

CHRISTMAS morning.

Guy woke, as was his custom, at five a.m. There was nothing to do.

There had to be something. One of the biggest celebrity weddings of the year was scheduled for five this afternoon.

He lay and watched the weak rays of dawn flitter across his counterpane, mentally ticking off everything that had to be done.

He'd made huge lists, and Jenny had delegated.

Every person in the town seemed to have something to do. The normal sleeping-in-front-of-television end to Christmas Day was not going to happen in Sandpiper Bay. Jenny had hauled in every local, and a few tourists as well, and she'd given everyone a job.

And the best thing was that nearly all of them were doing it for nothing.

'Barret and Anna can pay,' Guy had growled, when Jenny had told him.

'Yes, but most of the town's folk believe in Christmas.'

'So what's *that* got to do with it?'

'They believe it's wrong to work on Christmas Day. But if it's for something like aiding the tsunami effort it'll strike a chord. One of our local kids is working in the international aid effort and...'

'You're asking Barret and Anna to give a donation to *charity*?'

'No. I'm asking Barret and Anna to pay a fair price for labour and then we'll give it away.'

'It doesn't make sense.'

'Maybe for you it doesn't,' she agreed. 'But for us…it's our way.' She glared at him. 'If you want to take our profits for yourself…'

'Whoa,' he told her. And then he thought, What sort of employer/employee relationship was this? She'd just given away his profits.

But there had been no arguing, and now the whole town had jobs to do for the good of the tsunami relief effort. He could lie in bed and stare at the ceiling and think he should be back in New York.

Why should he be back in New York? Christmases back home were simply an excuse for ostentation.

He hated Christmas. Even before Christa had died he'd hated Christmas.

Five a.m. Nothing to do until nine.

He hated Christmas.

NINE. HE WALKED up the veranda steps, carrying expensive truffles and vintage wine. The screen door slammed open and a pyjama-clad urchin catapulted through, crutches tumbling as Henry toppled forward to hug his legs.

A Labrador puppy came bouncing after him. The puppy reached Henry and Henry abandoned Guy. He sat down on the veranda and shoved his nose into the puppy's soft fur.

'This is Patsy,' he told Guy, his voice muffled by puppy. 'She was on my bed when I woke up, and she's all mine, and I have to train her.'

'That's great,' Guy said, feeling…emotional. That was the end of that resolution, then.

'And there's more.' Small boy and pup looked up at him, eyes glistening with Christmas joy. 'We've been waiting and waiting, and Santa's been, and there's stockings for every-one. But Mummy says we can't open them until you come.'

'Come on in,' Jenny said, and he raised his eyes from her son and smiled at Jenny.

She was simply dressed in clean jeans and T-shirt—a T-shirt adorned with sequins carefully sewn on to make a picture of Rudolph the Red-Nosed Reindeer.

She had two glowing Santa Clauses hanging from her ears.

She was smiling. Who needed grinning Santa Clauses when there was a smile like this?

'You're overdressed,' she told him. 'A suit at nine on Christmas morning? Pyjamas are more the go.'

'I don't wear them,' he told her, and she blushed. A great blush. It made him want to...

Keep it impersonal, he told himself harshly.

'Well, at least wear a Christmas hat,' she said, and handed him a hat. Then, when he didn't react, she took it back, reached up and placed it on his head. A red and white Santa hat.

Forget the hat. She was so close. She smelled of pine nee-dles and mince pies and...and Jenny.

There was mistletoe over his head. He couldn't see it but he was sure of it. The desire to take her into his arms and kiss her senseless was suddenly overwhelming.

But Lorna was at the door, with Jack behind her, laughing and calling for them to come in.

'It's all very well for Henry,' Jack complained, 'he's got his puppy. But every single one of my presents is still wrapped, and if we don't get to these stockings soon I'm going to bust.'

COMPARISONS OF THIS Christmas to every other Christmas he'd known were ludicrous. As a child he remembered formal Christmas mornings, drinks with business acquaintances where children were seen and not heard. A ludicrously over-the-top lunch where he was the only child—he hated the food and he hated the waiting, the waiting… Then his parents would sleep off their lunch, and some time towards evening his mother would call him in and they'd open their gifts. They weren't permitted to open them early as 'the tree looks so much better with gifts under it, and we'll keep that effect until all our guests have gone.'

Whatever his gift was, it would have been exquisitely wrapped and he'd have to admire the wrapping.

It was never anything he wanted. It was always something someone had recommended. 'Oh, we gave Guy a miniature violin—so sweet—I'm sure he's musical. He takes after my side of the family, not his father's…'

There was no violin today. This little family lived on a shoestring. The major present was the puppy. The rest of the gifts were…silly?

Some were silly, some were sensible—but it was a great mix. He watched as Henry unwrapped coloured pencils, a new collar and lead for his dog, and a vast parcel that turned out to be three months' supply of puppy food—Henry was so delighted he couldn't stop giggling, and there was a pause in the proceedings so Patsy could be photographed sitting on top of her future dinners… A rubber toy in the shape of a chook for Patsy, a game of wooden blocks that Henry received with joy…

Interspersed with these—for they took turns to open gifts—were the adult presents. Romance novels for Lorna, and a crazy device for massaging feet that Patsy took instant exception to. A new summer hat for Jack—he had to take off the reindeer antlers he was wearing, so he placed his new hat on and then propped his reindeer antlers over the top.

And for Guy…

He'd expected nothing. Of course he'd expected nothing. But there was a whole stocking stuffed with silly things. When he saw the stocking he felt his heart sink, expecting to be embarrassed that this family had spent money on his behalf, but the stocking simply made him laugh.

His very own pair of Christmas antlers—to go on top of his Santa hat. A red nose that flashed—'Wear it now,' Henry decreed, and he did. A mango—a perfect piece of fruit, wrapped with care, a vast red ribbon around it. He stared at the mango, and Jack grinned and handed him a knife and a plate and said, 'Eat it now, mate—cos it's Christmas.' So he took off his red nose and spread mango from one ear to the other and it was the best thing he'd ever eaten.

What else? A boat made of ice lolly sticks—'I wanted to make you a Ferrari,' Henry told him, 'but you've already got one. And this floats. I've put water in the bath all ready. You want to see?' So they had to troop into the bathroom and watch Henry's boat—the *Jennifer-Patsy*—take her maiden voyage round the bath, and then they had to rescue the *Jennifer-Patsy* and haul Patsy out of the bathtub and dry her, and then dry themselves, and then watch as Guy opened his last present, which was a glitzy magazine titled *How to Plan Your Perfect Wedding*.

'Lorna's idea, mate, not ours,' Jack said hastily, and then they were all laughing, and Lorna was handing round mince pies and it was time to take the Ferrari on its Santa run.

Which was crazy all by itself.

Santa—the local police chief—was waiting at the police station. With a paper bag of mince pies at his side to keep his strength up, Guy collected Santa and his lollies. Then he followed Santa's directions and made a clean sweep of Sandpiper Bay. Santa rang his bell with such strength that Guy's ears would take months to recover. From every house came children and adults and oldies, and Santa tossed lollies indiscriminately. Even from the vast houses owned by the squillionaires came kids and dogs and men and women, all at various stages of Christmas, all smiling, all cheering as they got their lollies and then disappearing back into their homes to celebrate the festive season.

Their last stop was back at the farm. Santa had arranged for his wife to collect him from there. Santa emptied the remains of his sack onto their veranda, and then drove away in state in the town's police car.

'Now dinner,' Lorna declared, and Guy wondered how he could eat any more. But of course he did—and how could he ever have thought he couldn't? He remembered the sophisticated Christmases he'd endured as a kid. There was no comparison. He ate turkey and gravy and crispy roast potatoes and every sort of vegetable he could imagine with relish. Then Jack demanded he light the pudding—and how could he not eat pudding after that?

'Brandy sauce, brandy butter, cream or ice-cream?' Lorna asked.

Jenny grinned and said, 'He'll have all four, Mum, just like everyone else.'

And Guy looked across the table and thought, She's calling Lorna Mum and suddenly…suddenly he wanted to do exactly the same.

If he married Jenny he could…

Henry was down on the floor, subsiding into an afternoon nap with Patsy, and Guy thought, I wonder what the quarantine regulations are for taking dogs into the US.

'It's not going to happen,' Jenny said softly, and he looked across the table and saw a flash of sadness behind the laughter that had been there all morning.

It was as if she knew that what he was offering was serious—but it wasn't enough.

He couldn't leave her.

He couldn't.

'No one sleeps before the washing up,' Lorna said.

And Guy heard himself saying, 'I'll wash up. That's my Christmas gift to you.' He'd brought excellent wine and chocolates as gifts, but he knew now that they were dumb gifts. Sure, they liked them, but mangoes were better.

'I won't let you do it alone,' Jenny said, and grinned. 'Nobility is my middle name. Jack, Lorna—that means you sleep. Immediately. Henry and Patsy already are asleep. Guy, into the kitchen.'

'Aren't I the boss?' he asked, and everyone smiled.

'Not around here, mate,' Jack told him, gripping his wife's hand and holding it tight. 'The women in this family make the rules.'

So they stood in the kitchen, and he washed and she wiped, and suddenly the noisy fun gossip faded to nothing. There was a silence which should have been a contented silence, but it was...tense.

'Jenny?' he tried softly, but when he glanced at her, her smile had faded and her face was rigid with strain.

'Don't say it, Guy,' she whispered. 'This is my family. This is my place. I'm not going anywhere.'

THE WEDDING WAS due to take place at five p.m. They left at three. Only Patsy opened one eye and wagged a weary tail as they departed.

They drove in Jenny's wagon as they had final supplies in the back. 'Everything's there,' Guy told Jenny. 'I ran a final check before I came to your place.'

'And I ran a final check before everyone woke up,' Jenny retorted. 'Too many cooks, Mr Carver?'

'Double-checking doesn't hurt anyone,' he replied as they drove down the magnificent eucalypt-lined driveway of Anna's mansion. There was a cluster of expensive cars parked in front, obviously belonging to in-house guests. Within two hours there'd be hundreds of cars.

'I'll check the bride; you check the groom,' Jenny told Guy, forgetting she was the employee again, but acting on a rule they both knew. The most important duty in any wedding ceremony is to make sure you have two live bodies willing to say *I do*.

They rang the bell, a butler opened the door—and here was the first discordant note of the day. A man's voice was raised in fury.

'You can't do this, you bitch. I'll ruin you. I'll see your name raked across every tabloid and it's no holds barred. If you call this off just because of some moralistic damned scruples then I'll see you in hell. Have you got any idea of what this'll do to your PR?'

Before they had time to step inside—and before the butler had time to do what he should have done in times of crisis—refuse admittance—Barret himself shoved his way past them. They stared after him as the movie star disappeared behind the house. There was the sound of a motor being gunned into life—and then the squeal of a car being turned too fast and driven too fast away.

'There's your groom, Mr Carver,' Jenny murmured, wincing. 'Now for the bride.'

ANNA, SURPRISINGLY, SEEMED to still be in control. She was sitting on the second top step of the great staircase, as if her legs had given way, but as Jenny approached she even managed a shaky smile.

'That's two less guests for the wedding,' she murmured. 'We're minus one groom and we're minus one bridesmaid. Happy Christmas.' She sniffed. 'Oh, help.'

'Happy Christmas to you, too,' Jenny murmured, and sat down beside her while Guy looked on from below stairs. 'Um…was that what I think it was? Have you just called off the wedding?'

'You bet,' Anna whispered. 'I may live to regret it, but I don't think so.' She looked down to her butler. 'Max, I won't be needing you for a bit.'

'Should I start phoning a few people?' Max asked, sounding horrified. 'Maybe I can stop a few coming.'

'There's three hundred people coming to this wedding,' Guy said. 'They're coming from all over the world, and the wedding's less than two hours away. Our chances of stopping the crowd are negligible.'

'In that case go and have a stiff drink,' Anna told the butler. 'Or two.'

'Stay sober, Max,' Guy warned. 'We're going to need you.'

'Yes, sir,' the butler said. He looked at his mistress in concern. Then he looked from Guy to Jenny and back again. 'Fix it if you can,' he said softly. 'I don't think she's seeing what she's done.'

'I'm seeing what I've done all too clearly,' Anna retorted. 'I found him with one of my bridesmaids. In Georgia's bedroom. In Georgia's bed. *I* haven't done anything. Barret, on the other hand…'

'Can you verify this?' Guy asked the butler, and Max nodded.

'I was coming upstairs to remind Miss Anna that you were to be here at three. Miss Anna was standing at Miss Georgia's bedroom door looking…'

'Gobsmacked,' Anna said, and suddenly she giggled. It sounded dangerously close to hysterics. 'You saw them, too, didn't you, Max?'

'Yes, miss. But…'

'There are indeed buts,' Guy said gravely. 'I'd imagine Barret's heading straight back to Hollywood. Anna, if he's true to form he'll slur your name in every ear that matters. People *expect* Barret to play around. They won't feel sorry for Barret. They'll feel sorry for you.'

'I don't care,' Anna said, defiant, but Jenny saw the tremor in her fingers and knelt to sit beside her and take her hand. To her surprise, the woman gripped and held. Hard.

'Where's everyone else?' Guy was asking, and Jenny

thought, He's done this before. He's coped with disasters like this.

'We had eggnog for brunch,' Anna explained. 'Barret made it. Everyone's half-drunk already, so they're sleeping it off. Or I thought they were sleeping it off. I don't know how Barret managed...' Her voice trailed away in disgust.

Good, Jenny thought. If she was up to technical thinking then maybe other sorts of thinking were possible, too. She glanced down at Guy, their eyes locked, and she could see that he was thinking exactly what she was thinking.

Guy had agreed to do this wedding because he felt sorry for Anna. Nothing had changed. And if Anna had to be protected...

'*No one* must feel sorry for you,' she said, and Guy nodded, as if he'd just been about to say the same thing.

'What do you mean?' Anna demanded, and Guy took over.

'Anna, you've just come out of rehab. Everyone's looking at you. If I know Hollywood, they're expecting you to fail, and they're half hoping you will. Half the people coming to this wedding will be coming out of curiosity.' He hesitated, but then he went straight to the hard question. 'Did you touch the eggnog?'

'I drink soda water,' she said stiffly, and Guy nodded.

'I knew you'd say that. It's why I'm giving you a Carver Wedding. You deserve a second chance. But, the way I'm seeing it, this could be your ruin. Unless we turn it around. Unless we make this into a celebration regardless. You've ditched all the other bad habits. Barret was simply the last habit you ditched.'

'What...?' said Anna.

'Let's get this organised,' he said, striding up the stairs to join them. Anna and Jenny were still sitting on the second top stair. They shifted sideways and he sat down, too, so Anna had Jenny on one side and Guy on the other, with Max watching, stunned, from below. 'We need to move fast.'

'What...?' said Jenny.

'If people have flown from London and New York and wherever to see a celebration, and they don't see one, they're going to be disappointed,' Guy said. 'And it's Christmas Day, which makes it worse. They'll be hugely disappointed if they're turned away without food. And hungry, disappointed celebrities can get nasty. If they don't see you, they'll talk about you until the next sensation happens.'

Anna shuddered. 'Don't.'

'What should we do?' Jenny asked simply, and waited.

'We go ahead as if it was meant to happen,' he said. 'Anna, you need to act. When all your in-house guests wake and your other guests arrive, you greet them as if this is the best thing that can possibly have happened.'

'I don't know how...'

'I know how,' Guy said. 'Jenny, the time to be taken for the ceremony needs to be taken up with something else. I want a map of the way to the beach—that's about half a mile from here, isn't it? Down through the hills? An easy walk? I thought so. As every guest arrives they're to be handed a champagne cocktail, a tube of sunscreen and a bathing costume and sarong if they don't have their own. Jenny, get onto the local store owners now. Tell them we'll pay ten times face value if they have the stuff we need here in half an hour. Oh, and the camping store. I want as many folding tables as they have, plus beach umbrellas. Same price applies. Double it if you need to. As the workers arrive—our people are due here at four—they'll start ferrying the wedding breakfast to the beach. I want people toddling over the sandhills, cocktail in hand—we'll have people along the way replenishing glasses—arriving at the beach and seeing Anna in all her glory.'

'All my glory?' Anna said, gulping and looking awed.

'You'll be floating on a sea of flowers. You'll be wearing a tiny bikini and holding a fruit cocktail—something nonalcoholic, but no one need know—something that looks truly splendid. We'll have your bridesmaids—minus one, who I trust will take herself the way of your bridegroom—floating round on air mattresses. We'll use all the wedding flowers and make them look sumptuous. And you'll be saying *Welcome to the rest of my life. This is who I am. A woman who can put on the best party in the world.* It'll make Barret look stupid and you look magnificent.'

'But...' Anna whispered. 'But...'

'But what?'

'There's still the celebrant,' she whispered. 'There's all the pink tulle. I have editors from the top celebrity magazines flying in especially to see a wedding.'

'They *will* see a wedding,' Guy said.

'Whose?'

He took a deep breath.

'Mine.' And then he looked at Jenny. 'Ours.'

FOR A MOMENT there was nothing but silence. Jenny stared at Guy. Anna stared at Guy. And then Anna turned to Jenny.

'You'd pretend to get married? But...'

'There'd be no pretend about it,' Guy said softly. 'Anna, I love this woman.'

That's me, Jenny thought dumbly. He's talking about me.

'I've already said I wouldn't,' she whispered, and Guy nodded and reached across Anna and took her hand.

'I know. I was dumb.'

'Excuse me, but you don't want me sitting in the middle here,' Anna said, sounding close to hysterics, and Guy grinned.

'I've already proposed to the woman in moonlight. It didn't work. I'm trying again. Stay where you are.'

'Harumph,' said Max from below, and Guy nodded.

'You, too. I need witnesses.'

'What...?' said Jenny, and paused.

'You mean what am I asking?' Guy said. He hesitated, then ploughed on, a man making a confession before all. 'This morning I opened my stocking and found a boat made with ice lolly sticks.'

'So what?' she whispered, and he smiled.

'Let me finish,' he said. 'I need to. Jenny, fifteen years ago I turned my back on a career in law and used my savings to buy what must have been the most battered van our side of the Mississippi. I was so proud of that van. I used to walk round and pat it. But then...'

'Then Christa was killed.'

'She was,' Guy said. 'And the shock of her death made me think...well, that her values were true. I wanted to show myself that the sacrifice was worth it, and some warped, twisted part of my brain said the way to do that was make money.'

'And you have,' Anna said. 'You're such a success.'

'Not a success if I can't have my Jenny,' he said, and his eyes were holding Jenny's and they might as well be alone. 'I met Jenny a little more than a week ago, and I love everything about her. I love her bravery and her honesty and her caring and her laughter. I love her son and her son's puppy, and her mother-in-law and her father-in-law. I love the place where she lives. I was dumb enough to think maybe I could marry part of that and cart it back to New York, set it down as a possession. But it's not like that, is it, Jenny? You refused me for all the right reasons.'

'I...'

'I'm not asking you that same question now,' Guy said softly. 'I'm asking if you'll let me share your life. If you'll let me take over where Ben left off—loving you, loving what you are and where you are, just...loving.'

'Guy...'

'I've been thinking,' he went on, as if he was nervous that she'd say no before he'd fully explained. 'After the Christmas stocking…all the way round Sandpiper Bay with Santa beside me…I thought.'

'What did you think?' Anna asked, awed, and Jenny thought she'd asked the right question. She should have asked it herself, but the words wouldn't quite come out.

'I thought I could move my base to here,' he said. 'I thought we could make Sandpiper Bay the wedding capital of the world.' He grinned. 'Though I think we'd need two sets of premises. We'll take over the haberdashery and use part of it to incorporate Bridal Fluff. For any bride who wants fluff. And we'll have a special rate for locals—kids who've lived in the district for years and can't afford normal rates.' He hesitated. 'Maybe we could extend that idea to our other smaller premises, too,' he said. 'It takes thinking about, but then I'm not going to be working so hard in the future. I'm going to be doing a lot of lying on the beach, with our son and our puppy, and I can think things through then.'

'Our son?' Jenny said, astounded, and Guy's smile became almost shamefaced.

'It's not my right to share Henry's life,' he told Jenny. 'But if you'll let me…I want to so much. You have no idea how much I want to share.'

'You love Henry?'

'Almost as much as you,' he said, still gripping her hand, still holding her eyes, while Anna sat hornswoggled in between. 'I thought I loved Christa, and my shock at her death left me thinking I didn't know what love was. But I *do* know what it is. I know who it is. It's you. My love. My Jenny.'

There was a moment's stunned silence while everyone held their breath. Jenny didn't move. It was left to Anna to respond.

'Well,' Anna said. *'Well!'*

'Well,' echoed Jenny. She shook her head, as if shaking off disbelief. 'My thoughts exactly.'

'Are you going to accept?' Anna asked. 'I only ask because…'

'Time's getting on,' Max said from below, grinning broadly. 'And I've thought of something. You can't just swap from one wedding to another. There's laws in this country. Four weeks' notice before a wedding can take place.'

'But we could make our promises today,' Jenny whispered, and the whole world held its breath.

'You mean it?' Guy asked at last, and she smiled.

'Of course I mean it. I shouldn't. I loved Ben so much. But these last few days…I've been thinking and thinking, and the more I think the more I know Ben would say to grab life with both hands.' She hesitated. 'And I've been following your logic. Does this mean you want a shonky van again and not a Ferrari?'

'It might,' Guy said, cautious, and Jenny beamed.

'Hooray,' she said. 'Then let's do it. We'll write it into the wedding vows. You get my wagon and I get the Ferrari.'

He lunged at her across Anna's knees—and Anna, movie idol of millions, a woman who'd just been betrayed and whose wedding plans were in the dust, dissolved into helpless laughter while Guy Carver of the Carver corporation reached across her and kissed his intended bride as if there was no tomorrow.

CHAPTER NINE

GUY CARVER was a wedding planner extraordinaire. His own wedding was no exception. He would have liked to have had more than a few hours' notice but, given the circumstances, what was achieved was little short of miraculous.

Firstly he barked orders at everyone, while Jenny and Anna looked on in admiration—and with just a touch of the giggles. Then he swept Jenny into her wagon and carried her back to the farm.

'For I'm not doing this without consent,' he said. Ignoring Jenny's protest that Jack was her father-in-law, and no consent was needed, he carried her into the farmhouse as a groom carried his bride. He woke the startled Lorna and Jack and Henry and Patsy from their afternoon nap and asked with all the deference in the world whether there were any objections to his taking Jenny for his bride.

They were delighted.

'It's so lovely,' Lorna sniffed. 'We'll miss you, sweetheart, but we always knew you'd move on.'

'Then you'll be disappointed,' Guy said roundly. 'You're stuck with the lot of us for ever. Me and Jenny and Henry and Patsy and whoever else comes along. Mind, I'll have to make the odd trip overseas—but maybe we can all go. Maybe you'll even like New York.'

They were speechless—for a whole two minutes—and then Lorna started to plan.

'So you're getting married this afternoon?'

'We're having a ceremony this afternoon, to get Anna out

of a hole,' Jenny told her. 'The press will indeed see a Carver Wedding. We'll repeat our vows in a month for the legalities.'

'We'll repeat our vows night and morning for the rest of our lives,' Guy said exultantly, but Lorna was concentrating on more important issues.

'You need a dress, Jenny. Not the one you wore for Ben.'

'No,' Jenny said. She grinned, delirious with happiness and ready to be silly. 'Maybe I can wear togs and thongs?'

'Togs and thongs?' Guy queried.

'Bikini and flip-flops,' Jack translated, and Guy's face brightened.

'I can cope with that.'

'You can. She can't,' Lorna said roundly. 'Jenny, dear...'

'Mmm?' Jenny was hugging Henry, who was carefully thinking about all the rides he was now going to get in a Ferrari. 'Yes?'

'I never suggested it when you married Ben—to be honest I loved it that we made your wedding dress together. But now...I don't suppose you'd consider wearing mine?'

'Yours?' Jenny said, awed. 'Oh...'

'You're practically the same size as I was forty years ago, and the fashions have come back...' So they all trooped into the bedroom to Lorna's camphor chest, and then Lorna realised that this was serious and turned and shooed out the menfolk.

'You get back to Anna's,' she told Guy. 'You'll see Jenny at the ceremony and not before.'

'Yes, ma'am.'

But as Guy made his way out through the front door Lorna wheeled herself out of the bedroom in a hurry.

'I know it's a minor detail,' she called, 'but we need to know when and we need to know where.'

THE WHEN WAS eight p.m. The where was on the beach. The very loveliest time of day.

The beach was crowded with celebrities from all over the world, and almost every inhabitant of Sandpiper Bay. In their midst was Anna, bouncing around as if she had the world at her feet. Whatever mortification she was feeling, she was hiding it with brilliance.

It would be Barret who was mortified now, Guy thought, watching as Anna attracted everyone's admiration. He could even feel sorry for Barret. Anna was lovely.

She wasn't as lovely as Jenny.

Guy was standing on the shoreline, where sun-warmed sand gave way to sand made damp by the receding tide. There was a temporary altar behind him, and the celebrant was beaming before it. In truth, the celebrant was a little put out— she'd expected to marry superstars—but the fact that she was marrying Guy Carver and the wonderful Jenny, who everyone knew, almost made up for it.

There was only one attendant. Guy's best man was Henry, who held the ring—the Sandpiper Bay jeweller had been delighted to open for such a need—with the reverence it deserved. Henry had his own attendant—Patsy was right by his side—but she wasn't diverting Henry from ring-minding. His hero was at stake—a stepfather who had the marks of life upon him. He kept glancing up to Guy as if he might evaporate, and every time he did Guy looked down at him and winked.

Henry was practising winking back.

'They look like two cats with one canary,' one of the reporters said to her photographer, and the photographer sniffed her agreement.

'It's beautiful.'

'If you get that lens wet you're dead meat,' the reporter said, but she sniffed, too.

And then the bride arrived. By tractor. You couldn't get over these sand hills except by foot or all-terrain vehicle, so Lorna, dressed in her wedding best, drove a trifle erratically but with aplomb, while Jenny stood on the side and held on for dear life. The crowd—wisely—parted before them. Lorna reached her destination, flushed with success. Jack helped his daughter-in-law down and Jenny was deposited by Guy's side. To be married.

'With this ring I thee wed...'

Maybe the photographer's camera did get wet then, for there was hardly a dry eye on the beach as Jenny and Guy stood together against a backdrop of setting sun and sea and mountains and were made one.

'It's a perfect Carver Wedding,' Jenny whispered as their wedding kiss finally ended, and Guy smiled at her with a smile that said life for both of them was just beginning.

'I brought you lousy Christmas presents,' he told her. 'I had to make up somehow. Merry Christmas, Mrs Carver. With all my love.'

* * * * *

*Discover the magic of the holiday season in
SLEIGH RIDE WITH THE RANCHER,
an enchanting new Harlequin® Romance story
from award-winning author Donna Alward.*

Enjoy a sneak peek now!

* * *

"BUNDLE UP," he suggested, standing in the doorway. "Night's not over yet."

A strange sort of twirling started through her tummy as his gaze seemed to bore straight through to the heart of her. "It's not?"

"Not by a long shot. I have something to show you. I hope. Meet me outside in five minutes?"

She nodded. It was their last night. She couldn't imagine *not* going along with whatever he had planned.

When Hope stepped outside she first heard the bells. Once down the steps and past the snowbank she saw that Blake had hitched the horses to the sleigh again. It was dark but the sliver of moon cast an ethereal glow on the snow and the stars twinkled in the inky sky. A moonlight sleigh ride. She'd guessed there was something of the romantic in him, but this went beyond her imagining.

The practical side of her cautioned her to be careful. But the other side, the side that craved warmth and romance and intimacy…the side that she'd packaged carefully away years ago so as to protect it, urged her to get inside the sleigh and take advantage of every last bit of holiday romance she could. It was fleeting, after all. And too good to miss.

Blake sat on the bench of the driver's seat, reins in his left hand while he held out his right. "Come with me?"

She gripped his hand and stepped up and onto the seat. He'd placed a blanket on the wood this time, a cushion against the hard surface. A basket sat in between their feet and Blake smiled. "Ready?"

Ready for what? She knew he meant the ride but right now the word seemed to ask so much more. She nodded, half exhilarated, half terrified, as he drove them out of the barnyard and on a different route now—back to the pasture where they'd first taken the snowmobile. The bells called out in rhythm with hoofbeats, the sound keeping them company in the quiet night.

* * *

Pick up a copy of SLEIGH RIDE WITH THE RANCHER by Donna Alward in November 2012.

And enjoy other stories in the Harlequin® Romance **HOLIDAY MIRACLES** *trilogy:*

SNOWBOUND IN THE EARL'S CASTLE by Fiona Harper • Available now

MISTLETOE KISSES WITH THE BILLIONAIRE by Shirley Jump • December 2012

REQUEST YOUR FREE BOOKS!

2 FREE NOVELS
FROM THE ROMANCE COLLECTION
PLUS 2 FREE GIFTS!

YES! Please send me 2 FREE novels from the Romance Collection and my 2 FREE gifts (gifts are worth about $10). After receiving them, if I don't wish to receive any more books, I can return the shipping statement marked "cancel." If I don't cancel, I will receive 4 brand-new novels every month and be billed just $5.99 per book in the U.S. or $6.49 per book in Canada. That's a saving of at least 25% off the cover price. It's quite a bargain! Shipping and handling is just 50¢ per book in the U.S. and 75¢ per book in Canada.* I understand that accepting the 2 free books and gifts places me under no obligation to buy anything. I can always return a shipment and cancel at any time. Even if I never buy another book, the two free books and gifts are mine to keep forever.

194/394 MDN FELQ

Name	(PLEASE PRINT)	

Address		Apt. #

City	State/Prov.	Zip/Postal Code

Signature (if under 18, a parent or guardian must sign)

Mail to the **Reader Service:**
IN U.S.A.: P.O. Box 1867, Buffalo, NY 14240-1867
IN CANADA: P.O. Box 609, Fort Erie, Ontario L2A 5X3

Not valid for current subscribers to the Romance Collection
or the Romance/Suspense Collection.

Want to try two free books from another line?
Call 1-800-873-8635 or visit www.ReaderService.com.

* Terms and prices subject to change without notice. Prices do not include applicable taxes. Sales tax applicable in N.Y. Canadian residents will be charged applicable taxes. Offer not valid in Quebec. This offer is limited to one order per household. All orders subject to credit approval. Credit or debit balances in a customer's account(s) may be offset by any other outstanding balance owed by or to the customer. Please allow 4 to 6 weeks for delivery. Offer available while quantities last.

Your Privacy—The Reader Service is committed to protecting your privacy. Our Privacy Policy is available online at www.ReaderService.com or upon request from the Reader Service.

We make a portion of our mailing list available to reputable third parties that offer products we believe may interest you. If you prefer that we not exchange your name with third parties, or if you wish to clarify or modify your communication preferences, please visit us at www.ReaderService.com/consumerschoice or write to us at Reader Service Preference Service, P.O. Box 9062, Buffalo, NY 14269. Include your complete name and address.

ROM11

Find yourself
BANISHED TO THE HAREM
in a glamorous and tantalizing new tale from

Carol Marinelli

Playboy Sheikh Prince Rakhal Alzirz has time for
one more fling in London before he must return
to his desert kingdom—and Natasha Winters has
caught his eye. He seizes the chance to discover if
Natasha is as fiery in bed as her flaming red hair,
but their recklessness has consequences.... She
might be carrying the Alzirz heir!

BANISHED
TO THE HAREM

Available October 16!

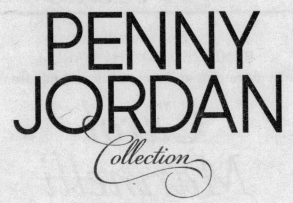